For An Eye, won the Pitlochry Award for the best crime novel by an unpublished writer, and the second, *Hand For A Hand*, continues to garner great reviews.

He is now working on his next Gilchrist novel, another story suffused with dark alleyways, cobbled streets and all things gruesome.

A DCI Gilchrist Novel

DEAD CATCH

T. F. MUIR

ROBINSON

CONSTABLE

First published in hardback in Great Britain in 2019 by Constable

This paperback edition published in Great Britain in 2020 by Constable

ISBN: 978-1-47212-879-9

Typeset in Dante MT by Hewer Text UK Ltd, Edinburgh
Printed and bound in Great Britain by Clays Ltd, Elcograf S.p.A.

Papers used by Constable are from well-managed forests
and other responsible sources.

Constable
An imprint of
Little, Brown Book Group
Carmelite House
50 Victoria Embankment
London EC4Y 0DZ

An Hachette UK Company
www.hachette.co.uk

www.littlebrown.co.uk

For Anna

AUTHOR'S NOTE

First and foremost, this book is a work of fiction. Those readers familiar with St Andrews and the East Neuk may notice that I have taken creative licence with respect to some local geography and history, and with the names of several police forces, which have now changed. The North Street Police Station has closed, too, but its proximity to the town centre with its many pubs and restaurants would have been too sorely missed by DCI Gilchrist for me to abandon it. I'm also pleased to note that the Criterion has recovered its original name from Lafferty's Bar. Any resemblance to real persons, living or dead, is unintentional and purely coincidental.

Any and all mistakes are mine.

www.frankmuir.com

CHAPTER 1

Thursday, Mid-March
Tentsmuir Forest, Fife, Scotland

Detective Chief Inspector Andy Gilchrist stepped from his car into the full force of an easterly gale. Overhead, tree limbs creaked and groaned as the wind gusted in from the North Sea. Leaves, twigs, broken branches, tumbled across the forest floor as if running for cover.

Gilchrist lowered his head and strode into the teeth of the storm.

Beyond the forest's edge, in the open, the wind seemed to strengthen, the temperature to drop a few degrees. Dune grass whipped and danced as if keeping time with some crazy tune, flicking up sand that stung his face. He tripped as he stumbled seawards, but once he crossed the hillocked spread of grassed dunes, the landscape opened up to a panoramic view of white beach and endless waves.

He turned and walked northwards, whistling sea to his right, creaking forest to his left. Sand lifted off the beach in fog-like waves.

He shivered off the cold, and mumbled to himself that at least it wasn't raining. But a backward glance across the Eden Estuary warned him that any such optimism might be short-lived.

He was still some fifty yards from his destination when his mobile rang – ID Jessie. He turned his back to the wind and took the call, cupping a hand to his ear. 'How soon can you get here?' he shouted.

'That's the problem, sir. I've got a family emergency.'

Something slumped in his stomach. Detective Sergeant Jessie Janes lived alone with her only son, Robert, who was stone-deaf with no hope of ever hearing. He knew Jessie well enough to know that when she said *family emergency*, it was serious. 'Take whatever time you need,' he said, 'and get back to me once Robert's recovered.'

'It's not Robert, sir.' A pause, then, 'It's Tommy.'

For one confusing moment the name failed to register. Then it hit him. Jessie's older brother, Tommy Janes, lifelong criminal, prime suspect in a double murder, and on the run for the last four months. But her call didn't make sense. How could Tommy be a family emergency? Unless . . .

'Has he contacted you?' he asked.

'Early this morning. Out of the blue. Told him to piss off and turn himself in. But he can be a persuasive bastard when he puts his mind to it.'

'He didn't threaten you, did he?'

'Of course he did. That's what he's good at.'

Gilchrist gritted his teeth, turned to face the wind. Waves rushed shoreward. White horses chased their own spindrift. Tommy was street-smart and prison-tough and knew how to apply pressure where it hurt. He would have threatened Jessie with Robert's safety. That's what he would've done. 'We could settle you and Robert into a safe-house until—'

'Sir. No.' A pause, then, 'Tommy's in trouble.'

'I know he's in bloody trouble. He's wanted by Strathclyde Police for—'

'It's not that, sir. He's scared. He's *really* scared.'

Gilchrist frowned at Jessie's concern. Not like her to worry over her criminal brother, someone who'd spent more time behind bars than not. 'So what're you saying?'

'I need to take the morning off, sir. I'll be back by midday.'

'Please tell me you're not going to meet him.'

'I'm not going to meet him.' She let out a heavy sigh, then said, 'I'll be all right, sir. He says he's got something that I . . . that *we* . . . need to see.'

'Like what?'

'He wouldn't say.'

Gilchrist knew she wouldn't tell him, but thought it worth a try anyway. 'So where are you going?'

'I don't know, sir. Tommy said he'll find me.'

Gilchrist didn't like the sound of that. 'I'll call the Office,' he said, 'and arrange for someone to shadow you.'

'No, sir. Don't. Please. If he thinks I'm being followed, he'll run. I have to do this by myself.'

'He wouldn't notice—'

'No, sir. Please.'

'For crying out loud, Jessie. I don't want you putting your life at risk.'

'Tommy talks tough. But he won't harm me. I know that, sir.'

'I don't like it, Jessie . . .'

But the line had already died.

'Ah, fuck,' he said, then phoned Detective Constable Mhairi McBride, the newest and youngest member of his team – and one of the brightest, he had to say. 'Get the Telecoms Unit to trace Jessie's mobile. Then take the biggest officer you can find, and follow her.' He didn't mention Tommy Janes by name, but hinted at the possibility of Jessie putting herself in harm's way.

'If we have an opportunity, sir, would you like us to make a formal arrest?'

Gilchrist's thoughts were for Jessie's safety. Even though Tommy Janes had a history of violence, Jessie had confronted him only last year. If Tommy had intended to harm her, he could have done so then. But God only knew how he would react if he found out Jessie had betrayed him. Of course, that wasn't the only problem. Jessie consorting with a criminal on the run – a prime suspect in a double murder no less – and not making a formal arrest, was breaking every rule in the book, and probably a dozen more.

'No,' he said. 'Keep well back. Step in only if it looks like it could get out of hand.'

He pocketed his mobile and tried to convince himself that he'd done all he could to safeguard Jessie. But if word of Jessie's contact with Tommy, and Gilchrist's knowledge of it, ever got back to Chief Superintendent Diane Smiley, they could both find themselves collecting their dole money by the end of the week.

He grunted in frustrated anger, and walked on towards the crime scene – a fishing boat washed up on the sands of Tentsmuir Beach, driven there by one of the worst storms to hit the east coast in over twenty years. He thought he recognised Colin, the lead SOCO, but swirling sand made one forensic-suited Scenes of Crime Officer look like the next.

From what little Gilchrist knew about it, the Maritime and Coastguard Agency picked up the boat on radar during the night. When it failed to respond to radio calls, the Coastguard Rescue Service prepared to launch a helicopter. But with gusts touching one hundred miles an hour, the rescue flight was cancelled. All they could do was monitor the vessel's progress on their screens, and from the ground.

A rescue party had been despatched to Tentsmuir Beach in readiness for the boat being driven ashore, which it had done at 2.42 that morning. But when a team boarded it and found it crewless, they assumed it had broken free of its moorings, and been left to the mercy of the tide and the wind.

Which had been the general consensus amongst the Rescue Service team . . .

Until they opened the hold.

CHAPTER 2

Gilchrist arrived at the beached boat just as his mobile vibrated in his pocket. He sought respite from the wind by sheltering behind the hull. Standing there, it seemed as if the storm had lessened. Even so, sand rustled past in eye-blinding waves.

He took the call – ID Mhairi – and said, 'Problems?'

'We can't track her, sir. She must have removed her SIM card.'

'Bugger it.' He raked his fingers through his hair. 'Can we locate her on the ANPR?' The Automatic Number Plate Recognition system was not intended for tracking officers in the line of their duty, but it was worth a shot.

'Can we do that, sir?'

'We can,' he said, 'if we suspect a life is in danger.'

'I'll get onto it right away, sir.'

'Get back to me as soon as,' he said, and ended the call.

Shit and fuck it. It had been over a year since Jessie joined Fife Constabulary after transferring from Strathclyde Police in Glasgow. Since her arrival she had proven herself to be a valuable member of his team. But her lively spirit, and her brazen disregard of authority – a bit like his own maverick attitude – could land her in trouble. More than once he'd been tempted to rein her in, give her a right old bollocking, but her instinctive investigative skills – second only to his own, he liked to believe – had caused him to soften his tone and give her cautionary advice. But this time, by going *underground* for a morning, Jessie had crossed his unspoken line. When he got her within his reach, he would have it out with her.

He slipped his mobile into his pocket, ventured out from behind the hull. The wind hit him with renewed strength, it seemed. He was signed in by the Crime Scene Manager, DC Alan Bowers, then slipped on a pair of latex gloves, and lifted the crime-scene tape.

The tide had ebbed, leaving the boat high and dry. Beached as it was, the shallow keel deep in sand, the vessel now lay on its side at a steep angle. He worked his way with care up a slippery rope ladder secured to the gunwale – courtesy of the Coastguard Rescue Service – and onto a straked deck permeated with the latent stench of fish and kelp. Some subconscious part of his olfactory senses picked up another underlying aroma – nothing to do with the sea and all things maritime – a deeper more pungent guff with which he was more familiar; the unmistakable tongue-coating stench of putrefying flesh.

From the open hold he caught the scuffling sounds of SOCOs going about their grisly task below, trying to make forensic sense of an untimely death. A sudden shift in the wind left him in no doubt that the hold was where the stench was coming from. He held onto the edge of the bulkhead to avoid sliding down the slanted deck, easing his way aft, until he was close enough to grasp onto the hold's coaming.

Before he could enter, one of the suited SOCOs skipped up the ladder with an agility that confounded Gilchrist. Even before the man pulled off his face mask, Gilchrist recognised Colin, the lead forensics analyst.

'What have we got?' Gilchrist asked.

Colin took in a few lungfuls of sea air, as if to clear his being of the smell of death, then said, 'Not a pretty sight. Black male in his thirties, maybe forties. Been dead about a week, maybe ten days, I'd say. Locked in the hold—'

'Locked?' Gilchrist glanced at the access hatch. It had been pulled back and now lay flat on the deck.

'When the Coastguard Rescue Service boarded,' Colin said, 'the hold was closed, the hatch chained and padlocked. They had to cut through it with a bolt cropper.' He shook his head. 'Someone must have got a right blast of guff when they pulled it open.'

'Not a pretty sight, you said.'

'As well as being a week or so post-mortem,' Colin said, 'cuts and abrasions on the body suggest that the poor punter was tortured.'

Jesus Christ. Gilchrist closed his eyes for a long second. He'd seen bodies mutilated by torture before – broken bones, missing fingers, toes and worse, faces beaten and swollen beyond recognition and his own comprehension – but when he opened his eyes, something in the way Colin returned his gaze warned him that this was bad.

'Cause of death?' he tried.

'Difficult to say without a formal PM. The beatings might

have killed him. Or maybe loss of blood. Or maybe he was just left to die. I'll leave that for Cooper to confirm. Talking of which,' Colin said, and nodded with his chin over Gilchrist's shoulder.

Gilchrist glanced along Colin's line of sight. Even though the figure was still some fifty yards or so distant, he could not fail to catch the mass of strawberry blonde hair whipping in the wind. Dr Rebecca Cooper, Fife's foremost forensic pathologist, and old flame of his, was making her way along the beach – not without some difficulty, he had to say.

He turned, and nodded to Colin. 'I'd better have a look then.'

'He's all yours.'

Gilchrist gripped the hold's ladder, and placed a foot on the third rung down. Because of the way the hull was lying, he found his foot coming to rest where the handrail connected to it. But he took his time, and eased himself down into the hold one rung at a time.

The floor of the hold was wooden planking, worn smooth from years of storing fish. In the confined space, the stench was all-pervasive, thick enough to taste, and strong enough to overpower the rotting odour of death. But the way the sea-wind played on the access hatch, Gilchrist soon caught the whiff of putrefaction stirred up from the hold's darker spots.

He turned to the body, and caught his breath.

The SOCOs had set up lights in close proximity to the body, but no one would blame you for thinking that the bloodied mass was a lump of butchered meat, and not human at all. From where he stood, no more than ten feet from the mess, if he hadn't been told the victim was male, he would have struggled to determine the gender with any confidence.

Despite the body being bloated from a week of post-mortem putrefaction, Gilchrist's first thought was that the man when alive had been slight in build. He pulled up an image of athletes from Ethiopia, Kenya and other African nations who now seem to dominate long-distance running events. The face gaped cracked-tooth at him, eyes swollen closed like a dead boxer's, open mouth oozing purged fluids as black as old blood.

One of the SOCOs was swabbing the wooden hull to the side, while another seemed more intent on scraping under the body's toenails. They both appeared so focused on their respective tasks that Gilchrist coughed as he approached the SOCO working on the body.

'Any thoughts?' he said, and leaned forward to study a series of cuts like chevrons that ran from the left shoulder along the arm to the wrist – ten or twelve cuts in total, he estimated.

The SOCO released the man's foot, and looked at Gilchrist with clear blue eyes, then said, 'With respect to?'

'Cause of death?'

She shook her head. 'Above my pay grade.'

'Best guess?'

'As long as you don't hold me to it, I'd say strangulation.'

Intrigued, Gilchrist said, 'Strangled by what?'

'Only just noticed this,' she said, and pointed to the man's neck. 'Looks like a ligature of some sort. A wire. Like cheese wire, perhaps.'

Gilchrist had to strain to make out the wire. Because of the swelling, the wire was buried deep into the soft flesh of the neck, making it more or less invisible to the naked eye. But now it had been pointed out to him, he came to realise that the man's upper arms had been strapped by wire to nails driven into the hull planking behind him, as had his neck. And the longer he studied the arrangement, the more he came to suspect that if the man struggled to escape, the wire would have tightened around his arms and neck, until he eventually choked to death.

At the sound of movement on the deck overhead, Gilchrist pushed himself to his feet. Down here, in the cold dark of the hold, riding the waves of a rough sea – even a calm sea for that matter – it would have been impossible to sit for any length of time without moving. So, strapped up like the man was, any movement – forced or accidental – would have been as good as signing his death warrant.

Still, cheese wire didn't explain the bloodied face and slashed arms.

He ran his gaze along the chevron cuts, noted the clotted blood, which told him that the man had been alive when these wounds had been inflicted, probably for the purpose of torture. He puzzled at the logic, and thought the chevrons were too perfect, too symmetrical, to have been done at sea. So, it was probable that the boat had been docked during the man's initial imprisonment in the hold. Of course, all of this was conjecture at the moment, and he knew he could be so far off base that he could be outside looking in.

A shadow shifted across the hatch opening, and he watched with interest as first one Hunter-wellington clad leg, then another, searched for, and found, the ladder rungs. He knew how slippery the floor was, and he managed to work his way over to the ladder and offer his hand as support.

To his surprise, Cooper took it.

'A gentleman to the last,' she said.

'Not sure I like the sound of *to the last*, but other than that, what can I say?' He gave her a smile, which she failed to reciprocate. Well, what had he been expecting? 'Body's that way.'

'So I see,' she said, and pulled free.

It irked him that she could cast him off with such apparent ease, as if all he had ever been to her was someone to fill the void left by a philandering husband until she could decide whether or not to go through with their divorce. Last Gilchrist had heard, she had chosen not to. But with Cooper, nothing was ever straightforward.

He was saved by his mobile ringing.

Gripping the ladder with one hand, he removed his phone from his jacket with the other – ID Mhairi. 'Yes, Mhairi. What've you got?'

'Nothing, sir. Her car's still in the driveway. It looks like she decided to walk to wherever she was going.'

'What the hell's Jessie playing at?' he said.

Cooper cast him a knowing look, as if to say, *I told you she would let you down*. But he ignored her, and clambered up the ladder, feet slipping on the rungs. He staggered onto the deck, and braced himself as he faced an easterly wind that carried with it more than a hint of rain. A glance over the Eden Estuary told him it would be pelting it down in five minutes. But raining or not, he needed to have a word with Jessie that afternoon, the firmer the better.

In the meantime, he had a murder investigation to get started.

'Drop what you're doing, Mhairi. I need you at Tentsmuir Beach.'

'Yes, sir.'

He shivered off a chill, and said, 'And mine's a latte, no sugar.'

'On its way, sir.'

CHAPTER 3

Jessie waited for a gap in the traffic, then scurried across Largo Road and into ALDI supermarket. After the blustering winds, the store felt quiet, safe. She walked to the end of the first aisle, as instructed – so that Tommy could watch her from afar, she knew, to see if anyone was following her. Then she returned to the front of the store, purchased a newspaper – the *Daily Record* – and paid for it at the till.

Back outside, the cold wind felt like a punch to the face. She zipped her anorak up to her neck, flipped up the hood, then turned into the teeth of the wind. She walked along the side of the store, crossed the street and into Tom Stewart Lane, which ran beside an open green space with goalposts at either end. But with the weather so fierce, that morning the park lay empty. Trees that lined the chain-link fence swayed and bent in the gale. Leaves and pieces of paper trapped in the mesh flapped like fish in netting.

The lane was nothing more than a paved footpath, which brought her out to a parking area and a double row of lock-ups that served the surrounding terraced homes. Despite the quietness of the area, she didn't think Tommy would make an appearance here, it being too exposed. Where she stood could be seen from a number of windows. She noticed a curtain twitch on one of the upper windows – not Tommy, she was sure, but a nosy neighbour. She slipped her hand into her pocket and removed a mobile phone – the one she'd found ringing on the hall floor that morning – just to give her something else to hold. Then she scowled at the screen to let Tommy know – if he was watching – that he was beginning to piss her off.

No texts. No missed calls. Nothing.

She cursed under her breath and slipped the mobile back into her pocket as her mind replayed Tommy's words to her – *Once you're out of Tom Stewart Lane, keep walking. I'll be watching you.*

'Aye, right, Tommy,' she said to herself. 'I'll keep walking. But which way?'

She was unfamiliar with the housing estate in which she now stood, and didn't know where any of the roads led. Not that you could get lost in St Andrews, more likely you could walk for miles and end up at some spot you'd driven past for years without knowing how you got there. Of course, she could look the street up on the internet, check it out on Google Maps if she'd had her own mobile. But the phone Tommy had slotted through her letterbox in the early hours was bottom of the range.

Nothing for it, she thought, but to carry on walking.

Rather than head deeper into the estate or walk beside the double row of garages – something about lock-ups always made her feel ill at ease – she decided to take James Robb Avenue. She turned left into the avenue, relieved to be out of the full blast of the wind. She had gone only a few yards when the mobile rang.

She stopped, and took the call.

'Turn round,' a man's voice said. 'You're going the wrong way.'

'You told me to keep walking—'

The connection died.

Jessie kept the mobile to her ear as she eyed the nearest windows, then those beyond, trying to work out where Tommy had called from. If he could see her, then surely she could see him. But Tommy had been on the run since last November, and despite Strathclyde's best efforts, no one had found a trace of him. Her brother could be the Artful Dodger for all anyone knew. If a full police force couldn't find him, what chance did she have?

She stuffed the mobile into her pocket, tucked the *Daily Record* under her arm, and said, 'Fuck you, Tommy. I've got better things to do than fanny around after you.' As if to make matters worse, it started raining, but she put her head down, and retraced her steps.

She returned to James Robb Avenue, turned left, and walked past the lock-ups. When she reached Fraser Avenue, she stopped, expecting the mobile to ring and Tommy to tell her she was going the wrong way again. But it lay in her pocket, silent. The rain had turned into a downpour. Drops bounced off the road like liquid bullets. From the distance, she caught the growling grumble of thunder. Above, the sky blackened. She hoped Tommy would make an appearance soon, and she wondered for the umpteenth time why he hadn't insisted she do this under cover of darkness—

The mobile rang.

She turned her back to the wind and rain, and made the connection.

'Eyes left,' Tommy said.

Jessie shifted her body. 'Now what?'

'See that silver car, the one with the broken tail-light?'

It took her a few seconds to pick it out from others parked there. 'Got it.'

'It's in there. On the back seat.'

'What is?'

'You'll see.'

'Then what?'

'You'll know, once you see it.'

'And what do you want me to do with this bloody *Daily Record*?'

'Shove it up your arse for all I care.'

'Then why did you tell me to buy it?'

'So's you wouldnae look suspicious in ALDI, walking in and back out again.'

'Oh that's fucking brilliant, Tommy, that is.'

The line died.

Jessie slid the mobile into her jacket, and walked towards the car. She glanced left and right, searching for movement, anything that might give her a clue as to where her brother was. But by the time she reached the car, she was none the wiser.

The car was a Vauxhall Vectra, with soft tyres that bulged from low pressure. The windscreen, bonnet and roof were splattered with bird droppings. Dirt gathered on the road around the wheels told her that the car had neither been cleaned nor moved in weeks, maybe months. She slipped on a pair of latex gloves, took a quick look around her.

The worst of the storm had passed, but it was still raining hard.

She tried the rear door handle. It clicked open.

There, on the back seat, lay a small padded envelope. She reached inside, picked it up, and slipped it between the pages of the *Daily Record*. Door closed, newspaper tucked inside her jacket, and off she went, conscious that her actions might have been seen from one of the neighbouring homes, and already the police were being notified of a car theft.

She retraced her steps, walking smartly, but not running. Striding with the wind, the rain seemed less harsh, the temperature less chilling, and by the time she arrived at ALDI again, she found herself out of breath and sweating. Christ in a bucket, she needed to get fit, or cut out all the junk food – pizza, fish and chips, samosas, curries. But she shared meals at home with her boy, and where would Robert be if all of a sudden she stopped buying what he liked to eat?

She thought of stopping off for a coffee somewhere and opening Tommy's envelope. But she decided against that. She was already running late, and with this latest crime – dead body found on grounded fishing boat – she knew that Andy needed all the help he could get. So she carried on, working her way back along Largo Road, towards her home where her car was parked, all the while expecting the mobile to ring, and Tommy to tell her what to do.

By the time she arrived back home, she was sweating like a sumo wrestler. But she didn't stop for a coffee, or a shower, or a change of clothes. Instead she picked up her own mobile, then slid into her car, a Fiat 500 that Lachie – CS Lachlan McKellar of Strathclyde Police – ex-friend, ex-associate, ex-everything for that matter, had arranged for her to buy in a sweetheart deal. At the time she hadn't asked what the term *sweetheart deal* had meant, but soon found out that it had much to do with the lowering of knickers.

Christ, how could she have been so stupid?

She had just driven through the mini-roundabout at the Whey Pat Tavern onto City Road, when she decided not to drive straight to Tentsmuir Beach, but to find out what was in the package. She needed to know what she was dealing with. It was all far too close to home, and could snap up and bite her. So, she drove into St Marys Place, and eased her way through early morning traffic – where do all these cars come from? In Market Street, she found a parking spot within spitting distance of Starbucks.

With skinny latte and blueberry muffin in hand – well, she had missed breakfast – she found a seat in the back room, devoid of students, visitors or others taking shelter from the storm. She broke her muffin, took a nibble and a sip of coffee, before daring to retrieve the package from her jacket pocket. She laid it on the table, and for a fleeting moment wondered if she should bypass Gilchrist and go through the formal process of logging it in at the Office. Then, just as quickly she discarded that idea. Instead, she retrieved Tommy's mobile, and returned the last incoming number.

She held her breath as the call went through the connection process to end with a recorded message telling her that *the number you have called does not exist*. Well, no surprise there, she thought. Tommy had not evaded half of the national police forces by being stupid. But it did tell her that she would have to wait for him to contact her.

She picked up the padded envelope, turned it over just to check she wasn't missing anything – an address, printed message, even a name – which she wasn't. Then she slipped her car key under the flap and pulled it along the edge. Even so, she peered inside before sliding out its contents, a pocket diary – last year's edition – no more than four inches in size, the kind she used to write in when she was in primary school. Although the cover appeared to be in good condition, the diary had a permanent bend to it, as if it had spent most of its life in someone's back pocket.

She flipped through the pages, mostly blank, until she came across what Tommy had wanted her to find – a list of six names in child-like printing in ink near the spine, so that anyone flipping through the diary might not notice. None of the names meant anything to her. But clearly this information was of value to someone, and important enough for Tommy to risk his freedom getting it to her. Were these names somehow associated with the murders for which Tommy was wanted? But more worrying, now she had the diary in hand, she realised she could not simply present these names as evidence of anything, as they'd been given to her by the prime suspect in a double murder investigation.

She came to understand that she really only had one option.

And she didn't think Andy would like it.

CHAPTER 4

'Thanks, Mhairi,' Gilchrist said. 'You're a darling.' He took a sip of his Costa coffee, and felt the warm liquid slide into his stomach. Just that first mouthful made him realise how cold he was, how an east wind off the North Sea could suck the warmth from your body without mercy.

Mhairi had almost finished her own coffee, and nodded to the fishing boat. 'What do you think, sir?'

'I think you don't need to see it,' he said.

She grimaced, as if offended. 'Sir?'

'It's bad, Mhairi,' he said, then regretted having said that. He shouldn't minimise her by trying to shield her from a gruesome murder scene. *Baptism by fire*, he'd been told when he first joined the Constabulary. But truth be told, of the three of them – Jessie, Mhairi and himself – he had the weakest stomach. He often suffered visceral nausea at the scenes of horrific killings he'd been forced to study in detail in order to solve the crime.

'I meant,' he said, 'that with the hull lying the way it is, and with the wind and all the rain we've just had, the deck is super slippery. Best to wait until they've got the body in the mortuary.'

'I see, sir.'

Gilchrist hid his face in his coffee as Mhairi eased away from him, the magnetic pull of the crime scene seemingly irresistible despite slick decking. He watched her eye the side of the ship, lean forward and touch the hull, run a hand over it as she walked to the stern. Then she stood there, tilted her head as if all the better to read the name of the boat.

Something about that action intrigued Gilchrist, the way she frowned as she read the name, then stepped forward to scrape a fingernail over the paint. Then coffee cup stuffed into the sand at her feet, hand into her jacket pocket to remove her car keys. It didn't take much scraping before she looked at Gilchrist, brow raised, eyes wide.

'What've you got?' he said, and walked towards her.

'The name's been painted over, sir.'

He looked at it – *Golden Plover* – in bold yellow paintwork against the dark blue hull, beneath which the town – *St Combs* – was painted in the same colour, but in smaller, squarer letters. He couldn't place the town of St Combs, only knew it was on the coast north of Fife. Part of the stem of the *l* in *Plover* had been scraped off by Mhairi where the paint had already been flaking. As he scanned the letters, he saw that the paint was in poor condition, and that the hull needed to be stripped and repainted if it was to be maintained in good order.

Back to the *l* in *Plover*, below which he thought he could make out the faintest shape of another letter, as if the paint beneath was embossed. Or maybe nothing more dramatic than a run in the paintwork. 'What're you thinking?' he asked Mhairi.

She tore a sheet of paper from her notepad. 'That there's another name underneath.'

22

Gilchrist watched Mhairi press the paper flat to the hull, over the *l*, then run a pencil back and forth across it, until the ghostly shape of another letter took form – the tail end of an upper case G.

She removed the paper, held it out to him. 'What do you think, sir?'

'How often are names changed on boats?'

'Don't know, sir. But I phoned the Maritime and Coastguard Agency before I left the Office, and they confirmed they have no records of a *Golden Plover* out of St Combs. They had a *Golden Eagle*, but no *Plover*.'

Mhairi was proving herself to be an invaluable team member, prepared to take the initiative, and always willing to learn. He nodded. 'So we have an unregistered fishing boat beached on the shores of Fife last night, with no crew, only the mutilated body of a black male.' He stared off across the Eden Estuary, and had to shield his eyes against a sharp burst of rain. Black clouds, low enough to touch, were about to drop their lot – a *thunderplump* his mother used to call it. But with the rain came a slackening in the wind, no longer whistling from the east, but bustling from the south.

He turned back to Mhairi. 'So what're we looking at? Drugs? Smuggling? Human trafficking?' He nodded to the boat. 'Or just plain old murder.'

Mhairi's lips pressed into a white line, causing him to reflect on what he'd just said. Was this a sign that he'd been in the job too long, that he was now inured to the horrors of a brutal killing? How could he breeze over such a gruesome crime scene by calling it *plain old murder*? He cleared his throat, and said, 'Whatever's going on, no one deserves to have their life ended like that. So let's get cracking.'

23

'Yes, sir.'

'I want you to find out the original name of this boat, who it's registered to, and when it was last at sea under its original name. It's likely too much to expect to find the logbook, but maybe the Maritime and Coastguard Agency have records of its whereabouts in the last couple of months. Get Jackie to help you. Give me everything you can. I want the works. OK?'

'I'm on it, sir.'

With that, he tugged his collar up, and clambered up the rope ladder again, intent on finding out if Cooper had any news for him. The hold would also provide cover from the rain, now picking up to a steady downpour.

Back below deck, the stench seemed much worse. He almost gagged as he turned and looked at the body. Cooper was on her knees, trying to pry the man's mouth wide. But with a rictus smile in a swollen face, Gilchrist doubted there was much to be gained. Rain thudded the decking overhead, a constant drumming magnified by the echo-chamber effects of the confined space. He pressed a hand for support against the roof as he kneeled beside Cooper.

'Anything?' he asked.

She glanced at him. 'Other than a dead body?'

He ignored her quip. 'How about cause of death?'

'Too early to say, but I'm inclined to agree with Sheena, that he choked himself to death on these wires here.' She tapped the wire, gave it a firm shake, and the body moved as if in annoyance.

'He choked himself?' he said. 'As opposed to someone choking him?'

'Why do you always look for the dramatic in the obvious?'

'I would've thought being wired to nails in the hull was dramatic enough, and that there's nothing obvious about what's happened here.'

The SOCO by Cooper's side – Sheena, if he had to take a guess – seemed to catch the nip in Gilchrist's tone, and looked off to the side, as if she'd found something of interest in her notes. Cooper, on the other hand, was going about her task as if he hadn't spoken.

His annoyance faded when Cooper said, 'This is interesting,' and he leaned in beside her, intrigued as she worked a pair of tweezers into the body's mouth, then eased what looked like a clump of cardboard from the purged fluid.

'What's that?' he said.

'Patience, for God's sake.' The tweezers slipped free. She tutted and reinserted them, frowning as she concentrated on snagging the slime-covered item. That time, she managed to clasp it, and pulled it free, then placed it in the flat of her hand. When she held it between her thumb and forefinger, she said, 'Looks like it's a folded piece of paper.'

'Maybe it's a note,' he said.

'It's a note, all right. But not the type you're looking for.' She unfolded it, once, twice, then again, until she held it out to him.

He took it from her. 'What the . . .? It's a fiver?' He stretched it tight, turned it over, then back again, puzzling as to why anyone would stuff a five-pound note into the mouth of a man they were about to kill, or had already killed. He stared at it like a simpleton confounded by a magician's trick, knowing what he was seeing, but unable to work out how it had been done. What was the significance of a five-pound note? He held it up to the light, turned it one way, then the next. But as far as he could see, there was nothing unusual about it. Just a typical Clydesdale Bank fiver.

He handed it back to Cooper, and said, 'Bag it.' Then a thought struck him. 'Is there anything else in his mouth?'

'Not that I can see,' she said.

'Maybe in his stomach?'

'Unlikely. I'd say the fiver was inserted into his mouth post-mortem.'

'Why do you say that?'

She shrugged. 'To leave some kind of message? A calling card, perhaps?'

Gilchrist stared at the dead man by their side, a silent witness to their conversation and all that had gone on before in this hold. What could he tell them if he were still alive? He looked hard at the swollen eyes, almost willing the man to explain what it all meant. His gaze drifted over the bloodied face, down across his bruised shoulder, onto the row of chevron slashes, several deep enough to see the white of the bone.

'Dear God,' he whispered. 'What utter hell you must have gone through.'

And with these words, he pushed himself off his knees. He had a job to do, a murder investigation to lead. He needed to ID the body, find out who killed the man, and bring him or her to justice. He pressed his hand against the hull to steady himself. Cooper was still on her knees, shining a light into the man's ears. She'd suggested the fiver was stuffed into the man's mouth as *some kind of message – a calling card?*

But if so, who was the message intended for?

The police force in general? Fife Constabulary? Himself specifically?

He thought not, for as he worked through the rationale and nibbled away at the logic, he came to see what the fiver was intended to be.

Not a calling card. And not any old message.

But a warning.

CHAPTER 5

Jessie parked her Fiat 500 next to Gilchrist's BMW, relieved to see that he was still at the crime scene. She hadn't wanted to speak to him over the phone, instead wanted to talk to him face to face, seek his advice on what to do with Tommy's diary, and the names within.

But before she got out of her car, she tried Tommy's mobile again.

To her surprise, her call was answered on the first ring.

'What the fuck kept you?'

'Jesus, Tommy, your phone's been down.'

'Aye, well, there's a reason for that.'

'You're bloody right there is.'

'So what d'you think?'

'I think I'm a detective sergeant talking to a suspect in a double murder investigation is what I think. And I think I can get myself in a whole lot of bother over this.'

'Naw, what d'you think about the names?'

'I don't give a shit about the names, Tommy. The names mean nothing to me. Jesus, Tommy, just talking to you could get me fired and probably charged as an accomplice.'

'Fuck sake, Jessie. That diary's gold dust, is what it is. It'll no get you fucking fired. It'll get you promoted. Jesus Christ, you're some thick-as-shite bitch, so you are.'

'If you want me to hang up on you, Tommy, you're going about it the right way.'

'Don't you get it?' he shouted. 'You done nothing with the other stuff I gave you.'

'Wrong, Tommy. I passed it on to those who could do something about it.'

'Aye, and they done fuck all about it, is what they done.' He grunted then, a throaty growl, followed by a hard spit. A bit closer, and she could have heard the ricochet. Then the voice was back. 'I knew youse lot would shite yoursels. Youse don't have the fuckin' balls to take on that bastard Maxwell.'

'So that's what this is about, is it?'

'For fuck sake, do I have to fuckin' spell it out for you?'

'Listen, Tommy, and you listen to me well.' Jessie struggled to calm the anger that fired through her. 'If anyone's being thick-as-shite here, it's you. You seem to forget that I work for Fife Constabulary. In other words, I'm the polis, Tommy. Don't you get it? You and me shouldn't be talking to each other unless there's metal bars between us.'

Silence.

'Jesus, Tommy, what the hell are you playing at? Why'd you contact me anyway? Why not just mail the bloody diary to me? Why all the subterfuge and cryptic messages and pick it up in the back seat of some stupid car as if you're James-fucking-Bond?'

Silence.

She held the mobile to her ear for a long moment, waiting for Tommy to respond. But it took her a few more seconds to catch the faintest scratching, leaving her with the strangest feeling that her brother was crying. Dear God, that would be a first.

'You still there, Tommy?'

A sniff, then, 'Listen to me, Jessie. You're all I've got. I've no one else. You're the only one who'll listen to me.' Another sniff. 'I'm shit scared, so I am. I've never been so fucking scared in all my life. I cannae keep going like this. They're after me, and they're no gonnie stop until I'm deid.'

'Who's after you?'

'Maxwell and his mob. All of them. I'm fucked, Jessie. Truly fucked. They done Terry and Maw. It wisnae me. They done them. Then they set me up for it.' Another sniff. 'You're my last hope, Jessie. Help me. Please, dear God, Jessie. Help me.'

The line faded to silence again.

Jessie let out her breath, long and hard, knowing some difficult decision had already been made in her subconscious. No matter how distant she and Tommy had been, no matter how different the paths of their lives, or how much they had argued in the past, how little they saw eye to eye, of all her family, Tommy had been the least cruel to her. And whether she liked it or not, he was still her brother.

On the spur of the moment, and against her better judgement, she said, 'OK, Tommy, I hear you. But give me a clue. I don't know any of these names. What do they matter?'

'Pass them up the line to someone you trust, Jessie. They'll know.'

'Listen, Tommy, I can help you. But you need to turn yourself in.'

'Aw, for fuck sake,' he snapped. 'Have you no listened to a fuckin' word I said?'

That's better. Now they were back on track. 'Every single one of them,' she said. 'But I'm still the polis, and you're still on the run, and there's only—'

'I heard you ID'd them,' Tommy interrupted. 'Terry and Maw.'

Jessie blinked once, twice, struggling to keep out the memory of her mother's body in the mortuary – skin on bones, face and body emaciated and scarred from a life of prostitution, alcohol and hard drugs—

'I'm telling you, Jessie, if you don't jump on this, I'll be the next one you're gonnie have to ID.'

The line died.

Jessie closed her eyes and cursed under her breath. What had she done to deserve this, born into a dysfunctional family of social misfits and criminals? Now only Tommy was left. But even so, he could still be the death of her. She had moved from Glasgow to the east coast to get away from it all, get away from her criminal family and their criminal connections. But one year later, here she was, still being hounded—

She jolted at the rap on the window.

DC Mhairi McBride gave her a concerned smile.

Jessie opened the door. 'What's up?'

'The boss is looking for you.'

'So what's new?' She stepped from her car. Shielded by the forest canopy, raindrops splashed around them in soft spatters. 'Where is he?'

'On the beach.' Mhairi held her gaze for a moment, then said, 'You all right?'

'Sure. I'm fine.' She tried a smile, but it could have been a grimace. 'On the beach, you said.' She closed her car door, locked it with her key fob, and strode off towards the sand dunes. Small

31

as Tommy's diary was, in her pocket it felt as large and as heavy as a brick. She called Tommy's mobile again, but got through to a message telling her the number did not exist. She cleared the dunes and the North Sea spread before her, waves chopping and wild despite the fall in the wind. The rain, too, had softened, and white clouds were peeling back a blue sky in the east. For all anyone knew in Scotland, it could be barbecue weather by teatime. She tugged her anorak hood tighter, and strode along the beach.

She hadn't known what to expect when she'd been told that a fishing boat had been swept ashore – flotsam scattered around the beach, perhaps, a body lying face down in the sand – but the vessel appeared to be intact, although stranded high and dry and tilted on its side. Blue crime-scene tape stretched around the hull like a fence, flapping in the wind. The receding sea swept ashore, some twenty yards distant.

The SOCOs were already there, manhandling a body bag from the decking, the angle of the hull making a relatively simple task all the more difficult. She noticed Gilchrist at the boat's stern, his attention focused on something on the hull. He looked up as she approached, then turned back to whatever he was looking at.

She walked up beside him. 'Didn't bring you any coffee,' she said. 'Sorry. Forgot.'

'Had more important things on your mind, no doubt.'

She said nothing as he ran the tips of his fingers over the name painted on the stern, his touch gentle, searching, almost inquisitive, like a blind man struggling to read Braille.

'Did you meet Tommy?' he asked, closing his eyes, continuing to play with the wood, as if trying to find some flaw in the finish.

But with all that flaking paint, it seemed to Jessie that all he had to do was open his eyes.

'No. Just spoke to him.'

'By phone?'

'Well, yeah. How else? Morse code?'

'Do you have his number?'

'He's removed the SIM card by now.'

'That's not what I asked.'

'Jesus, Andy. What the hell are you doing? You look as if you're getting off on the wood. It's creeping me out.'

He lowered his hands to his sides, then turned to face her. 'Do you have his number?'

'Yeah, but it'll be a waste of time.'

'Let's have it.' He removed his mobile from his pocket, and tapped in the number as Jessie read it out to him. A few seconds later, he ended the call. 'Where were you when you didn't meet him?' he said.

'In some housing estate at the back of ALDI on Largo Road.'

He tapped another number, got through right away. 'Find out which masts pinged this number earlier today.' He read it out. 'And get back to me soonest.' He stuffed his mobile into his pocket, and said, 'Want to tell me what the hell you were playing at?'

She couldn't fail to catch the change in his manner, the biting nip in his voice. But she retrieved Tommy's diary from her inside pocket, and held it out to him.

'I was hoping *you'd* be able to tell *me*.'

CHAPTER 6

Gilchrist took the diary from Jessie, and flipped through it.

He looked at her, puzzled.

'Try the nineteenth of March,' she said.

'What's significant about that date?'

'Nothing, I guess. Other than that's where the names are.'

He opened the diary to the date and, sure enough, there they were, six names printed in a child-like hand, parallel to and set deep into the page near the spine. He mouthed each one as he read them off, but none triggered any memories. Then he looked at Jessie. 'Chippie Smith? Who's he? A joiner? Or someone who likes fish suppers?'

'That's the problem,' Jessie said. 'I don't know any of them either. But Tommy told me to pass these names to someone I trusted. Which I've now done. By passing them to you.'

Jessie was one of the brightest detectives he'd ever worked with, but here she was, wading deeper into the swamp at the beck and call of her lunatic brother. 'Tommy gave us more names last year before Christmas, if you remember,' he said.

'How could I forget?'

'And as far as I know nothing came of it.'

'No.' Her eyes seemed to die for a moment, before reigniting. 'But these were names of officers in Strathclyde Police. No one would dare go after them without irrefutable proof of something criminal,' she said.

Gilchrist weighed up her words before holding up the diary. 'You do realise that this isn't worth a toss now,' he said. 'Any lawyer in the land would deem it inadmissible, if it ever got to court, even if we were ever able to work out what the *it* is.'

'I know that, sir.'

'So why the hell are you fooling around with a half-brained lunatic who's wanted by every police force in the country for God's sake when all he can give you is a diary worth next to eff all that we can't even use in court?' He took a quick breath. 'Jesus Christ, Jessie, you traipsed off this morning without your phone or your car. What if anyone had to contact you in an emergency? How would we have done that? Not to mention putting your life at risk at the hands of a known violent criminal.' He slapped a hand against the stern. 'I've told you before, and I'm telling you this for the last time. I need to be able to contact you 24/7. Which means that you don't just go walkies for a morning and turn up waving a few names in my face as if nothing's happened. And if you can't or won't or are unwilling to agree to that, then that's fine. You can move on.' He glared at her. '*Got it?*'

'Having a tiff, are we?'

Gilchrist jerked his head to the side, and caught Cooper at the corner of the stern, eyes gleaming, lips struggling to contain a smile.

'Ah, fuck,' Jessie said, and turned on her heels and strode off.

'Jessie,' he said, then shouted, '*DS Janes.*'

But she kept her head down as if she hadn't heard, and strode along the beach, away from the crime scene, away from the beached boat with all its blood-covered secrets yet to be discovered, and away from the embarrassment of being dressed down in front of none other than Dr Rebecca Cooper, or *Her Majesty*, as Jessie preferred to call her.

Gilchrist felt his heart go out to Jessie, and regretted having spoken to her so sternly. Truth be told, he was angry with himself for having raised his voice, and annoyed for ladling into Jessie within earshot of Cooper. He watched her parting figure from the corner of his eye as he faced Cooper.

'Yes, Becky. You got anything for me?'

'Other than take a couple of Panadol and call me in the morning?' She smirked for a moment, before her face deadpanned as if only then realising he was not amused. 'I'll be better able to advise you after I've performed the post mortem.'

'How soon?'

'You must learn to curb that impatience of yours, Andy.'

'How soon, Becky? For God's sake, it's not rocket science.'

'No, it's more difficult than that.' She levelled her gaze at him, and he found himself struggling not to look away. 'But I've come across something interesting,' she said, 'which might help you ID the body.'

'Go on.'

'A scar on the left thigh, relatively new I'd say. To me it looks consistent with that of an operation.'

'What kind of operation?'

'There you go again, demanding answers. I can't say for sure, but from the length and direction of the wound, I'd say he's had a broken femur.'

'Why operate on a broken leg?'

'The femur's the strongest bone in the body, and it might have been shattered.' She smiled at him. 'It takes a lot to do that to a femur. A car crash might do it. Or a bullet.'

Gilchrist cocked his head. This was Cooper at her worst, and best, drip-feeding him information piece by teasing piece. Somehow it reminded him of their foreplay, years ago it seemed now. 'So you must've found a bullet wound,' he said.

She chuckled. 'Through and through. And from the angle, I'd say he was lucky not to have been hit in the femoral artery. He could've died from loss of blood. Of course, the bullet could have ricocheted off the femur, shattering it in the process.'

Gilchrist thought it odd using the word *lucky* to describe anything about the dead man. What on earth was lucky about surviving being shot in the leg, only to be wired to nails in the hold of some godforsaken fishing boat, and tortured to death? Make that, *choked* to death. He couldn't imagine the pain the poor soul must have gone through before letting Death carry him away. It might be argued that it would have been luckier if he'd simply died from being shot in the leg in the first place.

Just then, another thought struck him.

'So, with the bone shattered, the operation was performed to screw it together?'

'Possibly.'

'Which would show up in X-rays.'

'Yes.'

'From which we could determine exactly what kind and how many screws or plates or whatever were used.'

Silent, she smiled at him.

'So there would be a record of that operation somewhere.'

'But in which hospital is anybody's guess.'

This had Gilchrist thinking they could start with local hospitals, then spread farther afield until they found the one they were looking for. But doing so could be man-hour intensive. Still, the end result could be worth it.

'How old is the bullet wound?' he asked.

She shrugged. 'Difficult to say, given the conditions in the hold.'

'Best guess?'

'Within the last couple of years. But I'll be better placed to advise you after the PM.'

'Let's get his DNA analysed as a priority. And if you find a match, get on to the SCRO.' He stepped away from the stern. If the victim had a criminal record, the Scottish Criminal Records Office would have a number for him, and all his crimes recorded. 'Get back to me as soon as you have something.'

'Do you know what the boat was used for?' she called out after him.

He stopped, and faced her. Silhouetted against the dark sea, hair blowing around her face in golden waves, he thought she looked striking. As if knowing that, she tucked a thick wave behind her ear. He said, 'As in – what was he doing in the hold in the first place?'

'Check the galley. I'd say the white powder in the cracks isn't flour.'

He smiled at her, and she smiled back.

Rather than struggle up the rope ladder to go back onboard, he found Colin near the water's edge, smoking a cigarette – Marlboro. Silent, they stood together looking out over the North Sea. The storm could have been a dream. The wind had stilled, the rain stopped, and he enjoyed the peaceful moment breathing in the acrid warmth of second-hand smoke. He could still remember the day he gave up smoking – 13 September, sixteen years ago, the day of his mother's funeral. It had been several years since he'd last bought a packet of cigarettes. He had succumbed more than once to the irresistible pull of that residual habit, of course. But even so, he liked to believe he was more or less done with it now.

'Penny for your thoughts,' he said to Colin.

Colin's cheeks sunk as he inhaled. 'That I've just about had it with the day job.'

'Getting to you?'

Colin exhaled, as if emptying his lungs for good. 'And then some.'

Gilchrist thought silence was as good an answer as any.

Colin drew his cigarette down to the filter, and crushed it between his thumb and forefinger. He flicked the dout at the sea, gave a sideways nod to the boat. 'I don't know how anyone could do that to another human being. I mean, what kind of nutters are out there?'

'All kinds,' Gilchrist said. 'But it's our job to find them, and bring them to justice.'

'Aye, sure we will. It's like an incoming tide. It just keeps coming.' He gritted his teeth, shivered off the chill.

Gilchrist put his hand on Colin's shoulder, gave a fatherly squeeze. 'You can't look at the big picture,' he said. 'It's too overwhelming. All you can do is take each one as it comes. Consider that poor soul in the hold. He might have had a wife, a child, someone who loves him and is wondering what's happened to him. As bad as the job might seem, think of what you're doing for them – the wife, the children. They need you. They need us. Someone to account for that man's life, and give closure to it, in whatever form that takes.'

Colin ran a hand under his nose. 'It still doesn't make it any easier.' He flickered a smile. 'Which I suppose is why we drink whisky by the gallons.'

'That, and the weather,' Gilchrist said.

Colin glanced at the sky. 'You think it's going to clear up?'

'That's anybody's guess. But before you head out to the golf course, could you have your guys check the galley for drugs? I'm thinking along the lines that the *Golden Plover*'s changed its name for a good reason.'

'Running drugs?'

'It's early days. But it's a thought.'

Colin nodded. 'I'll get back to you,' he said, then walked off up the beach.

Gilchrist removed his hands from his pockets, and saw that he'd been nursing Tommy Janes's pocket diary. He turned it over in his fingers. No matter what he thought of Jessie and her brother, Jessie was right. These names had to mean something to someone.

He would pass them on, just the one phone call.

And he knew who that someone could be.

CHAPTER 7

Gilchrist phoned DCI Peter 'Dainty' Small of Strathclyde Police HQ, Glasgow. He and Dainty had joined Fife Constabulary around the same time, but even though Dainty had since moved to Glasgow, they still kept in contact, exchanging information on cases from time to time.

Dainty answered in a large voice that belied his size. 'DCI Small speaking.'

'It's Andy Gilchrist, Dainty. How are you?'

'Fighting off alligators and fuck knows what else. What can I do you for?'

Typical Dainty. Busy and straight to the point. 'I'd like to run some more names past you.'

'Hope they're less fucking troublesome than that last lot you sent. Fuck sake, Andy, I had to come to the Office wearing a fucking crash helmet. Didn't know from which side the flak was going to come. Maxwell tried it on with me, but I told him to fuck off. After that, he backed off. But I couldn't do a thing with them. No incriminating evidence of any kind. Zip. Nada. Fuck all. How's Jessie doing?'

'As good as,' Gilchrist said.

'Good. Maxwell had it in for her at one time. But I'm glad the shit passed.' A grunt for a cough, then, 'So these names, what about them?'

'We hand-delivered the last ones to you. Are you OK to speak?'

'Got all that sorted, so yeah, let's have them.'

'Chippie Smith?'

'Oh, for fuck sake. Fucking wanker of the first order. What's he done?'

'I was hoping you could tell me.'

'He's into everything, Chippie is. Can you give me a clue?'

'How about I give you the other names?'

'Shoot.'

Gilchrist ran them off, one by one, without any comment from Dainty. When he had gone through the short list of six, he said, 'Anything?'

'Here's what I can tell you, Andy. And you didn't hear this from me, OK?'

'OK.'

'They're all snitches. Every one of them. They all take a bit here, a bit there, from whichever hand will feed them.' His voice lowered to that of a co-conspirator. 'But what they all have in common is that they're all *allegedly*, and I'm fucking emphasising allegedly here, they are all *allegedly* on the payroll of Jock Shepherd.'

Just the mention of that name had a queasiness stirring in Gilchrist's stomach with the speed of a triple dose of liver salts. As Scotland's alleged – there was that word again – crime patriarch, he was reputed to have a finger in every pie going, sometimes as much as the hand and the arm all the way up to the elbow, maybe even the armpit. If it was illegal, then big Jock Shepherd was bound to have some involvement in it. He should have been put away years ago, but not only did he have the brightest – and most expensive – legal team in the country, it was generally accepted that he ran his family business the old-fashioned way, with a gentleman's unspoken code of conduct. If you crossed big Jock, well, that was the end of it. But if you played the game, and acknowledged that in the world of crime someone had to be king, who better to have than big Jock who would be happy to shop lesser criminals to the police if he thought his business enterprises were being encroached upon. In exchange for a certain level of lassitude with respect to prosecution, of course.

In short, better the devil you know—

'But two weeks ago,' Dainty said, interrupting Gilchrist's thoughts, 'Cutter Boyd was found with his throat cut in a construction skip at the back of the King's Theatre. And rumour has it that Stooky Dee's gone and vanished. There's some serious shit going on in the local underworld at the moment. The lads are expecting Stooky to turn up any day now, probably in bits.'

Cutter Boyd and Stooky Dee were two of the names on Tommy's list, so Gilchrist said, 'If they're both on Shepherd's payroll, what's he saying about that?'

'*Allegedly* on Shepherd's payroll, Andy. *Allegedly*. Big Jock's keeping a low profile. It's what he does when some turf gets overturned. Lies low until the dust settles, then pokes his head over the parapet and sends his boys in to clear up the mess.' A pause, then, 'Where did you get these names from anyway?'

That was the question Gilchrist didn't want to have to answer. He'd been hoping that Dainty would just take the names on board and leave it at that. He was only passing them on to keep Jessie safe, maybe even get Tommy out of her life for good.

'They were written in a diary,' he said.

'And the diary belongs to . . .?'

'Couldn't say. It just turned up.'

'Like turned up in the mail?'

'No. Like left in the back seat of a car.'

'Don't keep me guessing here, Andy. This could get me burned big time.'

Gilchrist decided to come clean – well, sort of. 'Jessie got a call from her brother, Tommy, telling her where the diary was—'

'You do know we've got half the fucking force looking for that bastard, don't you?'

'I do, yes, but she didn't meet him, just got some cryptic phone calls.'

'Were you able to trace the calls?'

'We're working on it.'

'And where was the car?'

'We're checking CCTV footage, too. Give me some credit, for crying out loud.'

'Sure, Andy. Sorry. But keep me posted.'

To get off the subject of Tommy Janes, Gilchrist said, 'A fishing boat washed ashore last night with a body on board. Haven't yet confirmed cause of death, but it looks like the poor guy went through the mill. Beaten up pretty badly, but here's the thing, we found a fiver stuffed into his mouth. Any ideas?'

The line fell silent for a few seconds, then Dainty said, 'Years ago, and I'm talking twenty-plus years here, the first murder I was ever involved with in Glasgow was a junkie who'd been beaten to a pulp. Every bone in his body broken. Like a fucking teabag he was. We found a fiver stuffed down his throat. We were never able to charge anyone, but it all pointed to it being one team squaring off with another for fucking grassing.

'Back then,' he continued, 'a fiver was almost worth something. Now it barely buys you a pint. Looks like the cost of living's affecting everyone. I'm surprised they never put it in a self-addressed stamped envelope.' He tried a laugh, but he seemed not to have the spirit for it. 'What I'm saying, Andy, is that your man looks like he's been done in by the pros. I don't mean hitmen, I mean he's been killed by someone with a criminal record.' A pause, then, 'It did occur to me that that fucker Tommy Janes fits the bill.'

Gilchrist had already thought of that, but Tommy seemed more interested in passing the diary to Jessie than trying to distance himself from the body on the fishing boat. He explained that to Dainty, then said, 'Let me know what you come up with on any of the other names.'

'Will do, Andy.' And with that, the line died.

Gilchrist stared out across the North Sea. Something in the conversation with Dainty niggled. Or maybe it was just the mention of big Jock Shepherd. Gilchrist had confronted the man once before, in a face-to-face meeting that had him fearing for his life, after which he'd brought a cruel criminal to justice, someone who'd overstepped the unmarked boundaries of the criminal world and encroached on Shepherd's enterprises. And just as Dainty had said, big Jock Shepherd had provided the vital evidence that enabled the police – Gilchrist – to put the man away for life, and thus end any interference in Shepherd's businesses – the criminal version of quid pro quo, it might be called.

But it had been the fiver stuffed down the junkie's throat that intrigued Gilchrist, and although he hadn't mentioned it to Dainty, he decided to send crime scene photographs to him, just to cover all the bases. He slipped the diary into his jacket pocket, then set off along the beach, following Jessie's footprints in the damp sand.

CHAPTER 8

He found Jessie in her Fiat 500, seated behind the steering wheel, mobile to her ear. When she saw him approaching, she raised a couple of fingers – two minutes, he would like to believe she was telling him, rather than giving him the Vicky.

Instead of waiting for her to finish her call, he phoned Cooper.

'I haven't started the PM yet, if that's why you're calling.'

'I'm sure you'll jump on it just as fast as you can,' he said, not rising to her quip. 'I need you to email photographs of our man in the hold to DCI Peter Small of Strathclyde Police. He might be able to ID him.'

'I doubt it,' she said. 'I doubt anyone could.'

'It's a long shot, I know. But it's still a shot.'

'You seem to have forgotten that I'm a forensic pathologist, not a photographer.'

'The body's on its way to Bell Street. I can have someone pop over within the hour if you can't afford the time.'

'Do that,' she said, and hung up.

He cursed under his breath, struggling to stifle his anger. Since ending their affair, Becky had become unreachable. He had hoped they might continue to show fondness for each other, but it was becoming clear to him that she wanted him out of her life. He would like to believe he had managed to maintain a professional relationship, but in truth, once the rules had been broken, nothing he could do or say would ever repair them.

His anger had settled to irritation by the time Jessie emerged from her car.

She held up a hand in mock surrender as she walked towards him. 'You were right to give me a ticking off,' she said. 'I'm sorry for doing what I did this morning. From now on I'll make sure I'm contactable 24/7.'

'You said that last time.'

Her confidence evaporated, but only for a second. 'But I don't take kindly to being chewed out in front of Becky-are-we-having-a-tiff-Cooper. God, she's such a condescending bitch. No wonder she gets on my nerves.'

Gilchrist waited a few seconds while Jessie settled down. 'In case it slipped your notice,' he said, 'Rebecca was nowhere in sight when you arrived.'

'But she was when I left.'

He nodded. 'Which brings me to my next point.'

Jessie seemed to square her shoulders, as if ready for the onslaught.

'Next time you walk away from me like that,' he said, 'I'll expect your request for a transfer on my desk within the hour.'

Something went out of Jessie then, and her body seemed to slump. 'Yes, sir,' she said. 'I'm sorry. It won't happen again.'

He held her eyes for a few beats longer, before saying, 'Right. Let's get on with some work.'

He spent the next several minutes bringing her up to speed – bullet wounds on the body's leg; possible shattered bones; scar from an operation; possible evidence of drugs on board; passing Tommy's list of names to Dainty; Chippie Smith and the others *allegedly* on the payroll of big Jock Shepherd; and, 'Oh, one final thing, there's no boat from St Combs registered under the name *Golden Plover*. Mhairi's been tasked with finding out the original name. Give her a call, and see if she's getting anywhere with that.'

While Jessie accessed her phone, he decided to shelter from the wind. He pressed his remote fob, and his BMW winked at him. Inside, he switched on the engine, turned the heater to full. It took less than a minute for the cabin to warm up, when his mobile announced the arrival of a text – Hi dad can you call?

His daughter, Maureen, was having a tough time since returning to St Andrews last November after a short trip to Australia. The planned emigration to Perth on the west coast to begin a new life with her fiancé, Tom, had been a disaster. Rather than take up his position with an IT company as planned, for some inexplicable reason Tom abandoned his job almost before it began, and embarked on a spontaneous trans-Australian trip expecting Mo just to tag along. But Mo'd had other ideas, and Tom's persuasive skills had fallen on deaf ears. Which put an end to that – possibly the shortest engagement on the planet.

He got through on the second ring. 'Hi, princess. You wanted me to call.'

'I need to see you,' she said.

Need, not *would like*, which warned him that something had come up. Maybe Tom had decided to come back from Australia, and she needed fatherly advice. But he thought her voice sounded . . . what? . . . unsteady?

'Is everything all right?' he said.

She sniffed, and he realised she might have been crying. 'Not really.'

'It's not about Tom, is it?'

'No, it's not,' she said. 'It's nothing to do with Tom. Why do you always have to jump to that conclusion?'

Well, if he thought she was still pining after her ex-fiancé, he was mistaken. Rather than tread through the minefield of Mo's personal life, he said, 'I can swing by your flat later, Mo. I'm kind of busy at the moment—'

'You're always busy, Dad. And for goodness sake, I'm not asking you to spend the whole day with me. Can't you just slip out for a few minutes? It's not like Fife Constabulary is going to collapse just because you're not there.'

'A few minutes, you say?'

But the line was already dead.

He gritted his teeth. This was the side to Mo he truly despised, her selfish impatience that bordered on the downright rude, an ugly trait she'd inherited from her late mother – not from himself, he was sure of that. But at this stage of a murder investigation, he just couldn't take time off. So, rather than phone her back, he typed a text – Will swing by tonight. Love you. Xxx – hit the *Send* button, then slipped his mobile into his jacket pocket just as Jessie tapped his window.

He wound it down.

Jessie leaned forward. 'Mhairi took some photographs of the boat, and sent them to the Maritime and Coastguard Agency in Aberdeen. And guess what? She got lucky.'

'Lucky?'

'Struck gold, more like. One of the staff recognised the boat from an unusual wood pattern on the cabin, a repair from being hit by a shipyard crane hook. Said he'd recognise it anywhere because he'd been on the actual boat when it happened. His father used to be a shipwright, and he'd offered to do the repair for a good price, but was turned down. Said that Joe insisted on doing the repair himself, and that he'd recognise his botched up handiwork anywhere.'

A frisson of electricity iced Gilchrist's spine. 'Joe?'

Jessie gave a grim smile. 'Joe Christie. From your neck of the woods. Crail. His boat *Brenda Girl* was lost at sea three years ago, and old Joe with it.' She sniffed, then twisted her mouth in a grimace. 'They never found his body.'

Gilchrist struggled to pull up the memory, and slowly the mist lifted.

That winter had been milder than normal, and Joe Christie – he could see him now; tousled white hair, ruddy complexion, fingers thick and scarred from a lifetime's fishing for a living – had set out to sea one Friday morning, as he'd done for the past fifty years. Gilchrist hadn't known Joe personally. He'd seen him about town, and recalled the talk in the bars at the time, the general consensus being that eff all had happened to Joe, that he'd just got fed up being married to Brenda – who wouldn't? – and done a runner, and hadn't he been talking to that young Jenny McKie who worked in the Co-op? She's up for it, now her man's left her.

It had taken his wife, Brenda, ten days to report Joe missing, by which time whatever trail there might have been had gone stone cold. When questioned by the Anstruther Office at the time, Brenda said that she and Joe had been married for too many years, and she thought he'd gone away for a week to have a wee break from life in general, just like he'd done the last ten years or so. But never this long. Which was why she was reporting him missing.

51

Jenny McKie was found to be alive and well and not quite so young – late fifties – still working behind the till in the Co-op. She hadn't seen Joe since that Friday morning when he'd stopped in for a packet of Rizla Kingsize Slim, and a can of Bugler's tobacco. And that was the last anyone had seen or heard of Joe Christie and his boat *Brenda Girl*.

Gilchrist opened the car door. 'Phone Mhairi again,' he said, 'and tell her we need Anstruther's records of the Christie investigation.'

'I can get these for you.'

'No. I need you to follow up with the SOCOs for photos of the victim, and email them to Dainty for ID. And if you can't get any decent photos from Colin, the body's in the Bell Street mortuary.' He winked at her, and smiled as the penny dropped.

Then he set off towards the sand dunes.

CHAPTER 9

Sure enough, now it had been pointed out to him, even from thirty yards the repair to the cabin roof was noticeable. But he didn't bother clambering on board to check the repair close up. Instead he walked to the stern and removed his car keys.

He reached up and scraped his key against the paint where Mhairi had scratched a bit loose. He took care not to gouge too deep, and tried to ease the top layer of paint free. It came away surprisingly easily, enabling him to pry a piece off to reveal a burgundy-coloured hull over which a small portion of the still shining golden letters of the boat's name had been painted. He thought the letter could be a G. But he needed to make sure.

He scraped again, and several minutes later had enough of the top layer removed to confirm the letter under the *l* for *Plover* was in fact a G – for *Girl*? He pressed on, scraping over the name from beginning to end, and found a patch where the paint flaked at the letter *o* in *Golden*, underneath which he found what looked like the top of a *B*. He was confused for a moment, until he realised that *Golden Plover* was longer than *Brenda Girl*, and could explain why the letter *B* was slightly offset. He scraped some more, but the paint stuck fast. The top coat would need to be buffed off, or removed with Nitromors or some other paint stripper. But even without the repair job in the cabin, Gilchrist now felt certain that the fishing boat was indeed Joe Christie's long-lost *Brenda Girl*.

He slipped his keys into his pocket and walked around the hull to the rope ladder. He pulled himself on board, then eased up and across the slanted hull until he gripped a corner of the cabin, and pulled himself around it to face the repair.

Jessie was correct. The repair was a bit of a botched job.

It looked as if the crane hook had smashed through a corner of the cabin, and broken the windows. Rather than replace an entire section of panelling, an attempt had been made to cut out the damage and fit in the new. Wood-filler had been used to repair the gaps where the new didn't quite match the old. The windows had been replaced, too, but again the fitting was poor. All in all, a cheap job, and not the level of workmanship you would want to trust your life with, particularly in waters off the Fife coast, which could turn perilous in a heartbeat.

Gilchrist removed his mobile and took photos of the repair to the cabin, then emailed them to Jessie in the first instance. Once downloaded for their records, he might have Mhairi deliver hard copies to the Maritime and Coastguard Agency for further verification. He was making his shaky way back down the rope ladder when Colin popped his head out of the hold, and said, 'I think you were right. Looks like they could've been running drugs.'

'Let's hear it.'

'I'd say a bag of the stuff burst, and someone tried to sweep it up, but missed a bit in one of the corners. Could be heroin. But I'll get it analysed in the lab, just to make sure.' He slipped from view, back into the hold.

Gilchrist stepped off the ladder onto the safety of the beach. Overhead, the skies had cleared and the sun was doing what it could to remind the people of Scotland that spring was just around the corner. An unpleasant aroma clung to his clothes and a tangible coating on his tongue had him walking to the water's edge where he took his time breathing in clear, crisp air. Despite the chill, the water looked inviting, and it struck him that he hadn't swum in the sea, or really had a decent holiday overseas, for several years.

Maybe it was time for a break. But that would come later.

First, he had not only a missing-person case to look into, but a murder to solve.

Logic told him that drugs must surely have been smuggled on Christie's boat. People didn't get tortured to death just for the hell of it. For some criminal businesses, drugs were the necessary evil that generated vital cashflow, and that lifeline was worth killing for. The echo of Colin's earlier words reverberated through his mind – *It's like an incoming tide . . . it just keeps coming*. How right he was. It seemed that the more they tried to clear up the drugs problem, the more it spread – like the criminal equivalent of Japanese knotweed.

But with drugs came the side-line activities, a thriving industry of drug-fuelled and drug-related criminality that fed off the main engine and kept an entire sub-culture in money or stoned oblivion. Gilchrist had once been convinced his son, Jack, had taken hard drugs, which Jack had repeatedly and vehemently denied, of course, claiming to have dabbled in soft drugs only – cannabis, mescaline – then taking pleasure in reminding his father that alcohol – which Gilchrist drank in copious quantities – was far more addictive than any of the soft drugs Jack enjoyed.

Which reminded him that he hadn't spoken to Jack in several weeks.

He checked the time – 10.44 – which might be considered an early rise for his artist son, then dialled his number. To his surprise, Jack was up and about and sounding lively.

'Hey, Andy,' Jack said. 'It's been a while. How you keeping?'

'Better than your mobile, it seems. Has it died on you?'

Jack laughed, a hard rattle that pulled a smile to Gilchrist's lips. 'The phone works both ways.'

'Not where you're concerned, it doesn't.'

'So,' Jack said, 'what's up?'

He didn't want to home straight in on the purpose of his call, so said, 'Thought I'd phone my favourite son for a wee chat between breaks at work.'

'Your *only* son, you mean. And I keep telling you to give up the day job. It's doing your nut in. As for me, things are looking up this end. One of the bigger galleries in Dundee has agreed to show my stuff on a trial basis for a month. They're linked with another gallery in Edinburgh, and if there's enough interest then, hey, you never know.'

'That's great, Jack. Why don't we meet up for a pint sometime soon, and you can tell me all about it.'

'No pints. I'm off the bevvy. Been off it for a month now.'

Gilchrist tried to hide his surprise with, 'Are you on antibiotics?'

'No, the wagon.'

'Why?' he asked. He couldn't remember a day when Jack had not had a pint in the pub. In fact, since turning eighteen, it was possible that Jack had the perfect attendance record.

'Met someone,' Jack said. 'And she's keeping me on the straight and narrow.'

Gilchrist almost groaned. Jack might have the perfect attendance in the local pubs, but where women were concerned he was definitely mentally AWOL, maybe even MIA. 'Well, that's good to hear, Jack. Anyone I know?'

'Shouldn't think so. If you're free later, we can meet for a pint and I'll introduce you.'

'Thought you weren't drinking.'

'We're not, but you are, right? The Central tonight at six? Does that work?'

'Provided nothing turns up.'

'Me and Kris'll be in there anyway, having a coffee or something.'

Jack having a *coffee or something*? In a pub? Gilchrist was so surprised he almost forgot the purpose of his call. 'Have you been in touch with Mo recently?'

Jack sighed, then said, 'Me and Kris popped round to her flat last week. She barely said a word. You know what Mo's like.'

No, he thought. It had been so long since he and Mo had sat down and had a chat that he felt as if he didn't know what his daughter was like at all any more. 'Maybe she didn't like Kris,' he tried.

'*Not like* and *Kris* are words that just don't go together. There's no way anyone can't like Kris. She's great. You'll love her.'

Gilchrist felt his heart slump. This was Jack at his worst, head over heels in love with a woman, blinded to everything in life including common sense and logic. Kris had already talked his son out of drinking alcohol – not that there was anything wrong with that – but the image of Jack in a bar without an alcoholic drink in sight just didn't compute.

He kept his options open by saying, 'If I can make it, I'll be there, Jack. OK?'

When the call ended, Gilchrist stared off across the North Sea. He should be proud of Jack for overcoming his reliance on alcohol, and pleased he'd met a woman who could make him feel positive about his life. He should be supportive of his son's latest relationship, safe in the knowledge that she was good for him.

But Gilchrist suspected that somehow it would all be short-lived.

CHAPTER 10

Gilchrist's first break arrived at 2.51 that afternoon in the form of a phone call from Dainty. 'Just had the boys looking through these photos you sent over, and we're pretty sure it's Stooky Dee.'

'Pretty sure?'

'Ninety-nine per cent sure. To be a hundred, you need a match on his DNA.'

'Should have results back soon.'

'If the body's got a tattoo behind the right ear, a bumblebee – don't fucking ask – then it's him.'

'We'll check that out,' Gilchrist said, then added, 'So how do you know Stooky?'

The line hung for several seconds, as if Dainty was considering what to tell him, and how much. 'A couple of years ago Stooky got involved in a stakeout that went to fuck,' he said. 'Took a bullet in his left thigh, and had to be carted off to the Royal. Hobbled about on crutches for months after, threatening to sue the police and everyone in it until we reminded him what side his fucking bread was buttered—'

'Wait a minute,' said Gilchrist. 'Are you saying Stooky's one of ours?'

'Yes and no. He ducked and dived. Worked for whoever paid him.'

'I thought he was on Jock Shepherd's payroll.'

'That's why we put the emphasis on *allegedly*, Andy. He's *allegedly* on Shepherd's payroll. Big Jock knows how the fucking system works. To survive in his business, he has to give a bit, take a bit. From time to time he helps us, and we help him, exchange a bit of this for a bit of that. As far as Shepherd's concerned, it's business as usual. That's the good news,' Dainty said.

'And the bad?'

'A body was fished from the Clyde at lunchtime. Been in the water a couple of days, but we've already been able to ID the poor sod as Hatchet McBirn.'

Gilchrist jolted. Hatchet McBirn was another name in Tommy's diary. 'So of the six names on that list, three are already dead,' he said. 'And all *allegedly* on Shepherd's payroll.' A pause then, 'So it's gang warfare?'

'Word on the street is that no one wants to take on big Jock. But just keep the status quo, keep their heads down, earn a living, albeit a fucking corrupt one.'

'And what about the remaining names on the list?' Gilchrist asked, struggling to recall them – Chippie Smith, Angel Thomson, Bruiser Mann.

'They're on their fucking ownie-oh,' Dainty said. 'Just punters on the side, watching what's what. We've had no dealings with them.'

Something niggled Gilchrist. If Dainty had no interest in the other three, then why were he and Gilchrist still on the phone?

He edged into it with, 'But those who are dead are of interest to you – Boyd, Dee, McBirn. Is that what you're saying?'

'Correct.'

Then it struck him. 'But not all three. Only Stooky?'

Dainty chuckled. 'Only Stooky,' he agreed.

'Because . . .?'

'Because he was tortured.'

Even then, all the pieces didn't fit. Dainty was holding something back, he was sure of it. But what? And why such a fuss over a small-time criminal who worked on both sides of the law for whoever paid him the most? Then the penny dropped.

'The fiver stuffed into his mouth,' he said. 'It's a calling card.'

'I can't say.'

'Can't say because you don't know? Or because you don't want to tell me?'

'Some questions are best left unanswered, Andy. Let's put it that way.'

'You need to do better than that, Dainty. The body's turned up on my doorstep, and I've a professional and moral obligation to find out how and why he died, and who killed him. You're duty bound to pass over any information that could assist in the—'

'Cut the fucking protocol crap, Andy. Under normal circumstances I would. But listen to me when I tell you this. These are not normal circumstances.' A pause, then, 'Something's going on. It's big. And it's fucking dangerous—'

'And it's to do with an imminent major drug shipment.'

Dainty didn't speak for so long that Gilchrist thought he had hung up. Then he came back with, 'Was that a fucking educated guess, or have you found something?'

'What would I have found, other than a dead body?'

'You need to tell me what's going on, Andy—'

'Isn't that the pot calling the kettle black?'

Another pause, then, 'I'm sending a man up. He'll be with you by the end of the day.'

'Anyone I know?'

'DS Nathanial Fox.'

'Never heard of him.'

'You'll like Nat. He's a good guy. Got to go.'

And with that, the connection died.

Gilchrist held onto the phone for a few seconds before returning it to its cradle. He churned through their conversation in his mind, troubled by the way Dainty hadn't taken him into his confidence. They'd been friends for more years than he could remember, but this was the first time he'd felt any kind of resentment against Dainty. It irked that Dainty had hung up without explanation, and annoyed him that he'd wanted Gilchrist to tell all, while keeping his own cards close to his chest.

But as their words echoed through his mind, Gilchrist came to understand that Dainty didn't want to be the one to update him, but instead had presented him with an alternative in the form of DS Nathanial Fox. *You'll like Nat. He's a good guy*. Was that Dainty's way of telling Gilchrist that Nat had all the answers to Gilchrist's unanswered questions?

He glanced at the time. Just after three. If Dainty jumped right on it – and it sounded like he would – then DS Nathanial Fox could be with Gilchrist sometime after 5 p.m., in time for that day's debriefing. He retrieved his mobile, and dialled Cooper's number.

'Cause of death, strangulation by a wire ligature around his neck,' she said without introduction. 'The wire is similar to the kind gardeners use to tie back plants, and was tied with a slipknot.

So he could have choked himself simply by trying to struggle free. He'd also lost a great deal of blood, so he's not likely to have been conscious at the time of his passing.'

'Does he have any tattoos?' Gilchrist asked.

'He has several.'

'How about behind the right ear?'

'Yes,' she said. 'An insect. Could be a wasp.'

'How about a bee?'

'It's a poor tattoo if it is.'

Gilchrist felt confident enough to say, 'His name is Stooky Dee, and you should find a DNA match on the database.'

'Stooky Dee? Who's he?'

'A petty criminal known to Strathclyde Police. I've been on the phone with Dainty who confirmed the bullet wound in the left thigh was from a stakeout a couple of years ago that went wrong. He had an operation in the Glasgow Royal Infirmary. What else can you tell me from the body?'

'The slashes on his left arm were done before he died, and by a sharp knife with a fine blade, the blade of a scalpel, perhaps, or something like that.'

'So he'd been tortured?'

'I'd say so.'

'Any alcohol, illegal substances in his blood?'

'Don't have the toxicology reports back yet, but if he was tortured, it'd be unlikely that whoever was doing the torturing would lessen the pain by giving him drugs.' She let out a heavy sigh, which had Gilchrist thinking she was irritated by his questions. Or maybe she was having difficulty understanding, just like he was, how any human being could do that to another—

'They also tortured him with his toes.'

'Say that again.'

'His toes. The metatarsal-phalange joint, where the toe connects to the foot. Every one of them was torn.'

'All five?'

'All ten. Both feet.'

Gilchrist had to close his eyes, but an image of the man's toes being pulled back until the joints snapped hit him with such clarity that he pushed away from his desk and looked out the window. He took a couple of deep breaths to steady his heart. White clouds dotted blue skies, nature's way of fooling you into thinking summer was close.

'Anything else?' he asked.

'Of course,' she said, with a coldness that reminded him of how heartless she'd been with him at times. 'Open wounds on his back are indicative of him having been whipped.'

'Ah, fuck.' He squeezed his nose with his thumb and forefinger. 'Jesus, Becky, the poor soul's gone through hell. And for what? To get him to cough up the goods on someone? Don't they have drugs that can do that now?'

'They do,' she said. 'But they're expensive, and not readily available.'

Neither's crack cocaine, he wanted to say. But they can still get their hands on that, whoever *they* are. But Cooper's coldness was getting to him. It took a certain individual to carry out post-mortem examinations day in day out. You had to be capable of switching off emotions with the ease of turning a tap, which in a way helped him understand how Cooper could just blank whatever feelings she'd once had for him.

He turned from the window as the oddest thought passed through his mind.

'Send me a copy of what you've got so far,' he said, and ended the call.

The date. That's what had jumped into his mind.

The date in the diary. The nineteenth of March.

Which happened to be next Monday.

His mention of an imminent drug shipment had stopped Dainty in his tracks. *Was that a fucking educated guess, or have you found something?* Yes, Gilchrist thought. I've found something all right. I've found the date of the drugs shipment . . .

Which you, Dainty, weren't going to mention.

CHAPTER 11

He found Jessie in her office at her computer, staring at the screen, opened folders strewn across her desk like discarded cards. Her eyes widened as he walked towards her.

'What've I done now?' she said.

'I need you to get hold of Tommy.'

'I don't know where he is.'

'Did you get a location on his mobile number?'

'We got a couple, yeah. But he'll be long gone by now.'

'That's not what I want to hear.'

Without another word, she picked up her mobile and dialled a number. She tapped the screen, and the sound of the dialling tone filled the room. When the connection was made, a recorded voice said, *The number you have called is not in service.* She ended the call, looked up at him, and said, 'That's the only number I've got for him.'

'And your point is?'

Jessie frowned. 'Even if I was able to contact him, sir – which I'm not – what would you want me to do with him if I found him?'

Gilchrist leaned forward and placed his hands on the desk so that their eyes were level. 'You're not listening to me, Jessie. I want you to find Tommy Janes. And when you do, I want him to tell you where and exactly when the drug shipment's coming in—'

'What drug shipment?'

'Tommy knows.'

'You've lost me, sir.'

It might be argued that he was lost himself. He didn't have a clear understanding of what had happened, only that something was niggling that sixth sense of his, telling him that the answer to Stooky Dee's murder and, just as importantly, Joe Christie's disappearance all these years ago, somehow lay with Tommy. But Tommy was prison-smart, and could be one step ahead of him, maybe more. Which raised the worrying thought, that what if Tommy was up to his ears in the killings, and had handed over the diary to throw the police off his trail?

He pushed back from Jessie's desk, and said, 'There were six names in that diary. Three are now dead. We can't rule out the possibility that Tommy—'

'Hold it.' Jessie held up her hands. 'I know my brother's a nutcase, but he's no killer.'

'It's no giant leap from GBH to murder,' he tried.

'It's not Tommy.' She shook her head, her eyes almost pleading. 'Tommy's a hard bastard, I'll give you that, but he's not a killer, Andy. He had a tough upbringing—'

'As had you.' He returned her look with one of hard fact. 'But *you* don't go about killing people—'

'And neither does Tommy.'

'How can you be sure?' he said. 'Tommy's spent more time inside than out. He even shared a cell with Bully Reid, for God's sake. If there was one born killer on the planet, then Bully was it. And after being released on licence, Tommy found himself back inside within six months—'

'He's changed, Andy. Believe me, I know he's changed.'

'Like a leopard changes its spots?'

Something passed behind Jessie's eyes at that comment, some thought that stilled her, as if time had backtracked and she found herself staring at Tommy as a youngster. Then the scene rebooted. 'Tommy can't swim,' she said.

'And . . .?'

'When we were young, me and Tommy and Terry were playing by the River Cart, searching for frogs. Tommy slipped on a rock, and fell in. He panicked. Started screaming and flapping his arms like he was drowning. Terry walked in and pulled him out. The water was only waist high. Ever since then, Tommy's been scared to death of water. He won't go anywhere near it. He'll barely walk across a bridge if there's water flowing under it.' She shook her head with absolute certainty. 'Even if that boat had been high and dry in a shipyard waiting to be launched, there's no way Tommy would've gone onto it to kill that guy—'

'Stooky Dee.'

Jessie gawked at him. 'What?'

'Our tortured guy's name is Stooky Dee. Dainty's team ID'd him. Cooper expects the DNA results back any time now, which will confirm it.'

She still seemed puzzled. 'You said three on the list were dead.'

'Dainty confirmed that Cutter Boyd was found in a dumpster at the back of the King's Theatre two weeks ago, with his throat cut. Lunchtime today, Hatchet McBirn was pulled from the River Clyde.'

Jessie said, 'And about a week ago, Stooky Dee was killed in the hold of a fishing boat. So . . .' She let out a lungful of air. 'One killing a week? Is that significant?'

Gilchrist raised an eyebrow. 'I hadn't thought of it like that. But maybe.' He walked across the room, turned his back to the window, and sat on the sill. Jessie looked small and wounded, as if hurt by his accusations about Tommy. But sometimes you just have to push.

'How would Tommy know these six names?' he asked.

'That's anybody's guess.'

'They're all on Jock Shepherd's payroll. *Allegedly*,' he emphasised. 'Does Tommy know big Jock?'

'Wouldn't put it past him.'

'What if it's not just the names we should be thinking about, but the date?'

'What date?'

'The date in the diary. The page Tommy wrote the names on. The nineteenth of March.'

'Is that significant?'

He pushed off the sill. 'Dainty said something big is going on, and that it's dangerous. But he wouldn't tell me what. But I think Tommy knows. And he knows when. Monday's the nineteenth, so if Tommy knows the date, then logically he must know what's about to happen.' He returned Jessie's gaze, but she was offering him nothing.

'The SOCOs found evidence of hard drugs on Joe Christie's boat,' he said. 'So I think it was being used for shipping drugs.'

'I'd heard,' she said. 'Maybe for social use?'

'Too much for that. Colin thought it was spillage from a burst bag.' Gilchrist pulled out a chair. 'Tommy's the key. He knows what's going on. So we need to find him. And you're the best person to do that.'

'How the hell am I going to do that?' she said. 'Sir.'

'You once said that you and Tommy used to be close—'

'*Used* to be. Past tense.'

'But you know who his friends are, who he'd confide in, where he'd likely go to lie low for a while.'

'I've hardly spoken to Tommy in years,' she said. 'I've no idea who his friends are. If word gets to Tommy that I'm looking for him, he'll think I'm after him. And believe me, when Tommy's cornered, he's scary. I don't know if I'd like to meet him *anywhere* under these circumstances.'

'You might if you were to give him good news.'

Jessie stared at him. 'And what good news would that be?'

'A new life in exchange for his testimony.'

'Witness protection?'

Gilchrist nodded.

Jessie puffed out her cheeks, then let it out. 'Jeezo, Andy, I wouldn't know where to start to look for him. I really wouldn't.'

'He's got your phone number, hasn't he?'

'Hello? Earth to Andy?' She tapped an imaginary head with her knuckles. 'Tommy might have my number, but I can't get through to his. Duh . . .'

'So make him call you.'

'What am I missing?'

'I don't care how much of a loner Tommy is. He must have

some friends somewhere. Or one friend, only *one* that he trusts.' He tried to hold her gaze, but she offered a blank look at the floor in response. 'Tommy's never married. Right?'

'Right.'

'But there must be someone he's close to.'

Jessie pursed her lips.

'*Think*,' he demanded. 'Was he ever in love? Did he ever lose his heart to a woman?'

'This is Tommy Janes we're talking about. Love and Tommy are two words that don't go well together.'

Gilchrist raked his fingers through his hair. 'A girl maybe, when he was younger.' But still he was not breaking through. 'When you were *all* younger. Before Tommy grew up and became wild.' He caught his breath as something seemed to shift behind Jessie's eyes, like the faintest of shadows. 'Yes?' he urged.

Then she stared through him. 'Izzy,' she said. 'Izzy Sinclair. She lived in the same close as us in Easterhouse. She had a soft spot for Tommy. I remember Tommy and Terry fighting out the back one day over something Terry had said to Izzy. Tommy gave him a right doing. Izzy must've been only fourteen or fifteen, but after that she doted on Tommy. But Tommy being Tommy, played the big man, wanting nothing to do with a wee girl. Not long after that, Izzy's old man got a new job and they moved away. Years later, I heard that Tommy and Izzy had met up again and had an on-off relationship for some time. But I don't think it lasted. Probably got pissed off visiting him in Barlinnie.' She grimaced at Gilchrist. 'And that's about it.'

'It's thin, I know. But it's a start.' He pushed to his feet. 'Get Jackie to find out what she can about Izzy, where she is, what she's doing. And if she's still in the country, go and talk to her face to face. She might know something.'

'And if she doesn't?'

He shrugged. 'Then we're back to square one.'

CHAPTER 12

With Jessie assigned to finding Tommy with the help of Jackie Canning – researcher extraordinaire – Gilchrist went in search of Mhairi. He found her at her desk, headphones on, eyes fixated on her computer screen.

When she noticed him, she whipped off her headphones. 'Sir?'

'Any luck with Joe Christie's files?'

She held up a large Manila folder. 'Got them here, sir.'

'Is his wife still alive?'

'She is, sir, and she still lives in Crail.'

'Let's go. And update me on the way.'

He had just pulled his BMW onto North Street when his phone rang – ID Cooper. He took the call through his car's system, and said, 'Yes, Becky.'

'The DNA is a match for Stooky Dee,' she said.

'Toxicology results?'

'God, Andy, you really are impatient.'

'I take it that's a no. So when will you have them?'

'Tomorrow.'

'I'll talk to you then.' He ended the call, and said, 'Tell me what you've found on Joe Christie.'

Mhairi flipped the folder open, and slipped out several sheets with notes scribbled on them. 'The SIO assigned to his case was DS May Pearson. She's since left the service and the area, and moved to Calgary in Canada with her husband and two children.'

'That's a bad start.' He turned left into Abbey Street, and accelerated downhill. 'We can still contact her if we need to. Keep going,' he said.

'The last person to see Joe Christie was Ivan McIver, who owned the fishing boat *Seagull Bait*. He died last year.'

Gilchrist gritted his teeth, gripped the steering wheel, and hissed, 'Jesus.'

'But we've got Ivan's statement here. He says that Joe was never a talker, that he was a loner who just got on with the day job of setting out to sea and laying his creels. He says here, that the last time he saw Joe, he thought he looked troubled—'

'Troubled? In what way?'

'He doesn't say.' She flipped through a number of pages, then read, '*That morning, Joe was quieter than usual. I said Good morning to him, but he ignored me. He looked awful worried, as if some major problem was troubling him. He was always tight with money, and I remember thinking he must have had a bad weekend in the bookies.*' She flipped a page over. '*The last sighting I had of him was at the wheel of* Brenda Girl *heading east. The swell was rising and the winds were picking up from the north. I wondered why Joe was heading into deeper waters.*'

'So Joe was going somewhere different that day?'

'Looks like that. But McIver didn't know where.'

'Did the Anstruther Office look into that?'

Mhairi brushed through some more pages, then shook her head. 'No, it looks like that was it. Joe sailed into the sunset, so to speak, and was never seen again.'

'Surely someone somewhere must have a sighting of him.' Gilchrist let out a gasp of frustration. 'I mean, the North Sea's got to be one of the busiest fishing areas on the planet.'

'But how would we find that out after all this time?'

'The Coastguard must have some records of shipping, surely.' But even as the words left his mouth, he realised he could be setting his team an impossible task, trying to track down evidence of a sighting of Christie's *Brenda Girl* before he and his boat vanished. And all for what? It didn't matter where the boat had gone to. What mattered was that it had been found again, albeit with a new name. Joe Christie was dead, Gilchrist felt sure. They might be able to glean more about what had happened to Joe, and where he had gone, if they spoke to the one person who must have known him better than anyone else – his wife.

'Tell me what else you've found,' he said, and drove on.

But by the time they reached the fishing village of Crail, and turned into Kirkwynd, Gilchrist was none the wiser. He parked opposite the address, a small terraced cottage on Nethergate with a clay-coloured pan-tiled roof. Weeds grew from the roof gutter, paint peeled from the fascia, a once-tidy home now tired and rundown, as if it needed a man's presence. Grey smoke from the single chimney trailed across the adjacent rooftops.

Someone was at home.

Mhairi rang the bell.

Gilchrist counted to twelve, then Mhairi rang the bell again.

A few seconds later, she cocked her head. 'Someone's coming.'

'There's nothing wrong with your hearing.' He stood back as the door cracked open, and an elderly woman's face, lined and grey, topped with dishevelled hair, filled the gap. The door creaked wider to reveal a stained dressing gown that draped over worn slippers.

'Mrs Christie?' he said.

'That's what it says on the door.'

He held out his warrant card. 'DCI Gilchrist from St Andrews CID, and this is DC McBride.'

Mhairi smiled, and said, 'We'd like a few minutes of your time.'

'What for?'

'To talk to you about your late husband, Joe.'

'Have you found the old bugger?'

Mhairi grimaced. 'I'm afraid not, ma'am.'

She tutted. 'Well, how d'you know he's deid, then?'

Gilchrist said, 'It might be best if we talked inside?' For an awkward moment, he thought she might slam the door in his face, but then she stepped back, and he held out his hand for Mhairi to enter first.

'Straight through to the kitchen,' Mrs Christie said. 'I've just finished hoovering.'

Gilchrist thanked her as he eased past her and followed Mhairi along a short hallway into a small kitchen. They both stood and waited for Mrs Christie to join them.

She shuffled into the kitchen and ignored them as she walked to the back door and pulled it open. Four cats spilled in, tails high, bodies curling around the old woman's legs. Only then did Gilchrist notice food trays on the floor in the corner. Two of the cats were already nuzzling the bowls, as if expecting to find them filled with morsels.

He leaned down and clawed his fingers into the fur of what looked like the oldest of the four, and the only tomcat from the look of things. The tom arched its back against the rub of his hand, throat purring like an engine. 'Does he have a name?' he asked her.

'What for? They cannae speak.'

Well, now it had been pointed out to him, he supposed it had been a silly question. He stood upright, while the tom continued to brush against his legs. 'I've only got one cat,' he said. 'Blackie, she's called.'

The old woman topped her cup from the teapot, and poured in a good helping of milk.

Gilchrist noticed the cats now sat on their haunches next to their food bowls. 'We can wait until you feed them,' he suggested.

'Hunger's good kitchen,' she said, and took a sip of her tea.

Mhairi had her notebook open, pen poised, and gave him a look that said she didn't want to spend more time in the cattery than was necessary. Well, if the cats weren't going to be fed until after they left, it seemed only fair that they got on with it.

'Right,' he said. 'The last you saw of your husband, Joe, was that morning he sailed from Crail three years ago. And you haven't heard from him since.'

She stared at him as she took another sip of tea.

'Is that correct?'

'Aye. Not one word.'

He let several seconds pass before saying, 'A fishing boat was washed ashore during last night's storm. Over on Tentsmuir Beach. It's had a change of name, but isn't registered with the

Coastguard.' One of the cats meowed, a feline reminder for him to hurry up, we're hungry. 'The boat's original name was *Brenda Girl*,' he said, and watched recognition shift across her face to end in a scowl that curled her lips.

'The old bugger sold it, so he did.'

'Why do you say that?'

'He said he would do that. Sell it. Fish prices had gone to cock. Working his arse off to pay the taxman. Nae money in it any more.' She shook her head. 'I always knew he'd do a runner on me someday.'

Mhairi said, 'Why do you say that, Mrs Christie?'

'Because he's a man.'

'A man who earned a dangerous living by fishing,' Mhairi tried.

'And a man who would get into bed with anything that moved, given half a chance.' She pulled a chair out from the kitchen table, and slumped herself onto it.

Gilchrist felt his eyebrows rise. The words *until death do you part* drifted through his mind in a wave that pulled up memories of his own failed marriage. Men the world over were mostly driven by their desire for sex. Or maybe it was their desire of the chase, the thought of some different body to explore. Look how Harry had beguiled Gilchrist's own wife, Gail. But Mhairi's voice reading Ivan's statement echoed, too – *a loner who just got on with the day job of setting out to sea and laying his creels*. That didn't sound to Gilchrist like a man who would *get into bed with anything that moved*.

He walked towards the kitchen table, taking care not to tread on any cats' paws – the pack shifting about their bowls with renewed energy, it seemed. 'Who do you think Joe sold the boat to?' he asked.

She shrugged. 'The first person stupit enough to buy it.'

He thought for a moment, then said, 'When Joe went out that day, Ivan McIver said he last saw him heading east. Out into deeper waters.'

'To Holland,' she said. 'That's where he wanted to end up.'

Gilchrist glanced at Mhairi, but her eyes told him this was news to her, too. 'Did you tell Detective Sergeant May Pearson that?'

'Who?'

'The Senior Investigating Officer.'

'Don't know about that, but whoever I spoke to, they weren't bothered.'

'Why not?'

'Don't know. They never asked. If they were bothered, they would've.'

'And you never offered?'

'Why would I? Joe's head was full of big plans for this, and big plans for that. But the stupit old bugger done nothing except go out on that bloody boat of his and spend any money he had left over from that day's catch in the bookies.'

With a married woman disinterested in finding her husband's whereabouts, or even if he was alive or not, Gilchrist couldn't help feeling that DS May Pearson had not delved into Christie's disappearance as deeply as she might have. Probably a matter of going through the investigative process, dotting an 'i' here, crossing a 't' there, until all the boxes were ticked, more or less.

'Where do you think Joe would have gone to if he sailed to Holland?' Gilchrist asked.

'Amsterdam.'

'Why there?'

'He'd been there as a wee boy, and loved it.'

Gilchrist nodded. He was about to wade his way through the cats again, when he noticed a carton of cat food on a shelf by the side of the fridge. He reached for it. 'Do you mind?'

She slurped a mouthful of tea.

The cats seemed to sense what was about to happen. They burst into activity, brushing themselves around his legs, tails high, one on its hind legs almost clawing its way up his new chinos. He had difficulty pouring the dried food into the bowls without spilling any, his hand being nudged this way and that as he topped the bowls. Satisfied that he'd taken care of all of them, he returned the carton to the shelf. With the cats busy feeding, he felt as if he could get back to the interview without further distraction.

'Do you know Ivan McIver?' he asked.

'No really.'

'Do you know anybody who might throw some light on Joe's disappearance?'

'Cannae think of anyone.'

Gilchrist nodded to Mhairi, who shook her head. He hadn't expected to learn anything new from talking to Joe's widow, but sometimes you just have to go through the motions. He leaned down and chucked the big tom's neck, but he was too busy eating to show any feline interest in being petted.

'I would call this one Tom,' he said.

'Aye, I'm sure that'll help him find his way home,' she said.

He smiled and pushed to his feet. 'We'll see ourselves out, Mrs Christie. Thanks for your help, and we're sorry we couldn't bring you better news on Joe.'

She grimaced, and gave a silent nod.

He led the way down the hallway, and had his hand on the front door handle, when Mrs Christie called out, 'Now you've found his boat, did you manage to find his logbook?'

Gilchrist and Mhairi turned to face her.

'If there was one good thing I could say about that old bugger,' she said, 'it would be that he kept his logbook up to date. At the end of every trip he would fill it out. Come hail or shine. Never missed a day. Said it was his insurance.'

'Insurance?' Gilchrist said. 'Insurance against what?'

'How would I know? But that's what he told me after the break-in. And a few days later he went missing.'

Gilchrist walked back towards Mrs Christie, Mhairi behind him. 'The reports never mentioned anything about a break-in,' he said.

'No, they wouldn't, would they? Yon lot down the police station couldn't close the book fast enough.'

'Why do you say that?' It seemed the sensible thing to ask.

'They just came in with their big boots and stood in the hall. They barely took a look around. Every drawer in the place had been pulled out. But after five minutes, they just took a note of my name and said they'd get back to me.'

'Where was Joe when the police came?'

'Out in his boat. Where else?'

The bookies, Gilchrist thought. But he kept his tongue in check. 'Was there anything stolen or missing?' he asked.

'No that I could tell. When Joe came home that night, he'd had a few. He cursed and punched a hole in the wall, he was that mad. But that's when he told me about the logbook being his insurance. Said he'd sort it out.'

'Sort what out?'

'How would I know? That's all he would say. Nothing more.'

Gilchrist said, 'We found the boat, but not the logbook.'

'Aye, that's what I thought. You'd need to know where to look, wouldn't you?'

CHAPTER 13

Jessie stared at Jackie's computer screen. 'This is it?' she asked.

Jackie nodded, her unruly bob of rust-coloured hair bouncing like a loose-curled Afro. She worked the mouse, placed the cursor at the start of the address, and ran it through all the letters. Her stammer was now so bad she had given up trying to speak. Besides, cursors for pointers were as effective as any tongue. A click of the mouse, and the printer whirred alive, printing out the address and contact information, as well as Google Maps directions.

Jessie removed the page from the printer tray. It had taken Jackie only fifty minutes to locate Izzy Sinclair – now Izzy McLure with two teenaged children, divorced for four years, living in a council house in Inchkeith Drive, Dunfermline, on the dole for three years, her last period of employment lasting only six months in the local Tesco.

Jessie thought of phoning Izzy, but if Tommy had indeed been in contact with her, it would be better to talk to her face to face – more difficult for her to get away with telling lies that way. According to Google Maps, it would take her about an hour to drive there. If she set off now, she could be back before 7 p.m. – if she didn't hit traffic.

Mind made up, she headed for the door.

Gilchrist parked in Tentsmuir Forest.

The skies had cleared, the wind had died, and although the temperature was in single figures, the sun close to setting, the walk across the sand dunes offered the promise of longer days and lighter nights. He was now finding that the older he became, the more he longed for those wonderful late summer sunsets, when darkness didn't settle on the Fife coast until after 11 p.m. Years ago, in the Shetland Islands farther north, during a midsummer's week he'd experienced the *simmer dim* as a teenager, where the sun never set and twilight ran through the midnight hours. He'd promised himself that he would return one day, but life has a habit of taking over, and he never had.

He and Mhairi cleared the dunes, and the winds picked up as if from nowhere. Ahead, the sea seemed alive with rows of white horses. 'Christ,' he said. 'What is it about Scotland? It could be snowing by the time we get home.'

Mhairi said, 'Yes, sir,' and kept her hands stuffed deep into her pockets.

Joe's boat was still high and dry, having been driven beyond the high tide mark by the previous night's storm. And being a crime scene, it had attracted a crowd of spectators, some interested in seeing a beached boat close up, others more intrigued by the workings of the SOCOs still going about their business.

The crime-scene tape had been moved, too, to take in a wider area and keep the nosy spectators at a more respectful distance.

He and Mhairi signed in again, and he held the tape high for her to slip under. The climb up the rope ladder was still as tricky, but he took his time, then helped Mhairi on board.

The cloying stench of decaying meat and rotting fish, which had pervaded every pore of his being earlier, had lessened, and was now the occasional putrid whiff that seemed to lift off the decking at the random stirring of a sea breeze. He wasn't sure if it was his imagination or not, but it seemed to him that the boat now lay at a sharper angle, as if the hull had found some comfortable spot on the beach and settled deeper. He gripped the corner of the cabin, pulled himself up the deck, and swung inside. Mhairi was more limber than he, and seemed more at home on canted decking than he could ever be.

'It should be over there,' she said, nodding to the starboard corner of the cabin.

Gilchrist worked his way over, using his hands against the window frame to steady himself. When he reached the corner, he leaned down, one foot on the deck, the other on the inside of the hull. It took him several minutes of tapping and pressing the cabin panels before he found the removable panel Mrs Christie had told them about, a ten-inch length of tongue-and-groove that he pried out to reveal a slotted opening from which he pulled a tired-looking logbook, its hardback cover pliable from dampness and stained with mildew.

It felt soggy, and when he tried to open it, the pages stuck together. Further attempts to peel them wider only threatened to tear the paper. He tried to separate several pages with a fingernail, but it was like opening damp puff pastry layer by flaking layer.

'We'll have to let someone look at this,' he said.

'I've a friend who works in the library,' Mhairi said. 'And I know she's been involved in recovering damaged books. I could ask her.'

'Perfect,' he said. 'Get her to jump on it.'

Back in his car, Gilchrist had to shiver off the cold. The sun had already set and night had arrived with a dark winter chill. He started the engine, and worked his way back out of the forest. By the time he cleared the exit, the cabin had warmed, heat once again circulating through his system.

Back in the North Street Office, he found a message from Dainty confirming that DS Nathanial Fox had ID-ed the body in the Bell Street mortuary as Stooky Dee. Gilchrist was surprised to find out that Fox had visited Bell Street without forewarning, and annoyed that Dainty had not left a phone number for Gilchrist to contact Fox. He was about to call Dainty when a hard rap on his office door had him replacing the handset in its cradle.

'Yes, ma'am,' he said.

Chief Superintendent Diane Smiley entered his office with a tight grimace. Her hair seemed blonder, the roots less dark, and shorter, too. 'Just had a call from the Chief,' she said. 'And he's not happy.'

Gilchrist tried to show his best poker face, but the inference that the Chief Constable had issues with his ongoing investigation – and at such an early stage – had him frowning and cocking his head. 'About?' he said.

'About why Strathclyde are providing resources to a Fife Constabulary investigation.'

'I wouldn't use the term *providing resources*, ma'am. I contacted Strathclyde to assist in ID-ing the murder victim. So, *sharing information* would be a more appropriate term. In my opinion. ma'am.'

'And have they?' she said. 'ID-ed the victim?'

'I've only just had it confirmed that the victim's name is Stooky Dee, a small-time crook *allegedly* on the payroll of Jock Shepherd. Glasgow's crime patriarch,' he added, 'if you're unfamiliar with the name.' Not that he thought she would be, as Shepherd's criminal enterprises were sufficiently widespread for some to consider him Scotland's crime patriarch, let alone Glasgow's.

'Ah,' she said. 'Now I see.'

But something in the narrowing of her eyes warned Gilchrist that whatever Smiler thought she could see, she wasn't about to share it. 'Did you contact Lothian and Borders?' she asked.

His frown deepened. 'No. Why?'

'Northern? Or Tayside?'

'No.'

'Any other forces?'

'No.'

Her scowl shifted to curiosity. 'Well,' she said. 'I have to ask why?'

'Why what?'

'Why contact Strathclyde Police at all?'

Gilchrist held her hard gaze, his mind crackling like wildfire, warning him that for Fife Constabulary's Chief Constable Archie McVicar to have become involved, someone in Strathclyde must have had their feathers ruffled. Or perhaps more correctly, Gilchrist had turned over some stone that no one in Strathclyde wanted turned over. But how could he have done that? He'd spoken to Dainty only that afternoon, which was when he realised that it was all to do with Tommy Janes being on the run, and the man determined to bring him in at all costs – Chief Superintendent Victor Maxwell of Strathclyde's BAD Squad.

What had Dainty once told Gilchrist about Maxwell?

Maxwell's not normal, Andy. He's got fucking eyes everywhere. So watch your back. And tell Jessie to do the same. Until that nutcase of a brother of hers turns up more likely dead than alive, then we all need to steer clear of Maxwell and the rest of his fucking team.

Maxwell was someone you wouldn't want to fall out with. But even if his rationale was wrong, Gilchrist didn't think it wise to offer up any personal link to Tommy Janes and his list of names. At least not yet. Well, in for a penny, so they say . . .

'Stooky Dee's name popped up on the PNC,' he lied, 'as recently reported missing. His home address was Glasgow, so Strathclyde seemed the obvious choice.' He gave her a quick smile. 'They've since sent up one of their own to ID the body – a Detective Sergeant Nathanial Fox.'

Smiler nodded, as if giving his comment some thought.

Gilchrist snatched the opportunity to move on. He glanced at his watch. 'As it turns out, I'm expecting DS Fox here any time now. I've no way of contacting him directly, so we'll just have to press on with today's debriefing without him.' He held his arm out, an invitation for Smiler to precede him. 'Shall we?'

He almost breathed a sigh of relief when she turned to the door.

As they walked along the upper hallway, she said, 'So I'll call the Chief back and tell him what? That we're not stealing resources from Strathclyde, but instead are providing them with information which could . . .?'

It took Gilchrist three steps before he realised he was expected to answer. 'Which could assist them in their own ongoing murder investigations.'

A pause, then, 'Investigations? Plural?'

'Yes.'

Smiler stopped, as did Gilchrist. 'For God's sake, Andy, will you stop drip-feeding me. What bloody investigations plural are you talking about?'

'Stooky Dee is one of three people on Jock Shepherd's payroll – *allegedly* – to turn up dead in the past two weeks.' He nodded to the staircase, and said, 'I'll bring this up at the debriefing, ma'am,' escorting her by the arm as they headed downstairs. 'But what puzzles me is why the Chief would be so unhappy with my investigation thus far. In my experience,' he continued, 'when someone complains upstairs about misuse of resources, or interference in this, that or the other, it usually means that they're trying to point the finger of blame to someone else.'

'Or divert attention from some*where* else,' she said.

Smiler's comment took Gilchrist by surprise, a level of mental acuity that told him she was more than capable of running the St Andrews Office. 'Or some*thing* else?' he tried.

'Like a murder investigation they don't want us to be involved in?'

'Could be,' he said, and held the door to the briefing room open. 'I'd be interested in finding out who phoned the Chief in the first instance.'

Rather than enter the room, Smiler stood back. 'Carry on with your debriefing, Andy. And let me get back to you.'

As she walked away from him, black shoes clicking the tiled flooring, navy-blue uniform pressed as crisp as new, he puzzled as to how their thought processes seemed to work in parallel, how their sense of logic ran the same path with barely a word of conflict, and wondered if they would ultimately reach the same conclusion.

Whoever had tried to stir up big Archie would have made sure to distance themselves from all evidence. If Gilchrist wanted to find out whatever was going on – the *something big* – he knew it was not about who killed Stooky Dee or Cutter Boyd or Hatchet McBirn. No, he thought, it was about finding out *why* they had been murdered in the first place.

CHAPTER 14

Jessie pulled her Fiat 500 off the road and parked half-on half-off the pavement. She switched off the engine and lights, and spent a couple of minutes taking a careful look around her to make sure that brother of hers was nowhere in sight. The likelihood of Tommy having been to Izzy's home was slim to zero. But where her brother was concerned, Jessie knew to leave nothing to chance. She eyed the houses along the street, not sure what she was looking for, but just trying to convince herself that Tommy wasn't here.

Eventually, she opened the door and stepped into the damp night chill.

From where she stood, she counted the house numbers all the way to Izzy's address, a mid-terrace house on the opposite side of the street. A light was on in her front room and spilled onto a dark footpath to the front door. The upstairs windows lay in darkness, whereas all the homes either side, and the adjacent home at the end of the terrace of four, glowed with warmth from within.

Jessie tightened her scarf around her neck, and crossed the road.

Where most residents had replaced their front lawns with paving to provide off-road parking, Izzy's was the only house that sported a hedge and a lawn – if it could be called that. A bulging privet hedge in need of a right good pruning came chest-high, and fronted an area of overgrown grass, flattened from the wind and the weight of the rain.

She walked to the front door and, using the light from her mobile, checked the house number. No mistake. This was Izzy's. She turned around and scanned the street one last time. It lay quiet and empty, as if everyone had fled the town, or were indoors watching *Coronation Street* or *Emmerdale*.

She took a deep breath, faced the door, and pressed the doorbell.

She heard a toneless buzzing from deep within. A flicker of light from the window to her right revealed a face for an instant before the curtain settled into darkness again. Moments later, locks clicked and scraped as keys were turned. Then the door eased open with a sticky slap, to be stopped by a chain that snapped tight at a four-inch gap through which Jessie saw only darkness.

'Yeah?' a woman's voice said.

'Izzy McLure?'

The gap narrowed as the door almost closed. 'Who is it?'

'I'm looking for Izzy McLure.'

'She's no here.'

'This is her address,' Jessie said. 'So she should be here.'

Silence. But at least the door stayed open.

'I'm with Fife Constabulary,' Jessie said, not wanting to mention her surname in case Izzy – if it was indeed Izzy behind the door – made the connection and slammed the door in her face. 'I can show you my warrant card if you open the door. Or I can push it through the letterbox if you'd prefer. But I'd need to get it back, which would mean opening the door anyway. So I might as well show it to you.'

'What d'you want?'

'A cup of tea if you've got the kettle on.' Jessie pushed her warrant card into the gap at the edge of the door, and shone her mobile phone onto it. 'It'd be easier to see if you put the hall light on.'

Again, silence.

Jessie retrieved her warrant card and phone, then said, 'I'd just like to have a wee chat with you. That's all.'

'I'm getting ready for bed.'

Well, she thought, nothing for it but to come clean. 'You probably don't remember me, Izzy. But I'm Tommy's wee sister.'

The door closed, and Jessie whispered a silent curse.

Then, to her surprise, it eased open again, this time chain-free.

In the hallway darkness, Jessie could make out the waif-like figure of a woman in denim jeans tight enough to be the second skin of anorexic-thin legs. A man-sized cardigan hid her upper body. Long sleeves covered her hands.

'Jessie?' she said.

Jessie nodded. 'Detective Sergeant Jessica Janes, to be exact.'

'Aye,' she said. 'I'd heard.'

A surge of excitement flashed through Jessie. The only way Izzy could know she'd joined the police was from Tommy himself. But just to be sure, she said, 'Who'd you hear that from?'

Izzy realised her slip-up, and pushed at the door.

93

Jessie stamped her foot on the threshold. 'I'm here to help, Izzy.' She felt the pressure slacken off her foot as Izzy relaxed her grip. 'I've come alone. I only want to talk. Tommy's got himself in a lot of trouble. And we believe his life is in danger.' It took a few seconds for her to realise that Izzy was crying. She removed her foot from the threshold, and said, 'Why don't I come in and make us both a cuppa?'

Izzy sniffed, nodded her head, and pulled back.

Jessie stepped inside and, as she closed the door, cast her gaze along the street, unable to shift the strangest feeling of being watched. She followed Izzy along a narrow hallway into a tiny kitchen redolent of cooking fat and chips, and overly bright from a cluster of spotlights on the ceiling. A single dinner plate stood alone on a dripping tray. Venetian blinds blanked out a small window by the sink. A glance around the work surfaces, shelves, small kitchen table, confirmed that Izzy lived and ate alone.

She turned to find Izzy staring at her.

'You look different,' Izzy said.

'It's been years.'

Izzy squeezed her hands together and pressed them to her mouth, as if to prevent her saying something she might regret. Brown eyes that seemed darker than Jessie remembered studied her with an alertness that could be mistaken for animal cunning. 'You've Tommy's eyes,' she said.

At the mention of Tommy, Jessie struggled to keep her excitement hidden. She'd been right. Tommy had been in contact with Izzy. Rather than press her, Jessie offered a smile of friendship. 'There's just the two of us now. Me and Tommy.'

Something shifted across Izzy's face like a shadow. A frown ruptured her forehead. 'He didnae do it,' she said. 'He's innocent.'

Jessie nodded, certain now that Tommy had been in recent contact. *He didnae do it. He's innocent.* How did Izzy even know what the *it* was? Who would have told her, if not Tommy? She waited for Izzy to offer up more, but it seemed she'd said all she was going to say about Tommy's guilt or innocence.

Jessie looked around the kitchen. 'Do you have a kettle?'

Izzy shook her head. 'Plug needs a fuse. Been microwaving everything.' She reached up and removed two mugs from a cupboard, which she filled with tap water then placed in the microwave.

When she pressed the timer, Jessie said, 'Even the chips?'

'Leftover from the chippie.'

Just the action of moving around the kitchen revealed to Jessie how skinny Izzy was. Pipe-cleaner jeans flattened a shapeless backside, and when she reached up for the teabags, her cardigan slipped loose to give Jessie a fleeting glimpse of porcelain skin and a waist that could be the envy of any teenager.

'You live alone?' Jessie said.

Izzy's eyes widened at the question, as if afraid of the answer. 'The kids've went with their father. Lazy conniving bastard. That way he says he disnae have to pay me a thing. Nae maintenance. Nothing. It's no right, so it's no. They're my kids, too.' The microwave beeped and Izzy jerked an angry look at it.

'Let me.' Jessie opened the microwave, and removed both mugs.

Izzy took a seat at the table. 'Milk's off,' she said, dabbing a teabag into one of the mugs. 'So it's gonnae have to be black.'

'Just the way I like my men,' Jessie said.

Izzy's gaze darted to Jessie, and her lips parted in a white smile of perfect teeth – a real surprise. 'You never, did you?'

Jessie smiled. 'It's been that long I can hardly remember.' Izzy grinned as she dunked the teabag from one mug to the other, leaving Jessie with the impression that it hadn't been that long ago for Izzy. She waited until Izzy shoved a mug her way, teabag included, before saying, "Tell me about Tommy.'

'Whit about him?'

Jessie took a sip of tea, and eyed Izzy over the rim. 'I know you're seeing him, Izzy,' she lied. 'And I know you and Tommy go back years. So I'm happy for you.' She rolled her eyes to the ceiling. 'Now that lazy conniving bastard of a husband of yours is out the way.'

Izzy stared at her mug of tea so long that Jessie thought she had clammed up for good. Then she turned her gaze full bore at Jessie, and said, 'You're polis—'

'And I'm also Tommy's sister.' Jessie put some force into her voice. 'I'm not here to arrest him, Izzy. You got that? I said I'm here to help.'

Izzy's lips tightened. 'Here to help? How can you help? Tommy's in too deep—'

'Tommy's innocent. I know he is.' She let out a sigh that sounded harsh even to her own ears, then she focused on keeping her tone level, her voice more gentle. 'Tommy might be a right nutter, but he was nothing like Terry. There was always a soft side to Tommy that he showed to only a few.'

Izzy's lips wavered. Tears squeezed from the corners of her eyes, and Jessie reached over and took hold of her hands.

'I can't help Tommy if you won't help me, Izzy.'

She shook her head. 'The polis'll no help him.'

'We will.'

'You cannae. It disnae matter if he's no guilty,' she said. 'It's the polis that're after him. And they'll no let up until they get him.'

Jessie massaged Izzy's hand. 'Look at me, Izzy.' She waited until Izzy's tearful gaze lifted. 'I know you and Tommy go back years. And I know Tommy's not the man they say he is. So there's a life for Tommy. A life for you and Tommy. Together. If you want it.'

Izzy's gaze flickered with uncertainty. She sniffed, shook her head. 'But how . . .?'

'Witness protection.'

The words hit Izzy like a slap to the face. She stared at Jessie, then her gaze danced left and right, as if her mind were trying to solve some incalculable equation.

Jessie sensed her chance. And took it. 'For the two of you,' she said. 'New identities. New place to live. Overseas if you'd like. Spain seems to be in fashion at the moment.' Christ, she'd really done it now.

But Izzy's whole being seemed to soar with the promise of a way out. Her eyes sparkled at the chance to make a fresh start, a new life in a new country, away from the depressing gloom of the Scottish weather. It seemed as if she was already there, sipping champagne cocktails on some Costa del-wherever beach, skin glowing from a Spanish sun, purse lightened by recent purchases – jewellery, shoes, handbags, colourful kaftans.

Then, as reality settled in, her spirits thumped back to earth.

'What's the catch?' she said.

'No catch, Izzy. Tommy helps us, and we help Tommy.'

Izzy turned her head to the window by the sink, eyes focusing on the far distance, as if searching for the Spanish sun beyond the venetian blinds.

Jessie knew she had no authority to make any such deal, and she made a silent prayer, hoping to God that she hadn't oversold it. 'But first,' she said, 'you need to get Tommy to contact me.'

Izzy returned her gaze. She could have aged ten years in as many seconds. 'I cannae guarantee that.'

'I know you can't.'

Izzy nodded. 'I'll try.'

'Thanks, Izzy.' It was all she could say.

CHAPTER 15

With the day's debriefing behind him, Gilchrist pushed through the door to the car park at the rear of the North Street Office. He'd not heard back from CS Smiley about Chief Constable McVicar, so he assumed she would catch up with him in the morning. In the bitter March chill, he checked his mobile for texts, to find one from DS Fox – Staying at west port. Can I buy you a pint? – at least he now had Fox's mobile number; and another from his daughter, Maureen – R u coming tonite?

Disappointment flushed through him, not because he didn't want to speak to either, but because he wanted to spend more time with each. But he couldn't let Maureen down, so he sent a text – Will be there by 8 – then fired up the ignition, and drove off to meet Fox in the West Port Bar and Kitchen.

In South Street he found a parking spot outside Drouthy Neebors, across the road from the West Port. A light drizzle as fine as smirr misted the air as he pulled up his jacket collar and crossed the street.

Only one person was seated at the bar on the left as he entered – a local by the look of him; blue-striped Fair Isle sweater over a denim shirt; Angus leather jacket hanging over the back of the chair. He seemed more interested in his mobile than his Amstel beer. Gilchrist ignored him and veered right, stepping into a lower lounge that seemed quiet for that time of night. A young couple in the corner glanced his way then returned to their mobile phones. An elderly couple in deep conversation paid him no attention.

Back upstairs, he was about to walk to the bar through the back when a man's voice called out, 'Gilchrist?'

He turned, surprised to find the local walking towards him, hand outstretched.

The grip was dry and firm, almost too firm. 'DS Fox,' the local said, then raised a hand to the bartender. 'Miss? Whatever this guy's having. My tab.'

Gilchrist said, 'Pint of 80 Shilling would do the trick, thank you.'

'You got it.' Fox returned to his chair, pushed one Gilchrist's way.

Gilchrist took some time removing his jacket, slipping it over the back of his seat, then lifted his pint as it arrived. 'Can't stay long. Promised I'd visit my daughter.'

Fox nodded, and held his bottle out. 'To daughters.'

Gilchrist chinked his pint to the bottle. 'I'll drink to that.' He took a sip. 'So tell me, do I detect a slight American accent?'

'Spent seven years in Winston Salem, North Carolina. Worked with the County Fire Department. Loved it. Great weather, plenty of money and good-looking women. Just throwing themselves at you. I tell you, the good old US of A knows what it's about.'

'Why return to Scotland?' It seemed the sensible thing to ask.

'Health. Ticker's not what it used to be.'

What Gilchrist had first taken as a ruddy flush of wellbeing on Fox's face, he came to realise was the rubicund evidence of blood pressure the high side of healthy. Tiredness below the eyes, and a general uneven pallor, hinted of too much alcohol and just as many cigarettes.

Fox finished his Amstel, nodded to the bartender. 'I'll have a Glenlivet. On the rocks. More Glenlivet than rocks, if you get my meaning.' Then he turned to Gilchrist. 'Don't know what it is about Scotland. You make the stuff, but it gets dished out like you don't wanna share it.'

When Fox's Glenlivet came up, he scowled at it and pushed it back. 'Put some more in it, will you?'

The bartender, who looked as young as a student, said, 'Another double, sir?'

'You got it, miss.'

Gilchrist waited while Fox's quadruple was served. 'For a moment there, I thought you were going to need a pint tumbler.'

Fox chuckled. 'Up yours,' he said, and took a quaff that drained it halfway. He ran his tongue over his lips, then looked at Gilchrist as if stunned to see he still had company.

Gilchrist was aware of time passing. Despite the attraction of an evening at the bar, he needed to focus while Fox was still on the right side of sober. 'You visited the Bell Street mortuary,' he said.

'That Dr Cooper's something else, isn't she?'

'She knows her stuff. I'll give her that.'

'And her ass. Man oh man, you'd need both hands just to hold on.'

101

'You ID-ed the victim?' Gilchrist said. 'How did you know Stooky?'

'Used to be one of my snitches,' he said.

'Used to be?'

'We had a falling out about money. He wanted more. But that wasn't gonna happen. So he moved on.' His smile could have fooled Gilchrist into believing he was pleased that Stooky had been tortured and murdered.

'You don't seem upset.'

Fox's lips flickered into a grimace. 'After the falling out, Stooky turned nasty. Even threatened me. Told me to watch my back.' He shook his head. 'That was a big mistake. So, no, I'm not upset. Good riddance, if you ask me.'

'When did you last see him?'

'About six months ago. Not long after the fallout.' Fox sipped his whisky, lips curling as if it now tasted bitter. 'Stooky wasn't in the business of making friends. He had a job to do. Kept that to himself, too. And always flush with cash. Did collection work for big Jock.'

There was that name again. But just to be sure, Gilchrist said, 'Jock Shepherd?'

'You got it.'

'You don't want to mess with that man.'

Fox nodded, took another sip. 'World's full of people who don't wanna pay what they owe. Stooky was good at getting them to cough up. Might've been small in stature, but man, he could be a mean mother. It would be a foolhardy person who tried to avoid paying big Jock. Particularly with Stooky chasing you down.' He turned to Gilchrist. 'But you know all about that, don't you?'

Surprised, Gilchrist said, 'What do you mean?'

'Just something Dainty said in the passing. Gave the impression that you'd run foul of big Jock once before. But, hey, I wouldn't worry. Most of us've run foul of big Jock at one time or another. Nature of the beast, I guess.'

Gilchrist frowned. He'd last met Shepherd about a year or so ago. Although he hadn't *run foul* of the man, he'd been left in no doubt that Shepherd was the boss, and that he would allow no one – no matter on which side of the law they worked – to stand in his way. And all for the benefit of business – Shepherd's business – making sure he was churning in the cash, legal or not.

But Gilchrist still had unanswered questions. 'So you think one of big Jock's debtors didn't want to pay, and was sending him a message by killing Stooky?'

Fox shook his head. 'Stooky's killing was nothing to do with collections.'

Gilchrist lifted his pint. 'I'm listening.'

'Stooky died the old-fashioned way. A good old gangland killing.'

Gilchrist said nothing while Fox did what he could to drain his glass. The whisky could have been acid from the way the man's face screwed up. Then he took another sip, and returned his glass to the bartop with a crack that startled the bartender.

'Another one of these, miss.'

Gilchrist sensed the bartender felt she was too young to refuse a customer a drink, and the look on her face warned him she was about to seek managerial assistance. 'I'll vouch for him,' he said. 'One more, then we're on our way.' He gave her a smile of reassurance, then faced Fox. 'Told you I can't stay long.'

'Speak for yourself.'

Gilchrist pressed his pint to his lips. Fox was well on his way to having one too many, maybe several too many. For all he knew, Fox could have stopped in a couple of bars before the West Port. 'So why do you think Stooky's killing is gang related?'

'The note in the mouth. The Clydesdale Bank fiver.'

'Which means . . .?'

'Which means sweet eff-all in a court of law.' Fox smiled at the bartender as she slid a filled glass across the bar. 'Thanks, miss.' He leaned forward to take a sip, careful not to spill any. Then he straightened up, and said, 'It might not be well known to the public, but it's big Jock Shepherd's calling card.'

'Are you saying Shepherd killed Stooky?'

'Not Shepherd in person *per se.*'

'But if Stooky worked for Shepherd, why would he have him killed?'

'Cleaning shop. Moving house. Time for a change.' Fox grimaced at Gilchrist, then said, 'Shepherd's not well. Word is he won't see the summer out. Maybe not even see it in.' He nodded, as if at the wisdom of his words. 'And not just Stooky,' he added. 'But Hatchet McBirn, *and* Cutter Boyd.'

'All three?'

'Yep.'

'Well,' said Gilchrist, trying to put his thoughts in order. 'If it's not a secret that the fiver's Shepherd's calling card, who's to say they're not copycat killings?'

'That's what we're *supposed* to think.'

Gilchrist's head was spinning from the convoluted logic. Even if Shepherd *won't see the summer out or even in,* why would he kill his own men? It made no sense. He waited until Fox returned his glass to the bar, then said, 'So you know for sure who's behind the killings?'

'We've got our suspicions.'

'Sounds like there's a but coming up.'

'But . . . we've got to tread carefully.'

Gilchrist almost cursed. Fox was not opening up, and seemed more intent on having a good night out rather than sharing information. He'd likely had no intention of ever doing so. Just come up to ID Stooky's body, and see for himself that the fiver was indeed a Clydesdale Bank fiver – whatever that proved. But if you asked the question – who knew the fiver was Jock Shepherd's calling card? – *alleged* calling card – then it could cut the list of suspects to the troubling few: someone in the police service.

And with that thought, Jessie's voice echoed through his mind – *Tommy might be a right nutter, but he was nothing like Terry*. No, he thought, Terry was the wild brother who could slice and dice you to death, just as soon as look at you.

Which brought him full circle, back to Tommy's list.

'What about the others?' he asked Fox.

Fox stilled, as if the question had frozen him to the spot. 'What others?'

From memory, Gilchrist rattled off the other three names on Tommy's list, those who had survived the supposed gangland cull. 'Bruiser Mann. Chippie Smith. Angel Thomson.'

A shadow of sorts passed behind Fox's eyes. 'Doing fine, last I heard.'

'And Tommy Janes?'

Fox's eyes narrowed, but only for a moment. 'I was hoping young Jessie might have come along with you this evening.'

'Why not phone her, speak to her directly?'

Fox cocked his head, as if giving the question some thought. 'Don't want to trouble her,' he said. 'So that won't be necessary.'

'Because . . .?'

'Because of what she's gone through.'

Gilchrist downed the last of his pint. Fox was not letting him in, just feeding him bits and pieces to tag him along. Well, he wasn't up for listening to any more of Fox's saccharine drivel. He slid from his chair, picked up his jacket. 'Can I ask you one last question before I go?'

'So soon?' He held out his hand.

Gilchrist took it. 'The other names,' he said. 'Bruiser, Chippie, Angel.'

'What about them?'

'You didn't ask, Where did you get them?'

'So?'

'That's because you already knew about them.'

Fox managed to pull his hand free. 'You're looking for something that's not there, Gilchrist. They're small-time criminals. Operating out of Glasgow. On big Jock's ticket. Most of their adult lives spent behind bars. Everyone in Strathclyde knows them.'

'But not everyone in Strathclyde knows about the list.'

Fox stilled.

Gilchrist offered a wry smile. 'Do you know what I've learned from our meeting tonight?'

'Is that it? Your last question?'

'Absolutely nothing,' Gilchrist said, then turned and walked from the bar.

Outside, he bustled through the drizzle to his car parked on the opposite side of the street. He switched on the ignition, slipped into gear. He hadn't been altogether honest with DS Nathanial Fox. Because he hadn't learned *absolutely nothing* from their meeting. He'd learned not to believe a word that came out of Fox's mouth.

But worse than that. Much worse.

He'd learned that he could no longer trust Dainty.

CHAPTER 16

He thought Maureen looked tired, as if she'd stayed awake into the small hours for him to get there. But it was still early – five minutes shy of 8 p.m. – and before he could work out what was troubling her, she reached up and gave him a hug.

He hugged her back, pecked her cheek. 'How are you?'

She hooked a finger in her hair, tucked it behind her ear. 'Have you eaten?' she said, then turned and headed to the kitchen.

He closed the door behind him, and followed her.

'I know that was a silly question,' she said, 'because you usually go to the pub and have a pint without ordering any food.'

'Well, that's not exactly true.'

'And you always say that.'

'Not always.'

'See?'

'See what?'

'You haven't eaten yet.'

'I'm not hungry.'

'And you always say that, too.' She opened the fridge, slid out three sliced quarters of pizza on a dinner plate covered with cling film, which she placed on a circular oak table large enough to sit four at a push. He said nothing as she stripped the cling film, crumpled it into a ball, and dumped it into the bin. 'Your favourite,' she said. 'Cold pizza.'

Well, he could never argue with her over that. Unpalatable as it may sound, cold pizza was indeed one of his favourites, a fondness he'd developed during that first year of living by himself after Gail thundered from the family home, young Jack and Maureen in tow, to settle in Glasgow with her new fellow, Harry – that wife-shagging bastard. Still, if he could ever take the good out of being cuckolded, it would be his discovery of cold pizza.

Of course, not having a microwave at the time helped – that, too, had found its way to Glasgow. After ordering a large pizza for home delivery, which was usually partially eaten no more than an hour or so before crashing out for the night, following mornings were mostly rushed affairs back then, made worse by nursing a hangover, with no time for toast or tea, or the boiling of an egg. So it was only natural for leftover pizza straight from the fridge to become standard breakfast fare by default, and often eaten on the drive to the Office.

'I've also got you this,' she said, and held up a chilled bottle of Deuchars IPA. She snicked off the metal cap with a bottle opener, and handed it to him.

'I'm impressed,' he said.

'Don't be. Feeding you's not rocket science.' She removed the cling film from a small bowl of salad, and set it on the table beside an assortment of salad dressings he'd failed to notice until that moment.

'You shouldn't have gone to so much trouble,' he said.

'It's leftover pizza and salad, for crying out loud. Have a seat, Dad, and start eating.'

'Before it gets warm, you mean?' She didn't laugh at his silly joke, and he held out his bottle and chinked an imaginary glass. 'Cheers.' The beer tasted cold, releasing a nip at the back of his throat, just the way he liked it. He helped himself to a dollop of fresh salad, spooned some onto Maureen's plate. Then he slid a quarter-slice of pizza onto his plate, then Maureen's, then waited for her to sit down and join him.

But she was busying herself in a cupboard, as if searching for something misplaced. He looked around her flat, his gaze settling on the two-seater sofa which, from the guddle lying around it, could be the nerve centre of her home. Crushed cushions filled one corner by the arm closer to the window. A tartan woollen throw lay crumpled on the carpet by the legs of a coffee table on which opened books lay face-down and broken-spined, as if fatigued, amidst a haphazard array of A4 pages thick with scribbled notes.

'You studying again?' he asked.

'Thinking of taking an Open University course.'

'Which one?'

'Ah, here we are.' She handed him a plastic bottle of black peppercorns from the cupboard. 'Can you fill the peppermill? I've got to go to the bathroom.'

By the time Maureen took her seat at the table, the peppermill had been filled to the brim, the plastic bottle returned to the cupboard, and his salad well dressed and seasoned.

'Cheers,' she said, and chinked her glass of iced water against his IPA.

He replied with a 'Cheers' of his own, and waited until she had taken that first nibble of pizza, before saying, 'You're not having a wine?'

'You'd make a good detective chief inspector. You're very observant.'

He chuckled as required, and bit into his pizza – no knife and fork for this task – then washed it down with a mouthful of beer. 'That was a question,' he said.

'What was?'

'About the wine.'

'Oh.'

'Any particular reason?'

'You could say, but I'm not sure.'

This was another trait he disliked about Maureen, her irritating habit of not giving a straight answer, just like her mother – her *late* mother. But he smiled at her, took one more bite, and said, 'So what reason?'

'You always told us never to talk with our mouths full.'

He nodded, took another slug of beer. 'That's wonderful,' he said. 'The beer. And the pizza, too.'

'Glad you like it.'

He forked some lettuce and cucumber, lifted it to his mouth, then held it there. 'You wanted to talk to me,' he said. 'I can't remember the last time you didn't have wine with your meal.'

'Changed days, Dad.'

'Changed because of . . .?'

She bit into her pizza, as if to tell him to work it out for himself.

Which he did . . . well . . . he already *had* . . . but was struggling with how to say it, just in case he was wrong. 'Well,' he tried, 'most women avoid alcohol during pregnancy. But if that's the case, I would say I'm confused about your earlier answer.'

'Which was . . .?'

'Why you weren't sure. About the particular reason. For not having wine.' He took the forkful of salad, then followed it with a mouthful of pizza. He smiled, and eyed her from behind his bottle of beer.

She said nothing, which told him everything. Then she got up from the table, walked to the sink, and stared out the kitchen window. He slid his plate to the side, and stood. When he reached her, he put his arm around her, surprised to feel the tremors of her sobbing. He pulled her closer, her head tilting onto his shoulder, and together they stared in silence at the night darkness.

It took a few moments before he sensed her recovering. 'Does Tom know?' he said.

She shook her head, sniffed back a sob. 'I haven't told him.'

'Which is why you weren't sure?'

'Sort of.' She pushed away, and as she turned to face him, he knew from the tightness in her lips that there was more to come. 'I'm pretty sure it's not Tom's.'

Well, there he had it. Like mother, like daughter. Tom a cuckold, just as Gilchrist had been. Although he wasn't sure if you had to be married first, before you could be cuckolded.

No matter, he knew the feeling. But Tom was not his primary concern.

He offered an understanding grimace, and said, 'Which complicates matters.'

'You always were the master of the understatement.'

He caught her furtive glance over his shoulder, which helped him better understand her dilemma. 'You're wondering how you're going to be able to fit in studying for your Open University course if you're going to have a child.'

'No, Dad. I'm wondering how and where I'm going to have a termination.'

He tried to keep his surprise hidden, but didn't think he pulled it off. Maureen's lips jerked a quick smile, then she returned to the kitchen table as if they'd been talking about the weather. Silent, he took his own chair and picked up what was left of his pizza. But the base tasted cold and hard, the pepperoni limp, the cheese bland. He sipped it down with a mouthful of beer, no longer fresh and crisp, but lukewarm and flat. Maureen, on the other hand, now she had offloaded her worries and come clean in a sense, ate with gusto.

He finished his beer, pushed his plate away. 'Mind if I have another one of these?'

'Help yourself. I bought four.'

'Perfect.'

Not that he intended to drink four bottles of Deuchars. Rather, he couldn't think of anything meaningful to say. He ran his empty bottle under the tap, stood it on the draining board, and pulled another from the fridge. He picked up the opener, snecked off the top, and was saved by Maureen saying, 'So you don't approve?'

He might be the master of the understatement, but Mo was the master of the loaded question. Don't approve of her considering terminating her pregnancy? Don't approve of her being a woman with more than one lover? Don't approve of her taking an Open University course? Don't approve of the salad? Or what? For all he knew, it could be all four, maybe more. But logic guided him to the correct question.

'Terminating a pregnancy is a big decision,' he answered.

'And so is going through with it,' she snapped.

He let a couple of beats pass. 'What you're feeling at the moment is only natural.'

'And what am I feeling?'

Well, he'd walked straight into that one, he supposed. Just like her mother, Maureen had that unsettling ability to wrongfoot him when he least expected it – another character trait she could do without. 'Mostly confusion, I'd say. And worry, of course. You're worried about how you're going to cope financially. You're worried about how you're going to raise a child on your own, and all the other worries you'd given no thought to until this moment.' He tried a smile, but his lips might as well have belonged to someone else. He took a sip of beer that drained it past the halfway mark.

He shrugged his shoulders at her. 'Anyway, that's how I felt when your mum told me she was pregnant with you. All of the above. And then some. Not only was I petrified at the thought of being the father to some helpless child who would look to me for support through her life . . . into adulthood,' he added, just to avoid argument. 'But I was worried that I might not be able to provide for you. What if I lost my job? What if I died, or was killed, or took some incurable disease? What if . . . what if . . .?'

He took another sip of his beer. 'So I understand how you feel, Mo. At the moment, you're scared. And overwhelmed. It's almost too much to take in.' He smiled at her, placed his beer on the table, reached out for her hand, and massaged her fingers. 'But don't worry. That's life. These feelings of uncertainty and insecurity will pass.' He searched her eyes for any signs of having made an impact, but she stared back at him with a cold look that warned him he might have it all wrong.

Then she said, 'I'll think about it.'

'You already have.'

She frowned. 'What do you mean?'

He nodded to her iced water. 'Your subconscious already knows your decision.'

She stared at her glass as if confused, then looked up at him and said, 'Maybe I'll have a large wine before I go to bed.'

'Maybe you will.' He released her hand. 'But if I was a betting man, I'd put money on you not wanting to harm your own child.' He pushed his chair back. 'I need to go. I've got a lot on. But thanks for the meal. And the beers.' He slid the half-finished bottle to the side. 'I'll call you tomorrow.'

She lowered her gaze to the iced water.

He let himself out.

CHAPTER 17

Back in his car, Gilchrist sat for several minutes trying to still the sickening feeling in his gut. Maureen was pregnant. A surprise, but not the end of the world. Nowhere near it. In fact, it was the *beginning* of the world for her child. He felt his lips stretch into a smile, then shift to a tight grimace as he tried to stifle a sense of rising panic. He hadn't been convincing enough for Maureen. She was determined, single-minded, a woman who might – and there was a difficult question in that might – go through with the termination just to prove him wrong. Oh, dear God. Surely never.

He replayed their conversation, and saw that he had not handled it well. It wasn't too late to go back to her flat and try to offer fatherly advice. But Maureen was no pushover. For years he'd struggled with their relationship. One moment she was loving and understanding, the next the switch would click, and it was as if she would do the exact opposite of what he was saying, just because she could. And tonight, he feared, was one of these moments.

But her own pregnancy . . .?

'No way,' he said to himself, and made a mental note to phone her first thing in the morning. Then he did what he always did when life's problems appeared overwhelming, he went back to work. He retrieved his mobile from the glove compartment, and powered it up.

Maureen often accused him of loving his job more than he loved his family, so he'd not taken his mobile with him, a concession he was certain she hadn't even noticed. But the manner in which their evening had ended niggled away at him. Should he have been more understanding, more patient? Had he rushed away? Should he have stayed longer?

But these thoughts were getting him nowhere.

He checked his mobile, and saw that he'd missed four calls, one from Cooper – now wasn't that a surprise? – one from Jessie, one from Smiler and, most recently, one from DS Fox, in reverse incoming order.

He returned Fox's call first, only to be dumped into voicemail. He left a message asking Fox to call back, then he called Smiler.

'Sorry for calling so late, ma'am. But I've just picked up your message.'

'Thanks, Andy. I'm not long off the phone with the Chief. I told him what you'd told me, but he's still not happy about your contacting Strathclyde for help in resources.'

'Did he listen to what you were telling him?'

'He did. But he's not interested.'

Gilchrist almost cursed with frustration. For big Archie to make such a fuss about resources from other constabularies, there had to be something more going on. But what, he was not being made privy to. He accelerated past the mini-roundabout at the foot of Kinkell Brae, and into open countryside. Off to his

117

left, beyond the caravan park, the North Sea lay as black as ink. Ahead, the road lay clear, his rearview mirror, too. He could have the night stars all to himself. His car responded to his foot on the pedal, its three-litre engine powering him into the night with effortless ease.

'So you're instructing me to do what, ma'am?'

'I'm instructing you to drop any and all involvement with Strathclyde,' she said.

'Someone's pulling the Chief's strings,' he said. 'Did he tell you who he spoke to?'

Her deep sigh could have been anger. 'Don't try to second guess the Chief Constable on this. There could be a hundred reasons for him being upset at your interference.'

Gilchrist didn't like the word interference. As far as he was concerned, he'd not been interfering in anything, only trying to move his murder investigation forward. 'Such as . . .?'

'Such as some ongoing operation that is relying on discretion and stealth, as opposed to some other constabulary, specifically Fife, marching in with their bloody heavy boots, and interfering with carefully prepared plans.'

'Did McVicar say that?'

'Not word for word.'

'So you're reading between the lines—'

'What I'm reading, DCI Gilchrist, is that you are to have no further contact with anyone in Strathclyde, or any other constabulary for that matter, with respect to the murder of Mr Stooky Dee.'

Gilchrist put his foot on the brake, pulled the car to a skidding halt, tyres kicking up dirt and gravel as he bumped onto the grass verge. 'With all due respect, ma'am—'

'And with all due respect, DCI Gilchrist, I will not have you challenging my direct instructions. You are off the case. End of. Is that clear? You and your staff are to have no further involvement in Dee's murder investigation. You are to hand over all files to DS Fox of Strathclyde Police first thing in the morning.'

Gilchrist hissed a curse.

'I've already spoken to DS Fox,' she said. 'He'll be here at eight, first thing.'

Which explained the earlier phone message from Fox, but also the real reason why he was staying overnight in St Andrews. To ensure that all files pertaining to Stooky's murder were delivered to Strathclyde in person. ID-ing the body, or confirming the five-pound note, could be considered a bonus—

'You've gone quiet on me, Andy.'

The use of his first name told him that Smiler had got over her hissy-fit, and might be feeling regret at having snapped. Not regret at letting him have it, but regret at not controlling her temper as precisely as she liked to portray.

'I'm thinking,' he said.

'There's nothing to think about. The powers that be have taken us – *you* – off the case. In doesn't matter that Stooky Dee turned up dead in Fife waters. He lived in Glasgow, and his death in all proba-bility occurred nowhere near Fife. So, it makes sense for Strathclyde to take control. Besides, it's all part of a much wider investigation. There's too much at stake. This is beyond our scope.' She let several seconds elapse, then said, 'I'm sorry, Andy. But that's the way it is.'

Part of a much wider investigation? Well, shouldn't Fife Constabulary be called upon to assist? It seemed the logical thing to ask, but instead he said, 'Very well, ma'am. I'll be at the Office first thing to make sure DS Fox is given every file as required.'

119

'Good,' she said. 'You and I will have a word then.'

'Before you go, ma'am?'

'Yes?'

He could not fail to catch the bite of impatience in her tone. 'For the avoidance of any misunderstanding, ma'am, I should tell you that I intend to retain some original files and hand over copies of—'

'What did I just tell you?' she snapped. 'You are *off* the case.'

'I know that, ma'am, but—'

'*Stop*,' she shouted. 'That's enough.' She paused, as if to catch her breath, and when she next spoke, her tone possessed a clinical coldness that warned him he might have pushed too far. 'Be in my office tomorrow morning at eight,' she said. 'At which time you will place every file, record and note pertaining to Stooky Dee's murder investigation, *every* single one of them, all originals, on my desk.'

It took him a few seconds of silence to realise she was waiting for him to agree. 'If you say so, ma'am.'

'I will then witness you handing over every single original file to DS Fox. Is that clear, DCI Gilchrist?'

'It is indeed, ma'am.' But the line was already dead.

He slipped into gear and bumped back onto the road. Within seconds, he accelerated to seventy. If he'd been in Smiler's position, would he have been so determined to stamp his authority on the Office staff? He would like to think not. But the odds of him reaching any rank loftier than Detective Chief Inspector at this stage in his career were slim to zero, maybe even one hundred below. Still, he would like to think he would be more willing to listen to his subordinates, take on board what they were saying. So, for what he was about to do, he reasoned, Smiler had only herself to blame.

He dialled Jackie Canning's number, and she answered with, 'Uh-huh?'

'Evening, Jackie. Sorry to call at this hour. I haven't disturbed you, have I?'

'Nuh-uh.'

'Got an easy job for you,' he said. 'I'm meeting the Chief Superintendent tomorrow morning first thing, and I need you to make a copy of all files and notes on the investigation into the body on the boat. Think you can do that before I meet her?'

'Uh-huh.'

'Might be simpler if you created a separate folder and just dumped all the computer files into it. Would you need a hand to scan and copy any handwritten notes?'

'Nuh-uh.'

'It shouldn't take you too long, should it?'

'A c . . . a c . . .'

'A couple of hours?'

'Uh-huh.'

'Thanks, Jackie. You're the best.' He gave a squelchy *mwah* over the phone, and felt a smile tug his lips at her chuckle.

Next he dialled DS Fox and was dumped into voicemail again. 'Just letting you know that I've spoken to Chief Superintendent Smiley, and she's instructed me to hand over files to you tomorrow morning. It'll take my team some time to pull them all together, so why don't you swing by at, say, nine o'clock? We should have everything good to go by then.'

He ended the call.

Next, he phoned Jessie.

'How did you get on with Izzy?' he asked.

'She didn't come right out and say it, but she's been in contact with Tommy.'

'And . . .?'

'And she's going to have a talk with him.'

'Well, the brown stuff's hit the fan big time,' he said. 'McVicar's been on to Smiler, and we're off the case.'

'Hang on 'til I clean my ears,' she said. 'For a moment there, I thought you said we were off the case.'

He chuckled, and said, 'Get hold of Izzy again, tonight if possible, and tell her we need to speak to Tommy as a matter of urgency.'

'So what're you thinking?'

'That someone somewhere has got something on McVicar, and until we know who it is or what's going on, I wouldn't trust anyone. Least of all DS Fox.'

'You met him?'

Gilchrist explained that evening's events, ending with, 'Let's talk first thing in the morning.'

'Define first thing.'

'I'll pick you up at six.'

'Will I have time to put on my mascara?'

'Only if you're quick.'

She giggled, and said, 'See you then.'

He was driving into Crail when his phone rang again – ID Cooper. With all that had gone on that night, he'd forgotten she'd called. Or maybe his subconscious was warning him that it was for the best that they no longer communicated. On the other hand, recent contact between them had been nothing but professional. Even so, it still irked to hear her voice.

He took the call, and said, 'Evening, Becky.'

'I called earlier.'

'Had my mobile switched off, but it's switched on now.'

She tutted. 'Have you heard from Smiler?'

The use of CS Smiley's nickname surprised him, although nothing should surprise him where Cooper was concerned. 'I have,' he said, 'which I suspect is why you're calling.'

'I don't trust her, Andy. She told me that Strathclyde Police are now handling your murder investigation, and I've to coordinate all PM and forensic reports with a DS Nathanial Fox.' She tutted again. 'Have you seen him? He was here earlier in the day, ID-ing the body. God, what a creep.' She paused, then said, 'You don't seem upset.'

'Should I be?'

'I've never known you to be so blasé about being pulled off a case.'

'Have you had the toxicology results back yet?'

She gushed out a short laugh, and said, 'I have, yes.'

'And . . .?'

'And I don't believe I'm authorised to divulge that information to the *ex*-SIO.'

Something in her tone hinted at playful impudence, reminding him of her teasing in the past. God, it would be all too easy to pick up from where they'd left off. He forced these thoughts away, and said, 'Maybe not directly through the office in the form of a formal report. But by slip-of-the-tongue, perhaps?'

'As in – the toxicology results show high levels of cocaine, alcohol, and lower levels of Rohypnol . . .? Oops.'

Rohypnol was a date-rape drug, but Gilchrist knew it hadn't been administered to take sexual advantage of Stooky, rather to subdue the man, make him more compliant. Cooper's giggle at her deliberate slip-up had him struggling not to smile. 'So, Dr Cooper,' he said, 'in your slip-of-the-tongue opinion, are the levels of that cocktail of drugs high enough to anaesthetise pain?'

'They most definitely are.'

Gilchrist let out a sigh of relief. For all Stooky had been tortured, any pain his captors had intended to inflict would have been lessened by the drugs they used to make him cough up whatever secrets he'd been holding. 'Thank God for small mercies,' he said. 'It would of course be nice to see a slip-of-the-tongue copy of that report.'

'Already sent it,' she said, her tone all business again. 'I meant what I said, Andy. I don't trust Smiler. And you would be wise to do likewise. Ciao.' She hung up.

A few seconds later, he pulled into South Castle Street and drew to a halt. One more phone call to make. He got through on the second ring, Mhairi's voice high with surprise to hear from him. 'Did you get anywhere with restoring the logbook?' Gilchrist asked.

'Not as badly damaged as I first thought, sir. Some mould, but mostly damage from dampness. The spine's not separated from the text block, which is good. So, it's in not too bad nick.'

'Think you might have something ready for us first thing in the morning?'

'We dried what we could by interleaving, and have an oscil-lating fan on it. Problem is the ink's run on some pages, which makes many entries illegible. Might be able to have a look at it in the morning, sir, but it would need to be handled with care.'

'Good. If anyone mentions it, you don't know what they're talking about.'

'Sir?'

'We're being pulled off the case, Mhairi. We'll talk in the morning.'

He ended the call, and stepped into the damp chill of a darkening March night.

CHAPTER 18

Fisherman's Cottage, Crail

Gilchrist walked through the lounge and noticed his answering machine blinking. He frowned at it. Everyone he knew had mobile phones, so who would call his landline? He was slipping off his jacket when movement at his dining-room window startled him.

Even in the blackness of his back garden, he could make out the dark shadow of a cat on his windowsill, brushing itself against the glass, doing a balancing act as it turned on the narrow ledge and brushed along its other side, tail as upright as a flagpole.

He walked to the window, hissing, 'Puss, puss,' knowing that Blackie wouldn't hear him through the glass and, once he stepped outside, would run away to hide in the tight gap behind his garden shed at the back wall. Even though Blackie had never let him any closer than six feet, he had found to his amazement that she showed no fear through the glass. He could even pretend to run his hand along her fur through the glass, with Blackie arching her back and rubbing her whiskers against his hand with vicarious feline pleasure.

On four separate occasions he had opened the window mid-rub, but the instant the catchment cracked, Blackie made a dash for it. In the end, he had given up, settling for the questionable pleasure of petting a cat through the window.

If only relationships could be that simple, he thought.

In the kitchen, he removed a carton of cat food, and opened the back door. A glance at the dining-room window ledge confirmed that Blackie had done her usual, vanished into the depths of his garden. Sure enough, when he cleaned the bowls with the garden hose, twin pinpricks stared back at him from the corner of the hut. He rattled the carton. 'Here puss, puss.' But he was wasting his breath. Blackie was as good as deaf.

On the walk back along his garden path, it struck him for some reason that he hadn't noticed Maureen's cat in her flat. A Ragamuffin with the thickest coat and a long brush-like tail, Charlie was one of the friendliest house cats Gilchrist had ever come across. Or perhaps it had been Blackie's unapproachable coldness that led him to that conclusion. Maureen had arranged for a friend of hers – Jen, as best he could recall – to look after Charlie once she and Tom emigrated to Australia. But maybe the agreement Jen made was for Charlie's move to be permanent. Hence, the missing cat from Maureen's flat.

He locked the kitchen door behind him, and shivered off the chill. He returned the cat food to the cupboard, wondering if Maureen might consider adopting Blackie. But he quickly dispelled that idea. A cat that refused to be touched would not be the most suitable pet for a pregnant woman. He strode into his living room, and pressed the button on his answering machine.

Hey, Andy, we waited a couple of hours, but you never showed. Told Kris your head was wasted with work, but what can I say? Bummed you up so much, she's gagging to meet you, so we're heading out to the Golf Hotel. We'll be there until the back of ten. Hope you can stick your head in. But if you can't, no worries, we'll maybe just pop down the road to yours, and knock you up. Catch you.

Gilchrist blew out a silent curse. This was Jack at his worst. Besotted with a woman, blind-sided to everything else – even alcohol, for crying out loud. *Jack* and *sober* were words that hadn't been seen together for years. And the last thing he wanted was for Jack to come to his house this side of midnight, with his girlfriend of the month. Once seated comfortably, Jack was renowned for staying the course.

On the other hand, this new sober Jack could be completely different. But Gilchrist didn't want to take the chance. He had an early rise in the morning. The Golf Hotel was no more than a five-minute walk from his cottage. He pulled a scarf from the hall cupboard, wrapped it round his neck and set off.

He found Jack seated at a table near the corner by the fire, prodding it with the poker, logs turning over, sparks flying. When he saw Gilchrist, he almost jumped to his feet and came over and gave him a hug.

'Hey, you got my message.'

'I most surely did,' Gilchrist said, hugging him tight in return. When they parted, he noticed no drinks on the table. He looked around. But the bar seemed devoid of anyone he could consider being Kris. 'Where's this Kris of yours?' He frowned. 'Has she left?'

Jack beamed a smile. 'She's just popped out to make a call.' His gaze drifted beyond the bar, and from the brightness in his son's eyes Gilchrist knew that Kris had just returned.

He turned to face her, and struggled to hide his surprise. Where he'd imagined Kris to be a contemporary of Jack's, lines around her eyes and wrinkles on her neck gave the impression of her being closer to Gilchrist's age.

'Lovely to meet you at last,' she said, and gave him a firm handshake. 'I'm Kris.' She stretched up to peck his cheek, then back and over for the other side.

Her face felt warm, her skin soft, and the sparkle in her eyes spoke of happiness and youth, despite first impressions.

'Can I get you a drink, Andy?' she said. 'You don't mind me calling you Andy?'

'That's my name,' he said, although he had a suspicion that it wouldn't have mattered however he'd replied.

'Jack said you prefer real ale.'

'Here,' he said. 'Let me get these. What'll you have?'

'Told you,' said Jack.

'That's very kind of you, Andy. I'll have a soda water and lime. Not juice. Two slices of lime. Preferably freshly cut, if they can manage that.'

'And you?' he said to Jack.

'The same.'

Gilchrist nodded, and said, 'Any ice?'

'No way. It's too cold.'

Gilchrist glanced at the fire, the logs flaring from Jack's pokering. Well, it was March, he supposed, and officially still winter – only just.

When he returned with the drinks and placed them on the table, Kris and Jack were happily ensconced in the corner, cuddling in like young lovers.

Jack said, 'You're having a Corona? Never thought I'd see the day.'

'Wanted something light,' he said. 'Got an early start in the morning.'

'So what's new?' Jack lifted his glass of soda water, chinked it against Kris's, then Andy's. 'Sláinte,' he said, and took a sip that almost drained it.

Gilchrist necked his Corona, the sliced lime refreshing in the log-fired air. 'So tell me, Kris, how did you and Jack meet?'

'At an art exhibition in Dundee,' Jack said.

'Thanks, Kris.'

Kris choked out a laugh, and Jack raised his glass. 'Touché,' he said, then drained it, seemingly unaccustomed to pacing non-alcoholic intake.

'Like another?' Gilchrist asked.

'No. I was just thirsty. I'll wait.'

Kris on the other hand had taken a sip that barely made a difference. 'Jack's right,' she said. 'I'd been exhibiting in Edinburgh for over a year, and wanted to expand beyond the city. So I arranged an exhibition in Dundee. And that's when I met Jack.'

'And it was electric, I'm telling you. Pure electricity.' Jack huddled closer.

Kris gave a demure smile, and nodded. 'When Jack and I first set eyes on each other, I can't explain it. It truly was remarkable. Electricity is a good way of describing it.'

'So you're an artist,' Gilchrist said.

'Sculptor. Mostly metal.'

'Like welding, soldering? That sort of thing?'

'Sort of.'

He took another sip of Corona, conscious of Jack's eyes on him. 'So why Dundee?' he asked. 'That's north. Most Scottish creatives want to have their name spreading south, into England, especially London if they could.'

She smiled at him. 'I'm not interested in money.'

'I never said you were.'

'I'm more interested in exhibiting my work in cities and towns that are not famous for being steeped in artistic history.'

Gilchrist said, 'Dundee? For example.'

'You could say.'

'The home of the *Beano*, the *Dandy* and a host of other comics, all of them steeped in creative history.'

'There's a difference,' she said.

'I'm sure there is.' He took another sip. 'I suspect Jack would like to have his work shown farther south.' He glanced at Jack. 'Yes?'

'Used to think that, but Kris is showing me another side to my art. One that's the by-product of persistence and dedication. More a marathon than a sprint.' He nodded to her, as if seeking confirmation.

She smiled in return.

Gilchrist hid behind a mouthful of beer. He'd watched Jack over the years strive to make the most meagre living from his art. But as recently as six months ago, for the first time in his life Jack appeared to be selling his stuff, making decent money – five figures for one or two pieces – and seemingly flush with cash, at long bloody last. Which raised the question; what had he done with it? He forced the worrying answer away.

'Jack tells me you're a policeman, Andy.'

'Detective,' he said. 'So only two years in Edinburgh?'

'And you work in St Andrews CID?'

'Hence the early start in the morning.' He removed a business card from his pocket and placed it on the table. 'Sure I can't get you another one, Jack?'

'I'm fine.'

'So.' He faced Kris. 'Before Edinburgh you lived . . .?'

'In London.'

'The centre of the universe for arty-farty types.'

'Arty-farty types,' Jack repeated. 'What did I tell you?'

'Not so much nowadays,' Kris said.

He shoved his business card towards her. 'Do you have a card?'

'I'm afraid I don't, Andy. No need. Most of my contacts are word-of-mouth.'

'Best way to network, so they tell me.' He took another sip, almost finished it, and said, 'It was good to meet you. But you have to excuse me. I really do have an early start.'

Something that looked like relief washed over Jack's face, and he almost jumped to his feet, held out his hand in a man-to-man handshake. Whatever happened to the customary high-five? Gilchrist turned to Kris, and before he could shake her hand, she said, 'Can I have a chat with you, Andy? Before you head off?'

'Sure.'

'Outside?'

He nodded, then smiled at Jack. 'Keep that phone of yours alive.'

Jack guffawed, and said, 'Catch you, man.'

Outside, Gilchrist turned left and walked onto the paved area between the Golf Hotel and the adjacent Tea Room. He stepped past a couple of windows – just to make sure they were out of Jack's line of sight – then turned to face Kris, and rested his elbow on the hotel's stone wall.

Kris already had a cigarette in her mouth, filter tight between her teeth, lighter in her hand. She held the packet out to him – Silk Cut – and he declined. She nodded. 'Jack told me you'd given up.' Then she lit her cigarette, inhaled as if her life depended on it, twisted her mouth and blew out.

'What else did he tell you?'

'That you're naturally inquisitive, which makes you a perfect fit for your job.'

He returned her cool gaze, trying to ignore the warm waft of second-hand smoke that seemed to drift his way no matter which way he turned. 'You wanted to talk.'

She took another deep hit. 'I'm not as old as I look, Andy. I'm still in my thirties.'

He found her confession strange, but said, 'Jack's twenty-four.'

'Twenty-five on Saturday.'

Christ. He'd forgotten all about that. He hadn't bought a card, let alone a present.

'I've had a tough life,' she said. 'Hence, what I like to call, my mature look.'

'By tough, you mean addicted?'

'I'm clean now.'

'How long?'

'Five years.'

'Hard drugs?'

She sniffed, nodded. 'You name it, I've tried it.'

He said nothing, just stared at her, and fought off the urge to snatch her cigarette from her and take a deep draw. He breathed in the acrid night air. Christ, it smelled great. 'Do you have a criminal record?' Well, he might as well come straight out and ask.

She blew smoke from the side of her mouth. 'Possession of illegal substances. Muled for a year. Maybe longer.' She shook her head. 'But never distributing. Only using.'

He resisted reminding her that muling was a form of distributing, and instead said, 'So you spent time inside?'

'Community service only.'

He turned away, eyed the length of the street. How many youngsters had he arrested over the years for drug-related crimes? It didn't bear thinking about. He faced her again. 'Does Jack know?'

'Of course.' She smiled. 'There are no secrets between Jack and me.' She finished her cigarette, dropped the dout to the paving, and ground it out with a flat-shoed foot. She ran a hand through her short hair, and sniffed the air. 'I care for your son, Andy. I care for him very much. And he cares for me.'

Gilchrist said nothing, just held her gaze.

'I don't know if you're aware or not, but Jack is gifted. He has an incredible talent.'

'So I've heard.'

Something in the tone of his voice drained her, as if it struck her all of a sudden that she was wasting her time trying to explain anything to a boring old detective chief inspector. 'Anyway, I thought you should know,' she said.

'You didn't have a business card,' he said. 'But you have a surname.'

'Hedström. Kristen Hedström. It's Swedish. Not me. My parents.' She turned from him. 'That's another thing Jack warned me about you.'

'What's that?'

'That you would check me out.' She shrugged her shoulders. 'Go ahead. I don't care. I've nothing to hide. It's not me you'll be upsetting.' She gave a quick smile that failed to reach her eyes, then walked away from him, back to the bar.

When she slipped around the corner, Gilchrist just stood there, feeling like a fool. She had tried to explain herself to him, let him know her feelings for his son, try to allay concerns he might have had about their age difference, even come clean about her past dependency on drugs, her present reliance on art – Jack's reliance, too, for that matter.

Why the hell wasn't that enough? What was it about Jack that he found so difficult to trust? He'd made a promise to himself months ago that he would believe Jack when he said he'd never done drugs, despite his own demented concerns. And if you stopped to think about it, that's exactly how he should describe himself – demented.

He tightened his scarf around his neck, upped his jacket collar, and set off for home, deep in the discomfort of his own misery.

CHAPTER 19

The following morning arrived dark and dreary. The bedroom skylights could have been black ceiling posters. Gilchrist switched off his alarm, checked the time – 5.00 – and groaned. Not that rising early was the difficulty, rather it was avoiding that last one-for-the-road – the road being the short walk from the lounge to his bedroom, as it turned out last night – that often proved irresistible.

Brushing his teeth almost had him throwing up, but a piping hot shower and a shave with his waterproof electric razor had him feeling good to go – well, as good as he was ever going to feel at that time on a Friday morning.

In the kitchen, with a fresh mug of tea in front of him, he checked his text messages, pleased to see one from Jackie Canning confirming that all files on the Stooky Dee murder investigation had been copied and saved. A link to the Constabulary website provided him immediate access. A quick check – he really was beginning to get a handle on all this digital stuff now – let him thumb his way through them. While doing so, he managed to crunch his way through two slices of dry toast and marmalade, which was about all his stomach would permit.

In the lounge, he replaced the top on the bottle of whisky – Aberlour – and struggled to recall if it had been full when he'd started. Bloody hell, he hoped not. He returned it to his *cocktail cabinet*, nothing more than a trolley on wheels, on which stood a number of bottles – whisky, gin, Bacardi – and of course that unavoidable bottle of vodka, Jack's go-to drink; well, at least it used to be.

He gathered up several sheets of scribbled notes off the chair and table, picked up his notebook from the floor. He fluffed up the cushions, then grabbed his scarf and leather jacket from the hook in the hall, and headed out.

His breath puffed white in the cold morning air as he strode up Rose Wynd, the wind picking up, hinting that the Fife coast was in for a mid-March battering. Behind, he caught the shrill call of seagulls fighting over scraps of food, or with each other – he couldn't say – the distant thunder of waves as they thumped against the harbour wall. If the rain stayed off, most Scots could handle a cold wind, no matter how strong. But bloody hell, it could be an Arctic morning. He tugged at his scarf, and blew off the chill. Hands deep in his pockets, he pressed the remote fob, and his BMW winked at him.

Inside, he powered up and drove off, fan on high to take whatever heat the engine could offer. He checked the time – 5.39 – then phoned Jessie.

She picked up on the first ring. 'You said six. Not half-five.'

'I'm on my way.'

'Well, I guessed that. How else are you going to get from Crail to St Andrews?'

'Good morning to you, too, Jessie.'

'Oh, for crying out loud,' she said. 'It's pitch black outside.'

'At least it's not raining.'

'Not yet.' The line died.

He took his time on the drive to St Andrews, and pulled up outside Jessie's home in Canongate at six on the dot. She rushed down the drive, one hand on her head, pulled the door open and clambered inside. 'Where's summer when you need it?'

'It'll be Christmas soon.'

'Piss off. How fast can you make it to the coffee shop?'

'Seatbelt on?'

'Stop talking, and just drive. My mouth feels like the bottom of a parrot's cage.'

'What kind of parrot?'

'The kind that shits on your tongue.'

She slipped out her mobile, and tapped the screen.

He guessed she was texting a message, and said, 'Anyone I know?'

'Angie. I'm asking her to stick her head in and check on Robert this morning.'

At the mention of Jessie's son, Gilchrist felt his heart sink. Late last year, Robert had been given the devastating news that his hearing loss was permanent, and nothing – not even a cochlear implant – could help. His hearing nerves weren't just dead, they'd never developed in the first place.

'So how is Robert?' he said.

'He's something else, let me tell you.' She looked up from her texting. 'He said he hasn't spoken to his girlfriend in three weeks—'

'He has a girlfriend? You never told me that.'

'No, you dumpling. It's one of his jokes he's come up with. For his book.'

'Oh. Right. Sorry.'

'Anyway, he's not spoken to her in three weeks. He doesn't want to interrupt her.' She coughed out a laugh, and slapped her knee. 'I don't know where it comes from,' she said. 'But I just love him to bits, you know.'

Gilchrist smiled. He did know. With her irrepressible sense of humour and her vigour for life, Jessie smothered her son with heartfelt love. If it was ever possible to love someone to the max, that was Jessie with Robert. And if you ever spoke out against Robert, or harmed him in any way, even without intention, you'd better be ready for war.

Gilchrist drove into Market Street. 'Robert gets his zest for life from you, I'd say.'

'It's the Glasgow sense of humour. Doesn't matter how bad it gets, there's always a funny side to it.'

'Not always,' he said, wondering what she found amusing about being hauled off the Stooky Dee investigation.

She tapped her mobile again, then said, 'That's it. Job done. Don't know what I'd do without Angie. And all these tutors for Robert's costing me a fortune. But d'you know the good news?'

'What's that?'

'He doesn't want to go to university.'

Gilchrist frowned. 'That's good?'

'He's decided he wants to be a chippy.'

'You mean a joiner?' Gilchrist said.

'Same as Angie's brother, Carson. Even said he would take Robert on part-time some weekends and show him the ropes. And pay him, too. Like, whoah, my wee boy's turned into a man all of a sudden.'

'But what about his writing? I thought he wanted be an author.'

139

'He's still going to do that. Which is why he's working on his one-liners.'

Gilchrist pulled into a parking space opposite Starbucks.

'Here,' she said. 'Let me get these.' She handed him a tenner.

'Thought you were going to get them.'

'It's blowing a gale. I've washed my hair. I'll pay. You know? I'll *get* them. You go pick them up. And I'll share a muffin. Blueberry. And don't forget the paper towels. Oh, and make mine a skinny.'

'And I'll have a fatty?'

She giggled at that. 'I wish I had your metabolism. You never put on weight.'

'Anything else?'

'Keep the engine running and the fan on. I'm still shivering.'

'Right.' He stepped into a stiff breeze, thankful that Starbucks had been opening earlier than normal – 5.45 – ever since a new manager had taken over. Where would they be if they couldn't get their daily caffeine injection? He ordered two tall lattes – one skinny, one fatty – which failed to extract a smile from the young barista. Maybe the new manager liked to start early, but it seemed that some of his employees didn't. He chose a cranberry muffin – no blueberries – paid at the till, and dropped a pound coin into the tips mug – not so much as a thank you. Oh, well.

Coffees, muffin and napkins in hand, he managed to open the shop door with his foot and make his way back to his car without spilling a drop. Jessie was deep in conversation on her mobile, and he had to elbow the side window to get her attention.

She started with surprise, then pushed the door open, stepped out, and brushed past him on her way across the cobbled street, mobile hard to her ear. Gilchrist set the coffees in the cup holders in the centre console, balanced the muffin and napkins beside them, then took his seat behind the wheel.

He turned the fan to low, adjusted the heat from high to medium, then picked up his latte. He'd taken only a few sips when Jessie opened the car door and slid in with a rush of cold air.

'Problems?' he said.

'That was Izzy. She managed to talk to Tommy last night, and tried to convince him that Spain was a safe bet.' She shook her head. 'Long story short. Tommy's not up for it. He's done another runner.'

'He didn't like the idea of witness protection?' he asked.

'Says it won't work. Not for him, anyway. There's too many cops in the know who want his skin. Izzy's words.'

'Does she know where Tommy's gone?'

'No chance.'

'She must have some idea, surely.'

'This is Tommy Janes we're talking about. He's rubbed shoulders with some of the toughest criminals in Glasgow, maybe even Scotland, for all I know. If Tommy's shitting himself, then he's got good reason to.'

Gilchrist gave Jessie's words some thoughts. Nothing seemed to fit. The names on the list, small-time criminals being killed off one by one – three down, three to go. He struggled to recall the remaining names: Bruiser Mann, Chippie Smith, Angel Thomson.

Who was behind the killings? And why? What did it mean?

And it irked that Archie McVicar had instructed Smiler to take Gilchrist and his team off the Stooky Dee investigation. Once he'd handed over all the files to DS Fox that morning, witnessed by Smiler, then that really was it – a Fife murder being investigated by Strathclyde Police—

'You know what?' Jessie said. 'I'm thinking that Izzy knows how to contact Tommy.'

'I thought you said she didn't know.'

'I said she doesn't know where he's *gone*.'

'She's got a mobile number for him?'

'Maybe,' she said. 'There was something she said that made me think she hadn't met Tommy last night, but had only spoken to him on the phone.' She pulled out her mobile. 'It's time to have another chat with that dozy besom, this time an honest one.'

'Don't bother, Jessie. Forget it. We're off the case. Remember?'

'What's finding my brother got to do with Stooky Dee's murder?'

'Tommy gave us the list of names, Stooky's being one of them. And in case you've forgotten, Tommy's still wanted for questioning in a murder investigation being handled by Strathclyde Police. It's too close to home, and puts you in direct conflict with the powers that be in Strathclyde. Not a good position to be in.'

Jessie stared at him, finger poised over the screen.

'Hang up,' he said, 'and drink your coffee before it gets cold.'

Without a word, Jessie slid her mobile into her pocket, then removed her coffee from the cup holder. She took a couple of sips before breaking off a piece of muffin, and grumbled, 'What is it about blueberry that you don't understand?'

'They were out of them.' He eased along Market Street, and had to stop at the Whyte-Melville Memorial Fountain to let a woman with three handicapped adults cross the street. And all the while he was conscious of Jessie's silence. 'Something tells me you're upset,' he tried. 'And it's bugger all to do with the muffin not being blueberry.'

Jessie didn't answer until he turned into Union Street. 'I've been thinking,' she said. 'When are you meeting Smiler?'

'About eight.'

'Which is why we're heading to the Office for the back of six?'

He offered a quick smile. 'You think I'm up to something?'

She shook her head. 'No,' she said. 'I *know* you're up to something.'

'You're just going to have to join in then, won't you?'

CHAPTER 20

The call came at 7.45.

Gilchrist answered it with, 'Good morning, ma'am.'

'I'll see you now,' Smiler said. 'Bring all your files.'

'Will do, ma'am.' But she had already hung up.

Gilchrist picked up the pile of files that he and Jessie had agreed were relevant only to the Stooky Dee murder investigation. 'Check up on Mhairi,' he said. 'And wish me luck.'

Upstairs, he knocked on Smiler's door and pushed it open. His heart stuttered at the sight of Chief Constable Archie McVicar standing at the end of Smiler's desk, regal and stiff-backed, uniform immaculate, as if he'd just collected it from the cleaners. Gilchrist strode into the room, and laid the files on Smiler's desk.

He nodded to McVicar. 'Good morning, sir.' Then Smiler. 'Ma'am.'

Smiler frowned. 'Is this all there is?'

McVicar harrumphed. 'Looks rather thin, Andy, I have to say.'

'Me or the files, sir.' But that failed to elicit a smile. He opened the top folder, and removed the flashdrive that Jackie had created.

'The case was only opened yesterday,' he said. 'But everything should be on there, sir.'

Smiler said, 'Should be, or is?'

'Is.'

'Give me.'

Gilchrist handed her the flashdrive.

She inserted it into her computer. 'Password?'

'Didn't create one.'

She grunted, and took less than five seconds to access it and pull up a folder, which she opened. Standing at the opposite side of her desk, he watched her scan the screen, fingers clicking the mouse, opening files at random it seemed. When she appeared satisfied, she said, 'Is that everything, DCI Gilchrist?'

'Yes, ma'am.'

'You're holding nothing back?'

'These are all the files pertaining to Stooky Dee's murder investigation.'

'Good.'

'But to avoid any misunderstanding, you should know that I've made copies of—'

'I thought I made it perfectly clear that this Office was to retain nothing associated with that murder investigation, meaning that no files were to be copied, and that the matter in its *entirety* was to be handed over to Strathclyde Police in *full*; emphasis on *entirety* and *in full*, DCI Gilchrist. You did understand that?'

'I did, ma'am, yes.'

'So why did you not do as I instructed?' She sat back and stared at him, as if stunned by the absurdity of it all, cheeks colouring from the effort, or at being embarrassed in front of the Chief Constable.

'But I did, ma'am.'

Her gaze darted to McVicar, then back to Gilchrist. 'Do enlighten me.'

He turned to McVicar. 'I understand, sir, that your instruction was to hand deliver to Strathclyde Police all files relevant to the Stooky Dee murder investigation.' He waited for McVicar to grunt agreement, before nodding to the folders on Smiler's desk. 'These folders and that flashdrive accomplish that. Other files and reports have been entered directly into the PNC, and are accessible by any force. So, everything has been done in accordance with your directive, sir.'

McVicar tilted his head back a touch, as if to study Gilchrist down the length of his nose. With some men that might be seen as condescension. With McVicar, it was the calm before the storm. 'You haven't answered Chief Superintendent Smiley's question, Andy, as to why you copied files against her categorical instruction.'

'With due respect, sir.' He nodded to Smiler. 'Ma'am. I made copies of only those files that relate to another case—'

'What other case?' Smiler snapped.

'Joe Christie's disappearance, ma'am.'

McVicar said, 'Who's Joe Christie?'

'The owner of *Brenda Girl*.'

'Did you say *Brenda Girl*?'

'I did, sir, yes.'

'What in the name of God is *Brenda Girl*?'

The irritation in McVicar's tone warned him that he was pushing the man's patience to the limit, maybe even beyond. But he did not take kindly to being ordered about so readily, and even less kindly to having jurisdictional precedence overruled. 'It's the fishing boat that washed up on Tentsmuir Beach with Stooky Dee's body on board, sir. The boat's name had been changed from *Brenda Girl* to *Golden Plover*.'

'Well, in that case, it's relevant to the ongoing murder investigation, is it not?'

'It is, sir, yes.'

Smiler sighed. 'What am I missing, DCI Gilchrist?'

'I don't think you're missing anything, ma'am. The files I've copied are relevant to a missing person's enquiry. Joe Christie's not been seen for three years. His boat's now turned up with its name changed, and no sign of Christie.' He faced McVicar. 'We believe Christie is dead, or more likely has been murdered for his boat, sir.'

'And no one initiated an investigation at the time?'

'The Anstruther Office did, sir, but got nowhere. I've already spoken to Christie's widow who confirmed he was last seen heading east, and that was that. The fact that his boat ran aground on Tentsmuir Beach puts his disappearance into our jurisdiction, and nothing to do with the current murder investigation, sir. But if you want me to hand that case over to Strathclyde Police as well, then I would of course do so, although I would have to question the rationale for doing that. Sir.'

Well, there he'd said it. Laid the ball at their feet. McVicar's gaze slid to Smiler, the files on the table, then back to Smiler, who sat stone-faced and silent. Gilchrist had never seen the Chief Constable so . . . how would you say it . . . undecided?

Smiler saved McVicar. 'So, DCI Gilchrist, are you saying you're going to look into this Joe Christie's disappearance?'

'His disappearance has never been solved, ma'am. So, with his boat turning up, albeit under a different name, I believe we now have a duty to reopen the case.'

She eyed him with suspicion, but McVicar beat her to it. 'Tell me, Andy. What do you have that the Anstruther Office didn't have years ago?'

'Other than his boat, sir?'

McVicar grunted in annoyance, and said, 'Obviously.'

Gilchrist didn't want to mention the logbook. After all, it could turn up nothing. So he said, 'A fresh pair of eyes, sir.'

'Bit of a longshot, I'd say.'

'Most cold cases tend to be, sir. But it would be worthwhile revisiting Anstruther's files. And if we happen to come across anything remotely relevant to Strathclyde's ongoing investigation, you would of course be the first to know, sir.'

McVicar narrowed his eyes, as if knowing he was being tricked, but couldn't figure it out. 'Very well, Andy.' He turned to Smiler. 'Diane?'

She looked lost for a moment, then said, 'That'll be all, DCI Gilchrist.'

'One question before I go, ma'am.'

She frowned. 'Yes?'

He faced McVicar. 'I know that the murder victim lived in Glasgow, sir. Even so, the intervention of Strathclyde Police into a Fife Constabulary investigation is unusual, to say the least. My guess would be that it's part of a larger investigation.' He paused for feedback, but you didn't become Chief Constable by being gullible. So he continued. 'If I could hazard a guess, sir, it would be that Strathclyde's investigation involves a major drug shipment.'

McVicar displayed his best poker face. 'And your question is, Andy?'

'Why not let Fife Constabulary assist, sir?'

It seemed a simple enough question, but the answer appeared to elude McVicar. 'Keep me updated on the Joe Christie cold case,' he said. 'That'll be all. Thank you.'

'Very well, sir. Ma'am.'

Gilchrist turned and strode from the office, his mind burning with the need to push for more. But he and McVicar went back many years, and over time he had come to understand the subtleties of the Chief Constable's psyche. The fact that McVicar had failed to deny or acknowledge Gilchrist's comments told him that he was close to hitting the nail on the head, if he hadn't already hammered it home. He opened the door, and closed it behind him, more certain than ever of his next step.

CHAPTER 21

Back downstairs, he caught Jessie's eye and signalled for her to follow him outside.

In the car park, he walked straight to his BMW, had the engine running and the fan on high by the time Jessie slipped into the passenger seat. He slid into gear and eased through the pend into North Street. 'Any luck with Mhairi?' he asked.

'They've been able to dry the logbook, but some entries have bled into others. So it's all still a bit of a mess.'

Gilchrist cursed under his breath. What had he been expecting? A typed report with names, dates and signatures? 'Find out where Mhairi is, and let's check it out for ourselves.'

Mhairi's friend lived in a modern split-level house on Balnacarron Avenue. One half of the double garage had been converted into a workshop of sorts, and he parked his BMW on a steep, bricked driveway.

He found Mhairi seated at a wooden workbench, jotting down notes. She stood when she saw him, and shouted, 'Carol?'

A slender woman dressed in denim jeans and a white T-shirt, despite a cold draught funnelling into the workshop from an easterly wind, entered through a door that led to the other half of the garage.

Mhairi introduced the woman as Carol Granger, who gave him a firm handshake and a gap-toothed smile. 'I've heard a lot about you,' she said, then walked to the workbench, and took hold of a metal wheel that operated what looked like a pressing machine. 'Managed to dry most of it out last night,' she said, and turned the metal wheel.

The pressing machine clicked, and the top plate raised a tad from the floor.

At first Gilchrist didn't understand what was happening. Not until Granger turned the wheel some more then leaned down to slide a solid piece of wood from under the top plate, did he notice the logbook. As if answering his unspoken question, Granger said, 'If you don't press it when you've first dried the pages, they can become distorted and illegible as they dry out completely. The press avoids that.'

She slipped on a pair of blue latex gloves, then removed the logbook from the press with care. Then she carried the logbook to a cleared corner of the workbench covered with white butcher paper and overlain with paper towels. She placed the logbook onto the paper towels, and prised the hardcover open with such deliberate care that Gilchrist thought she was afraid the whole thing might evaporate into book dust.

She held the cover at right angles, as if not to break the spine, then eased it wider until the pages lay spread before them. At first glance, he thought it all looked legible, but a closer examination confirmed that ink on one page had bled into the opposite page, creating blurred hieroglyphics ringed with watermarks. It might all be legible, but it would clearly take time and effort to decipher.

'Are the pages like that the whole way through?' he asked.

'Mostly.' As if to prove her point, Granger peeled a clump of pages back to reveal similar inked hieroglyphics. 'When you dry a book by interleafing, you don't interleaf every page to begin with, just every dozen or so, or else you could distort the book, even split the spine. Once you've had a first go at it, you can then stand it upright in front of an oscillating fan. It's good to use the press now and again, to restore the book's shape.'

'Have you been through every page now?' he asked.

'Not yet. It was pretty damp throughout. It takes time to dry out completely.'

'How much time?'

'Impossible to say. Every book is different.'

He struggled to cover his frustration. They were getting nowhere fast. 'Can you show me the last entry?' he said.

'Here it is.' She eased back the pages. 'Twenty-fifth of October.'

Gilchrist slipped on a pair of latex gloves, then fingered the logbook, taking care as he turned over the pages, working his way back through time, examining them one by one. Each page was a printed form, identical in every way, with headed columns for *Hours*, *Knots* and *Tenths* – whatever they were. Another column with the heading *Wind* was subdivided into two thinner columns – *Direction* and *Speed*. Another for *Barometric Pressure in Bars*, and one for *Temperature*. But other than the date and time of entry, the only information noted in any of these columns was the wind direction and speed – *NE 12; NNE 14; NNE 18*. So much for keeping his logbook *up to date, come hail or shine*. Here was evidence to the contrary that not much maritime information had been logged at all.

Gilchrist studied the headings again, puzzled and irritated in equal measure when he saw that no columns were headed

Longitude or *Latitude*. He wasn't a seaman himself, but it seemed to him that in the open vastness of the North Sea you would want to know where you were at any point in time. Still, if you thought about it, perhaps that would be of little concern for the solitary captain of a small fishing boat that never ventured into deeper waters, but mostly hugged the coastline, laying and retrieving creels, the Scottish mainland close by, always in sight.

His hopes were kept afloat by the final column. Headed *Remarks*, this was a different matter altogether. Wider than the others – almost half a page in width – it was crammed with notes written in ink, in what looked like a childish hand, which he presumed was Christie's. He struggled to read the spiderlike handwriting, made more difficult by the water-damage bleeding, and managed to make sense only of the odd bit here, another bit there.

He turned to the preceding page, worried that the paper still felt soft and soggy. 'You can't dry this any faster, can you?'

'Not recommended,' Granger said. 'We might damage it irreparably.'

He gritted his teeth. Maybe Cooper was right. He really was becoming more impatient with age. 'Once it's dried,' he said, 'it's going to take time to examine this in detail. The ink seems to have bled badly in places.'

Granger nodded in grim-mouthed silence.

Mhairi said, 'I've had a go at working out what's written on that final entry, sir.' She screwed up her face as she opened her notebook. 'It's sketchy. But I've noted down what I think is reasonably clear, and tried to fill in the gaps with what I thought was obvious. I've left out what I couldn't read or guess. For example some of the bearings aren't clear,' she said. 'So I wouldn't bank on these until we got confirmation.'

Gilchrist felt his hopes soar. They might not have longitude and latitude noted, but if sufficient bearings had been noted in the *Remarks* column, then it might be possible to track *Brenda Girl*'s final course from Christie's last entry. If he was heading to Amsterdam as his wife suggested, then with help they might be able to identify which port he'd been heading to. He didn't want to get anybody's hopes up, for there was always a possibility that Christie had sold the boat. But even as that thought was blossoming, it evaporated just as quickly. If Christie had sold his boat, he would surely have taken his logbook with him; as insurance, just as his wife had said.

He nodded to Mhairi. 'Let's have it.'

'This is the last entry on twenty-fifth of October, sir. At the start, it's noted in the appropriate columns that the wind is *N6*, which I take to mean a north wind at six miles per hour.'

Nautical miles per hour? Or maybe kilometres per hour? Not that it really mattered, he supposed. So he nodded his agreement, and said, 'So it's relatively calm.'

'I'd say so, sir. The main entry starts off with numbers which I think are bearings, so filling in some of the gaps, and expanding known acronyms, it says – *Headed east-south-east* then indecipherable. *Swell six feet. Made steady progress for* . . . can't make it out, sir. *Set new heading south*, again illegible. *Sighted IOM to west. Rendezvoused* . . . at least that's what I think it says, sir, the spelling's wrong.'

'Let's see it on the entry,' he said, and peered at the blurred ink. But the writing was too faint, the craftsmanship too poor, for him to confirm it one way or the other. How Mhairi was able to decipher anything, he couldn't tell. 'I can't make head nor tail of it,' he said, then turned to Mhairi. 'You said he sighted IOM to the west. What's IOM?'

Mhairi grimaced. 'I could be wrong, sir, but heading easterly from Crail, then turning south, it could be the Isle of May.'

Gilchrist nodded. The Isle of May was an island at the outer mouth of the Firth of Forth where the German fleet surrendered all its warships at the end of the First World War. The island was now a nature reserve, and boat trips and a ferry service ran from Anstruther. But with respect to Christie's disappearance, did it mean anything? He couldn't say.

'Carry on, Mhairi.'

She returned to her notes. '*Rendezvoused with* . . . and again, I'm sorry, sir, it's illegible, and I wouldn't want to hazard a guess.'

He offered her a smile, and said, 'Keep going.'

'Yes, sir. *Rendezvoused with* . . . whatever. *Set course west-north-west. Swell rising to ten feet. Wind stiffening.* He's also got that in the wind column, sir, *N22*, so it looks like the weather's worsening.'

'Anything else in that entry?' he asked.

'Only . . . *Moored at Anstruther at 19:43*. And that's it.'

Gilchrist let out a gush of frustration. He'd been pinning his hopes on coming across something they might consider worthy enough to provide Christie insurance. But it seemed to be nothing more than worthless maritime entries. And insurance against what? Had Christie feared for his life? Had the break-in been a prelude to his disappearance? Were the break-in and his disappearance even related, for crying out loud?

'Let me see the logbook,' he said, and removed it from the workbench. He flipped it open to the back cover, to receive a reprimand from Granger.

'Careful. You'll break the spine.'

Fuck the spine, he wanted to say. If the logbook contained nothing more than the odd maritime note on wind speeds, sea swells, bearings out and bearings back, a day-trip to some unidentifiable destination, whatever that was – another fishing boat, perhaps; or some buoy where drugs or illegal merchandise could be dropped off and collected? – then they might as well throw the bloody thing in the rubbish bin. But he offered her a smile of apology, and handed it back.

'I was thinking, sir, that if the last entry was the twenty-fifth of October, where Christie moored in Anstruther, then he must have gone missing the following day, the twenty-sixth.'

Gilchrist narrowed his eyes as his mind fired its way through the logic of some other possibility. 'Why would he go to Anstruther at all?'

'The police report mentioned nothing about him mooring in Anstruther, sir.'

'Maybe he never got off his boat. Maybe he was meeting someone in another boat in the harbour. Maybe that someone took the boat and killed Christie.' Or maybe, he thought, he'd solved the equation to the square root of eff all. Christ, they were getting nowhere . . .

'This is interesting.'

Gilchrist and Mhairi turned together. Granger held up what looked like a decrepit business card. 'I've just found this stuck between a couple of pages.'

Gilchrist took it from her. The card had softened to such an extent that its edges were thin and frayed. But it had been placed between clean pages in the logbook so that no ink had bled into it. The card was plain white, one side blank, the other with a place name – Larach Mhor – and a phone number printed in plain type. But hand-printed in blue ink below that, in Christie's spidery penmanship, was a name that set off alarm bells for Gilchrist.

'Bloody hell,' he whispered.

CHAPTER 22

Gilchrist handed the business card to Jessie.

'V Maxwell?' she said. 'Is that who I think it is?'

But Gilchrist had already walked from the workshop and stood facing the wind, its icy breath refreshing against the flush of his brow. The fog that clouded his thoughts was lifting to reveal another possibility, one he did not like. His own words to McVicar echoed in his mind – *If I could hazard a guess, sir, it would be that Strathclyde's investigation involves a major drug shipment.*

No wonder McVicar had failed to respond. For if Victor Maxwell of the BAD Squad – Battle Against Drugs – was in any way involved in Christie's disappearance, then it did not bode well for Stooky Dee's murder investigation. What had been, until that moment, the single strand of a cold case of a missing person, all of a sudden had erupted into an interconnected web of drugs, murder and corruption.

And just how deep did that corruption run?

Victor Maxwell had been up in front of Complaints and Discipline on more than one occasion, but each time had managed to walk away with his reputation intact – watertight alibis, missing witnesses, unarguable corroboration, all seemingly above board and unassailable in a court of law.

But another, more worrying, thought flitted into Gilchrist's mind.

Had McVicar's insistence in ridding Fife Constabulary of any involvement in Stooky Dee's investigation exposed possible compliance in police wrongdoing? And Dainty, too? Was his relationship with DS Fox more than business? Fox had known about the names on Tommy's list. You didn't have to be Einstein to work through the possible links.

And worse was the thought that three names on the list had been murdered, all of whom were employees . . . *alleged* employees . . . of big Jock Shepherd.

The difficulty Gilchrist foresaw was not that the BAD Squad might be homing in on nailing Jock Shepherd's ass to the proverbial cross – taking him out, in other words – but that they might be contemplating taking over—

'Larach Mhor sounds familiar.'

Gilchrist jolted at the sound of Jessie's voice. 'What?'

'It's a bar in Pittenweem. Lachie took me on a date there once.'

He held Jessie's gaze, willing her to explain the joke to him. But her dark eyes told him there was nothing funny in what she'd said. She was serious. Lachie really had taken her on a date to Larach Mhor. Chief Superintendent Lachlan McKellar of Strathclyde Police had travelled from Glasgow to Fife for a night out in a small bar and restaurant in the tiny fishing village of Pittenweem. Nothing wrong with that, on the face of it, but McKellar had reputedly been involved in at least one of Maxwell's sting operations. So, adding two and two to make four – he hoped

– the reason Lachie knew about Larach Mhor was through his association with Maxwell. It all made perfect sense on one side of the coin. But on the other, he could be so far off base he was outside looking in.

He faced Jessie. 'You don't still keep in touch with Lachie, do you?'

'Who? Jabba the Hutt?' Jessie knuckled an imaginary head. 'Earth to Andy?'

'What I meant was, we're not likely to bump into him in Pittenweem, are we?'

'Fat chance. Oops,' she said, and giggled.

'Phone Jackie,' he said, 'and get her to print out some head-shots. We'll need them for our trip to Larach Mhor.' He ran off the names of those he wanted printed out, and opened the door to his car. Jessie slid inside, clipped on her seatbelt then busied herself with texting. Rather than drive off right away, he walked to the seafront and faced the harbour, intent on phoning Maureen.

When she answered, he thought she sounded tired.

'Just calling to see how you are, princess,' he said, 'and to follow up on last night.' He listened to digital silence for so long that he thought the line had died. 'You still there?'

'I'm waiting for you to follow up on last night.'

He squeezed the bridge of his nose with his thumb and fore-finger, and let his gaze drift to the distant horizon, the sky grey, as dark as the sea. Speaking to Maureen when she was in one of her moods was like petting a lion. You had no idea when it would turn on you.

'I was concerned about the way our evening went last night,' he said. 'I think we left a lot of things unanswered, and

I wanted to make sure you were all right.' He listened to silence fill the line. He wanted to tell Maureen that he cared for her, was there for her. But he also wanted to have another face-to-face chat with her, hopefully later that day. He seemed to have got off on the wrong foot with his call, so said, 'Can we start again?'

She tutted.

'Look, Mo, I'm sorry about last night if I came across as telling you what to do. I would never do that. But I hope you took on board what I said. About your subconscious already knowing what you want to do.' He paused for feedback, but she was not for giving up so readily. 'I hope I helped you overcome your initial worries. About being a mother. About how you're going to cope. I'll help in any way I can.' He paused again, but the line still lay silent. 'It's a big decision, so take your time. If you want to talk some more about it, let me know—'

'I've already made my decision.'

He swallowed the lump in his throat, then took his time saying, 'OK.'

'I'm not going to have a termination,' she said. 'I'm going to keep it.'

It took a couple of seconds for the impact of what she'd said to hit him. 'Well, that's wonderful,' he said. 'I'm so happy for you. And I'm so proud that you—'

'But.'

He clenched his jaw, closed his eyes. He didn't want to ask, but he really had no choice. 'But what?'

'But I'm going to have an amniocentesis.' She paused, but only for a moment, then said, 'If there's anything wrong with the foetus, I want to have a termination.'

161

'OK,' he said, dragging the word out, trying to recall how many weeks a pregnancy had to be before an amniocentesis could be carried out. Sixteen, he thought, although he couldn't be sure—

'Could I ask you to do something for me?'

'Yes. Of course. Anything.'

'I've scheduled an appointment at Ninewells on Monday, for ten in the morning.' A pause, then, 'Will you come along with me, Dad?'

'Of course I will.' The words were out before he could think. Of course he would go with his daughter to the hospital on Monday, but dreaded the possibility of the case being at some critical point. And in that moment, he made a promise to himself, that he would be with Maureen, come hell or high water. And if the worst came to the worst he would resign rather than be instructed otherwise.

'Thanks, Dad.'

'I'm here for you, Mo.'

'I know you are, Dad. I love you.'

'Love you, too, princess.'

He ended the call, surprised by the hot nip of tears. At the thought of his daughter becoming a mother? Or of him becoming a grandfather? Or because he'd known from the whispered rush of her voice that she truly did love him, that for once in his life she knew he would be there for her when she needed him most.

He walked back to his car and took his seat behind the wheel.

'Problems?' Jessie said.

He smiled at her. 'Sorted,' he said, then eased back onto the road.

Outside the Office, he double-parked on North Street while Jessie ran inside to collect the photographs from Jackie. He didn't want to see, or have to speak with Smiler, and gave a sigh of relief when Jessie returned only minutes later.

St Andrews to Pittenweem is about ten miles as the crow flies, and Gilchrist didn't hang about. He floored it to eighty in some stretches of country road and within minutes, it seemed, they drove into Charles Street, past the Anchor Inn on the right and down into the older part of town. Stone houses either side could have stood there for centuries.

He hadn't bothered to enter the destination on his GPS system, and soon found out that he didn't know his way around the back streets of Pittenweem as well as he thought he did. He crossed the main road – the A917 that ran through town and along the east coast – and continued into Routine Row. Not the shortest way as it turned out, but you can't get lost in a town the size of Pittenweem, particularly if your destination is the seafront. He worked his way downhill onto Mid Shore and found a parking spot that overlooked the harbour.

Outside, the air hung tangy with the smell of kelp and salt-water, and the less pleasant aroma of fish left in the open air too long. Gulls, on the constant search for food, quarrelled on the harbour walls, flapping and pecking, lifting webbed feet off the stone to hang in the air on buffeting wisps of wind. An engine burst into life as a fishing boat headed seaward, thumping pistons mingling with the day-to-day cacophony of a Scottish fishing harbour going about its daily business.

From the outside, the Larach Mhor looked as if it had once been a house. Its stone facade matched the homes either side, but a sign above the window – the name all one word, he noted – and a wooden bench beneath, gave the game away for the thirst-weary traveller.

Gilchrist followed Jessie over the threshold, and into the pub.

CHAPTER 23

Inside, Gilchrist was faced with a gantry the pride of any public bar. Whisky glowed with enticing warmth; gin with chilling freshness. Draft beer could be pulled from any one of four taps. A barmaid with hair dyed black, and matching tights and sweater that showed off a frame more suited for work on a fishing trawler than behind a bar, offered a warm smile.

'What can I get youse?' she said.

'A bit early for me,' Gilchrist said, and held out his warrant card. 'We're with St Andrews CID. Can you spare a few minutes?'

'Whatever it is, I didnae do it.' She laughed at that, which had Jessie bristling.

'How about serving underage customers?' Jessie said. 'You ever do that?' Which took the smile from the barmaid's face. 'Your name?'

'Jean,' she said, no longer so sure of herself.

'Surname?'

'Hartley.'

'How long have you worked in this bar, Jean?' Gilchrist asked her.

165

She shrugged. 'About four years. Why?'

Gilchrist removed one of Jackie's printouts from a brown envelope he pulled from his inside jacket pocket. He held it out to her. 'Have you ever served this man?' he asked. 'Or seen him in the pub, or anywhere else?'

She sniffed, ran a hand under her nose, then shook her head. 'Sorry.'

Gilchrist turned Victor Maxwell's photo face down on the bar. He hadn't expected her to have recognised Maxwell. Doing so would be proof that Maxwell had set foot in a bar that might connect him to the disappearance of Joe Christie on the night his boat was stolen. No, Maxwell was too smart for that. He would have sent one of his minions to do the nasty; DI Walter MacIntosh, for example, or Tosh, as he was more commonly known.

He held up a photo of Tosh.

Hartley narrowed her eyes for a moment, then shook her head again.

Gilchrist felt oddly deflated. 'You sure?'

'Positive.'

He laid Tosh's photo face down on top of Maxwell's then showed her a photo of Joe Christie. 'How about him?'

'He looks familiar. But it's been a while. I cannae be sure.'

'A while since you've seen him?'

'I think so.'

'A year? Longer? Three years?'

Hartley glanced at Jessie, then back to Gilchrist. 'I'm sorry. We get all sorts of people having a pint or a bite to eat here. I never really pay attention to them. I'm always too busy serving customers, rather than eyeing them up, if you get my meaning.'

'Who else works here?' Jessie said.

'Velly.'

'Who?'

'Velly Rangan. She hired me. She'd be your best bet.'

'She in?'

'Doesnae start 'til later.'

'She got a phone number?'

Hartley slipped her mobile from her back pocket, tapped the screen and read out a number. Gilchrist dialled it, and his call was answered straight away, a woman's voice that gave no hint of an Indian or ethnic accent. He strode back outside while he went through the introductions then, after explaining the purpose of his call, said, 'Where can we meet?'

'I'm just about to have a coffee on Shore Street in Anstruther.'

He asked for the name of the shop, and said, 'We'll be with you in five.'

It took him closer to fifteen minutes to hook up with Rangan. For some reason, the town was heaving – maybe because the sun was threatening to come out. The public car park was full, and he ended up having to abandon his car on the slope of the concrete ramp to the harbour. He sent Rangan a text in case she was thinking of leaving.

They found her inside, seated at the window, an Apple MacBook opened on the table, a large mug of coffee and a half-eaten slice of chocolate cake on a side plate. Gilchrist put her in her thirties, a thin woman with aquiline Indian features, and brown eyes enlarged behind black-rimmed spectacles. She didn't stand when Gilchrist approached. With only one chair available, and others taken up with customers chatting or texting, there was no room for the three of them.

Jessie said, 'You sit. I'll stand.'

Gilchrist obliged and took the only chair. He showed Rangan his warrant card, just to make the meeting a bit more formal than she seemed to think it was. She took the hint by closing her MacBook and hiding behind her coffee.

'How long have you worked at Larach Mhor?' he asked.

She lipped the rim. 'Coming up for ten years.'

'Are you the longest-serving employee?'

'You could say.'

He opened Jackie's envelope, and showed her Victor Maxwell's photograph first, which was met with a firm shake of her head, further proof that Maxwell did indeed know how to keep himself out of the spotlight.

Next came Tosh's photo. Another shake of the head.

Again, Gilchrist felt a flush of disappointment.

Then he showed her Joe Christie's.

'I know him,' she said.

'Do you have a name?'

She grimaced, as if struggling to recall. 'He's missing, isn't he?'

'Why do you say that?'

'Isn't he?'

Gilchrist said, 'Do you know his name?'

'No, but I recognise his face. Haven't seen him around for yonks, though.'

'When did you last see him?'

'Now you're asking. Years ago. Two maybe. Longer, even. I don't know.'

'How about his boat?'

'What about it?'

'Do you remember seeing that?'

She shook her head. 'I know nothing about his boat. I get seasick just walking along the harbour,' she said, as if that explained everything.

He tapped Christie's image again, pushed it closer to her. 'Try to remember,' he said. 'When you last saw him, what was he doing? Was he with anyone? Did he buy a pint? Did he buy some food? Did you serve him? Did he talk to anyone?'

She stared hard at the image, and Gilchrist could tell from the furrowing of her brow that something was coming to her. Her lips tightened, as if the moment had passed, then she looked at him. 'I'm not sure, but I have the vaguest memory of something years ago.'

Gilchrist focused on her deer-like eyes. 'I'm listening.'

'We hardly get any trouble in our bar. The odd drunk swearing, or someone spilling a pint. Nothing to write home about.' She turned her head and looked out the window, her gaze settling on something on the far horizon for several seconds, before returning. 'But one night I remember this man coming in.' She tapped her fingers on the photograph, pulled it closer. 'Him, I think. He was out of breath. As if he'd been running. He looked around, like he was searching for someone. Next thing, he's back out the door.'

Gilchrist retrieved the photograph. 'Are you sure it was him?'

'I think so.'

Not exactly a vote of confidence. He leaned back and returned her gaze. 'A police investigation was carried out when he went missing. Every home and every pub, shop and office in Anstruther was visited.' He knew what he was saying was not likely, but sometimes you just have to push. 'Did you tell the police what you saw?'

'They never asked me.'

'They never came to Larach Mhor?'

'They came, aye, but they didnae ask me. I remember I was on the late shift when they came round that day.'

'And they never came back?'

'No.'

'And you never went to the local police station to tell them what you saw?'

'Why would I? They'd asked the others.'

Gilchrist pursed his lips with frustration. Christie hadn't been reported missing by his wife for ten days, and even then she hadn't been convinced he was in trouble, but had sailed off into the sunset, so to speak – Amsterdam to be exact. With a less than interested wife, and a cooling trail already over a week old, no wonder the local police put in a half-hearted effort to find old Joe.

'Can you think of anything else?' he tried. 'Anything at all?'

'Only that he was wearing a fisherman's cagoule.'

'Why would you remember that?'

'Because it wasnae your bog-standard yellow cagoule, but bright red. Stood out like a sore thumb.' She scowled. 'And it had a tear in the shoulder. I remember that. If it had been mine, I would've binned it yonks ago.' She forked a piece of chocolate cake, as if to tell him that she'd said all she was going to say.

After thirty seconds of silence, he slid a business card to her. 'If you think of anything else, give me a call.' He slipped the photographs back into the brown envelope, was about to push his chair back, when he decided to show her one more.

He removed it from the envelope, and laid it on the table. 'How about this man? Do you recognise him?'

She studied the image for a couple of seconds, then shook her head. 'Sorry. No.'

Gilchrist returned Jock Shepherd's photo to the envelope, then stood. 'Thanks for meeting with me. Your description's been very helpful.'

'Except for one thing,' she said.

'What's that?'

'It might not have been that man at all.'

Well, there he had it. Never rely on human memory.

He gave a grim smile and pushed through the café door, Jessie behind him.

CHAPTER 24

They crossed Shore Street, heading for Gilchrist's car. 'Do you have Mrs Christie's phone number?' he asked.

Jessie checked her mobile, then rattled it off.

The call rang out, but didn't dump him in voicemail. He recited the number back to Jessie, to confirm he had it correct – he had – and dialled it again. This time it was answered on the second ring.

'Mrs Christie?'

'What?'

He introduced himself, and said, 'Did your husband ever wear a cagoule?'

'A what?'

'A fisherman's cagoule. A waterproof jacket. Did he ever wear one?'

'Aye. All the time.'

'Can you describe it for me?'

'It's just like any other waterproof jacket.'

'No, I meant what colour? And did it have any defects? That sort of thing.'

'He had two or three of they jackets,' she said.

Bugger it. The last thing he wanted to hear. He pressed his remote fob, and his car winked at him. 'Do you still have them?'

'Threw them in the bin years ago, when I realised he wisnae coming back.'

Gilchrist kept his tone level as he took his seat behind the wheel. 'Again, I'm sorry for your loss, Mrs Christie. But it would be helpful if you could remember what he was wearing when he left home that day.'

A pause, then, 'Naw, I couldnae tell you what one he had on.'

Gilchrist gritted his teeth. He'd hoped he wouldn't have to tease the answer he wanted from her, but she was leaving him with no choice. He switched his mobile onto speaker, and grimaced at Jessie, then tried, 'Did he ever wear a *yellow* cagoule?'

'Aye, he did. As well as a black one and a red one. But I could-nae tell you what one he had on that day.'

Gilchrist tried a more direct route. 'The red one. Can you tell me anything about it?'

'Like what?'

'Was it brand new?'

'Naw, it was torn to buggery. I'd told him to get a new one, but he wouldnae listen.'

'Where was it torn?'

'The sleeve was hanging off.'

'It had come away from the shoulder. Is that what you're saying?'

'Hanging by a thread.'

Jessie gave the thumbs up, and he said, 'OK, thanks for your help, Mrs Christie. If anything turns up, I'll be in touch.' He disconnected, and said, 'So it looks like it *was* Christie who turned up in Larach Mhor that night. If we can find out who he was looking for, that could help us figure out what happened to him.'

'Sounds like a dead end to me.'

Gilchrist almost agreed. 'Get on to the Coastguard and see if they've got any record of *Brenda Girl* sailing from Anstruther to Crail that night—'

'They don't have,' Jessie said. 'Or we would already have it. Remember? The last record they have of it is what we've found in the logbook.'

Gilchrist started the engine with a growl that sent a flock of seagulls over the harbour wall. Jessie was right. Christie was a dead end. He was missing, and his boat had been stolen, and no one – least of all the police who handled the initial investigation – had any idea what had happened. But the niggling thought he couldn't shift, was that Christie's disappearance – could he call it murder? – and Stooky Dee's murder were somehow connected. He was sure of that. But the answer as to how they were connected was beyond him at that moment.

Had Christie's disappearance and Dee's murder been carried out by the same criminal gang? Or, more worryingly, did the fine line between criminality and the law run through the middle of both cases? Once again, Victor Maxwell's name jumped to the fore, courtesy of the business card found in Christie's logbook.

Gilchrist slipped into reverse, and backed up the ramp onto Shore Street. At the lights, he turned onto Crail Road and had just passed Burial Brae when Jessie said, 'You're driving too fast.'

He glanced at the dashboard – 52 in a 30 limit – and eased back. 'Sorry. My mind was somewhere else.'

'Penny for your thoughts?'

'Need to be more than a penny,' he said.

'OK. I'll buy you a pint. Spit it out.'

He pursed his lips, kept his eyes on the road ahead. Maxwell was somehow involved, but they had no proof, and were unlikely to uncover proof anytime soon. But his mind tugged his thoughts in another direction, and he said, 'I'm thinking that I don't like DS Fox.'

'Yeah?' She twisted around on her seat, so she was facing him. 'Is this the famous Gilchrist sixth sense kicking in?'

'Don't know about that,' he said. 'But there's something false about him.'

'He lived in the States for a while, you said.'

'So he said.'

'You think he's lying?'

'Maybe not about living in the States, but he's holding something back. That's what I sensed, that he had some other agenda, as if ID-ing Stooky's body was an excuse for doing something else.'

'Like what?'

'I don't know.'

Jessie thought for a moment, then said, 'Dainty knows him. Right?'

'Right.'

'So you'd think Dainty would have told you if there was something going on.'

'You would think so, yes.' Which should have brought an end to his concerns.

But still his thoughts niggled.

He took the long road back to St Andrews, but by the time he drove through Kilrenny, he'd failed to come up with anything definitive. But he knew how gut feelings worked, and said, 'Let's get Jackie to look into DS Fox on the QT. She needs to be careful. I don't want to drag her into Smiler's bad books. Or you, for that matter.'

He had just driven past the entrance to the Castle Course when Jessie's mobile rang.

She stared at the screen, and said, 'Uh-oh,' then answered with, 'Yeah?'

Gilchrist drove on, conscious of a tightening in the air. Whoever Jessie was listening to had her pressing her lips tight. All of a sudden, she said, 'I swear to God, if you're having me on, I'm telling you, I will find you and arrest you myself.' Then she slapped her mobile shut, and let out her breath in a long gush. 'Holy shit,' she said. 'That was Tommy.'

'Get onto Telecoms,' he said, 'and get them to locate that call.'

'No need,' she said. 'He's back on side, provided he gets witness protection.'

'I thought he wasn't interested in Spain.'

'He's not. He wants Izzy and him to be set up in Thailand.'

Gilchrist slowed to a crawl on the Kinkell Braes. Off to his right, the tide had ebbed, leaving the East Sands glowing like a copper beach. 'Why there?' he said.

'Because Maxwell's reach doesn't stretch that far.'

Gilchrist jerked a glance at her. 'Did he mention Maxwell by name?'

'He certainly did.'

Gilchrist gripped the steering wheel tight enough to turn his knuckles white. Could Tommy provide them with proof that Maxwell was up to his neck in it?

'He also said that Bruiser Mann's body will turn up at a recycling plant in Whiteinch first thing in the morning.'

The name hit Gilchrist like a slap to the face. One of the remaining three on Tommy's list. 'Where's Whiteinch?'

'Glasgow. Near the Clyde Tunnel. And he said if you want him to side in with the Procurator Fiscal, then we'd better get our act together, *fast*.'

Gilchrist accelerated up Abbey Walk, the sound of the engine reverberating off the stone walls. He was missing something, some piece that didn't quite fit. 'Why now?' he said. 'Why come back now, ready to turn Queen's evidence?'

'I phoned Izzy this morning, and told her to tell Tommy that Strathclyde Police were now handling Stooky Dee's case, and that we'd been pulled off it.'

'So Tommy knew he'd lost any leverage he thought he had with us.'

'Got it in one.'

'And Bruiser Mann's another one of Shepherd's boys? *Allegedly*.'

'Tommy says Shepherd's being pushed to the brink. And that something big's about to happen.'

'And when it does, Tommy wants to make sure he's in with the right crowd?'

'You hit the nail smack dab on the head.'

Gilchrist switched on his car's phone. 'Call this number for me.' He read it out, while Jessie entered it. 'Not a word,' he said. 'You're not here.'

Jessie ran her thumb and forefinger across her lips as the phone rang. Then a man's voice said, 'Small.'

'Dainty,' said Gilchrist. 'How are you?'

'Better than you by the sounds of things. Heard you'd been pulled off the Stooky Dee investigation. I tell you, the mind fucking boggles.'

Gilchrist felt he had no time to waste, and went straight in with, 'What can you tell me about Bruiser Mann?'

'Fuck sake, Andy. That was quick. He's just turned up in a bin lorry in Whiteinch, face battered to fuck.'

Bloody hell. Tommy must be tight with someone in the know. 'So who's handling the case?'

'Vic Maxwell.'

Why was he not surprised at that? 'What's Shepherd saying?'

'Fuck knows,' Dainty said. 'But if I know big Jock, he'll be spitting nails.' A pause, then, 'Why the interest, Andy?'

'It's complicated,' he said. 'But we're looking into a cold case that might be linked to Stooky's murder.'

'What's the connection?'

'Too early to say. But Maxwell's name keeps popping up.'

'Watch yourself there, Andy. Best to steer clear of him. I mean it.'

'That list I gave you,' Gilchrist said. 'Only Chippie Smith and Angel Thomson are still standing.'

'Shepherd's got them in hiding.'

'Battening down the hatches, you mean. For the big shipment that's coming in.'

'Got to go. If anything turns up, you'll be the first to know.'

The line died.

Jessie looked at Gilchrist. 'He couldn't hang up quick enough, could he?'

No, he thought. Any mention of that *something big* had Dainty running for cover.

'What now?' Jessie said.

He drove on. 'I think it's time we talked to that brother of yours,' he said. 'You need to set it up for tonight.'

'For crying out loud, Andy. You're chancing your arm.'

'Give him a call, Jessie. If he wants a one-way ticket to Thailand for him and Izzy, then he needs to earn it. Tonight's his one-time opportunity. If he doesn't turn up, then we're walking away, and he's on his own.'

CHAPTER 25

The remainder of the day seemed to fly past with barely a glimmer of hope. Efforts to find more information on Christie's final journey to Amsterdam brought them to a dead end. Mhairi found nothing new in the logbook, obliging Gilchrist to conclude that the only useful information it provided had been the business card with Maxwell's name printed on it. With that in mind, he toyed with the idea of phoning Victor Maxwell, and just challenging him. But he had no proof of anything, and realised he would only be wasting his time, but more worryingly, could be showing Maxwell his hand.

Besides, Dainty's words of warning – *best to steer clear of him* – still echoed in his mind.

By close of play, Gilchrist had come up with nothing. The Maritime and Coastguard Agency had no records of the movement of *Golden Plover*, which he found more than a little troubling. It seemed to him that *Golden Plover* was even more elusive in its existence than *Brenda Girl*.

Calls to port authorities throughout Scotland were leading nowhere. None had any record of *Golden Plover*. No harbours, boat clubs, marinas or fishing clubs had any record of anchorage, berthing, repair or storage fees being paid for *Golden Plover*. Whoever owned, or was in possession of, *Golden Plover* must have berthed it in a private marina, or pulled it from the sea and dry-docked it out of sight. For all he knew, it could have been docked in some farmer's barn along the road.

The only good news, if it could be called that, was Jackie's report on Kristen, Jack's girlfriend of the month, which Gilchrist found late in the day, buried in his in-tray. Despite the misery of that first meeting, it turned out that Kristen Hedström graduated from Oxford University with a first-class honours in English Literature, then spent five years travelling through Europe, from which no record of any laws being broken surfaced. But in the UK, a minor scuffle with the police in London saw her fined fifty pounds for resisting arrest during a demonstration against the killing of animals for fur. And six years prior to that, she'd been arrested on suspicion of possessing illegal substances. She pled guilty and was given a six-month suspended sentence, and one hundred hours of community service. Not exactly a guilt-free history, but it was certainly miles from the stuff of mainlining addiction. If he could take the positive, it would be that Kristen might be good for his son, keeping him straight from her own experience, along the lines of once bitten, twice shy.

But the day had not been a complete waste. Jessie had managed to arrange for her and Gilchrist to meet Tommy at the back of the old paper mill in Guardbridge. The council was trying to encourage new businesses into the property, with abandoned space being rented out at unbeatable prices. The project was still in its early stages, and most of the building was still vacant. A time to meet had been agreed – 9 p.m. – when all start-ups were closed, the paper mill locked for the night, and the waste ground at the rear hidden in complete darkness.

By 6.30 p.m., Gilchrist's head was spinning.

He pulled in Mhairi and Jessie for a quick debriefing, and by 6.45 p.m. decided to call it a day. Being Friday, he offered to buy them a few drinks in the Central. Mhairi declined – she was meeting Colin in the Whey Pat Tavern, then off to Dundee to try a new Thai restaurant that had been getting rave reviews. Jessie had to head off home to sort out Robert's dinner – mince pie, chips and baked beans – and to settle up with Angie for that week's work.

Rather than drive home to Crail, Gilchrist decided to have a bite to eat in the Central Bar. Booths that backed against the walls were perfect for spreading out files and reviewing records in private while he relaxed with a pint.

He pushed through the College Street entrance into the crowded din of a Scottish bar at the start of the weekend. He squeezed between rowdy students and hungry tourists, past a pair of ruddy-faced caddies who looked surprised to see they were still standing. It didn't take him long to determine that all the booths were taken, and when a young couple slid off their bar stools, he managed to claim a spot at the bar with his elbow.

Behind the bar, the staff shimmied past each other in the narrow aisles like dancers searching for partners. He caught the eye of one of them, a slim woman with short black hair and a pleasing smile, and ordered a pint of Deuchars.

It came up dark and creamy, good enough to eat, and his first mouthful almost took it to the halfway mark. But the bar was too crowded to find a table and order food, so he paid for his pint, intending to drive back to Crail and have something to eat at home. He checked his mobile, and found to his surprise that he'd missed a text from Cooper – clocked in at 17:58, when he'd been deep into that day's summary – Am free tonight. Can I buy you a pint? Becky xx

He eyed the message, trying to work out Cooper's reason for wanting to meet him. It had taken him many painful hours to finally realise that he wasn't the type of man with whom Cooper was prepared to invest the rest of her life. Of course, add to that the annoying fact that her peripatetic husband, Max, had apparently resolved his unfaithful ways and returned to the matrimonial home, proverbial tail between his legs, and the writing was there for all to see.

Since the turn of the year, Gilchrist had struggled to put their failed affair behind him. Even so, Cooper would often appear before him, shape-shifting in his mind's eye, sensuous, smiling, hair falling over his face as she impaled herself upon him. He almost groaned at the thought, then cast his gaze around the bar in case she was already there. That would be typical Cooper – send him a text and watch how he reacted.

He took a sip of his pint, then tapped his response – Sorry. Busy. Maybe another time? His finger hovered over the *Send* button while he reread his message. Would she see his open-ended reply as an opportunity to rekindle their relationship? And if she did, would he readily agree? He looked around the bar again as the answer came to him. Then he eyed his mobile, pressed the *Back* button, and retyped his message – Can't. Working.

He pressed *Send*, slipped his mobile into his pocket and left his pint unfinished.

Outside, in the relative quiet of Market Street, he walked across the cobbled road. He had no destination in mind, only that he felt an overpowering need to breathe in the chilling night air, clear his mind of fogged thoughts. He tugged up his collar, shivered off the night chill – had the temperature dropped twenty degrees? – and strode on.

At the end of Church Street, he almost turned left to check out the Criterion, but a glance at the overspill clientele standing on the pavement – mostly smokers – forced him to change his mind. He turned right, walked along South Street, past the old Kirk on his right, and the walkway to the pend onto Market Street, then past the old Post Office building, now a modern eatery – the kind of place Cooper would like. As he walked, he came to understand that it was not Cooper's text message that was bothering him, nor his curt response to her, but his and Jessie's meeting with Tommy later that night.

Just thinking of facing Jessie's brother had his pulse rate spiking. Few criminals had that effect on him, but Tommy Janes did. Or maybe it was what he wanted to ask Tommy that had him worried, that in order to uncover the truth, Tommy would have to acknowledge his personal participation in several illegal episodes.

Still, the question had to be asked. No doubt about it.

He just had to be prepared for Tommy's response.

CHAPTER 26

St Andrews to the old paper mill in Guardbridge was some five miles, no more than a ten-minute drive. Once he cleared the town limits, Gilchrist said, 'In a way, I'm surprised Tommy agreed to meet.'

Jessie shuffled on her seat. 'I think he knows he's running out of time. He's a tough nut. But I've never heard him so scared.'

Gilchrist said nothing, kept his eyes on the road ahead.

What had started off as a body found on a beached fishing boat was now developing into something far more sinister and outreaching, like some giant web that caught all passing debris. But once trapped, there might be no getting out. And as he drove on, he could not shift the feeling that he was missing something, some vital link that pulled everything together.

'Is it worth getting Tommy on the phone?' he asked.

Jessie tapped her mobile, placed it to her ear, then shook her head. 'He's removed the SIM card.'

Well, what had he expected?

The countryside slid past in silence. Off to the right, the lights of Guardbridge and Leuchars broke the black darkness of the

North Sea and the Eden Estuary. He slowed down at the Guardbridge roundabout, swung a tight right, and kept his speed steady as he drove on towards the paper mill.

Soon the walls of the old building ran alongside on the right, rising some forty feet into the night sky. For just that moment, they could be on the outskirts of some major city. Tommy had agreed to meet them at the back of the old paper mill where renovation works had evolved into the demolition of smaller buildings, tearing out of concrete aprons, removal of steel reinforcement. A chain-link fence with security warnings ran along the heel of the footpath.

A glance in the rearview mirror confirmed that no one was behind him. Ahead, the road lay deserted as it cleared Guardbridge limits on its way to Leuchars. He touched the brakes, slowing down to twenty, then to fifteen as he cruised alongside the chain-link fence.

'You see anyone?' he said.

'Nothing. But that's Tommy for you.'

He'd not given any thought about the logistics of meeting Tommy until that moment, and said, 'I didn't expect it to be fenced off. It looks secure.'

'There must be an opening,' Jessie said.

He drove on, but the fence ran all the way to Motray Water. Beyond, the road entered dark countryside. His headlights sparkled on glittering asphalt. Although spring was almost here, night frost persisted. He braked hard at Toll Road, tyres slipping on the ice, loose stones clattering the underside as he did a hard U-turn.

Jessie had her mobile to her ear. 'He's still got it off.'

He eyed the dashboard. 'We're running early. If he's here, maybe it makes sense for him to power it down.'

'I told him I'd call when we got here.' She hissed a curse, and said, 'He's always been a mad bastard.'

He crossed Motray Water again, and turned right into River Terrace. The road was wide enough to swing the car around, and he bumped over the kerb onto the pavement, and parked facing the security fence. His headlights shone through the fence, into a darkened area of flattened waste ground. He turned the lights off, and killed the engine.

The wind hit them as they crossed the road to check out the security fence. A quick shake of a support post confirmed it was solid. At ground level, too, the tension in the wire was strong, with additional fixings that secured it to the ground – no way to crawl under, and too high to climb over.

They walked towards the main building, Gilchrist checking the fence every ten yards or so, hoping for a gap through which he and Jessie might slip under. But the fence was new, the fittings secure, and he realised the only way they were likely to gain access was through the entrance gate itself.

But at that time of night, the gate was locked. A double padlock secured it. With the days of night-watchmen long gone, Gilchrist searched for a webcam, and found it high up on a pole on the other side of the security fence. Somewhere, some bored security guard would be watching him and Jessie on screen monitors.

Jessie gripped the fenced gate with her fingers and gave it a hard shake. The posts rattled, but there was no give in them. 'Jesus,' she hissed. 'Where the hell are you, Tommy?'

'Try his mobile again.'

She did, but the result was the same.

'Have you tried sending a text?'

'What do you think I've been doing? He's removed the SIM card, or switched it off, or something.'

It was the *something* that troubled Gilchrist. Why would a career criminal as street-smart and prison-tough as Tommy Janes be scared? He stepped away from the fence, and backed onto the road. But the fence appeared solid either side of the entrance gate.

Was Tommy already here? Had he brought wire cutters with him?

To his left, the security fence ran into the country darkness. To his right, it connected with the gable end of the old brick building. 'There must be another way in,' he said. 'Where did Tommy say he would meet?'

'In the waste ground at the back of the paper mill,' she said. 'Exact words.'

'The back. Not the side. Which is where we're standing now.'

'Holy shit, Andy. The back, the side, does it really matter?'

'Well, if we were inside, I would say it doesn't. But as we're outside looking in, then I'd have to say it does.'

Jessie rattled the gate again. 'Fuck sake, Tommy.' Then she had her mobile to her ear again, and cursed when the connection failed.

'Maybe there's another way in,' he said. 'A side door off the street.' Which was when he noticed it, a car parked by the pavement, about a hundred yards from where he and Jessie stood. Had it been parked there when they first drove past? He couldn't say.

'Over there,' he said. 'Is that the car you got the list of names from?'

Jessie followed his line of sight, eyes straining to see in the dim light.

'Looks like a Vauxhall,' he offered.

'Is it silver?'

'Could be.'

She stuffed her hands into her pockets, and set off along the footpath. 'If the rear light's broken, then it's Tommy's.'

'Offside or nearside?' he asked.

'What?'

'Offside light or nearside light?'

'Jesus, Andy, you can be so bloody annoying at times.'

CHAPTER 27

Jessie reached the car before Gilchrist, and walked straight to the boot. She felt a surge of relief as she recognised it. Tommy was here after all.

'That's it,' she said. 'And it's the right-hand light.'

'You're sure it's the same car?'

'It's got the same bird-shitty roof. So it has to be.'

She said nothing as Gilchrist ran his hand over the broken tail-light. 'For future reference,' he said, 'this is the offside rear-light.'

'I'll remember that next time I'm watching football,' she snapped, and an image of Lachie flashed into her mind. He'd done that sweetheart deal with a car salesman, for which she was supposed to be forever grateful. This was the problem with men, their presumed superior knowledge when it came to cars. They could be birds displaying plumage to win a mate. Did they really think she would drop her knickers for a smooth-talking car mechanic? *Your spark plugs need changed. Oh, aye, right, well, your place or mine then?* Who could remember whether left was offside or nearside?

'Did I say something wrong?' Gilchrist asked.

She threw him a glance. 'Jesus, Andy, you're such a boring bastard.'

But he had moved away, was slipping latex gloves onto his hands – she pulled a pair from her own pocket – and trying the door handle . . .

The door opened. He leaned inside. 'Looks like it's been hotwired.'

'Well, this is Tommy Janes we're talking about.'

The interior cabin bulb wasn't working, but even so, in the dim street light she could see the car's state of disrepair – seats torn and stained, dashboard grey and fingered with dust, grease smudging the windscreen. The car could do with a proper valeting – or just driven to the scrappies and dumped. All in all it looked just as it had yesterday when she'd collected the envelope. Except that now there were wires dangling from the steering column.

'You'd think he'd have given it a clean,' she said. 'At least try to blend in.'

'Maybe he's only using it for this meeting.'

She turned to face the paper mill, the two-storey brick wall, the barn-sized door that ran along a metal rail on two metal wheels – pull the door, and it slid along the wall. She saw no padlock or keyhole, which told her the door could be locked only from the inside. But in the centre of that sliding door was a smaller hinged door through which staff could enter or exit without having to slide the main door open.

Gilchrist already had the flat of his hand against it.

'It's unlocked,' he said.

The door creaked open to reveal a black interior.

Jessie stepped over the threshold and followed Gilchrist inside. She stopped for a few beats to allow her eyes to grow accustomed to the gloom. A gust of wind rushed through the opening, slamming the door behind her with a clatter that echoed like a drumbeat. A shadow shifted to her side, and her heart leaped to her mouth. She whipped her mobile towards it. From the dim light of its screen she caught a figure approaching her—

'Can't find a light switch,' Gilchrist said.

Her legs almost gave way. 'Bloody hell, Andy. I nearly peed myself.'

'Sorry.'

'Have you got X-ray eyes or something?'

'I saw a light switch as I entered, but it doesn't work.'

Jessie fiddled with her mobile, and switched on its beam.

The room lit up like a crypt.

Cardboard boxes, as large as shipping cartons, clustered one corner. Stocks of paper as bulky as rolled rugs stood against the wall like dummy Scotsmen. Metal buckets, tins of paint and two extension ladders gave the impression that workmen had only just finished for the day. The air hung thick with the smell of fresh paint and oiled varnish, within which she thought she could detect the sour smell of something less pleasant.

'What is this place?' she asked.

'A storage area, maybe?'

'Strange place to have a storage area. Right at the main door.'

'That would be for ease of transport.'

'Oh, right. Why didn't I think of that?' It annoyed her that she wasn't thinking clearly, that the surreal fear of being trapped in a crypt had dulled her thought process. She shone her mobile at the far wall to reveal the black opening of another doorway.

'This way,' Gilchrist said.

'Where the hell is that idiot brother of mine?' All of a sudden she wished she hadn't agreed to meet Tommy here. She should have insisted on meeting him in some remote car park, or on a beach. It's not like the Fife coast was short on quiet spots. But she was here now, and once they found Tommy, they could—

'Wait.' Gilchrist stood still, head cocked to one side. 'You hear that?'

'Hear what?'

He turned his head, stared at some spot on the back wall.

She pointed her mobile at it, to reveal another door.

'It sounded like someone running,' he said.

'Tommy?'

'Why would he be running?'

Then Gilchrist was striding to the door, reaching for the handle. She rushed to keep up with him, mobile flickering shadows over the walls and ceiling like fleeing ghosts. The lock clicked, and Gilchrist stepped into another room, his hand already reaching for something on the inner wall—

The room lit up like a flash of lightning.

Jessie froze.

Gilchrist turned to face her, and from his eyes she could read his anguish.

It took another second of confusion before she noticed the dark pool in the corner of the room, her mind asking why the workmen would not have cleaned up their spilled paint. And for just that moment, her breath locked, as if time had stilled. Then her heart kick-started with a jolt that thumped a shudder to her core, and her mind at last took in what her eyes were telling her.

'Ah, fuck,' she said, and pushed past Gilchrist.

'Don't.'

She stopped, half-squatting, arms reaching out to the body at her feet.

'It's a crime scene,' he said. 'Don't touch anything.'

She knew from the way Tommy's eyes were opened and staring blindly at the ceiling that it was a crime scene. She knew from the blood that still dripped from a gaping wound in his throat and ran across the room to form a pool by the door like a red puddle, that he'd been murdered. And she knew from the warmth of his face as she brushed her hand across the scar on his cheek that whoever killed him had only just done so.

The person Andy heard running . . .? Shit . . .

Then she was on her feet and jogging back the way they'd come.

But Gilchrist was already ahead of her.

'He's still here,' she shouted to him.

'Outside,' he said. 'He's making a run for it.'

As she followed him back through the darkened rooms, across the concrete floor, to the street door that danced in the shadows from her phone's torchlight, it amazed her that he sounded so firm, so in control – nothing at all how she felt.

Then she was outside in the cold air, and standing with Gilchrist in the middle of the road. A quick look one way, then the other, told her nothing. But the departing echo of a car's racing engine from somewhere in the direction of Leuchars told her where the killer had fled – and told Gilchrist, too.

'Let's go,' he shouted.

Again she was running after him, his slim build more suited to being fleet of foot. She pressed a hand to steady her chest, her breath coming at her in hard hits. She was nowhere near as fast as Gilchrist, and lost sight of him as he ducked into the side street where he'd parked his car. But she gritted her teeth, held onto her boobs, and ran as fast as her legs would take her.

And as she ran, images of Tommy's gaping throat, the blood-ied mess that had once been a living body, flashed before her. Last year her mother had been murdered, then Terry, her brother – all in the space of a couple of days. And now Tommy. Gilchrist warned her that she might be next, but as long as Tommy had been alive, Jessie had felt safe – well, as safe as you could be in a family of criminals.

But now Tommy was dead, what next? Or should it be – *who* next?

Christ, Tommy, what the hell did you get yourself into?

She rushed across the junction, and had to jump to the side as Gilchrist's car slithered to a halt. The passenger door swung open as if on its own, and she jumped inside as the car careened onto the main road and accelerated into the country, engine roaring. She was still panting when they powered through Leuchars. A glance at the speedo – 85 – had her holding onto her seatbelt for dear life.

'Get onto the CCTV Control Centre,' Gilchrist said. 'And get them to check out the road from Leuchars to Dundee.'

'What are they looking for?'

'Any car that's breaking the speed limit.'

'That'll be us then.'

'We're looking for a description, hopefully a number plate.'

She had to hold onto the dashboard as he slammed on the brakes then powered out of town, taking the car up to 90 mph in a heartbeat, it seemed. 'Jesus, Andy, I'm wearing clean knickers.'

'There's a couple of junctions up ahead. We need to catch him before then.'

St Michael's Golf Course flew past on the left and, within seconds, the 30-mph speed limit of St Michaels flashed by doing close to the ton. A heavy dose of the brakes took the breath from her as her seatbelt crushed her chest. She'd travelled this road many times, on trips to Dundee with her son, Robert, for appointments with ENT specialists at Ninewells Hospital. So she knew why Gilchrist was driving so fast.

'Which way?' he shouted.

'Straight on.' She wondered why she had chosen that. The junction flashed past – left to Edinburgh, right to Dundee – and in no time at all they hit another junction.

'Which way?' Gilchrist shouted.

'Straight on.'

She had to slap her hands to the dashboard as the car veered left, tyres struggling for grip on the cold road. The road sign for Wormit flickered in the headlights for a millisecond, then sank into darkness at the speed of light.

'You need your ears cleaned,' she said. 'This isn't straight on.'

'I have a feeling he's going this way.'

'He?'

'Figure of speech.'

'I would've gone straight on,' she said.

'I know. You said that.'

Jessie stared into the blackness ahead, the headlights piercing the night inkiness like tunnels of light. Overhead, the sky could be a black blanket. She felt the power go out of the car's engine, and for a moment thought they'd run out of petrol. But the grim tightness of Gilchrist's face told her that he knew he'd lost him . . . or her . . . or them.

'Still want me to contact the CCTV Control Centre?'

'Yes,' he said. 'I was hoping to give a description of the car, but . . .' He tightened his grip on the steering wheel. 'They could be anywhere now.'

Jessie got onto the CCTV Control Centre as Gilchrist worked through a three-point turn on the narrow country road. He now seemed resigned to the fact that whoever they'd been chasing had vanished into the network of Scottish country roads. At night, and with limited CCTV coverage in open countryside, Tommy's killer – if that was indeed who they'd been chasing – could be well on his way to Dundee, or Edinburgh, or Glasgow by now. By daybreak, he could be in London or across the Channel.

Gilchrist swung his car onto the grass verge, then slid to a halt. He opened the door, and stepped out, mobile to his ear. Jessie followed. The night chill squeezed tears from her eyes, or maybe her subconscious was reminding her that the last member of her childhood family had just been murdered. A tremor took hold of her lips, and all of a sudden she struggled to fill her lungs.

What the hell was happening?

It's not like she and Tommy had been close. Maybe her sadness was for Izzy, whose hopes for a better life in sunny climes abroad had been snuffed out with the cruel slash of a razor-sharp blade. She stared across the dark countryside, catching bits of Gilchrist's phone conversation as he organised a team of SOCOs, and gave instruction for someone to contact Dr Rebecca Cooper, the police pathologist. Odd that he didn't just call Becky himself, she thought. Or maybe he truly was over her. Then he finished his calls, slipped his mobile into his pocket, and walked over to her.

'How're you doing?'

She sniffed, shrugged her shoulders. 'I never really got on with Tommy.'

He nodded. 'I'm really sorry, Jessie. It's been a tough time for you.'

She sniffed again.

'We need to distance you from the investigation,' he said. 'It's too personal.'

She knew she couldn't be involved, and shook her head to let him know it was OK. Then her eyes stung from the nip of tears, and she couldn't stop a sob escaping from her throat as Gilchrist placed his arms around her and held her close.

CHAPTER 28

Saturday morning
North Street Office, St Andrews

Despite a late night, Gilchrist arrived at the Office at 7.30 a.m.

He'd told Jessie to take the weekend off – no excuses – and to give him a call in the morning, any time that worked for her, any time at all, as long as she felt up to it. He'd also phoned Colin – spoiled his date with Mhairi, as it turned out – and told him to have a draft report on his desk first thing.

He took a sip of his Starbuck's coffee, opened Colin's file, and removed a series of photographs. As he flipped through them, he had the oddest feeling that Colin had taken these to upset him, or perhaps to remind him that he didn't care for having his Friday-evening date with a good-looking woman cut short.

Another sip of coffee to wash back the nip of bile as his stomach threatened to eject last night's sandwich – tinned tuna and sliced tomato after midnight. Tommy's eyes, as flat as a dead fish's, stared back at him in high definition, close enough for Gilchrist to count the bloodied veins beneath the cornea. Images of the fatal wound to the throat, the cut so deep that the head seemed to be held on by only the spinal column and a flap of skin, flipped past him, one after the other. Gilchrist took another sip of coffee, pressed his lips tight, then hissed out a curse. How close did you have to be to take a photograph of a fatal wound? Close-ups could be valuable, but bloody hell, this lot verged on the sadistic. Maybe he should have a word with Colin. Or better still, next time just let the lad enjoy his Friday night.

More images of Tommy's slaughter slid from hand to hand, until one photo stopped him cold. Another close-up, this time of Tommy's stomach, his bloodied shirt pulled open. It struck him that there was not much blood from a wound such as this. But if Tommy had been almost decapitated first, then the stomach wound inflicted second, that would explain it.

He stared at the wound, a diagonal cut over twelve inches long that sliced through the belly-button. He felt his blood run cold, the hairs on the back of his neck rise, and swallowed another spurt of bile that nipped the back of his throat. He took another sip of coffee to kill the taste, and forced himself to study the image. He'd noticed that wound last night, but thought only that Tommy's shirt had been slashed. But in this image, the cut was so clean and deep that the camera caught the glistening pink of Tommy's intestines.

Gilchrist's stomach gave another involuntary spasm, and he pressed his hand to his mouth to avoid throwing up. Yet he still forced himself to study the image, his mind pulling up the memory of a similar wound that had him pushing back from his desk and walking to the window. He fumbled with the latch, and threw the window open, the damp air cool and clean against the sweat on his face.

It had been the angle of the wound that first caught his attention, the specific spot – the belly-button – through which the blade had sliced, the second. At first glance he could be forgiven for thinking it was just another madman's act of slaughter. But lay the two bodies side by side, and they could be twins.

Last year. That was when he'd seen it.

And the victim had been Terry Janes, Jessie's older brother.

Standing at the window, his mind fired at the logic. Whoever had killed Terry had also killed Tommy. But was that brutal, gut-slicing wound the killer's signature, his calling card? And if so, who was the killer's card for? Last year, when Jessie's mother and brother, Terry, had been murdered, Dainty had alerted Gilchrist to the possibility that Jessie could be next. Was this calling card a warning for Gilchrist that more was to come?

He jolted at the hard rapping on his door.

He forced a smile to his face. 'Didn't expect you in today.'

Mhairi entered his office. 'Just wanted to follow up on a few things from last night, sir.' She nodded at the photographs on Gilchrist's desk. 'Are these of Tommy Janes?'

'They are. Anything jump out at you?'

She picked them up, flipped through them with the poker face of a gambler staring at a full house. Then she found what she was looking for, and held the photograph out to him. 'We found this, sir.'

Gilchrist noticed the *we*, and realised that Mhairi had gone to the old paper mill with Colin, as part of the investigation team. Of course, she would have. They were out on a date, and Mhairi wouldn't have missed an opportunity to add to her growing port-folio of first-hand murder scenes. Once he'd organised the SOCOs and pathologist, Gilchrist had spent no more than fifteen minutes at the crime scene. He'd been conscious of the fact that both Smiler and McVicar had pulled him off the Stooky Dee investigation, and was concerned that she might turn up out of the blue – she was known to do that from time to time – and ask some difficult questions like – *Why were you meeting a known criminal whose involvement with Strathclyde Police is well known, despite being personally ordered off a murder investigation handled by Strathclyde? And don't try and tell me they're not related. Because I know they are. So what do you say, DCI Gilchrist?*

The question would come. No doubt about it. But last night he'd decided that he and Jessie should first work on their stories before facing Smiler's inquisition. So, he'd left with Jessie and driven her home. Which explained why he hadn't noticed the bloodied footprint in the photograph Mhairi now held out to him.

He took it from her, and pulled it close – part of a footprint, with sufficient definition to see the pattern on the sole. A tape measure lay across the edge of the toe to give a clear indication of the print's size.

'Could be a work boot,' he said. 'Or a running shoe.' He thought he could make out a crack in the sole's pattern, but couldn't say for sure. He nodded to the folder. 'Any others like this?'

'That's the best of the lot, sir. We found some scuff marks near the body, but this one was by the door. We were able to track his escape route through the building, and find out which way he left. You said at the time, sir, that you heard him running?'

It took him a few seconds to realise she'd asked a question. He nodded, and said, 'So how did he get out of the place?'

'A door at the rear that opened onto waste ground.'

'What about the security fence? How did he get onto the road?'

Mhairi frowned. 'I don't know, sir. I just—'

'Call the security firm, and get a copy of last night's CCTV footage from them,' he said. 'And follow up with the Control Centre, too. We put in a request for coverage on the Leuchars to Dundee road.'

When Mhairi left his office, he studied the image of the foot-print again. Something was niggling. How long had it taken from the moment in the darkness of the paper mill when he'd first heard someone running, until he heard the departing roar of a racing engine?

One minute? Two? Longer?

He couldn't say for sure. But what he did know was that the security fence had been tight and sound last night. Mhairi's words came back to him – *a door at the rear that opened onto waste ground*. But once the killer was in that waste ground, how had he escaped? And just as troubling – where had he parked his car?

Had Tommy's killer been familiar with the paper mill's layout? Somehow that didn't fit, because Gilchrist had it in his mind that the murder had been opportunistic, that the killer had lain in wait for Tommy, and killed him the moment he arrived. But how had he known of their meeting? Had Tommy let it slip? But again, for someone so street-smart and prison-tough, that scenario just didn't compute.

But the second question raised all sorts of probabilities. Tommy's wrecked Vauxhall Vectra had been the only parked car on the main road. If there were no other cars parked in the imme-diate vicinity, did that mean the killer had not acted alone, but had an accomplice, a driver who'd hung around in the back streets, waiting to be called upon when the time was right?

Bloody hell, he was digging up more questions than answers.

Only one thing for it.

He slipped on his jacket and strode to the door.

CHAPTER 29

In mid-morning sunlight, the old brick building appeared less ominous, smaller, too. What had looked to be solid walls that soared overhead into the night sky turned out to be no more than three storeys tall in one block, two storeys in others. The paper mill formed only one part of a terraced row of interconnected buildings and walls that ran along the back of the pavement for over a couple of hundred yards. He drove the full length of it, then beyond, and parked his car on the same spot as he had last night.

The SOCOs had opened the large sliding door, and reversed their Transit van inside. Crime-scene tape flapped across the open entrance. A group of bystanders watched from the opposite side of the street, taking photos with mobiles, and conversing amongst themselves.

Tommy's body had been removed to Bell Street mortuary in Dundee in the small hours of the morning. Gilchrist hadn't yet heard from Cooper, but expected she would carry out her PM examination as early as possible, despite it being the start of the weekend. He made a mental note to give her a call if he'd heard nothing by midday. Then he stuffed his hands into his pockets, and set off for the waste ground.

When he reached the security fence, he walked its length, from the paper mill to the bridge that crossed Motray Water. He took his time, checking for breaks in the fence, tugging the chain links between the metal stanchions. But when he reached the bridge, he'd found nowhere that would let anyone slip through, or under. It was not beyond reason for the killer to have climbed up and over the fence, but Gilchrist's gut was telling him that was not how he'd made his escape.

At the bridge, the fence ran back into the site, along the edge of Motray Water, which was when Gilchrist saw a possibility. From the paper mill to the spot on which he stood, the security fence was sound, with metal stanchions concreted into the ground. But where it ran alongside Motray Water, the fence consisted of a row of interconnected chain-link panels that stood on the ground on metal feet. A gap at the base of the panels was deep enough for someone to slide under.

Gilchrist visualised the killer running over the waste ground, then a quick slide under the fence to put himself at the edge of a vertical wall that dropped some eight feet to Motray Water. He walked farther, onto the bridge, and looked seawards. And there it was, as plain as day, a concrete walkway that ran across the shallow river and connected the waste ground to the opposite bank.

At the other end of the bridge, Gilchrist came across a side road, nothing more than a paved track wide enough for a car. But what caught his attention was a pair of skid marks close to a padlocked farm gate, beyond which lay an open field that led to the walkway.

He squatted, and studied the skid marks. No doubt about it. A car had left that spot in a hurry. Twenty yards up the slight incline put him back on the main road. He'd driven past this side road twice last night. But parked down there, off the main road, on a dark night, any vehicle with its lights off would never be noticed by anyone driving by.

He pushed himself to his feet and eyed the field. Last night had been damp, the grass winter-soft and March-soggy. They might be lucky enough to make a cast of footprints if the killer had stepped in some mud. The forecast for the weekend was cloudy and no rain, but in Scotland you would never bet on that. The SOCOs had a narrow window of opportunity. He stepped back from the gate and realised that as it was padlocked, the killer would have had to clamber over it. If he hadn't been wearing gloves, then the SOCOs might be able to lift fingerprints from the metal railing—

His mobile rang – ID Mhairi.

'Some bad news, sir. The security firm had a glitch in the CCTV system last night.'

'Let me guess,' he said. 'They've no footage from six until midnight.'

'About that, sir, yes.'

Gilchrist walked up towards the main road. The glitch in the CCTV system was not accidental. No, someone in the security firm had been paid to shut it down for the night while someone else got on with the business of murdering Tommy. He could assign a couple of uniforms to look into the security firm's records, interview a string of employees if they had to. But what would that give him?

Bugger all, came the answer.

It troubled him that their arranged meeting had led to Tommy's murder. But it told him that whoever was responsible for it – and likely Stooky Dee's murder, too – had money and power and tentacles that stretched from Glasgow to the Fife coast with the speed of light – or more correctly, with the speed of a phone call. But with the body count mounting, it also told him that something big was about to break, some criminal operation with millions of pounds at stake, maybe hundreds of millions for all he knew.

'Jesus,' he hissed.

'Sir?'

'Sorry, Mhairi, just thinking out loud.' He turned to look across the waste ground and the paper mill beyond. Overhead, clouds were thinning, revealing patches of blue. Maybe the forecast would be right for once. The rain would stay off, and they could make casts of the killer's footprints and have the case wrapped up by the end of the day.

Or maybe pigs could fly.

'Any luck with our CCTV Control Centre?'

'Not yet, sir.'

'Chase them up, Mhairi. We need a description of that car. And get back to me the instant you find anything.' He then phoned Colin and arranged for the SOCOs to examine the padlocked gate for fingerprints, the adjacent field for footprints.

You never could tell. They might just get lucky.

A gull wheeled overhead.

For a fleeting moment he thought it was a pig.

By midday, Gilchrist was none the wiser.

Mac Fountain, manager of the CCTV Control Centre in Glenrothes, had called. 'A car driving fast, you said.'

Gilchrist closed his eyes, pinched his nose. Hearing his request spoken like that, made it sound as ridiculous as it was. 'Not just fast,' he said. 'But speeding.'

'On the Leuchars to Dundee road?'

'Yes.'

'Do you know how long that road is?'

'Not off the top of my head, no.'

'Or how many cut-offs?'

Gilchrist exhaled, hard, letting Mac know that he was frustrated, too. 'Look, Mac, I know it's a long shot, but it's all we've got at the moment. I've given you an accurate time frame, and was hoping you might pick up something in Leuchars before it hit open country.'

'We got one in Leuchars all right. Two actually.'

'You did?' His hopes soared until the pause on the line told him that one of the cars was his own. 'Let me guess. My Beemer, and one other.'

'I guessed it was yours,' Mac said. 'But the quality's so bad it's more or less useless. You wouldn't recognise it yourself.'

Gilchrist hissed a curse. What was the point of being the most CCTV'd country on the planet if all they showed was worthless recordings?

'The cameras aren't set up for traffic,' Mac said, as if reading his mind. 'But for—'

'Got it.' Gilchrist didn't need to know the details, only that he was getting nowhere fast. Cameras were likely located at the railway station, maybe the Post Office, or some other spot, mostly for public safety, not necessarily for accident hot spots or tricky road junctions.

'Want me to keep looking?'

Mac's question sounded innocent, but what he was asking was approval to commit resources to it, and some department he could assign his time to. Gilchrist tilted his head back and resisted the urge to shout at the sky. It was always about money, not justice. A man had been killed last night, brutally murdered, for fuck sake, and money shouldn't come into it.

But it did, and he really had no option.

'Don't waste any more time on it, Mac. I'll get back to you if we come up with something else.'

The second call that morning had come from Smiler. 'I'll be at the Office in twenty minutes,' she said. 'I'll see you there.'

And she had.

She knuckled Gilchrist's door and entered without introduction.

Gilchrist had never seen the Chief Superintendent in anything other than her uniform. But that morning, being the weekend, she was wearing thigh-hugging bootcut chinos and a white silk blouse that did what it could to hide striking cleavage – where had that come from? He found himself struggling to maintain professional eye contact as she stood before him, legs astride, arms crossed.

'Morning, ma'am.'

'I've been advised that a known criminal by the name of Tommy Janes was murdered in Guardbridge last night.'

Gilchrist nodded. 'That's correct, ma'am.'

'And I've been told he was DS Janes's brother.'

Well, so much for professional condolences. 'He was, yes.'

'I've also been told that you and DS Janes had scheduled to meet this Tommy Janes last night, but that he was murdered before you got there.'

Gilchrist nodded. 'Correct.'

'Mind telling me what the purpose of your meeting was?'

Nothing like going straight to the point. Even though he and Jessie had their stories straight, now the question had been asked, he realised it wasn't going to be any easier trying to bend the truth. 'Of course not, ma'am.' He took a moment to focus his mind. 'Tommy Janes was a lifetime criminal,' he said, 'who met a woman and decided it was time to get out of his life of crime. And to do that, he was prepared to give evidence against a number of major criminals in exchange for witness protection.'

'And had you discussed granting this lifetime criminal witness protection with anyone other than DS Janes?'

'No, ma'am. It was early days. And it took some persuading to get him to agree to meet at all. But I needed to know what information he could provide that would justify the effort and expense of assigning him to the witness protection programme.'

She nodded. 'I see. And did you not think that DS Janes meeting with this lifetime criminal, her own brother, was a violation of police protocol?'

'I did, ma'am, yes. But it was the only way Tommy Janes was prepared to meet us.'

'So you went ahead, regardless.'

'Without DS Janes present, ma'am, there would have been no meeting. So, yes, we agreed to meet him, but regrettably he was killed before we did. So now that we have a new murder investigation initiated, I've removed DS Janes from my team. As you said, having her involved in the investigation would be against protocol.'

'I see.' She unfolded her arms and stared at some spot on the wall behind him, as if giving thought to her next question. Then her eyes settled on his. 'I'm expecting the Chief Constable to put forward an argument for pulling in Strathclyde Police again.'

'I'd be happy to share whatever we—'

'No,' she said. 'To take over the investigation.'

Gilchrist struggled to hide his surprise. 'On what grounds?'

'On the grounds that Tommy Janes's and Stooky Dee's murders are connected.'

'More of a coincidence I would say, ma'am.'

'You really think so?'

The sneer in her tone did not go unnoticed. Like Gilchrist, it seemed that Smiler did not believe in coincidence. If two separate things happened around the same time, then they were related, plain and simple. It was clear to Gilchrist that Tommy's murder was connected to Stooky Dee's, but exactly how was another question. The answer lay within Strathclyde Police, he was sure of it. McVicar meeting with Smiler to confirm he handed over all files to Strathclyde didn't just speak volumes, it roared. Some other investigation was underway, a case so big that the Chief Constable had become personally involved. But having a team from Strathclyde Police trying to commandeer another investigation away from Gilchrist was not going to work for him. Not this time.

He had to play this long. So he lied.

'I do believe it's coincidence, ma'am, yes.'

'Explain.'

He didn't like the way she seemed intent on making him pay for breaking protocol. But as he held her look, he came to understand that she was not grilling him in the hope he would shoot himself in the foot, rather she was looking for him to provide answers she might need herself when she had to stand up for him and his team, not to mention the Constabulary itself.

So he decided to take a chance, a wild one, and took her into his confidence.

'If *I* was ever questioned by the Chief Constable,' he said, 'I would tell him that the investigation into Joe Christie's disappearance and his suspected murder three years ago has turned up some unusual connections.' He didn't want to mention the logbook, because it had still to be logged in as evidence. So he said, 'We found an old business card in Joe Christie's belongings, which had the name V Maxwell hand-printed on it.'

'You never mentioned that.'

'It's in the reports,' he lied. 'But before jumping to the conclusion that the name was that of Chief Superintendent Victor Maxwell of Strathclyde, who incidentally was questioned by Complaints and Discipline with respect to a double murder in Glasgow last year, I thought it wise to first talk to someone who had evidence of criminal intent, which might . . . and it's a big might . . . help us solve Joe Christie's murder.'

The quantum leap in logic from Maxwell's name to Christie's murder was a stretch to say the least, but he hadn't wanted to point the finger directly at Maxwell in case it backfired. Dainty had warned him that Maxwell was as slippery as they come, and if Smiler presented that convoluted argument to McVicar, and it was later proven to be wrong, then it wouldn't just be his head for the chop, but Smiler's, too.

213

'We're at the start of our investigation into Tommy Janes's murder, ma'am, and until we have a better understanding of why he was murdered, and what information he might have been able to provide us, I would suggest we play our cards close to our chest.'

Smiler's eyes held his in an unblinking stare. Then she took a deep breath and let it out. 'Bloody hell, Andy. Did Janes tell you anything before he was killed? Anything at all?'

'Other than what we've already handed over to Strathclyde?'

'Of course.'

He grimaced in silence.

Her lips mouthed a silent curse – *for fuck sake* – then she shook her head. 'So you're telling me you have absolutely nothing new.'

Well, it was difficult to deny that. So he said, 'Which is exactly what Strathclyde would have if they took over the case, ma'am.'

'Hardly.'

Again, he could not fail to catch the sneer in her tone. 'Give me to the middle of next week,' he said, trying not to plead.

'And if the Chief confronts me before then?'

He shrugged. 'You have to do what you have to do.'

She offered a dry smile. 'He's already asked me to give him a call.' Then she turned and strode from his office.

Well, there he had it. Pushed to the side again. No way out now.

She stopped in the doorway and faced him. 'I'll see if I can stall him, Andy.'

He thought it best not to comment.

'Don't let me down.'

'I'll try not to, ma'am.'

She frowned, as if she found his answer disappointing. Then she gave him the tiniest of nods, and walked off.

CHAPTER 30

At 1 p.m. on the dot, Gilchrist's mobile rang – ID Jack. He answered with, 'Can I call you back, Jack? I'm up to my ears.'

'You always say that. Listen, you want to meet for a quick pint and a pie?'

Gilchrist blew out his breath. He didn't want to meet Jack for a pint and a pie, quick or otherwise. But his mind was clouding over with reading too many reports, and he really was getting nowhere. Maybe a breath of fresh air would do him good. But the memory of Smiler's earlier comments warned him that he had to press on.

'I really am tied up, Jack.'

'You've forgotten, haven't you?'

'Forgotten what?'

'See?'

Sometimes Jack could be as irritating as Maureen, which made Gilchrist realise with a spurt of regret that he hadn't phoned her as he'd intended to. 'OK, what've I forgotten?'

'I'll tell you when we meet for a pint.'

'Thought we were going to have a bite.'

'That, too.' The line scratched as if a hand was being dragged over the mouthpiece, then Jack came back with, 'The Central in five. Can you make it?'

Oh, what the hell? 'Sure,' he said.

The line died, and he pushed to his feet, feeling stiff. Maybe he was too old now for all that clambering around a fishing boat. As if to prove Jack's point, his stomach rumbled, and he reached for his jacket and strode from his office.

He entered the Central Bar from the College Street entrance, and squeezed into the post-midday crowd. The world was supposedly in a global recession, but from the buzzing throng you'd think they must be referring to some other planet. He almost missed Jack seated at the bar with Kris, both wearing what looked like new black leather jackets. Maybe Jack's paintings were selling well. Or Kris was his sugar mummy. A couple of half-finished drinks sat on the bar in front of them. He tapped Jack on the shoulder.

'You're either a fast drinker, or you've been here a while.'

Jack slipped off his stool, and surprised Gilchrist with a hug. 'Hey, Andy. What you having?'

Gilchrist recovered from Jack's grip. 'Nice jacket.'

Jack slipped his thumbs under the collar, tugged the leather. 'A present from Kris.'

Gilchrist glanced at Kris, but she gave him a blank stare in return. 'So what's the occasion?' he asked.

Jack smiled at Kris. 'See what I mean?'

Kris nodded, picked up her drink – a revolting-looking purple – and said, 'Cheers.'

Gilchrist said nothing, just smiled with compliance at their secret joke, until Jack said, 'It's my birthday.'

Shit, and bugger it. Of course it was. How the hell could he have let that slip? He tried to keep a straight face. 'Well, I suppose the drinks are on me, then.'

Jack guffawed, chinked his glass against Kris's, then drained it. 'Don't bother getting me anything. I'm getting too old for that now. It's just good to meet up in a bar.'

Gilchrist smiled at that. Not *meet up for a pint*, but *meet up in a bar*. So, his son must really be off alcohol, which was one positive thing about dating an older woman who bought leather jackets for birthdays, he supposed.

'Right,' Jack said. 'How long can you stay?'

'I can't stay long. I'm sorry. I've got a busy day ahead.'

'Jesus, Andy. What is it with you and work? You've got to ease up. I'm always telling you. It's Saturday, for crying out loud. What's so important that you can't take an hour or two off to have a pint or three with your only son on his birthday?' He caught the bartender's eye, made a swirling motion with his hand, and said, 'Same again.' Then to Gilchrist. 'What're you having? A Deuchars?'

Gilchrist nodded in defeat. 'Go on then. You've talked me into it.'

Jack ordered a pint of Deuchars, and as if as an afterthought, said, 'I'll have the same. And a vodka shooter on the side. Grey Goose.'

'Thought you weren't drinking.'

'A concession for birthdays.'

'Just yours? Or everyone's?'

Jack gave Gilchrist's arm a playful slap, then his gaze brightened as a shooter was pushed across the bar. He picked it up and passed it under his nose like a wine connoisseur sampling the bouquet of some vintage batch. 'Oh man, it's been a while.'

Gilchrist smiled. 'A month, you said.'

'A month too long.'

Give Jack his due. He didn't throw it back in a oner like days of old, but held onto it until the Deuchars arrived along with another glass of blackcurrant-something that rattled with ice.

Kris lifted her glass, chinked it against Jack's. 'Happy birthday, min kärlek. Skål.'

Jack tapped his shooter to the others, said, 'Skål,' then downed it.

In an odd sort of way, Gilchrist was relieved to see that things hadn't changed too much for Jack. He took a sip of his pint, and smiled at Kris. 'Was that Swedish?'

'You speak Swedish?'

He shook his head. 'Just recognised skol. From the beer. But you lost me with the min korlik.'

She chinked her glass to his. 'Min kärlek. It means – my love.'

'Ah,' he said. Well, there it was. Hooks already into his son, and no doubt telling him she loved him. Meanwhile, Jack had attracted the bartender's attention, and with pint in hand was ordering another shooter. Gilchrist tapped Jack's pint glass. 'Happy birthday.'

'Hey, Andy,' he said, and pulled in a mouthful that took the pint to halfway. Then he rubbed the back of his hand across his lips. 'Have I missed that, or what?'

'It's good to cut back every now and again.'

Jack laughed, then said, 'You're never going to change, are you? You went on at me for years about drugs. And now it's alcohol.' He faced Gilchrist, as if squaring up to him. 'I don't take drugs any more. I've told you that. But I drink alcohol, and I'll continue to drink alcohol—'

'Except when you don't.' He flickered his eyes at Kris.

Jack gave a sad smile, and nodded. 'Except when I don't.' He took another mouthful, turned to the bar, and picked up his second shooter. He tapped Gilchrist's pint. 'Sláinte,' and threw it back as if to prove his point.

Kris caught Gilchrist's eye, and held up her purple glass. 'Blackcurrant juice,' she said. 'I'm driving.'

'If you can't stay for a bite to eat,' Jack said, 'we'll just head off to Dundee.'

The change in tack surprised Gilchrist, but he said, 'What's on in Dundee?'

'Some of my stuff's being shown there. And Kris has set up a meeting with an agent up from London.'

Gilchrist felt as if he'd just been blind-sided, that he'd stuck his foot in it with Jack once again, and failed to live up to whatever image his son had of him – fatherly figure, sage older man, guiding light or just plain old drinking companion. He chinked his glass against Jack's in an attempt to bring him back onside. 'Well, that's good news, right? Great, even. The chance to sell your *stuff* in London. After London, then what? New York?'

Despite Gilchrist's forced bonhomie, Jack seemed disinterested, patting his jacket with both hands. A flush of disappointment swept through Gilchrist at the thought of Jack having started smoking again – worst thing you can do for your health, he'd told him.

Then Kris held up a set of car keys, and shook them. 'You already gave them to me.'

'Yeah, I know.'

'Thought you didn't drive,' Gilchrist said.

'Kris's giving me lessons.' Jack slipped his hand into his inside pocket, and removed a piece of paper. 'Here,' he said, and handed it to Gilchrist. 'Mo wants you to call her.'

Gilchrist took it, nothing more than a run of numbers scribbled onto what looked like a torn-off envelope flap. 'What's this?'

'Mo's number.'

He had a great memory for numbers, but this one meant nothing to him. 'Does she have a new mobile?'

Jack shrugged. 'Couldn't say. She just phoned and asked me to give you this number and tell you to call her on it.'

Gilchrist frowned in response.

'There's no criminal subterfuge going on here,' Jack said. He gave a short guffaw, and lifted his pint and finished it with a flourish. Then he pushed the empty glass across the bar, and turned to Kris. 'Right, min kärlek. Is that us?'

Kris placed her half-finished drink on the bar, then hooked an arm through Jack's.

Jack gave Gilchrist one of his high-fives, albeit shoulder-high, and a half-hearted hug that turned into little more than a weak shoulder-bump. 'Catch you.'

'Yes, stay in contact.'

But Jack and Kris were already pushing through the Saturday afternoon crowd.

Gilchrist said nothing, just watched his son walk away from him without a backward glance, and thump through the swing doors into Market Street. He turned to the bar, rested an elbow on it, tried to take in some football match being played in silence on one of the corner TVs high on the wall. He sipped his beer, but it was as tasteless as dishwater, and on impulse he placed his pint on the bar and left the pub.

A cold wind rushed along College Street, forcing him to put his hands into his pockets and keep his head down. In North Street, instead of turning towards the Office, he crossed the road and walked towards the Cathedral ruins. Something about the manner in which Jack left the pub troubled him. The suddenness with which he seemed to turn against him, as if he'd had enough of being told what to do, and was a man who now stood no nonsense. Of course, if he thought back to their childhood, and how seldom he'd been there for Jack or Maureen – some days not seeing them at all, only as sleeping children in bed in the morning, and sleeping children to be kissed goodnight on his return – it should be no surprise that Jack could live without a father in his life.

He kept walking, fighting off a cold shiver that threatened to have his teeth chattering like a clockwork toy. Spring in Scotland. It could be winter anywhere else on the planet. Why didn't he just hand in his notice, pack a suitcase and head off to warmer climes? He was past trying to climb up the professional ladder. Earlier fuck-ups in his career had put paid to that. But here he was again, working his arse off, pleading with the boss to give him a few extra days so he could move his investigation forward. And all for what? So Smiler could hand the whole thing over to Strathclyde Police at McVicar's pleasure, with some more hard-earned investigative summarising?

Talk about a thankless profession.

He found himself standing at the metal fence on East Scores, which overlooked the black rocks at the foot of the castle ruins. The tide was out, the sea dark, waves pummelling the shore in their endless cycle, just as they would continue to do until eternity. He gripped the fence, loving the feel of cold steel against the hot flush of his body.

Was he coming down with something? Or just tired from working too many long hours? Maybe Jack was right. Maybe it really was time to call it a day. He closed his eyes, breathed in the cold air, the salty smell of kelp. Still he could not shift that ominous feeling that he'd somehow upset Jack. He'd forgotten it was his birthday – how had he managed to let that happen? – and had to take a moment to work out how old his son was. Twenty-five today? He hissed out a curse. How could that be? Where had the years gone? It seemed that Jack and Maureen had been children one week, then adults the next, and all the while he'd been working in Fife Constabulary, the proverbial hamster on the wheel, running faster and faster, and getting nowhere.

Well, not exactly nowhere. It always amazed him how the subconscious worked, how the thought of one thing led to the thought of another, working away deep in the back of his brain somewhere, until it popped out as an answer to some unasked question.

He removed his mobile from his pocket, and phoned Jessie.

'How did you get on with Smiler?' she asked him.

Gilchrist hid his surprise, and said, 'You must have eyes in the Office.'

'Not really. Just logic. Smiler's proving herself to be difficult to slip anything by.'

Well, he couldn't argue against that. 'I told her I've taken you off the case,' he said. 'It being too personal and all that.' Jessie exhaled, a sigh or a curse he couldn't say. 'She said she's under pressure from McVicar to have Strathclyde take this case over, too.'

'Ah, for crying out loud, why's she letting them run all over her?'

'Maybe she's trying to get in with those at the top.'

'And when she does, she'll find out they pull on their knickers and pants one leg at a time, just the same as we do.'

'Joking aside,' Gilchrist said. 'How are you keeping?'

'You mean about Tommy?'

He nodded to himself. 'I know you didn't get on, but he was still your brother.'

The line remained silent for several seconds, then she said, 'D'you know, Andy, if it wasn't for that wasted piece of pisshead shit we had for a mother, Tommy might've turned out all right, maybe even made something of himself.'

'Why do you say that?'

'I don't know if this is true or not, but the old dear used to go on about how she was Peter Manuel's illegitimate child, the baby girl he never knew he had. But d'you know what I think? I think she was full of shit. I think she just said that to try to be someone bigger than she really was, the drunken trollop.'

Dainty had mentioned this rumour to Gilchrist, too, before Jessie moved to Fife from Strathclyde. Peter Manuel was the last man to be hanged in Barlinnie Prison back in the 1950s for a series of murders. As the alleged grandsons of an infamous serial killer, both Terry and Tommy Janes would have earned kudos in the backstreets of Glasgow's dark ganglands.

'But she was your mother, too,' he said. 'And look how you turned out.'

'It was different for boys,' she said. 'You should've seen the beatings Tommy used to get as a boy. And all because of that bitch for a mother.'

The line fell silent again, which gave him the chance to move on to the purpose of his call. 'But Tommy was getting out,' he said. 'He'd found a woman, and wanted to make a new life for him and her.' He let a couple of beats pass, then said, 'Does Izzy know about Tommy?'

'Shouldn't think so. Not yet, anyway.'

'Well,' he said, 'as you're officially not involved in his murder investigation, it might be the decent thing for you to offer Izzy your heartfelt condolences.'

A couple of beats, then Jessie said, 'You know, Andy, you're a sneaky bastard at times. But I like you.'

Gilchrist felt a smile tug his lips. 'So you'll do it?'

'Already got my car keys in hand.'

'Get back to me if you come up with anything new.'

'You bet I will.'

The line died.

Gilchrist shoved his free hand into his pocket, his fingers brushing Jack's scrap of paper. He removed it, read the number, then phoned Maureen.

CHAPTER 31

Something in the way Maureen answered his call, a hint of tension in her tone, told Gilchrist she was not alone. 'I met Jack today,' he said. 'He gave me this number. Did you buy a new mobile?'

'It's someone else's.'

He held on, waiting for her to offer more. But it seemed as if she wasn't for letting him in on her secret. 'Anyone I know?' he tried.

'I shouldn't think so, Dad.'

Well, what had he expected? 'You wanted me to call?' He stared off into the distance, waiting for her to respond. Gulls swept by on stiff cliff breezes, floating at a standstill in one direction, wheeling at reckless speed in the other. A silhouette for a ship dotted the horizon.

'Charlie's dead.'

For a moment, the name confounded him. Then he had it. 'What happened, Mo? He wasn't that old, was he?'

'He got run over yesterday.'

How had Charlie made it to the street? he wanted to ask. Maureen lived in a top-floor flat, and never let her cat outside, other than on the open kitchen windowsill, from where he would leap onto the roof of the adjacent extension. But this was a cat they were talking about. Of course Charlie would find his way to the ground, and eventually to the street.

'I'm sorry to hear that.' What else could he say?

She sniffed, and said, 'So I'm staying at a friend's for a few days.'

At the age of six, Maureen lost her first pet, Scruffy, a white Highland terrier and a nippy-tempered wee rascal who'd been attacked and killed by a pair of Dobermann pinschers. At the time, Gilchrist thought Scruffy with his snappy manner must have worked the larger dogs into a fury. But when he found Scruffy's bloodied carcass lying soaked and broken in his front garden, he realised that no amount of canine nipping could justify being savaged to death like that. He'd hidden Scruffy's body from Maureen, wrapped it in an old towel and carried it to the boot of his car, to be buried in farmland on the outskirts of St Andrews. To this day, he'd never told Maureen the truth, only telling her that wee Scruffy must have run away from home.

Even at such a young age, Maureen never believed him. It was as if she could see through him, even then, and for the following month she refused to enter the kitchen where Scruffy's basket had been. With Charlie now having been run over, he could understand why Maureen didn't want to stay at home.

But it didn't explain why he was calling her on someone else's number.

'What happened to your own mobile?' he asked.

'I left it in my flat.'

'Want me to pick it up and bring it to you?'

'It's OK, Dad. I just wanted to tell you that my hospital appointment's been pulled forward to first thing Monday. I know you're busy, but you said you would come with me.'

He could almost hear her holding her breath, waiting for him to confirm if he could take her or not. He was up against it if he wanted to keep Strathclyde away from Tommy Janes's murder investigation, and Smiler's voice was echoing in his mind – *Don't let me down.* First thing Monday was not a good time, and hospital appointments were renowned for overrunning their allotted time. But was there ever a good time during working hours to take care of personal business?

'Sure,' he said. 'When would you like me to pick you up?'

A hand brushed over the mouthpiece, then she came back with, 'Can you pick me up in Cupar?'

He struggled to hide his surprise. 'Not a problem. When and where?'

'I'll get back to you tomorrow. Thanks, Dad. You're a sweetheart. Love you.'

'Love you, too, princess. See you Monday.'

When the call ended, he accessed Jackie Canning's mobile number from his phone's memory. He tapped in Maureen's latest number, the one he'd just called, and added – Name and address? He sent the text, then stuffed his mobile into his pocket and headed back to the Office.

Inchkeith Drive, Dunfermline
2.14 p.m.

Jessie parked half-on half-off the pavement, almost on the same spot she'd parked a couple of nights ago. The rain-soaked street looked even more desolate in daylight hours, the homes more rundown. Izzy's house was four doors along on the opposite side, and seemed in a better state of repair than Jessie had first thought. At least the hedge looked trimmed.

She switched off the engine, was about to step outside, when Izzy's door opened and a man in denim jeans and heavy winter jacket strode down the slabbed path. The door closed behind him, and without so much as a backward glance he slid behind the wheel of an Audi. Seconds later, the car drove off, laying down a contrail of white exhaust in the cold afternoon air. Jessie noted the number plate before it rounded the corner and disappeared from sight. Then she sat tight, wondering if Izzy was at home by herself.

But after ten minutes, no one else appeared.

At Izzy's front door, she stood on the step, her heart heavy with what she was about to do. On the drive from St Andrews she'd tried to work out how best to break the news, if she should just blurt it out or play it gently. In the end, she realised that she didn't really know Izzy, or how she felt about Tommy, and decided it would be best if she showed her a certain level of sympathy.

She rang the doorbell.

A few seconds later, the locks clicked, and the door cracked open.

Izzy stood before her, wearing the same oversized cardigan as she had the other night. Light-grey sweatpants made her look slim, rather than anorexic skeletal. A pair of new-white trainers clashed with the dilapidated look. But dark shadows under eyes that stared back at her, wet and raw, warned Jessie that Izzy had been crying.

'What d'you want?' she said.

'Can I come in?'

'What for?'

Jessie had no way of knowing if Izzy already knew about Tommy's murder, but the pained look in her eyes made her mind up for her. 'Tommy was my brother,' she said. 'He was family.'

Izzy's eyes welled, and tears spilled down her cheeks.

Jessie ventured one foot over the threshold, and breathed a sigh of relief as Izzy took a step back to let her in.

The hallway was dark, the walls a woodchip cream devoid of pictures or photographs, as if Izzy had no interest in family history, or the outside world. Without invitation, Jessie walked along the hallway and into a kitchen redolent of burnt toast. She made her way to a spot in the corner, where she stood with her back to a small radio from which the tinny tones of some DJ she didn't recognise announced the next song. A couple of empty mugs stood on the draining board by the sink, along with two side plates. Whoever the man had been, he'd at least been invited to have tea and a slice of toast.

Izzy headed straight for the kettle – maybe the man who'd left had put in a new fuse. Drumming water drowned out the music, and Jessie said nothing as Izzy dropped two teabags into a ceramic teapot blackened with crazed cracks. Then she pottered about the sink, lifted a plate, put it back down, wiped her hands on a filthy dish towel, and hung it back over the oven door.

Finally, she looked at Jessie. 'They said he'd been tricked.'

'Who said?'

Izzy hesitated, as if worried that she'd given away too much. 'Tommy's friends.'

'The man driving the Audi?'

Izzy's gaze flickered wide-eyed at Jessie. 'Have you been spying on me? Because if you have, you can fuck off right now.'

'I wasn't spying on you, Izzy. I was phoning from my car,' she lied. 'I just happened to see him leaving.' She smiled. 'Honest.' The kettle clicked off, and she said, 'I'd love that cuppa if you don't mind.' She waited while Izzy filled the teapot. 'So who was he? The man who left.'

'Why d'you want to know?'

'Was it him who said Tommy'd been tricked?'

Silence.

'Did he say who'd tricked him?'

That time Izzy said, 'Didnae need to.' Then her eyes shifted from certainty to doubt.

Jessie needed a name. But she had to be careful. She was no longer a member of the investigation team, and any information she acquired could be deemed inadmissible. She eased into it with, 'So you know who tricked him, Izzy?'

Izzy lowered her gaze.

Jessie edged towards her, trying to catch her eyes. 'Can you give me a name?'

'I don't know any names. Tommy didnae tell me nothing.'

'What about the man who was here? What's his name?'

She shook her head. 'I don't know.'

'Don't lie to me, Izzy. I'm not stupid. I've got his number plate. I can find out one way or the other.' She hadn't meant to snap, and she struggled to keep her tone level. 'But you'll score some brownie points, Izzy, if you just tell me yourself.'

Something seemed to pass behind Izzy's eyes then, and she returned Jessie's look with the fire of defiance. 'Look at you,' she said. 'What were you to Tommy, eh? What did you ever do to

231

help him?' She pushed Jessie aside and took hold of a black handle jutting from a block of wood by the kettle.

Too late, Jessie realised it was a filleting knife.

She shouted, 'No,' as Izzy thrust the knife at her stomach.

CHAPTER 32

Jessie's training kicked in.

She struck at Izzy's arm, stepped in, grabbed her wrist and, with a hard twist and a quick turn, folded Izzy's arm up her back.

Izzy squealed in pain. The knife clattered to the linoleum flooring.

'Fuck sake, Izzy, I could put you away for that.'

'Why don't you?' she gasped.

That close, Jessie realised how frail Izzy was. She'd felt no weight behind the attack, as if Izzy's body was hollow. Her arm felt stick-thin, too, and Jessie relaxed her grip for fear of breaking it. As the fire went out of Izzy, she realised that Izzy's heart hadn't been in the attack, rather more defiant gesture than attempted murder. It could even be a cry for help.

Just to be safe, Jessie said, 'I'm not going to arrest you, Izzy. I know you're hurting for Tommy. I'm hurting, too. I want to help you. Nothing more. Do you understand?' She waited for Izzy to nod her head, then said, 'I'm going to let you go. And you're going to take a seat. And we're going to have a wee chat over a nice cup of tea. OK?'

Tears spilled off Izzy's chin as she nodded.

Jessie let Izzy's arm slide down her back, then she guided her by the shoulders to the kitchen table. No knives anywhere. Izzy sat, then stared at the table in muted silence. Jessie removed two mugs from the draining board.

'Milk and sugar?' she said.

'I've nae sugar. Nae milk neither.'

Jessie filled both mugs from the teapot, and placed one in front of Izzy. 'Take a sip,' she said. 'It'll make you feel better.'

Izzy reached for her tea, and said, 'I've nae biscuits.'

'That's good. I'm on a diet.'

Izzy's eyes took in Jessie's figure. 'You look good. Lost a wee bittie weight.'

'I always was the tubby one.'

Izzy sniffed. 'Me? I cannae put it on. Eat as much as I like, and nothing happens.' She hid behind another sip of tea.

Jessie knew what Izzy's problem was – smoking, or hard drugs. Stuff like that would kill your appetite. But rather than stir it up, she bunched up her boobs. 'Wouldn't mind losing a few pounds off of this lot.'

Izzy smiled, a change as striking as the sun emerging from thunderclouds. White teeth sparkled at odds with her grey pallor. Deep-set eyes glistened alive. And for just that moment, Jessie had a sense of how Tommy had been attracted to her. Then just as quickly the smile vanished, her face darkened. 'Tommy was up for the witness thingie. Said we could start a new life thigether. So what happens now?'

Jessie felt her heart sink. 'I'm not going to lie to you, Izzy. But without Tommy, it's not going to happen.' She watched Izzy's eyes shimmy left and right, as if some thought was coming to her. Then they settled on Jessie in a firm stare.

'Tommy had a book,' she said.

'Didn't know Tommy could read,' Jessie quipped.

'He did, you know. Have a book. Said it was his key.'

'His key to what?'

Izzy's face dropped again. 'Don't know. That's what he said.'

'Do you know where Tommy's book is?'

Izzy nodded.

'Can you show it to me?'

Tears welled in Izzy's eyes. Her lips trembled. 'I want to get away,' she said. 'Who wants to live like this?' Her gaze swept around her kitchen, taking in walls that could do with a coat of paint; cracked tiles that needed grouting; cabinet doors with missing handles, every piece of furniture it seemed, fit only for the tip. 'In this fucking place.'

Jessie reached across the table and took hold of Izzy's hands. They felt bloodless cold, bones like nails, knuckles like rivets. She massaged them, tried to rub warmth into them. 'I'm going to be honest with you. Because I'm Tommy's sister, I can't get involved in his murder investigation. So why don't you let me see Tommy's book, and if I think it's of any use, I'll pretend you never showed it to me, and I'll call in the team, and you can show it to them.'

'But I want to get away from here.'

Jessie could curse at herself for ever mentioning witness protection to Izzy. But Izzy was living hand-to-mouth, with nothing more in her life than what she possessed at any one moment. And what kind of life could she expect now Tommy was dead?

'First things first,' she said. 'The man who was here earlier. Who is he?'

'I don't know.'

Jessie held her tearful gaze. 'If you want away from here, Izzy, you need to do better than that. You've given me nothing.'

'Tommy's book,' she said, her eyes brightening. 'I can give you that.'

But Jessie persevered. The book could wait for now. 'You said he told you they'd tricked Tommy. *Who* tricked Tommy? *Who*, Izzy? I need to know.'

Then Izzy's eyes flattened with defeat. 'The polis,' she said.

Jessie almost gasped from the enormity of what she'd just been told. The police had tricked Tommy? Had they known Tommy was to be murdered in some gangland revenge and did nothing to stop it? Or were the police responsible for setting him up – *tricking* him – to be killed? Or worse, much worse, were they the perpetrators of Tommy's murder?

'Jesus, Izzy,' she hissed. 'Who in the polis? Did he mention any names?'

Izzy shook her head.

But Jessie knew from the shifting of Izzy's eyes that she was holding something back. If the man had stayed long enough to have a cup of tea, he'd likely said much more. But she didn't want to push for fear of Izzy shutting down. Besides, Jackie could do a search on the Audi's number plate. 'OK,' she said. 'So this book of Tommy's. Where is it?'

'Upstairs,' Izzy said, and pushed herself from the table.

Jessie followed her up a clatty staircase into a bedroom that stank of stale cigarettes and something more sour. Burn marks on the carpet told Jessie that Izzy smoked in bed. An image of Tommy lying in that bed with Izzy seared into her mind with a force that caused her to blink.

Izzy kneeled in front of a chest of drawers against the back wall. She pulled out the bottom drawer and removed folded T-shirts, socks, an unopened box of men's underwear. It struck Jessie that for Tommy to have evaded the police for so long by hiding here, then Izzy must have been living a double life – a single woman in public; Tommy's lover in secret.

'Here it is,' Izzy said, and held up a dog-eared Moleskine notebook.

Jessie turned it over. Nothing written on either the front or back cover. She opened it. Names of people she didn't know ran like a waterfall of letters down one side, each printed in ink in child-like penmanship. She turned to the next page – same thing – then flicked through the pages from the end. Many appeared blank at first sight, but a closer look revealed phone numbers written close to the spine. A cursory flip-through the notebook, and you wouldn't even notice them. All of a sudden, she caught her breath.

'What is it?' Izzy said.

Jessie pointed to the name. 'Do you know him?'

Izzy frowned at the name. 'Victor Maxwell?' she said, and shook her head.

Jessie didn't know how Maxwell was connected to the numbers beside his name, but logic told her that for Tommy to keep this notebook hidden, and call it the *key*, then what she was holding had to be nothing less powerful than dynamite. But she was still missing one piece of that day's puzzle, which irked her. She faced Izzy, and decided to go for it.

'Does anyone know about this book?' she said.

'Only me and Tommy.'

Jessie toughened her tone. 'I need more than this, Izzy.'

Izzy looked panic-stricken, as if seeing her dreams of a life overseas vanish like smoke in fog. 'I don't have anything else.'

Jessie held up the notebook. 'This could go a long way to helping you. But you've got to show that you're holding nothing back.' She let a couple of beats pass. 'The man who was here earlier. Who is he?'

Izzy closed her eyes for a long moment, then opened them.

'He's nobody,' she said. 'He's just my brother.'

CHAPTER 33

As it turned out, Izzy's brother wasn't nobody, but a player of sorts who was on Jock Shepherd's payroll. Despite being off the investigation team, Jessie had Jackie run the Audi's registration number through the PNC and the DVLA to confirm that it was registered as a company car – Dillanos Loans – and the company secretary, as registered with Companies House in Edinburgh, was Griffiths Sinclair, Izzy's brother.

When Jessie called Gilchrist, she said, 'You need to get down here.'

And he had.

Less than two hours after Jessie set foot in Izzy's house, Gilchrist, accompanied by DC Mhairi McBride, pulled up behind her Fiat 500. They had already agreed on a story of how Jessie had visited Tommy's girlfriend, Izzy McLure, to give Izzy her condolences, which was when Izzy said she had something of Tommy's that she wanted to hand in to the police. No, Jessie hadn't seen what it was. She only knew that Izzy thought it was something the police should have now that Tommy was dead.

Now Gilchrist was there, he walked up to Jessie's Fiat.

Jessie rolled down the window.

'I need you to give me a report on your meeting with Izzy,' he said. 'Let me have it first thing in the morning. I want to make sure this is watertight.'

'Got it.'

He nodded. 'Right. We'll take it from here.'

When Izzy opened the front door, he held out his warrant card, and introduced himself and Mhairi. 'Please come in,' she said, as she'd been instructed to say by Jessie.

Gilchrist followed her along the hallway into the kitchen where two seats were ready for them. Mhairi opened her notebook, and Gilchrist said, 'You have something you want to show us?'

Again, as directed, Izzy said, 'It's upstairs,' and together he and Mhairi followed Izzy into the bedroom where she removed the notebook from beneath a pile of folded underwear.

'It's Tommy's notebook,' she said. 'Tommy Janes. He was my boyfriend. He kept it here. He told me that if anything ever happened to him, that I was to hand it into the polis.'

Gilchrist took it from her. 'What's in it?'

'I'm no sure. I'm just doing what Tommy wanted.'

'Why not hand it into your local police station?'

'Tommy didnae trust them,' she said, again as instructed by Jessie. 'He said he trusted you, Mr Gilchrist. He said you would know what to do with it.'

Gilchrist opened the notebook, and ran his gaze down several lists of names. Some he recognised as crooks and other low-lifers he'd come across over the years, mostly small-time, but still career criminals. He counted nine names with an asterisk next to them, one of whom he recognised as having been killed years ago in a warehouse robbery in Glasgow that went awry, which had him thinking that the other asterisked names might be those who had died, or been killed, too.

Izzy said, 'Jessie pointed out Maxwell's name to me.'

'I thought she hadn't seen this.'

Izzy frowned with embarrassment. 'Oh, that's right. No, she hasn't.'

'You'd do well to remember that,' he said, and flipped through more pages until he came to Victor Maxwell's name. Christ, he thought, this was it. He scanned the numbers – not mobile phone numbers, but bank accounts, he was sure of that, five in total by the looks of things. And an address in the Channel Islands, which would be convenient for an offshore account if you lived in the UK.

He gave a silent prayer to a God he didn't believe in, then slapped the notebook shut.

His first thought was to have Jackie look into every account number, see if she could confirm the name of the account holder, but just as importantly, if money was flowing in and out of it, and if so, from where and to. Just that thought had him realising they could be about to open not just a can of worms, but an entire field of them. But first, he had to follow protocol, make sure his possession of Tommy's notebook could not be challenged in any way in court.

'DC McBride will take your statement,' he said, 'so that no one can argue you were coerced into handing over this notebook, or that we obtained it by illegal means. She'll then read your statement back to you, after which you'll be asked to read it yourself, then to sign and date it. All right?'

Izzy nodded, but Gilchrist had a sense that something was troubling her.

'You want to ask something?'

'When do I get to go?'

'Go where?'

'To the safe house. Abroad.' Izzy's eyes welled. 'That's why I'm giving you this. So's I can get away from here.'

Gilchrist felt his heart slump. Despite having anticipated this dilemma, having Izzy secured in the witness protection programme was not going to be an easy task. If Tommy had been alive, and his life had been in danger as a result of having turned Queen's evidence, then they could have put forward a strong case for a new identity for Tommy and his family. But with Tommy dead, having Izzy assigned witness protection alone was a big ask.

But he needed the notebook, and he needed Izzy on side. 'First,' he said, 'we need to examine the contents and see if these names and numbers mean anything—'

'No,' Izzy wailed. 'Tommy said there was enough in that book to put the whole of Scotland away.'

Gilchrist raised his hand to cut Izzy short. 'That's for us to determine,' he said. 'If we can't corroborate anything from this, then I'm afraid it's more or less useless.'

'Fuck you. I knew youse would screw me. I just fucking knew it.'

'Nobody's trying to screw anyone, Izzy. But we can't just take your word for it, or Tommy's for that matter. If we're going to put the whole of Scotland in jail,' he said, and gave a quick smile at her joke, 'then we need to make sure that what we have is watertight.' He could see his words were settling her down, but she was far from coming fully on board. 'I'll also start the ball rolling on the safe house,' he added, 'if that'll make you feel better.'

She sniffed, dragged the back of her hand under her nose. 'Aye, well, I'm no gonnie sit around on my arse if I find out youse've been screwing me.'

Gilchrist felt his hackles rise, the inference being that if they failed to get Izzy into the witness protection programme then she was going to dob them in it, or do something else that could jeopardise his investigation.

Time to let her know what was what.

'Let me put it this way, Izzy,' he said. 'We'll do what we can to help you, and you'll do what you can to help us.' He lowered his head, and toughened his tone. 'But if I find out that this notebook contains nothing but a worthless pile of names and numbers, then you'd better be well prepared to answer questions about why you've been harbouring a wanted criminal on the run.'

Izzy blinked. Her throat bobbed.

'Do you understand what I'm saying?'

Silent, she stared at him.

'Good,' he said. 'Now give DC McBride your statement. And leave nothing out.' He turned away, rattled down the stairs, and walked back to his car, Tommy's notebook in his hand.

Seated behind the wheel, he switched on the engine, turned the heat up and placed the notebook on his knees. Rather than spend time searching through it, he needed Jackie to look into the account numbers as a matter of priority. Once he had the account holders, he should have a better understanding of just how damning this notebook could be – *enough in that book to put the whole of Scotland away*. Now that was an interesting thought. He first texted Jackie telling her what he needed, then sent her another text listing the numbers against Maxwell's name.

Next, he phoned Dainty.

'Fuck sake, Andy. Just about to put my feet up and watch the footie.'

Gilchrist went straight in with, 'What can you tell me about Griffiths Sinclair?'

'Griff Sinclair?' A sigh so heavy that Gilchrist almost felt it. 'One of Jock Shepherd's boys. Handles accounts collections, for want of a better word. Fall behind with your monthly payments, and Griff's the man they send in to remind you you're late. He's been known to break a few arms and legs, that sort of stuff.'

Even though Gilchrist was staring at Izzy's house, his thoughts were miles beyond it. Here was another link to Jock Shepherd – the fiver stuffed into the mouths of those killed; the list of small-time crooks who were all employed by him. And now Griff Sinclair, involved in loan collections – just like Stooky, it struck him – and hardman tactics against those who fell behind.

'Has he killed anyone?'

'It's not in big Jock's interests. Can't get money from a corpse. Best to beat them up a bit to remind them what they owe. All fucking part and parcel of big Jock's loan enterprises. God help you if you had to borrow money from Shepherd. Exorbitant interest rates. Miss one payment, and you're on catch-up for the rest of your miserable fucking life.'

Gilchrist pinched his nose. He'd never been one to run up debt. Always paid by cash or debit card, and refused to fall behind in payments. He used to have credit cards, but made a point of bringing the balance current at the end of each month. But nowadays, it seemed that millions of people lived on credit, racking up bills they would be saddled with for life. How soul-destroying it must be to end up being buried in debt with no hope of clearing your feet. And then to be preyed on by the likes of big Jock Shepherd and his minders. Christ, it didn't bear thinking about—

'Why're you asking?' Dainty said.

'Better that you don't know. At least for the time being.'

'Understood.'

A thought flashed into Gilchrist's head. 'Would Victor Maxwell know Sinclair?'

'Now that's a fucking quantum leap.' Dainty chuckled. 'Can't say that he does. But funny you should bring it up . . .'

Gilchrist turned up the speakers.

'Just heard that Maxwell had the balls to bring in big Jock for questioning today. He's had to let him go, of course. But you don't fuck around with someone like big Jock and expect to walk away without being hurt.'

'What did Maxwell have on him?'

'Fuck all, as it turned out. But it does make you wonder.'

Yes, it did, thought Gilchrist, as another memory squirmed from the recesses of his subconscious. A date in Tommy's notes. This Monday, the nineteenth of March, as it turned out.

Anybody might think it was all a matter of coincidence.

But if you didn't believe in coincidence, where did that put you?

Smack dab in the middle of *something big*, if you thought about it.

CHAPTER 34

By 7 p.m., Gilchrist was no further forward.

Jackie's search for account details turned up nothing – a big, fat zero. The sort codes were correct, and the accounts did exist. But none of them matched any names in Tommy's notebook. Every account was under a different name, and all appeared to be normal everyday accounts for paying domestic bills or keeping savings. The largest sum in any was just over eleven thousand pounds in a savings account in the name of a Mrs Martha Sciplin, a widow in her nineties who lived in the outskirts of Glasgow.

He pushed himself to his feet and walked to his office window.

What was he missing? What the hell was Tommy's notebook all about?

Were the accounts nothing more than a con by Tommy to get him and Izzy into the witness protection programme? But that was pointless. Tommy would have known that if he fed the Constabulary faked accounts, then he could kiss goodbye to Thailand and a safe house beyond the reach of Victor Maxwell. What he'd provided with these accounts wouldn't get Tommy out of bed, let alone flown to Asia courtesy of the UK government.

It just didn't make sense. He had to be missing something.

But what, he had no idea.

Outside, night had already fallen. Beneath him, the car park lay as black as asphalt, his car hidden in the shadows of the boundary wall. Lamplight muted by curtains and blinds dotted the buildings beyond. His shoulders felt stiff, and an ache that throbbed at the back of his neck was threatening to turn into something more serious – the result of being seated in front of his computer screen for hours.

He felt a yawn take control of his jaw, and he stretched his arms, tried to nurse some life back into his tired body. But he would have to call it a day, take a break, get some sleep then tackle the problem in the morning with a fresh mind and new ideas. He shut down his computer, and had just closed his office door when his mobile rang – a number he failed to recognise, but with a 0141 prefix he knew was Glasgow.

He took the call as he walked down the stairs. 'DCI Gilchrist.'

'It's been a while, Mr Gilchrist.'

The timbre touched some long-forgotten memory but, try as he might, he couldn't pull it up. 'Who's this?' he said.

'Let's just say that you're dipping your toes into waters where you don't belong.'

The name Victor Maxwell flashed into his mind. But he'd never spoken to the man, so how could the voice sound familiar? He pushed through the door into North Street. 'I'm sorry,' he said. 'You've lost me.'

'Well, don't get lost tomorrow,' the voice said. 'King's Arms. Ten o'clock. And don't be fucking late this time.'

The connection died.

Gilchrist realised he'd stopped walking. He eyed his mobile, and called back the last number only to reach a recorded message – *the number you called does not exist*. Of course, it doesn't exist. That was how you survived a life of crime for so long. It had been the name of the pub that sparked the neural connection – the King's Arms – an eclectic working-man's pub in the heart of Dundee. Gilchrist had been in it once before, at the behest of Glasgow's crime patriarch, big Jock Shepherd.

And it was big Jock who wanted to meet him there again.

Back then, the meeting had gone reasonably well, with Gilchrist being handed enough evidence to put an up-and-coming criminal behind bars for the remainder of his life. The fact that this criminal had been one of big Jock's competitors, and that by dobbing him in to the cops, big Jock had strengthened his own business interests, was neither here nor there. To avoid out-and-out warfare, there had to be a certain equilibrium in the criminal underworld, and as long as big Jock remained at the top of his side of the equation, there was no need to upset the balance, so to speak. But this recent spate of deaths could mean an attempt was being made by some underling to take over Shepherd's empire.

Gilchrist slipped his mobile into his pocket and turned into Muttoes Lane, one of the many walkways that connect St Andrews' three main streets – North, Market and South. As he walked, his mind crackled with questions, coming up with answers that seemed only to open up more questions.

Why would Shepherd want to meet Gilchrist? Did he have more evidence to give him to use against his competitors? Why had Victor Maxwell pulled big Jock in for questioning, only to let him go hours later? Was it just a warning for big Jock, to remind him that no one – and certainly not Jock – was bigger than the law of the land? Or was there something more sinister going on? Had Strathclyde's investigation into Stooky's murder scratched through the surface of Glasgow's underworld to expose one of the city's other criminal families? Had Maxwell attempted to strike a deal with Shepherd?

Too many questions, not enough answers.

Gilchrist exited Muttoes Lane and crossed Market Street, destination the Criterion. By the time he turned the corner into South Street he was ready for a pint. He pushed through the Saturday-night crowd, all the more rowdy and merry from Premier League football being shown on the pub's TVs. He recognised West Ham United, or was it Aston Villa? – he never could tell the difference between their strips – but lost interest in the game when he noticed Colin – lead SOCO and one of the best Scenes of Crime Officers in the business – standing at the end of the bar, having a pint with Mhairi.

Colin caught his eye and nodded, which caused Mhairi to look his way, too. He thought Mhairi looked embarrassed at being caught drinking in a bar with a working associate – although strictly speaking, they weren't – so he nodded to the beer taps, a silent invitation over the evening din to buy the pair of them a drink.

Colin lifted his pint and mouthed 'Cheers', which Gilchrist took as a yes. He caught the eye of the bartender, a spiky-haired blonde girl with a white stained T-shirt and frayed denim shorts over black woollen tights – wasn't it still winter? – and ordered a Caledonian Eighty. 'And the same again for that couple,' he said, nodding to Colin. 'Whatever they had before.'

He paid for the round, lifted his pint and chinked it in Colin and Mhairi's direction, then stepped back from the bar and eyed one of the TV screens. He'd never really been into football, had played it now and again as a child – sweaters or scarves rolled up and laid on the grass for goalposts. But without fail he would be one of the last to be selected for the random teams, and always found himself playing in goal. Over the years, he'd developed into a fairly decent keeper, until he tried to block a shot and fractured his wrist. A roar went up from a ruddy-faced group in the corner, the video replay confirming a penalty had just been awarded against Man City—

'Thank you, sir.'

Gilchrist turned to face Mhairi, struck by how different she appeared with her brown hair tied back and a touch of mascara adding a subtle hint of kohl to her eyes. She seemed so young and vibrant, with a smile that set off white teeth and a flawless skin. He'd never paid attention to how attractive she was. It seemed as if DC Mhairi McBride had matured into a striking woman behind his back.

He glanced at the corner, and she said, 'Colin's gone to the loo, sir.'

He nodded. 'When we're off-duty, it's Andy, not sir.' He chinked his glass against hers – gin and tonic, maybe, or vodka, he didn't know. He'd just paid for the round, without asking what they were drinking. 'Haven't seen you in here before,' he said.

'I don't normally drink, sir . . . Andy.'

'Just Andy. Not Sir Andy.'

She chuckled at his silly joke, and he was saved by Colin push-ing his way through the crowd to put an arm around her.

'I've put one in the pipe for you,' Colin said.

'You didn't need to, but that's good of you.'

'Never let it be said.' Colin eyed the TV. 'Do you know the scores? Aberdeen were playing Celtic this afternoon. Probably got gubbed out the park.' Colin gulped a mouthful of beer, almost draining his glass, and Gilchrist came to understand that Mhairi's embarrassment could be due to Colin having had more alcohol than he could handle.

Well, it *was* a Saturday night.

He was about to move to the bar to allow Mhairi and Colin some time together – they wouldn't want to spend their evening chatting to the boss – when Colin said, 'Did Cooper get hold of you?'

Gilchrist sensed a revelation of sorts, and said, 'About?'

'About DS Fox wanting her to release the body asap.'

Gilchrist frowned, not clear on what the problem was. 'DS Fox is with Strathclyde Police,' he explained. 'Who are now in charge of the murder investigation.'

'Yeah, but she's refused.'

'Why?'

'Wouldn't say naught to little old me. But I bet she would speak to you.' He finished his pint. 'Would you like another?'

'No, thanks. Keep it in the pipe. I'm driving.'

Colin turned to Mhairi. 'You ready for another?'

'I'll pass.'

'Wrong answer. It's the weekend.' And with that, he turned to the bar, almost pushing an elderly man off his stool in his efforts to squeeze through.

'Looks like he's been enjoying himself,' Gilchrist said.

Mhairi gave a grim-faced nod in response.

He placed his empty glass beside others on an adjacent table, and said, 'I'm heading off. See you Monday.'

'Do you need me for anything tomorrow, sir?'

Gilchrist had spent most of his professional life working too many hours. He didn't feel he had the right to encourage others to do the same. His team worked more hours than was good for their health, each and every one of them.

He shook his head. 'Enjoy your weekend.'

Outside, the cold hit him anew. He pulled up his collar, and called Cooper.

She answered with, 'I really can't talk at the moment.'

He ignored her, and said, 'You refused to hand over Stooky Dee's body to Strathclyde Police—'

'And my files.'

'Your files?'

'That's the problem. They don't want any evidence of my PM report to be filed anywhere in Fife.'

'Why would they do that?'

'Oh, for God's sake, Andy. Sometimes you're just so . . . so . . . bloody naive.'

The call ended.

He frowned, puzzling over her comment.

He wouldn't say he was naive. Not at all.

Nor would he say he was gullible. Far from it.

But he would say one thing; he would say he was inquisitive. And when anyone tried to feed him crap, he would turn over hell and earth to find out why.

He slipped his mobile into his pocket, and strode back to his car.

CHAPTER 35

Morning arrived to the rattling hiss of rain on glass.

Through the bedroom skylight it could still be midnight.

Gilchrist pulled himself from bed, and groaned from the effort. He stumbled to the bathroom, trying to remember how last night ended. Had Jack called, and they'd argued? Or was that just part of a bad dream? Cooper's voice snapped away at his memory, too. Had he phoned her again? He stared at his grey face in the mirror and asked himself why he hadn't yet learned not to drink late at night, and particularly not whisky. Maybe it was time to cut it out altogether. When you can't distinguish dreams from memories, then that really was the start of the terminal slide.

A hard scrub with his toothbrush did little to remove the coating from his tongue, and a piping hot shower barely worked its magic. But a teapot's worth of strong tea and two slices of toast and banana helped settle his stomach. He chastised himself for drinking on an empty stomach, but if the truth be told, he hadn't been hungry last night.

Morning was still this side of eight o'clock. The rain had stopped, the wind had died and the sun was doing what it could to brighten the skies. He removed a carton of cat food from a cupboard, then stepped outside into the early morning chill. At the end of his garden he cleaned the cat's bowls with the garden hose, topped one with water, the other with dried food. He tried, 'Here, puss puss,' a couple of times, but Blackie was either not hungry or had decided she'd had enough of his inconsistent feeding regimen. He'd missed a day, or maybe two, he couldn't remember, and made a silent promise that he would be less forgetful in the future – if Blackie ever turned up again, that is.

Back inside, his living room looked like someone had partied the night before. His jacket lay crumpled over the back of a chair, his shoes kicked underneath the table. Ripped-open envelopes, the backs of their contents covered with scribbled notes and lines scratched from this circled number to that, littered the sofa and carpet in an indecipherable mess – his attempts last night to make sense of the innocent bank accounts. A half-finished bottle of The Arran Malt – his birthday / New Year present from Maureen – sat on the coffee table with the cork off. At its side stood a tumbler filled with melted ice the colour of weak whisky. Had he poured himself a wee *deoch an doris* – a last one for the road – and not finished it? Or had he staggered off to bed once he'd finally worked out why the account numbers had seemed senseless at first sight?

It really had been quite simple in the end, although coming up with the right solution now was more or less impossible. It had been the memory of Dainty telling him that Maxwell was as slippery as they come, which did it for him. Of course, the bank accounts in Tommy's notebook existed. He had no doubts about that now. None at all. But the numbers had to have been encrypted

– of course they had – for Tommy to have written them down. The troubling question was – had they been encrypted by Tommy, or had he copied down numbers already encrypted by someone else?

That was the point last night in the unwinding of his convoluted logic when Gilchrist had said, 'Fuck it,' and gone to bed. As he retrieved his scribbled notes from the floor, in the sobriety of a new day another answer bubbled to the fore. Rather than try to work out how the account numbers had been encrypted, why not work it out in reverse?

To do that, he would have the banks provide him with a printout of accounts through which large sums of money passed, but which were in the names of little-known companies or individuals. Once he had these numbers, they might see some pattern by comparing them to the accounts in the notebook. With fresh eyes on the problem, and not so much alcohol flowing through his system, he'd now convinced himself that the encryption would have to be simple, so simple that anyone – Victor Maxwell, he kept returning to – could readily read the correct account number from an encrypted one. It could even be as simple as adding 1 to each of the numbers, or deducting 1 from them.

Or . . . it could be much more complicated.

Which really brought him back to the beginning.

A glance at the time warned him that he would have to get a move on if he was to be at the King's Arms in Dundee for 10 a.m. He grabbed his jacket, his mobile, a couple of biscuits from a cupboard – Oaties to give him something for his stomach – then his car keys from a hook behind the kitchen door.

On the drive to Dundee, he phoned Jessie to run his latest thoughts on the account numbers past her. He valued her no-nonsense approach, but knew that his reverse encryption idea would be a tough sell.

Jessie did not disappoint. 'Do you have any idea how many accounts there are in the Bank of Scotland alone?' she said.

'I would imagine a lot.'

'And how many man-hours do you want to waste chasing this hare-brained idea of yours? Because that's what it is, Andy. It's hare-brained. You've got about as much chance of finding money-laundering accounts and linking them to Maxwell as I have of flying to the moon.'

'Any other suggestions?'

The line fell silent for several seconds before she came back with, 'OK. The FIU should be the ones to initiate an investigation with the Bank of Scotland. I can't see millions being laundered through any single account, so I'm thinking they should probably start with accounts that are shifting hundreds of thousands. Or maybe tens of thousands, but through a lot of transactions.'

Although Jessie had come round to his way of thinking, Gilchrist realised that trying to convince the Financial Investigation Unit to look into the possibility of drug money being laundered through bank accounts they had yet to identify was not a big ask, it was a *massive* ask. He wasn't sure he could pull it off, but if he could get the FIU onside, it would be a huge bonus.

The FIU had the power to obtain legal orders through the courts, which was critical in stripping assets from organised criminals. The Proceeds of Crime Act 2002 allowed them to seize cash and assets of anyone suspected of having profited from their crimes. The problem Gilchrist had with all this, of course, was trying to prove that crimes had been committed in the first place, by backing into money-laundering accounts he had yet to find.

Christ, talk about arse over tits in the extreme.

'OK,' he said. 'Get hold of Harvey Kenn. He's the best financial investigator in Scotland. And he's worked with us before. If anyone can do it, he's it.'

'Jeez, Andy. I thought I'd been pulled off the case.'

'You have. Officially you're off the books.'

'Which means . . .?'

'Which means I'm trying to keep costs down.'

'Does Smiler know?'

'Of course not.'

'That's brilliant, that is. Are you trying to get me suspended?'

'Just get on with it, Jessie, and get back to me as soon as.'

He killed the call, and pulled out from behind a couple of slow-moving vehicles. Then he floored the pedal, and tried to settle down for the drive to Dundee.

CHAPTER 36

Despite it being Sunday, rather than drift around the streets of Dundee in search of a parking space at a free meter, Gilchrist drove into the Gellatly Street car park. The King's Arms was no more than a ten-minute walk from there. Even so, he arrived at the bar just after 10 a.m. to find it closed.

He tried the door handle – locked – then backed a couple of steps into the pedestrian precinct. He thought back to yesterday's call and wondered if the meeting with Shepherd had been intended for ten in the evening, not the morning. But lights at the windows told him someone was inside, so he tried the door again, thumped it hard with the heel of his hand.

A few seconds later, the sound of locks clicking was followed by the door creaking open and the appearance of a small man in a black suit and waistcoat – no taller than five-six – with a scarred face that proved he'd been on the wrong side of a broken bottle, and eyes mean enough to warn all-comers that he was ready for another shot at it.

Without a word, he stepped aside.

Gilchrist brushed past him into an empty bar redolent of paint and varnish. Protective sheets of hessian backed with plastic covered the wooden floors, and folded over and around the central bar area as if someone had tried to put the place to bed. The only exposed areas were the walls and ceiling on which an attempt was being made to repair damaged cornicing. He felt his heart stutter at the sound of the door slamming shut, and the metallic clatter of locks being engaged. If they threw away the key, he might never get out.

But it was the hessian that worried him.

A good material in which to roll up a body for disposal later.

'This way,' the man grunted.

If they were going to do something to him, Gilchrist reasoned they would have done it by now. So he followed the man, heart stuck in his throat, along a short hall that led to the toilets. At an unmarked door, the man stopped and gestured for Gilchrist to enter.

'After you,' Gilchrist said.

Silent, the man stood back.

Well, he was here now, he thought, so he opened the door and entered an office of sorts. His heart jumped as the door thudded behind him.

If he hadn't been expecting to meet Jock Shepherd, Gilchrist would have been hard-pressed to recognise him. Where he had once been upright and broad-shouldered with a hefty bulk that easily filled out his six-foot-six frame, Shepherd now stooped bony-limbed and as gaunt-faced as a famine survivor. A couple of days' growth bearded jaundiced skin that hung from his neck in a loose fold as wrinkled as chicken wattle.

A skeletal hand waved at him. 'Have a seat, son.'

Gilchrist puzzled at the weak Glasgow rasp, nothing like the voice he'd heard on the phone. Only then did he notice a square table in the corner of the L-shaped room, beside which stood a younger, healthier version of Shepherd – his son from the looks of him – who pulled out a chair, an invitation for Gilchrist to sit.

But he didn't like the idea of being seated at a table for two with a third person behind him. He'd seen too many movies involving cheese wire. 'I'll stand,' he said.

Shepherd shrugged. 'Suit yourself.' Then he shuffled on unsteady legs towards the table. 'Fucking buggered, son . . . You don't mind if I sit, do you?'

Despite the question, Shepherd was not asking permission, and Gilchrist stood silent while the old man – once Glasgow's invincible crime patriarch – was helped into the chair by the younger man who then stood behind him like a palace bodyguard.

Once seated, Shepherd held out his hand for Gilchrist to sit opposite. 'I'm no gonnie bite, son.' His voice had no strength, as if the words were being spoken from the roof of his mouth, his lungs not strong enough to string more than a few words together. He paused to take a breath. 'Take a fucking seat . . . so's I can talk to you . . . without having to strain . . . my fucking neck.'

Gilchrist thought it surreal that he was standing in an office in a pub in Dundee, about to talk to a man who had once been widely acknowledged as the Godfather of Glasgow. Just the three of them – whoever the third man was.

As if sensing Gilchrist's unasked question, Shepherd said, 'Johnny . . . say hello to Mr Gilchrist.'

The young man stared at Gilchrist, and said, 'Hello, Mr Gilchrist.'

Gilchrist recognised the voice on the phone. Well, in for a penny, as they say, so he pulled out the seat opposite and sat down.

Shepherd rubbed spittle from his lips, and said, 'I didnae want to drag you . . . all the way down to Glasgow . . . Besides . . . the city's fucked now.'

'In what way?'

'It's no how it used to be . . . Cannae go for a shite . . . without some fucking high-flying cunt . . . asking questions . . . There's nae fucking respect any more . . . Isn't that right, Johnny?'

'That's right, Mr Shepherd.'

Gilchrist felt his eyebrows rise at the young man's deference. Maybe he wasn't Jock's son after all. He locked his eyes on Shepherd's, and said, 'I'd heard you'd been pulled in for questioning.'

Shepherd waved a hand in the air as if it was nothing. 'I'm dying, son . . . A man as smart as you . . . would've taken half a second . . . to work that out.'

Gilchrist thought silence his best option.

'We've all got to die . . . There's nae getting away from it . . . I've come to terms with my end . . . Now it's no longer a matter of when . . . but a matter of pride . . .' His eyes flared, and for just that moment Gilchrist saw into Shepherd's black soul, felt his once incontestable raw power. 'And dignity.'

Gilchrist thought it best just to nod in agreement.

'I'm a proud man, son . . . so I'm no gonnie give up my right . . . to die with fucking dignity.'

Gilchrist swallowed the lump in his throat, cast a glance Johnny's way. But Johnny just gave him a dead-eyed stare. In the hall outside, footsteps approached, then stopped at the door. He half-expected it to be kicked open and one of Shepherd's up-and-coming killers to burst in and machine-gun the room. Sweat trickled down his back, and he prayed that the tremor that gripped his legs would not shift to his hands. He clasped them together, just in case, then placed them under his chin, as if giving grave thought to Shepherd's words.

'But your lot . . . are no for showing any respect . . . to a dying man.'

The effort to speak seemed to be draining Shepherd. Gilchrist looked at Johnny, and said, 'I think he could use a glass of water.'

Shepherd flapped a hand with impatience, as if appalled by the idea. Then a silver hip flask appeared as if from nowhere, which he unscrewed with expert skill and pressed to his lips. He took a small mouthful, then another, then held the flask out to Gilchrist. 'Fuck knows where I'd be without the nectar of the gods.'

'No thanks,' Gilchrist said.

Shepherd screwed the top back on. 'You never were the whisky type, were you?'

'I have the occasional glass,' he agreed. 'But not during the day.'

'You don't know what you're missing, son.'

The sips of whisky seemed to have worked wonders for the big man, for his speech picked up, his eyes sparkled, and his mouth broke into a perfect smile that must have set him back thirty thousand, maybe more. Well, if you had the money to burn, Gilchrist supposed, setting out to be the gangster with the best teeth seemed as good a goal as any.

'I like you, son,' Shepherd said, the strength in his voice back, as if by magic. 'You listening to this, Johnny?'

'I'm listening, Mr Shepherd.'

'This man here done me a good turn a while back. Took care of some fucking wee nuisance for me. Banged the cunt up for the rest of his natural, so he did.' Shepherd leaned forward. 'D'you remember that, son?'

'How could I forget?' Gilchrist said, and meant it. The *wee nuisance* Shepherd was referring to had come within a hair's breadth – literally – of taking Gilchrist's life. Evidence given to him by Shepherd helped the Procurator Fiscal successfully argue a sentence for life without parole.

'Well, son, I've got another one for you.'

At some unspoken command, Johnny walked from his spot behind Shepherd over to the door. He gave one hard knock. The door opened, and he took hold of a folder. Without a word he walked back as the door closed behind him, then laid the folder on the table in front of Shepherd.

Shepherd stared at it for several long seconds before opening the cover and sliding out a colour photograph on glossy ten-by-eight paper, which he turned face-up to Gilchrist. 'You recognise him, son?'

Gilchrist almost caught his breath.

The image was a headshot – if it could be called that – of a dead man. Even without the open wound that showed the subcutaneous layer of fat and gristle, the oesophagus and airways of the throat, he could tell from the glazed look behind half-shut eyes that the man was never going to waken up.

He shook his head. 'Don't know him.'

'Cutter Boyd,' Shepherd said, and slid out the next image. 'How about this one?'

Despite the tingle of excitement that fired through Gilchrist at hearing Boyd's name – one of the six – he grimaced at the face before him, which looked as if it had been hammered from behind and turned inside out. No one, not even the man's mother, could have identified him – or her.

Again, he shook his head. 'No.'

'Bruiser Mann.' Shepherd slid another photo forward. 'Him?'

Gilchrist felt his stomach spasm, but managed to keep down an acidic lump of bile at the back of his throat. How anyone could inflict such brutality on another human being was beyond imagination. 'No.'

'Hatchet McBirn.' Then another one. 'How about him?' Shepherd said, then sat back as if to better study Gilchrist's reaction.

This one Gilchrist did recognise. Stooky Dee peered at him through swollen eyes. A metal wire cut deep into his throat. His split lips were partially open to reveal teeth cracked and broken from being hit with a hammer, or maybe from being pulled with a pair of pliers – same difference. But the significance of this image did not slip past him.

He lifted his eyes and glared at Shepherd. 'This was taken from police files.'

'I told you he was smart, Johnny.'

'You did, Mr Shepherd, yes.'

Gilchrist said, 'How did you get it?'

'You shouldnae be asking *how* I got it, son, but *why* I got it.'

After five seconds of silence, Gilchrist realised that Shepherd was waiting for him to ask the question. 'All right,' he said. 'Why have you got it?'

Shepherd narrowed his eyes and smiled. If Gilchrist had any doubts that the big man had lost any of his power, they were quashed right there and then. Shepherd leaned forward, his stare as sharp and piercing as a whetted blade of tempered steel. 'I got it for revenge,' he said. 'I got *all* of them for revenge.' He slapped spittle from the corners of his mouth.

Gilchrist returned Shepherd's hard look with one of his own, and came to understand that even though Shepherd might be dying, the man had lost not one iota of his psychopathic tendencies. He might be stark raving mad, for all anyone knew. Shepherd's vitriol might not be aimed his way, but Gilchrist knew he still needed to tread with care. 'If you know who's behind these killings,' he said, 'you should let the police take care of it.'

Shepherd's lips tightened, his eyes bulged, and for one frightening moment Gilchrist feared the man was going to launch himself at him, or instruct poker-faced Johnny behind him to do so.

'Do I look fucking stupit?' Shepherd spat.

Gilchrist tried to lower the heat. 'You look angry,' he suggested.

'Of course I'm fucking angry.' From the tremors in his jowls, the man looked beyond anger, as if he was having a stroke. 'Does the cunt that done this to my men . . .' He thudded two fingers against his chest so hard he should have broken his ribcage. '*My men,*' he roared. '*Mine* . . . think he's gonnie get away with it . . . by folding fivers . . . and stuffing them down their fucking throats?'

His anger seemed to have drained him. He sat back, retrieved his hip flask and, with shaky hands, managed to unscrew the top and press it hard to his lips.

Gilchrist tried to settle his thumping heart. He was still no clearer as to the purpose of this meeting, other than to witness the frightening force of Shepherd's rage. Another glance at Johnny left him none the wiser. He turned his attention back to Shepherd, and said, 'Cunt.'

Shepherd scowled at him. 'What the fuck did you say?'

'Cunt,' Gilchrist repeated, even though he hated the sound of that word and the way its consonants clipped the air. 'Single. Not plural. Not a group. Not a gang. But one man.'

Shepherd's anger vanished with a smile. He cast his gaze upwards. 'What did I tell you, Johnny? The man's smart.'

'You did tell me that, Mr Shepherd, yes.'

'And you know who this . . . this . . .' Gilchrist didn't want to use that word again, 'this one man is,' he said. Not a question, but a fact.

'Of course I fucking do.'

Gilchrist raised his eyebrows, a silent appeal to be given a name.

But Shepherd didn't tell him. Instead he pulled all four photographs together and cupped them like a hand of cards. 'And when I take that cunt out, by Christ he's gonnie suffer like this.' He slid Stooky Dee's image to Gilchrist. Then Hatchet McBirn's. 'And this.' Next, Bruiser Mann's. 'And this.' And finally, Cutter Boyd's. 'And this.'

Gilchrist picked the photographs up, one at a time. He had no doubts that whichever poor soul Shepherd was referring to was going to be tortured beyond recognition. But he was still no closer to why Shepherd wanted to meet. He rested his hands on the table, and leaned forward. 'And when you're happily taking your revenge by hammering some punter's head to a pulp, what am I expected to do?'

Shepherd held out his hands, palms up, one sane man beseeching another. 'I'll give you the name of the man who killed Tommy.'

Gilchrist almost jolted. 'Tommy Janes?'

'How many Tommys do you know?'

He let several seconds pass as he tried to work out if he was being toyed with or not. But Shepherd had come through for him once before. 'I'll need more than a name,' he said. 'I'll need proof.'

'Oh I'll give you proof, son. Don't you worry about that.'

Something in the way the words were spoken made Gilchrist say, 'But . . .?'

'But you're gonnie have to give me something in return.'

Gilchrist waited six beats before saying, 'Such as?'

But when the answer came, he could not have been more surprised.

Shepherd gave a victory smile, and said, 'Joe Christie's logbook.'

CHAPTER 37

Back in his car and out of the car park, Gilchrist forced himself to work through the convoluted rationale behind the meeting he'd just had. According to Shepherd, Joe Christie's logbook contained information that Shepherd needed to keep secret. What that information was, Shepherd had refused to say, and Gilchrist had wracked his brain trying to figure it out. From memory, the only thing of any worth had been the business card with Maxwell's name printed on the back. All the other entries had been notes about weather and bearings, which had to be completely worthless to a man like Shepherd, surely.

And how had he known that Gilchrist had the logbook in the first place? From Mrs Christie came the likely answer. Which in itself opened up a whole bucket of maggots. And Stooky Dee's photograph from police files? How the hell had Shepherd acquired that? Christ, the man seemed to have a reach that dipped deep into the pockets of the law and beyond. His head was reeling as he forced his thoughts back to the contents of the logbook.

What the bloody hell was he missing?

What was so important about that damned logbook?

Frustration surged through him as he failed to pull up an answer.

But he couldn't just hand it over without knowing what Shepherd needed to keep secret, could he? No, came the answer. Well, if he was going to exchange it for criminal evidence in the murder of Tommy Janes, he would need to have a copy made.

He phoned Mhairi, but the memory of Granger handling the damaged logbook as if the pages were as delicate as a butterfly's wings made him realise that she might damage it beyond repair. So, when she answered, he said, 'I need you to prepare a record of Christie's logbook. Go through each and every page and write down what's on them. Word for word. *Exactly*. And I want a separate sheet for every page.'

'Sir?'

'And I need that for Monday morning.'

'I'll do what I can, sir.'

'I'll explain later,' he said, and ended the call.

He hadn't known how long it would take Mhairi to hand-copy the logbook, so he'd settled for the following morning. That was as late as he dared leave it, because Johnny had told him as he was being escorted from the King's Arms, 'If Mr Shepherd doesn't have the logbook in his hands by tomorrow afternoon, then all deals are off.' Something in Johnny's tone warned Gilchrist of the critical importance of that time frame. So if Mhairi had it copied for the morning, he could have it hand-delivered to Shepherd by 3 p.m. Monday afternoon.

Next, he called Jessie. 'Did you get hold of Harvey Kenn?'

'I did, yeah. I ran past him what you'd said, but he ummhed and aahed until I told him you needed answers by close of business tomorrow.'

'How did that go down?'

'Surprisingly smoothly, although he did ask who he should send the bill to.'

Gilchrist pinched the bridge of his nose. With police forces around the nation being more and more cash-strapped, every unit, it seemed, was becoming more fiscally aware. As long as they had someone to pass the cost of their resources on to, their conscience could be considered clear. Well, if he was going to foot the bill, he'd better receive some benefit. 'Get back to Harvey,' he said, 'and tell him I want something by midday tomorrow. Any later, and he can shove his bill anywhere he likes.'

'With pleasure,' she said, and ended the call.

He kept to the inside lane as he drove across the Tay Bridge. Beneath him, the river slid seawards like some grey leviathan. Overhead, clouds spread like a jailer's blanket to a dull horizon. He glanced at his dashboard – outside temperature 5 °C. It seemed improbable that Midsummer's Day was only three months away. Well, that was if summer surfaced at all this year. He felt as if there was not much more he could do until he got back to the Office, so he decided to phone Maureen again on the number Jack had given him.

To his surprise, a man's voice said, 'Yeah?'

Gilchrist didn't care much for the man's tone, and said, 'Put Maureen on.'

'I don't think she's—'

'Put her on.'

The line fell silent with a clatter.

He accelerated from the Tay Bridge roundabout and booted it up to 80 mph in no time. Two miles farther, the line still hung in empty silence, and he was about to disconnect when the speakers clattered, and Maureen said, 'What's up, Dad?'

'Where are you?'

'I'm with Derek.'

'What I asked was – where are you?'

'Why?'

Gilchrist clenched his jaw. He cleared another roundabout and found himself racing along the A92 to Edinburgh as if he were late for a departing flight. He lifted his foot from the accelerator, let the car slow down, and forced his voice to sound neutral.

'Because I'd like to take you and Derek out for a coffee.'

'I'm not up for going out, Dad. Honestly.'

'I could stop off in Starbucks, and bring you a coffee.'

But Maureen seemed not up for talking.

'You still take a skinny latte?' he said. 'What does Derek take? And we could share a blueberry muffin? I know you like these. Or maybe cranberry?'

'You're not going to give up, are you?'

No, he wanted to say. I need to know what the hell is going on. But instead, he said, 'I'm concerned, Mo. That's all.' He thought he caught a sniffle, and wondered if she was crying. 'Talk to me, Mo. Tell me what's up. I'm here to help, if you'll only let me.'

'You can't help,' she said. 'It's too late.'

A freezing chill swept through him as if he'd just been flushed from head to toe with iced water. *It's too late*. Too late for what? Some decision had been taken, and he could not stop his heart sinking from the knowledge of what that decision had been.

It could mean only one thing.

It was too late to save her pregnancy.

Because . . .? Because . . . she'd had a termination?

He edged into it with, 'We have an appointment tomorrow morning.'

'Oh, Dad.' She sniffed, then said, 'I'm sorry, Dad. I'm so sorry.'

The line seemed to scuffle for a moment, as if a hand was brushing the mouthpiece. Then a man's voice said, 'This is Derek again, Mr Gilchrist—'

'What's your address?'

'I'm sorry, Mr Gilchrist, but Maureen doesn't—'

'Your address,' he said with more force than intended.

But the call ended with a heavy click.

He cursed under his breath, and realised with a nip of annoyance that Jackie Canning hadn't replied to yesterday's text asking for a name and address to match the number. Well, it was the weekend he supposed, and everyone was entitled to some time off. So he dialled another number, and got through on the second ring. 'It's Andy Gilchrist.'

'Andy? Long time, long time.'

'Are you still in business, Dick?'

'Doing a bit of ducking and diving. But what do you need?'

Gilchrist read out the number he'd just phoned, and said, 'Derek's his first name. But I'm looking for full name and address. Can you do that in fifteen minutes?'

'Should expect so. And would you like a printout of the last six months' calls?'

Gilchrist wasn't interested in that at this stage, and said, 'Just the name and address, and maybe highlight any obvious criminal history, if he has one.'

'Let me get back to you.'

The line died.

Gilchrist settled down for the drive to Cupar, which was where Maureen had told him she was staying. It had been some time since he'd last contacted Dick. A retired policeman, Dick had set up a small business building websites, but in reality did anything related to IT and computers. He'd once tried to sell his services to the Home Office as a cyber security advisor, but turned down the offer because of the way the *government twats* had talked down to him. The fact he could provide recorded phone conversations of more or less anyone in the UK or abroad – most definitely illegal – and had already done that for Gilchrist at his request, Gilchrist kept to himself. Finding a name and an address for a UK mobile number would be a doddle for someone with Dick's expertise.

Sure enough, five minutes later Dick called back with the surname – Scollan – and an address in Provost Wynd in Cupar. Scollan's driving licence was clean – three points for a speeding ticket ten years earlier had been cleared up. And as far as Dick could find, Scollan had no criminal history.

Gilchrist gritted his teeth, and tapped Scollan's address into his car's GPS system.

CHAPTER 38

Cupar is an old sheep and cattle market town, with some nine thousand plus residents, and a level of employment well above the national average. The town centre has avoided the curse of modern-day town planners with their irrational desire to flatten and rebuild anything that didn't fit in with their vision of modern living. Thankfully, many buildings still retained their historical charm and character, although most of the old stone facades could do with a good sandblasting.

Provost Wynd is a narrow road that runs perpendicular to Bonnygate, and bordered on one side along most of its length by two- and one-storey-high stone buildings. Scollan's address was a terraced cottage that looked more rundown than its neighbours.

Gilchrist rang the doorbell, and waited.

The door opened with a sticky slap.

A young man with a full beard and shorn head eyed Gilchrist with a look of suspicion.

Gilchrist failed to offer a smile. 'Derek Scollan?'

'Yeah?'

'I'm Maureen's father.'

'And?'

Not quite the welcome he'd hoped for, but he kept his tongue in check, and said, 'And I'm here to see her.'

'She's not well.'

'So where did you get your medical degree?'

Something akin to a flash of anger shifted across the man's face, and without warning he stepped back and closed the door; not slammed shut, but pushed hard enough for Gilchrist to blink with surprise. He slapped his hand against the doorbell, and held it down.

It took two minutes of non-stop ringing before the door opened.

Scollan said, 'You'd better come in.'

Gilchrist pushed past him and strode into a dark living room.

Seated in a chair next to a window with the curtains drawn, and swallowed in shadow, sat the figure of a woman slim enough to be Maureen. But she didn't stand as he entered, or say anything as he walked past and opened the curtains.

Light flooded the room.

Scollan scowled at him from the doorway.

Tucked up on one end of a corduroy sofa, surrounded by cushions, Maureen looked frail, almost helpless. Her face was alabaster white, her eyes swollen and reddened from too many tears. She seemed unable to return his gaze. Without invitation, he sat beside her and placed an arm around her.

She fell into him.

Her body shivered as she sobbed, and he hugged her tighter, buried his lips in her hair and whispered, 'It's OK, it's OK.' They sat like that for a couple of minutes, then he let his hand slide free as he relaxed his grip.

She sniffed, ran a hand under her nose.

'Are you able to talk?'

She sniffed again, and said, 'I'm sorry, Dad, it's . . . I couldn't . . . I didn't want . . .'

'I know you didn't want to,' he said. 'I know.' He had a sense that with each passing second she was regaining self-control. He retrieved his arm and gave her some space. 'Are you in any pain?' he asked.

She shook her head.

'Discomfort?'

'A bit.' She untucked her legs with a frown, and said, 'I'm OK.'

He watched the glimmer of tears well once more in her eyes, and felt his heart go out to this woman, this child, this daughter of his whom he'd known her entire life. He would do anything in his power to help her. But at that moment he felt utterly helpless.

'I'm sorry,' she whispered.

He gave a smile of understanding, took hold of her hand, and just sat with her for several silent minutes until he sensed she was recovering. 'Can I drive you home?' he said.

She glanced at Scollan still standing in the doorway, and he wondered how big a part the man had played in his daughter's decision. He squeezed her hand, and said, 'Only if *you* want me to.'

She seemed to catch his emphasis, and nodded.

He helped her to her feet, conscious of Scollan no longer in the doorway – where had he gone? – and said, 'Where are your things?'

'Derek's gone to fetch them.'

As if on cue, Scollan returned from the depths of the cottage carrying a large canvas holdall, which he held out for Gilchrist to take.

Maureen shook free from his grip, and said, 'Let me freshen up.'

Alone with Scollan, Gilchrist said, 'Did she see a doctor?'

Scollan shook his head. 'No. Pills.'

'She took them herself?'

'Yeah.'

'How many?'

Scollan shrugged as if he didn't care, or perhaps more correctly, didn't know.

Gilchrist tightened his grip on the holdall. 'She get them from you?'

Scollan's lips pressed into a white line, giving Gilchrist his answer. He made a silent promise to look into Scollan's past, and was saved from doing something he might regret by Maureen returning from the bathroom. Without a word, he led her from the room. When they stepped outside, the door closed behind them with a dull thud.

So much for farewell and good wishes.

On the road back to St Andrews, Gilchrist said, 'Derek said he gave you some pills.'

She turned away, stared out the side window.

'Where did he get them?'

'I don't know, Dad.'

'Does he work in the NHS?'

'Used to.'

Used to. Which told him that Scollan had past colleagues who could provide abortion pills without scrutiny. But why Maureen would acquire them from someone as unfriendly as Scollan, rather than by prescription through the NHS, was another question altogether.

'How many did you take?'

'One on Friday, another on Saturday.' She adjusted herself on the seat. 'Can we talk about something else?'

He waited until he had left the town limits and was accelerating on the A91 before he reached across and squeezed her hand. 'You look exhausted,' he said. 'I think you should keep tomorrow's appointment.'

'What good would that do?'

'You could be given an examination. Make sure everything's all right.'

'I'm fine, Dad. Really, I am.'

'I thought you said you were three months' pregnant.'

'I thought I was.'

Well, there he had it. What little he knew about the abortion pill was that it was not to be taken after the tenth week. And like fog clearing, the answer revealed itself to him. Maureen's ex-fiancé, Tom, was not the father. Derek Scollan was. And because of that, he thought he now understood why she had elected to self-terminate.

'Derek's married, isn't he?'

The stiffening of Maureen's body told him all. Scollan was married, could even have a family of his own. Maybe his infidelity would have come to light if Maureen had gone to an NHS doctor, something Scollan had not wanted to risk. So he'd acquired pills on the side, and taken care of his domestic problem on the QT.

'How long have you known Derek?' he asked.

'Just leave it, Dad. I don't want to talk about it. I'm fine. I'm moving forward. What's done's done. And I can't undo it.'

No, you can't, he thought to himself. No one can undo the past.

Which was a pity, because he still struggled to come to terms with not having been there for his children when they were growing up. He'd let work interfere with his family life and keep him away from home at a time when his children needed a father. And that absence from home had been the root cause of the demise of his marriage. But even now, when his children were adults and living close by, he still seemed unable to communicate with them.

He bit his tongue and drove on, Maureen's sullen silence suffocating the air.

CHAPTER 39

When the break in Gilchrist's investigation came, it hit from out of the blue.

He'd hoped – despite the ridiculous odds – that Harvey Kenn of the Constabulary's Financial Investigation Unit might have been able to provide them with bank account details by backing them out of the numbers in Tommy's notebook. But he hadn't heard from Kenn that morning, and attempts by Jessie and others to contact him had all but fallen on deaf ears or been abandoned in voicemail dumps.

And Mhairi's handwritten copy of Joe Christie's logbook hadn't solved the mystery. Yesterday's meeting with Shepherd had ended with the understanding that Gilchrist would hand-deliver the logbook in exchange for evidence on Tommy's killer, evidence that big Jock swore would be irrefutable. The first of several problems Gilchrist had with that arrangement was that only he and a select few knew of the logbook's existence, and that by not entering it as a piece of evidence they had violated investigative protocol, punishable by suspension or, more likely, termination with immediate effect. The second problem was that handing over the logbook to a known criminal could be described as an indefensible action bereft of logic or reason. Another problem was that he could not for the life of him figure out what was so important about the logbook in the first place. Mhairi had copied its contents letter for letter, number for number, and he still found himself struggling with the concept of exchanging it in blind faith.

And, of course, there was one more problem to overcome, one that might not raise its head until after he'd divested himself of the logbook, and that was the question Smiler would surely ask – how had he obtained such irrefutable evidence? But beneath it all lay the biggest problem, which was – could he really trust Jock Shepherd, knowing that he was a murderous psychopath who'd always managed to stay one step ahead of the law and never been brought to justice, whether or not he was terminally ill?

Christ, it didn't bear thinking about.

These thoughts were pulsing through his mind as he read Mhairi's notes once again, words and numbers blurring on the pages from boredom, when an entry tripped up his gaze. He skipped back a few lines and read that entry again. *Set course for south-south-east. Wind NE09.* Then the next line – *Wind NE01* – and the line below that – *Wind NE26.* He frowned as he studied these wind speeds. Not that he knew much about the intricacies of a north-east wind at sea. Rather, he'd seen these entries before, the exact same wind speeds.

He flipped through the pages, almost panting with excitement, and found the page he was looking for. He read the wind speeds

– *NE09; NE01; NE26* – then the entry immediately following – *Depth 206* – followed by a series of numbers that he'd first read as the longitude and latitude at the time of entry. And at that moment, he came to understand what he'd been looking at, but not seeing. He flipped back through Mhairi's notes, working from the earliest entries, jotted down other wind speeds. He was still not sure if his theory was just a stab in the dark, but if he could locate other groups of identical numbers he felt sure he'd found the answer to what they'd been looking for.

It didn't take him long. Not wind speeds that time, but depth markers that jumped out at him – 832 feet; 820 feet – followed by a series of numbers that he'd read as bearings. The same depth markers appeared on the same day the following week, but with a different set of numbers after them.

He pushed from his desk and walked to Jackie's room. She was seated at her desk, half-hidden by her computer, eyes fixed on its screen, fingers tapping the keyboard with the dexterity of a court reporter. She looked up as he entered, and gave him a wide smile.

'Are you busy?' he asked.

She wobbled her head, and managed to say, 'Duh . . .'

'I need you to do something for me.' He shoved his scribbled notes in front of her. 'These numbers,' he said, and pointed at the wind speeds. '09 – 01 – 06. And 832 – 820.'

She looked at him, and nodded.

'Find out which banks use these as their sort codes,' he said, then handed her a copy of Mhairi's notes, and instructed her to go through them, and see if she could find sort codes for other banks.

Back at his desk, he compared the numbers from Christie's logbook with those they'd passed to Harvey Kenn. But after fifteen minutes he was none the wiser. His theory of simple arithmetic cryptology seemed fatally flawed. He checked his emails to find one from Jackie confirming that the numbers were sort codes for the Royal Bank of Scotland and Santander, and that she'd found one more for Bank of Scotland. Assuming that the numbers following these codes were account numbers, then they had a total of ten bank accounts to investigate.

He collected his notes and went off in search of Mhairi.

He found her outside in the car park, on her mobile phone.

She ended the call when she saw him approaching.

'Here's a list of ten bank accounts,' he said. 'Get hold of Harvey Kenn as a matter of priority, and have him check them out. I want a printout of last year's statements on every one of them, and details of each of the account holders.'

'We can't get hold of him,' she said. 'He's not returning anyone's calls.'

'Try him again,' he said. 'And failing that, drive to Glenrothes and deliver them to him in person.'

'Yes, sir.'

He returned to the Office, feeling as if he was getting somewhere at last.

He found Jessie at her desk, on the phone, looking miserable. With his team being pulled off Stooky Dee's investigation, and Jessie being benched from her brother's murder, he'd assigned her the mundane task of creating a list of local fishermen and businessmen with whom Joe Christie might have had contact. Even though they knew that whatever she came up with would more than likely lead them nowhere, Jessie had delved into it with initial enthusiasm. But you could keep up appearances for only so long.

'Fancy a break?' he said.

She froze mid-dial, returned the handset to its cradle. 'Thought you'd never ask.'

'Grab your bag,' he said.

Jessie gathered her jacket and scarf from the back of her chair, picked up her bag from the floor, and chased after him. She just caught sight of him as he pushed through the main doors onto North Street, mobile to his ear. She was still some ten yards behind him when he stepped into College Street without a backward glance. But she knew from experience that he was keeping his phone conversation private.

She tucked her head down and scurried after him.

She expected him to enter the Central by the side door – he was known to like a pint with his pie, chips and beans, and it always puzzled her why he never put on weight – but he strode beyond the bar's side entrance and into Market Street where he turned right.

She caught up with him in the queue in Costa Coffee.

'Latte? Skinny?' he said.

'Make it a fatty latte. I lost a couple of pounds running after you. And order me one of these muffins while you're at it. I missed breakfast.'

He smiled, and placed the order. 'Two medium lattes, one skinny, and a couple of muffins. Blueberry and . . .?' He glanced at her. 'A cranberry?'

'Whatever.'

'And a cranberry,' he said.

'I might not have been joking about the fatty latte, you know.'

'Never known you to order anything but a skinny.' He removed his wallet. 'See if you can grab a couple of seats in the back. Somewhere quiet, if you can.'

She gathered a handful of napkins, and walked through to the back. Trying to find somewhere quiet in Costa Coffee was a tough ask that close to lunchtime, but she was surprised to find two tables deserted and cleared.

She took the table by the corner, then sat down, her back to the wall.

A moment later, Gilchrist appeared, balancing two coffee mugs on a tray.

He sat opposite her, and placed the mugs and plates on the table.

Silent, Jessie tried to read his face. His apparent reluctance to return her gaze warned her that he was about to share some bad news.

'There you go,' he said, and slid a plate with the cranberry muffin over. He tore a chunk from the blueberry muffin and held it out. 'Sure you don't want to share?'

She shook her head, took a sip of latte – hot and creamy.

'Got something I'd like you to do,' he said. 'But I don't want you to do it if you're not comfortable with it.'

'It's about Tommy, isn't it?'

He nodded. 'In one way, yes. In another, no.'

'I'm all ears.'

'Where's your bag?'

'On the floor.'

He waited until she placed it on her knees, then he removed a small parcel the size of a book from his jacket pocket, which he slipped into her bag. She didn't need to open it to know it was Christie's logbook.

'No one knows we found it,' he said.

'Except for Mhairi, and her friend, whatsherface.'

'Carol Granger.'

'That's the one.'

'We can trust her,' he said.

'Since when did *we* start trusting *anyone*?'

He ignored her comment, and leaned closer. 'If no one other than the four of us knows that we have it, then no one else will be surprised when they learn that we *don't* have it.'

Jessie frowned. 'We're going to toss it in the bin?'

'Not quite. I've agreed to give it to Jock Shepherd.'

'What?' She struggled to keep her composure.

'In exchange for information.'

She watched a smile touch the corners of his eyes, then fade as his look hardened. She knew she wasn't going to like what he was about to say. 'What information?' she said.

'The name of Tommy's killer.'

Time stopped, as if her senses had failed, her breathing, her heartbeat, the very life of her locked in that silenced moment for a stilled lifetime. Then her world rebooted, and she sucked in air with a hard gasp. 'One of Shepherd's men killed him?' she said.

'He didn't say that. He said he had information on Tommy's killer.' He shook his head. 'As you're off the case, and the logbook officially doesn't exist, I thought you should be the person to hand-deliver it to him. But I'm troubled by it all, I have to tell you. I'm not sure it's such a good idea.'

Jessie leaned forward. 'Was that who you were phoning on your way here?'

He nodded.

'When is he expecting to have it?'

'No later than three o'clock this afternoon,' he said. 'Or the deal's off.' He frowned with surprise as she slid from the table. 'You should finish your coffee.'

'I'm already on my way.'

'Well, in that case you'll need an address.' He handed her a business card.

She didn't look at it until she was seated in her car. She recognised the name of the street from her time with Strathclyde Police – Nithsdale Road – and knew it was somewhere in the south side of the city. If her memory held up, she might be able to drive straight to it.

'Right, you bastard,' she hissed. 'It's time you and I had a heart to heart.'

CHAPTER 40

Early afternoon
Nithsdale Road, Pollokshields, Glasgow

Pollokshields is known for its upmarket property, and Nithsdale Road slices through its middle, running east to west for almost a couple of kilometres. At its eastern end, where it connects with Pollokshaws Road, Nithsdale Road is lined on both sides with red and brown sandstone tenement buildings. But in general terms, the farther west you drive, the less urban the area, the more upmarket the residences become. In the most expensive enclave, lengthy driveways cut through striped lawns and pruned shrubbery to stone mansions large enough to cost a detective sergeant's annual salary just to keep heated.

Jessie's memory didn't fail her. She found Shepherd's address without difficulty and, just as she expected, although Shepherd's home might not have been the largest mansion, it couldn't be far off it. At the stone-pillared entrance, she had a decision to make – park her wee Fiat 500 kerbside, or drive up the paved driveway and park beside what she could only describe as a gleaming display of exotic cars.

She chose the former.

The driveway had to be a hundred yards long, and Jessie had walked no farther than five yards into the property when four men materialised from the corners of the mansion ahead, like silent warriors, hands inside black jackets, fingers no doubt gripping automatic pistols or whatever weapon was the order of the day for any self-respecting Glaswegian bodyguard. As she slipped her hand inside her own jacket to remove her warrant card, she had a surreal sense of the scene sizzling alive with tension.

'Hold it, miss.'

The voice had come from her left, and she turned to face a young man in his twenties, with shoulders out to here and a shorn head that glistened nutmeg brown, as if he'd spent the winter sunning in the Caribbean. For all she knew, he probably had.

'I'm with the police,' she said, and held her warrant card out to him.

But he seemed disinterested in it. His lips moved as he spoke out of earshot into a mouthpiece that scarred his cheek. His right hand slid Napoleon-like inside his suit, the material straining from the simple flexing of muscles. He still stood some ten feet from her, off the driveway, where he'd been stationed behind the stone wall. His gaze never left hers as he listened to instructions through his earpiece. Then he removed his hand from his jacket, and approached her.

'Arms out.'

Jessie did as she was told, expecting to have a set of hands feel their way over her, but the man produced a metal wand of sorts from a leather holster under his jacket, and ran it up and down her body, front, sides and back, then along her arms.

'No mobile?'

'It's in the car.'

'Spread your legs.'

'It's not in there.'

'Spread them.'

'Touch my crotch with that thing and you'll be singing soprano for the rest of your life.'

But Jessie needn't have worried. The wand swept up and around her inner thighs, hovering close but not quite touching. Then the man stood back and tapped his mouthpiece with his index finger. 'She's clean.' He waited for some response that was beyond Jessie's earshot, then nodded to the mansion.

'Nice talking to you,' Jessie quipped, as she returned her warrant card to her jacket.

By the time she arrived at the front entrance, she'd counted eleven cars parked on the cobbled driveway, all sparkling show-room new, all top of the range of whichever make they were. Two she recognised as Mercedes from the star logo on the front grille, but the others could be American classics for all she knew. What she did know was that her wee Fiat 500 could fit into the boot of any one of them.

At the mansion's front door, the four bodyguards stepped aside like hotel doormen. As she walked up the granite steps and into a marbled vestibule, the heady fragrance of spicy after-shave drifted after her. A small man in a white double-cuffed shirt and tartan waistcoat – no jacket – and a face that could have tested the blades of a meat grinder, greeted her with a gruff, 'Follow me.'

She was led along a carpeted hallway rich with the fragrance of polish, into a spacious lounge in the back of the house. A lawn as large as a football park stretched like a green blanket to a row of Scots pine. The door closed behind her, and she realised with a flutter of concern that she stood alone in the room with two men. One she recognised as a skeletal version of the patriarchal gangster, Jock Shepherd. The other could have been a younger version of the man.

Shepherd tried a welcoming smile, but it didn't suit him. 'Come in, hen,' he said, and waved a thin arm in the air. 'Come in. Have a seat.'

The room was redolent of varnish and something less appealing, more clinical, almost antiseptic, like the aftermath of a hospital party. She walked towards Shepherd, conscious of the younger man's eyes watching her every step, as if he feared that she was going to attack Shepherd all of a sudden and put him out of his misery. Shepherd, on the other hand, seemed more interested in dabbing his mouth with a white handkerchief.

He coughed as she sank into the chair facing him, a sound that seemed to rumble from a hollow chest. Then he swiped his mouth, and crushed the handkerchief into his hand. 'We'll no bother with the formality of shaking hands for obvious reasons.' He leaned forward, and Jessie had the feeling of being stripped from head to toe, then back again. As if satisfied by the result, Shepherd sat back. 'I cannae say you look like Jeannie,' he said. 'More like your brother, Tommy.' As if seeking affirmation, he glanced up at the young man who now stood behind him, hands on the back of his chair as if to make sure he couldn't get up and leave the room in a hurry. But from the look of him, Shepherd was not capable of going anywhere in a hurry.

'What's with the car auction?' Jessie said.

'We have guests,' Shepherd replied. 'A meeting of sorts.'

Jessie looked around her. 'They all hiding, are they?'

Shepherd tried another smile, but it looked like it hurt. 'I see you haven't lost your sense of humour.'

'I could tell you the joke about the Glasgow gangster who smoked forty a day and got fucked by cancer, but I don't think it would go down well.'

Shepherd dabbed his handkerchief to his mouth again, and managed to stifle a cough.

Behind him, the younger Shepherd's jaw rippled, and his fists tightened their grip on the chair. Then the moment passed, and he said, 'Would you like me to escort her to the door, Mr Shepherd?'

Shepherd raised his hand. 'That's awful tempting, son, but let's leave it for a wee while longer, yeah?' Then he stared hard at Jessie. 'You've brought something with you.'

Jessie said, 'Not on me. But I can lay my hands on it in a hurry if I need to.'

Shepherd scowled. 'I'm no here to play fucking games, hen. Do you have it or don't you?'

'I have it.'

'Right, then, fucking hand it over.'

Jessie felt the first stirrings of fear. This was not how she'd been told it was likely to play out. Shepherd had something to give Gilchrist in return for Christie's logbook – not to have a look through it first, then decide whether or not the exchange was worth it. But she managed to steady her nerves, and keep her voice strong. 'And what do I get in exchange?'

Shepherd gave an upward nod at the man behind him, who

removed a sealed envelope from his inside jacket pocket and handed it to him. Then Shepherd held it out to Jessie, and said, 'This.'

'Which is?'

'What you and your boss, DCI Gilchrist, *need* to see.'

The emphasis on the word *need* intrigued Jessie. Again, not what she'd expected. She stretched her arm out to take the envelope, but Shepherd pulled it back, out of reach.

'I'm waiting, hen.'

Jessie slipped her hand inside her jacket, and removed a small padded envelope. She jerked her lips in imitation of a smile, and said, 'I lied.'

'Now why am I no surprised at that?' Shepherd gave an upward nod, and the young man walked from behind the chair. Two steps and he was almost upon Jessie. He reached for the package, but Jessie tightened her grip. She held her other hand out to Shepherd. 'Quid pro quo,' she said.

Shepherd handed her the sealed envelope and she released the logbook.

The young man passed it over to Shepherd, then resumed his position behind his chair. Shepherd held the padded envelope in the palm of his hand, as if weighing a lump of meat.

'You can check it out,' Jessie said. 'It's what you asked for.'

'I know it is, hen. That boss of yours knows what's what. No like the others.'

'What others?' Jessie said.

Shepherd gave a hint of a smile as his gaze drifted to the sealed envelope.

'Would you like me to escort her to the door now, Mr Shepherd?'

Shepherd coughed into his handkerchief, then managed to say, 'A word of warning.' He stifled another cough. 'Tell that boss of yours no to let me down.'

Jessie frowned at that comment, but didn't question it. Instead, she said, 'I can find my own way out,' then strode to the door.

But the young man beat her to it.

A large hand with manicured nails took hold of her arm with a grip like a vice. She tried to shrug it off, but his steel-like hold tightened. 'If you want arrested for assaulting a police officer, you're going about it the right way.'

But the young man smirked at her as he opened the door, then held her as they walked – not quite arm in arm – along the hallway.

From behind a closed door on her left, Jessie thought she heard the murmur of voices, felt the vibration of movement, weight shifting through the floorboards. She had a sense of a large gathering in the front room, but the young man's grip almost carried her along as she was ushered to the front door.

Out into the marbled vestibule, the door closed behind her with a heavy click like a vault locking. At the bottom of the granite steps, she hesitated, and turned to her side as if to check the weather. Although the window was too high for her to see inside, she managed to catch sight of the back of an oil-slicked head, hair black and thick as a metal helmet, before two bodyguards as muscled as WWF wrestlers nudged her towards the pillared gate at the foot of the driveway. One of them gripped her arm, and she shrugged it free with, 'Get the fuck off.'

Together, the three of them marched down the driveway.

At the entrance gate, she saw no sign of the shorn-headed bodyguard, and an image of him walking the lengths of the boundary walls and fences like a daytime sentry brought a wry smile to her face. From the look of him, Jock Shepherd had no more than a few weeks to live, maybe even days. Yet here they were, guarding the place as if the Queen herself was about to pay a visit. She knew she had just witnessed something big, almost gate-crashed some private event, a major underworld clan gathering that could change the fundamentals of how crime in the city of Glasgow, maybe even Scotland and beyond, would be managed.

She walked to her car, unlocked it, then slid behind the steering wheel.

She inserted the key into the ignition, surprised to see her hands shaking.

CHAPTER 41

'What do you make of it?' Jessie said.

Gilchrist grunted in frustration, then turned his attention to the handwritten note again. As he read the simple words, he had no way of knowing if they'd been written by Shepherd or one of his minions. But more troubling, he had no way of knowing if he was being set up for a fall or being given a lead to an imminent crime. No matter what, the note was not what he'd expected in exchange for Christie's logbook.

Jessie had returned from Glasgow late that afternoon and handed the envelope to him, unopened, still sealed. She told him she hadn't opened it in case she did something she might have later regretted.

'Like take the law into your own hands?'

'Exactly.'

But the opening of the envelope and removal of its contents – a short note the size of a Post-it – turned out to be the epitome of an anti-climax. No name of Tommy's killer. Just a time, a date and a place – Wren's Garage in Pittenweem that evening at 7 p.m., to be exact. The note wasn't signed or dated, and the penmanship could have been that of a ten-year-old.

Gilchrist glanced at Jessie, and shook his head. 'I don't know what to think,' he said, 'other than – we're running out of time.'

'Which is probably why Shepherd put the three o'clock deadline on the exchange.'

'Any later,' Gilchrist agreed, 'and we would miss this evening's event. Whatever the hell it is.' He reached for his jacket and was about to stride to the door when Mhairi blocked his way. Her hair was ruffled, as if she'd just risen from bed, and her drawn face reminded him of how he looked after spending the night trying to work out some insoluble puzzle.

'Sorry, sir. But I've been going through these from Harvey Kenn.' She held out a pile of computer printouts.

'Give me the short version,' Gilchrist said.

Mhairi grimaced. 'Harvey dug into each of the accounts you gave me this morning, and none of them belong to anyone with a criminal record, sir.'

'You sure?'

'Yes, sir. But each of them has had revolving funds over the last year, mostly in the high six figures. And in one account the transactions topped two million in August.'

'These are high numbers to be moved through legitimate bank accounts,' he said, trying to keep the excitement from his voice. 'I mean, who has that amount of money floating about? Tens of thousands, maybe, but not millions.'

'They're company accounts, sir.'

That stopped him, but only for a moment. 'So they're operating accounts for large businesses?'

'That's what we're supposed to think, sir.'

He caught the smile at the corners of Mhairi's mouth. '*Supposed* to think?'

She nodded. 'Yes, sir. I checked Companies House this afternoon, and made a list of all the directors and company secretaries for each of them, and found that one person, a woman, is listed as the Chief Financial Officer in all four companies.'

A woman being at the centre of it all surprised Gilchrist. He'd expected Maxwell's name to have crawled from the pile by now. But instead of his investigation narrowing, it now seemed to be expanding. Still, you never could tell where any lead would take you.

'An executive,' he said. 'So we might find her signature on issued cheques.'

'I don't think we'd have any luck there, sir. It seems that all transactions were done by BACS transfer.'

Online banking was becoming the norm now, but if every transaction went through the Bank Automated Clearing System, that would create a digital trail, which they should be able to follow. 'What's the woman's name? The CFO?' he asked.

Mhairi referred to her notes. 'Lesley J. W. Duncan, sir.'

The name meant nothing to him, and the echo of Dainty's words rattled through his mind – *Maxwell's slippier than an eel in a barrel of oil.*

'Lesley could be a man's name,' he tried.

'Not how it's spelled. It would be Leslie ending in i-e if it was a man. Besides, the J is for Jennifer. But I can't find a Lesley J. W. Duncan listed in any electoral rolls.'

'Did you try searching with an i-e?' he asked. 'Just in case.'

'Yes, sir. Same result.'

'How about tax records, National Insurance number?'

'Nothing, sir. She doesn't appear to exist.'

'Except that she does,' Gilchrist said. 'At least on paper anyway. What about other directors? Are they imaginary, too?'

'They seem legitimate, sir, in the sense that they appear to exist, I mean. Although I haven't spoken to any of them in person yet, sir.'

He thought for a moment, then said, 'J for Jennifer. What does W stand for?'

'Wren, sir.'

Gilchrist jolted. He glanced at Jessie and saw that she'd picked up on it, too. The note from Shepherd referred to Wren's Garage, which seemed too much of a coincidence. But if you didn't believe in coincidence, where did that put it? Smack dab in the middle of his investigative sights came the answer.

He said to Mhairi, 'Get Jackie to find out everything she can about Wren's Garage in Pittenweem.'

'Do you have an address, sir?'

'No. But when Jackie finds it, call me with it.' He nodded to Jessie. 'Grab your coat.'

Outside, black clouds dulled the sky and a cold wind was stirring. Sunset on the Fife coast in the second half of March normally fell around seven o'clock. But with rainclouds low enough to touch, night-time could be less than an hour away. He clicked his remote fob, took his seat behind the wheel, and glanced at the clock on the dash – 17:46.

Which didn't give them much time.

To make matters worse, spots of rain splashed on the windscreen, which seconds later turned into a squall that shook the car from the force of the wind. Pittenweem was about ten miles due south of St Andrews, but at that time of day, the town would be busy. And from the North Street Office, driving on country roads slickened by a downpour, it could take twenty minutes to drive there. The trouble with April showers in March was that they often carried the threat of snow, and by the time Gilchrist eased through the pend that led from the car park the streets were turning white from hailstones.

The wind was doing what it could to slow them down as he drove up North Street, the buildings either side funnelling the storm, creating a bottleneck through which the squall whistled. He flipped on his wipers, but they barely cleared the screen.

'What is it about this place?' Jessie complained. 'It'll be the middle of summer in three months for crying out loud.'

Gilchrist's phone rang at that moment, and he put it through the speaker system. 'Yes, Mhairi.'

'Got the address for Wren's Garage, sir,' she said, then rattled off a street name and number. Jessie entered it into his car's GPS system.

'Who owns the property?' he asked Mhairi.

'Streetspace Ltd, sir.'

He'd never heard of it, didn't have any idea what it did for money, other than the fact that it owned the property on which Wren's Garage sat, and was probably banking a monthly rent. 'It's a limited company,' he said. 'So it'll be registered with Companies House. Check it out. For all we know, this Lesley Duncan might be the CFO for that, too.'

'Already done that, sir, and she is.'

Mhairi's comment did not surprise him, as if he'd already known that Ms Duncan was at the heart of the matter. But who she was, and what the matter was for it to have a heart, he was none the wiser. 'Get Jackie onto it,' he said. 'Find out who this Duncan is. She must exist somewhere.'

He ended the call, and accelerated past the cathedral ruins.

Heading south on Abbey Walk, he phoned Dainty. 'Got a name for you,' he said. 'A Ms Lesley J. W. Duncan. You heard of her?'

'Can't say that I have,' Dainty said. 'What's it in connection with?'

The purpose of calling Dainty was to find out information, not give it. And Gilchrist was conscious of Smiler's recent low profile in the Office, with rumours rearing that she was meeting with McVicar on some *important business*. Not that a DCI was normally made privy to such high and mighty matters between chief superintendents and chief constables, but it did seem to Gilchrist that he was being deliberately kept in the dark about something big that was about to break. And Fife Constabulary was not necessarily the focal point of whatever was going on, but was being contacted for support and advice – all of which was above and beyond Gilchrist's pay grade from the looks of it. Well, that's what he thought. Of course, Jessie's report on the criminal gathering at Shepherd's mansion only added to his suspicions.

Sometimes the only way to get an invite to the party was to gate-crash. With nothing to lose, he thought he'd give it a shot. A long shot, he knew. But if you didn't ask, you didn't get. 'Her name popped up on a PNC search,' he said. 'Thought I'd run it past you in case she was a player in this major drugs bust that's about to happen.'

The silence on the line told Gilchrist he'd hit the nail on the head, maybe not smack dab on the middle, but close enough. After a few beats, Dainty said, 'You're fishing, Andy.'

Nothing much slipped past Dainty, and experience had taught Gilchrist that honesty often pulled more from the man than deceit. 'I am, yes.'

'Why?'

Which was typical Dainty. Straight to the point. Might as well respond in kind, so he said, 'Jock Shepherd's dying. He's probably only got days to live. And we're guessing that he wants to go out on a high note.'

'Guessing?'

'*Educated* guessing. Hence the drugs bust.'

A pause, then, 'And you want me to tell you what?'

Jessie was staring at the phone system as if trying to read the spoken words. She glanced at Gilchrist, her eyebrows raised in question. He had no idea where this next question would take him, but it struck him all of a sudden that Shepherd's note might have already given him the answer.

'Tell me when it's happening,' he said. 'And where.'

'And what do I get in return?'

Gilchrist couldn't guarantee anything, of course, and didn't know if Shepherd was sending him on a wild errand or not. Maybe it was just a ploy of Shepherd's to keep Gilchrist out of the way of whatever *big something* was about to break. But again, he chose honesty.

'Truth be told, I don't know if I've got anything to give you.'

'Well, I can't help you, Andy. Sorry. But that's the way it has to be on this one.'

This one. Again, the reference to something unique, something big. Well, if Dainty wouldn't tell him directly, perhaps he could do so indirectly. 'Is Pittenweem close to the centre of anything?' he tried.

'Pittenweem? On the Fife coast?'

Gilchrist already knew from the tone of Dainty's voice that he was on the wrong path, that big Jock Shepherd really had sent them on a blind chase. But he said, 'The one and only.'

'You're way off, Andy. *Way* off.'

'And you've never heard of Lesley Duncan?'

'Never.' A pause, then, 'I'm sorry, Andy. I can't help you.'

But Gilchrist wasn't finished. He had one last dart to throw, a wild shot that could miss the board altogether. Shepherd didn't have long to live, and hosting criminal gatherings was not something you did for a farewell party. But if you thought about it logically, if Jock Shepherd really was trying to keep Gilchrist from interfering in this *big something*, then his handwritten note had to be correct on at least one point.

'So everything's in place for tonight?' he said.

His words could have frozen time, short-circuited the digital ether, for it took Dainty all of six seconds before he hung up.

Which gave Gilchrist his answer.

CHAPTER 42

By the time they arrived at Pittenweem's shoreline, the March squall had settled into full storm mode. Fishing boats anchored in calm waters seemed to come alive from the force of the wind. Ropes as thick and hairy as wrists strained on rusted anchor rings. Wooden hulls rolled and creaked as if in complaint. Beyond the relative quiet of the harbour waters, waves exploded over the stone pier with bursts of spray that swept landwards like spindrift.

On Mid Shore they found the address and name – Wren's Garage – painted on the inside wall of a narrow pend that led to the back of a row of terraced properties that fronted the harbour. Gilchrist slowed as he approached the entrance, snatched a quick glance through the pend, but saw nothing that looked like an ongoing business – no workshop, no cars, no mechanics with grubby hands and greased overalls – just a wooden building that looked like the ramshackle garage his parents' neighbours used to keep their car in.

He drove on and reached the end of the street, did a three-point turn and parked by the kerb. He switched off the lights, but kept the engine running and the fan on to keep the windscreen from steaming. With the wipers on slow intermittent, passers-by could think the car was empty.

Despite the rain, and the darkening night, Gilchrist had a clear view along Mid Shore and the mouth of the pend that led to Wren's Garage. A glance at the dash told him they had less than forty minutes until seven, at which time . . . well, who knew what would happen then? Probably nothing, if his mounting doubts were realised.

After ten minutes of waiting and watching, Jessie said, 'Looks like no one's around.'

'If they're here, they could be in the back.'

'Having a cup of tea in the garage?'

Gilchrist looked seawards. Black clouds hugged the horizon. 'Looks like this is on for the night.'

'So what's new?'

'It's not as bad as it was.'

Jessie glared at the horizon. 'It's just pissing down, you mean? Instead of torrential?'

Under such a blanket of dark clouds, you could be forgiven for thinking that night had settled early. Even so, Gilchrist said, 'Let's give it another ten minutes.'

'You think the rain's going to go off by then?'

'I think it'll be a bit darker.'

'Bloody hell,' she said, and stared out the windscreen. 'It's miserable, this place.'

'Pittenweem?'

'No. Scotland. Who would be stupid enough to emigrate to here?'

'Scotland has a lot to offer.'

'Sure, it does. If you're a wellington boots and umbrella sales-man. Oh, and raincoats.' She grunted, shifted in her seat. 'I knew someone who moved up to Glasgow from England. Born and bred somewhere south of London. She was here for two days before she bought a raincoat. Said it was the first raincoat she'd ever owned. Pissed off back south the following year. What does that tell you?'

'That she should've bought an umbrella instead?'

Jessie chuckled. 'Should've bought an umbrella as *well*, you mean.'

Gilchrist switched off the fan, then the engine. 'You ready?'

'No umbrella, so the jacket'll have to do.'

Outside, the wind hit them with renewed strength. Rain lashed in from the east, cold as ice and stinging like hail. Waves thumped the harbour wall, but something in the way the spray exploded told him that the worst of the storm was behind them.

They strode side by side along Mid Shore, and turned into Wren's Garage pend like a choreographed dance act seeking shelter.

'Jesus,' Jessie hissed. 'I'm soaked through.'

'Need to get yourself a waterproof jacket.'

'It *is* waterproof.'

'Showerproof.'

'What?'

'Your jacket's showerproof only.'

'And where did you get your sartorial degree?'

'Check the label.'

'Aye, right.'

In the shelter of the pend, Gilchrist raked his fingers through his hair, blew into his hands to take the chill from his fingers.

Then he walked to the far end of the pend, and eyed the deserted back area. Rainwater splashed onto the cobblestones from a broken downpipe. Runoff flowed past his shoes like a small burn. The garage, if it could be called that, looked larger than he'd first thought, and abandoned. But a curved mark that ran from the bottom of the right-hand door glistened like a scratch in the cobbles where the wood had scraped stone. The door had been opened recently. The padlock, too, shone as shiny as steel, and was large enough to suggest that whatever was being stored inside was of value and worth safekeeping.

Gilchrist looked at the area around him. The terraced buildings offered respite from the wind, and the downpour seemed to have lost its intensity. Wren's Garage – if that's what the wooden building was – overlooked a small yard hemmed in on three sides by eight-foot-high brick walls. The garage sat in one corner of the yard, and Gilchrist noted ruts in the gravel and dirt forecourt that hinted of vehicular access and turning. In his mind's eye he pictured a van driving through the pend, doing a hard turn to the left, then reversing up to the garage door. From there it would be a straight drive back through the pend.

Again, his attention was drawn to the hefty padlock.

What was stored in the garage? Contraband worth millions? He almost snorted at the absurdity of it. Probably nothing more than a mechanic's wrench set, or maybe just a pick and shovel. Big Jock Shepherd was more than likely having a laugh. Probably splitting his sides by now. If anything was going to happen here at seven, it was most likely not going to be the *something big* that they were hoping for. The wind shifted at that moment, throwing a gutter-load of rainwater over the area, as if telling Gilchrist to hurry up and get on with it.

He turned to Jessie. 'How's your lock-picking?'

'Could give it a try,' she said, and walked towards the garage.

Gilchrist followed her, troubled by the oddest sense of being watched. He ran his gaze along the back of the terraced homes. In the darkness of an early night, light shone from those windows he could see above the boundary wall. Curtains hung open. Blinds were pulled high. He watched a woman fill a kettle from the kitchen tap, before she stepped back and sank out of sight. At another window, a man adjusted a latch. From behind, he heard the scratch of metal on metal as Jessie worked the lock.

'I hope you realise,' she said, 'that without a warrant, anything we find inside would be compromised in court.'

'We have to get in first,' he said, and resisted telling her to hurry up.

All he wanted was to check it out before anyone arrived. He had burgeoning doubts about Shepherd's note, and the last thing he needed was his request for a search warrant to cross Smiler's desk, only for him to end up with egg on his face. If they found contraband inside, he could show Smiler the note from Shepherd, *then* apply for a search warrant.

Through the pend, headlights brightened Mid Shore. He held his breath as the shorehead lit up as if from a distress flare, then just as quickly settled into darkness as a car drove past, tyres hissing on the rain-soaked road, exhaust growling in the dying wind. Christ, he thought, if anyone happened to enter the pend, there was nowhere to hide.

Back to Jessie. 'Any luck?'

She hissed a curse, and said, 'Bloody hell, Andy. I'm trying, I'm trying.'

'I know you're trying. But do you think you can do it?'

'A key would be nice,' she said. 'Or a hacksaw.'

'Can't help you there.' Another glance at the windows did nothing to settle his nerves.

'Ah, shit,' Jessie said. 'That's it.'

'You're in?'

'It's snapped.'

Gilchrist caught the sudden whine of a high-revving engine, and felt his heart leap as a single headlight flashed across the mouth of the pend and disappeared along the shorehead, the sound of an engine fading into the darkness. Out on a motorbike on a night like this? Who would be so crazy? Movement above, a shadow of sorts, caught his peripheral vision, and he imagined – rather than saw – a face pulling back from one of the upper windows, two along from the roof of the pend . . .

Which was when he saw it.

High on the wall. Within arm's reach of a double sash window.

One through which no light shone from its uninhabited interior. The blinking light of a webcam. Only a fleeting flicker. Nothing more. But enough to tell him that somewhere, on someone's computer screen . . .

They were being watched.

CHAPTER 43

It all kicked off quickly after that.

Jessie managed to retract the broken lock-pick from the padlock, then rub the sleeve of her jacket across it, front and back, to remove her prints. Not the best way to do it, but as good as any in the time available.

For they had no time now, Gilchrist sensed that.

What he hadn't sensed, though, was the speed with which they would be confronted.

He and Jessie strode across the forecourt, intent on returning to his car to wait it out until 7 p.m., and had just entered the mouth of the pend when the blinding beam of a single flashlight stopped them. At the Mid Shore end of the pend, one flashlight beam became two, which ran up and down his and Jessie's respective lengths and settled on their faces.

Jessie raised her hand to shield her eyes. 'Douse the lights, boys,' she said.

Gilchrist thought he heard a snigger, and slid his hand inside his jacket to retrieve his warrant card. The beam slid from his face to his chest, followed by a man's voice saying, 'Steady,' the word drawn out hard and long as a warning, the timbre strangely familiar.

'We're with Fife Constabulary,' Gilchrist said.

'Hands where we can see them.'

With slow deliberation, Gilchrist removed his hand from inside his jacket.

'In the air.'

'Get real,' Jessie said.

The beam shivered with implied annoyance, but sufficient to show the metallic glint of a gun held in a steady hand. 'We're not fooling.' A pause, then, 'That's it. Higher.'

When Gilchrist and Jessie had their hands head-high, a figure emerged from between the two flashlights and walked towards them. As he neared, the silhouette shifted from blacks through greys to settle into the muscular form of DS Fox, holding what looked like a Glock in his left hand, although Gilchrist was never great at identifying makes of gun. The flashlights shivered as Fox's sidekicks – Gilchrist could count only three – approached and stood behind Fox, still in shadow. In the shivering light, Fox looked resolute, face grim, jaw tight. He was no longer the blasé Detective Sergeant ready to down whisky by the glass-load, but more like a man intent on protecting what was his, and his alone.

Despite that, Gilchrist tried to bluff it. He gave a smile of relief, and said, 'For a moment there, I thought we were in trouble,' and went to lower his arms—

'*Up*,' from a voice behind one of the flashlights.

Gilchrist froze. 'What's going on?' he asked Fox.

Fox grimaced. 'You present us with a problem.'

'In what way?'

'The fact that you're here.'

'We were trying to leave,' Jessie said. 'But you wouldn't let us.'

Fox's head swivelled like a robot to take Jessie in, and Gilchrist realised that standing where they were in the open mouth of the pend, whatever was about to happen would not be seen from any of the windows above. To stall what he feared was coming, Gilchrist resorted to the only defence he could think of – talking.

'Lesley Jennifer Wren Duncan,' he said. 'And Wren's Garage. That's why we're here. Which raises the question – why are you here?'

Fox turned his attention back to Gilchrist, and nodded, as if at the cleverness of the question. 'I'll tell you why I'm here,' he said, 'if you tell me how you happened to find this place.'

'Googled it,' Jessie said, which earned her another sharp look from Fox, with the added bonus of the fourth man in the group – the one without a flashlight – stepping forward from the shadows.

'You always were the cheeky bitch,' he said.

Gilchrist had never seen the man before, but from the disgusted look on Jessie's face, he could tell that she had.

'Well well well,' she said. 'Look what the dog's gone and dug up.'

The man approached Jessie, a glint of anger in his eyes, and pressed in close enough for Jessie to resist taking a step back.

'Last I heard of Detective Sergeant Brian Wheelan,' she said – and Gilchrist knew she was giving him a name for future reference, although that future was looking as if it might be shorter-lived than either of them hoped – 'you'd just been demoted.'

'No thanks to you, you fucking wee cow.'

Jessie spat in his face, and Wheelan's hand came up out of the darkness and hit her across her cheek with a punch that thudded her to the ground.

'Hold it right there, Andy.' Fox's voice purred with reason. 'She'd kept her mouth shut, she wouldn't be lying on the ground now, would she?' He nodded to the side, and one of the flashlights flicked off as a skinny man in a black biker jacket leaned down, slipped his hands under Jessie's armpits and dragged her upright.

Something about the scene put Gilchrist in mind of a fisherman going about his work, as if hauling limp bodies off cobbled courtyards was the same as pulling fish from a net. A prod in the ribs with the barrel of an automatic machine gun – surely not an Uzi – refocused Gilchrist's attention.

Fox said, 'Start walking,' and the other flashlight clicked off as the man at his side gave another prod.

Weak light from upper windows cast a yellow glow into the night. But at forecourt level, surrounded by three walls and two-storey buildings, the darkness was as good as total. Gilchrist stumbled towards the garage, hands still in the air, conscious that they were now out of the pend and in an area that in daylight would be visible to residents in the terraced homes. Surely one of them would see something suspicious and phone the police. On the other hand, what could they see in an unlit garage forecourt? And even if they did see something, would they know what it was, and could they be bothered to interfere?

Probably not on both counts, he reluctantly reasoned.

But Gilchrist was able to make out shapes in the darkness, and from the way the man ahead of him was carrying Jessie – her head down, feet dragging – he knew she was out cold. The speed

313

of Wheelan's punch had not only surprised Jessie, but Gilchrist, too. But it was the hard thud as Jessie hit the ground that warned him that she'd been knocked unconscious the moment the blow was struck. A pause at the garage door as a key clinked in the padlock, then a hard metallic click as it was unlocked and removed from its hasp, gave Gilchrist time to pull up what he could recall of DS Wheelan, a name that was coming back to him.

Jessie had once explained to him how she'd reached detective status while still in her twenties. Single-handedly, she'd exposed a father and his three sons as sexual abusers of the youngest member of their family. After she managed to convince the victim – Fiona – to seek help from the police, the matter went to trial, and it was DS Wheelan – who worked out of the Rutherglen Office at the time – who had provided character references for two of the sons, Fiona's oldest brothers. Jessie had been convinced Wheelan had done so because the sons muled drugs for him, but she'd been unable to find evidence to back up that theory. As it was, Wheelan's statements almost brought down the case, but ended up being sufficient only to mitigate some of the charges—

The garage door creaked open, its frame scraping the forecourt, and Jessie was carried into its blacker than black interior. A firm nudge in the ribs from that annoying gun barrel had Gilchrist following in short order, his heart pounding at what was about to happen. Several scenarios unfolded in his mind, none of which inspired hope, the most realistic being that they were going to shoot him and Jessie and leave their bodies to rot in the garage. For all he knew, the garage might lie from one year to the next without the door ever being opened.

The garage interior smelled musty dry. Rainwater hit the roof, a constant sound that thrummed in the background. Leather scuffed on the concrete floor as the others entered, and Gilchrist had the oddest sense that sacks of wheat, or bales of straw, were stored there. He slid one of his shoes over the floor, sensing the concrete smooth, with a coating of dust.

A hand with a grip as tight as a vice jerked him to a standstill, and everyone stood in the black silence as the door scraped shut. With a soft click, the world exploded into view. Gilchrist had to lower his head and screw his eyes against the brightness. The garage looked as if it had never been a workshop, but an office. Not much of an office, mind you, but good enough from which to access the internet, make a phone call, store what looked like wrapped and sealed bags of drugs on the floor – heroin, if he had to take a guess; thousands of pounds of it. The hand pressed down on his shoulder, hard, and before he could object he found himself slammed into a wooden chair.

'Right,' said Fox. 'Start talking.'

Gilchrist took hope from the fact that they hadn't tied his hands behind his back. On the other side of that argument, they hadn't been expecting to find anyone here, so wouldn't necessarily have reels of spare rope to hand. Not that he was about to jump to his feet any time soon and take them all on. A glance at the machine gun held in hands accustomed to automatic weaponry stiffened his resolve not to do anything that would give them cause to shoot. He looked down at Jessie on the floor by his side, eyes closed, blood seeping from her nose. The blow had struck her high on her cheek, where a raised bruise was taking shape. He hoped no bones had been broken. Of course, none of that might matter in an hour or so, maybe less.

'Is Jessie all right?' he said.

'Forget her. It's you I want to talk to.'

'Not until you convince me that Jessie's all right.'

Fox nodded to someone out of Gilchrist's line of sight, and the bulky figure of DS Wheelan crept into view, accompanied by a thinner man, the one who'd lugged Jessie into the garage. Between them, they manhandled her body upright onto another chair, similar to the one on which Gilchrist sat.

Wheelan took hold of Jessie's face in one hand, squeezing her cheeks, and tried to shake her awake. The other man had more of a clue, and removed a bottle of distilled water from a small fridge under a table, unscrewed the top, and poured it over Jessie's upturned face.

She came to with a spluttering curse.

'Satisfied?' Fox asked Gilchrist.

Gilchrist tried to push himself to his feet, but was restrained by that damn vice-like grip again.

'Stay put,' Fox snarled at him.

'Jessie?' Gilchrist said, and she managed to turn her head and look at him. 'Are you OK?' He thought her eyes were still swimming, but she gave him a half-nod and snorted a spray of blood down the front of her jacket, then sat back and eyed the group with venomous defiance. Gilchrist had to admire her courage. But no amount of glaring of eyes and snorting of blood was going to get them out of this mess anytime soon.

'Heh. Over here,' Fox said to Gilchrist, pointing two fingers at his own eyes.

Gilchrist did as he was told, and returned Fox's gaze.

'We'll try this one more friendly time,' he said. 'After which, if you're still playing funny buggers, we'll resort to less friendly means.' He jerked a quick smile that failed to touch his eyes. 'Capisci?'

'Sorry,' Gilchrist said. 'I don't speak French.'

Someone chuckled from behind Gilchrist, and he had a sense of the air tightening. He caught Fox giving the tiniest shake of his head, a movement that told Gilchrist who was the boss, and warned him that one false move could be his last. All of a sudden his memory cast up an image of Stooky Dee wired to the inside of the hull, and he realised that he could very well be talking to Stooky's killers. With that thought, a tremor did what it could to shiver his leg, but he pressed his foot hard on the floor and fought it off.

Fox leaned closer, his face no more than six inches from Gilchrist's, as if enticing Gilchrist to reach up with his free hands and try to choke him to death. And he came to see why they hadn't bothered to tie his hands behind his back. Why waste the effort? All they had to do was pull a trigger and it was end of the road for Gilchrist and all his memories.

What would happen to Jack and Maureen? What would they think?

The memory of talking to Joe Christie's wife appeared from nowhere. She'd lived for years believing Joe had deserted her, when in fact he was probably dead, his body never to be found. Would that be his own fate, too? Would Jack and Maureen have his body to cremate? Not buried. No, not buried. He'd written that into his will. And he found it strange how the mind worked at times of extreme stress, how despite the hopelessness of their situation he found himself thinking of a joke, of someone who wanted to be cremated, and being close to death, so close that they said they had one foot on the grate—

'How did you happen to find this place?' Fox said.

'Told you,' Jessie said. 'We Googled it.'

'Want me to shut her up, boss?'

Fox shook his head, then said to Gilchrist, 'Tell her if she doesn't keep her trap shut, we're going to put a bullet in your thigh.'

With that, one of the trio – a stocky man with hair like rusted wire – removed an automatic pistol from one pocket, a silencer from the other, and screwed the two together.

Fox smiled. 'Any preference?'

'Preference?' Gilchrist said.

'Which thigh? Left or right?'

Gilchrist turned to face Jessie. 'For once in your life, Jessie, can you keep that trap of yours shut?'

She nodded, and pressed her lips together.

But even that seemed not enough to satisfy them, for the stocky man stepped forward and pressed the suppressor's muzzle to the side of Gilchrist's head.

'Right,' Fox said. 'We'll try this one last time, shall we?'

CHAPTER 44

Gilchrist struggled to keep his tone light. 'My preference would be left thigh.'

Fox offered an appreciative smile.

The muzzle pressed harder.

Despite his best efforts at casual bravado, Gilchrist could not stop a fresh tremor from gripping his leg. He held his breath, waiting for the bullet that would end his life. Would he feel it? Would he die in a flash of pain? 'Even if I tell you what you want to know,' he gushed, 'you're still going to kill us.' He tried to give Fox his most defiant stare. But he doubted he would have won an Oscar. 'So why tell you anything at all?' he reasoned.

Fox frowned, as if giving his words some thought, then said, 'You know, I've got to tell you that there's some truth in what you're saying.' He nodded to the man with the gun to Gilchrist's head.

Gilchrist squeezed his eyes tight. Christ, no. This was it. He held his breath for one beat, two beats, three, then four, but when the pressure of the suppressor against the side of his head relaxed, he opened his eyes.

'Battie here,' Fox said, and nodded to the man with rust-coloured hair, 'is ex-SAS.'

Battie's lips parted in an imitation of a smile.

'I don't know if you would remember or not, or how old you would've been at the time, but the SAS were called into service during the Falklands War, doing all the usual stuff they're known for; secret missions, taking out this person, that unit, getting down and dirty in the thick of it all, doing the stuff that nobody liked doing.'

Gilchrist had no idea where Fox was going with this, but he was conscious of the man called Battie distancing himself from him, or perhaps more correctly, edging closer to Jessie.

'One of the nastier sides of war happens to be the interrogation of prisoners of war. It shouldn't be, of course, nasty I mean, with the Geneva Convention and all. But we're realists in the end. And when it comes to whether or not good old Private Francesco Pablova of the Argentinian Army knows something that might prevent Johnny Britain from getting blown up, well, there really are no rules, are there? Although we say there are.'

Fox reached out and placed a fatherly hand on the shoulder of the man called Battie who, Gilchrist was reluctant to admit, seemed to be perking up at the idea of some possibility that pleased him. 'And Battie here was one of your SAS interrogators. He never failed. Did you, Battie?'

'No, sir.'

'Not once. Not ever.' Fox's attention was back on Gilchrist with a vengeance. 'So would you like to know how it played out during the Falklands so that Battie boy scored the perfect record?'

320

Gilchrist grimaced, and managed to force down a sickening lump in his throat.

'Battie would have the prisoners lined up with their hands tied behind their backs, and he would walk up to the first one, waggle his gun in front of him and tell him that he would shoot him dead if he didn't answer the nice Army man's questions.' He paused for a moment, as if he'd just remembered something. 'Of course, Battie's fluent in Spanish. His dear mother married a Spanish bartender, God rest her soul. Did I tell you that?'

Silent, Gilchrist stared at him, now knowing with sickening dread where Fox was going with this.

'But that's by the way. So, where was I? Oh, yes, then Battie would stand aside while the nice Army interrogator asked the first question. And without fail, every soldier who was interrogated first, gave his name, rank, and serial number only. Nothing more. Because they'd been commanded to do so by their chiefs, who assured them that we British played the game clean, and by the rules.' Fox chuckled. 'This is the bit I like. Tell him, Battie.'

Battie stepped forward into Gilchrist's view, positioning himself in front of Jessie. He held his gun pointed at the garage roof, the suppressor long and black and looking clinically deadly. 'We never gave them second chances,' he said in a broad Glaswegian accent. 'We'd ask that first guy once, and if he spewed out his name, rank and serial number, I pressed the gun to his forehead and shot the bastard.' He laughed at that, a husky growl that flushed his cheeks. 'After that, the others were falling over themselves and pissing their pants to tell us everything.'

Fox clapped Battie's shoulder again. 'It never failed, did it, Battie?'

'Not once.'

'Show DCI Gilchrist how it's done, Battie.'

Battie lowered his gun, levelled it at Jessie's forehead and—

'*No.*' Gilchrist leaped from his chair and dived at Battie's arm, fearful that he was already too late. But Battie was prepared for the move. He stepped back like a ballet dancer, and thudded the butt of his gun into the back of Gilchrist's head in the passing with a force that should have cracked bone.

Gilchrist hit the floor with a heavy thud that pulled a grunt from his throat. But before he could push himself onto all fours, strong arms hooked him by his armpits and dragged him back onto his chair.

Fox's face swam in front of him, a Picasso painting that zoomed in close to peer into his eyes. Somebody shouted something, cursed maybe, he couldn't say. Then his stomach spasmed, and bile burned its way into his throat to dribble from his lips like spittle.

'That's the problem with the ex-SAS,' Fox said. 'They sometimes forget how well-trained they once were.' He leaned down, almost kneeling in front of Gilchrist, took hold of Gilchrist's hair and pulled his head back until they were looking at each other eye to eye. Well, Fox was doing the looking. Gilchrist was having difficulty focusing. But with every second he was coming round, although a throbbing pain at the back of his head had him wanting to lie down and just close his eyes.

'So,' Fox said, and glanced at Battie.

Battie spread his legs as if to steady himself, then pointed his gun at Jessie.

'I've got a son,' she whimpered. 'Please. My wee boy. He's deaf. He needs his mum.'

'Wait,' Gilchrist managed to grunt. It was now bluff or die. Maybe both. He spat up sputum, tried to lick his lips. But his tongue could've been connected to someone else's brain. 'Wait,' he said again, and wiped a hand across his lips, took a deep breath. 'If you shoot her, I'll tell you bugger all.'

'We'll see.'

'*I mean it.*'

The words were shouted loud enough for Battie's attention to be diverted.

'You'll fuck up your perfect record,' Gilchrist said. 'But that's how it'll be.'

Battie stepped back from Jessie at some signal from Fox, which Gilchrist failed to catch. Fox leaned close to Gilchrist again. 'OK,' he said. 'Maybe this time we break the rules and give you a second chance.'

Gilchrist tried to blink away the pain, but his head felt as if someone was tapping it with a hammer in time with his heart.

Fox offered a smile of sympathy. 'I'm waiting.'

'What's the question again?' Gilchrist said.

'How did you know to come here?'

'To Pittenweem?'

Fox let out a sigh of frustration. 'To Wren's Garage.'

'Joe Christie's logbook.'

His answer seemed to surprise Fox, for he frowned and cut a glance left and right at the others, then said, 'Joe Christie's dead.'

'I know he is.'

'So how did you find his logbook?'

'*Brenda Girl.*'

Fox scowled at him. '*Brenda Girl?*'

323

'His boat. It was swept ashore during that recent storm. The name had been changed to *Golden Plover*. The boat with Stooky Dee's body on board.'

Something passed behind Fox's eyes, calculations of sorts that set his eyes dancing as if his brain was having difficulty understanding English. 'And you found the logbook in the boat?' he asked at length.

'Yes.'

'I don't believe you.'

'I can't help you with that.'

Fox pulled himself upright, and stared down at Gilchrist as if deciding which part of him to chop off first, and where to get rid of the pieces.

'Can I speak?'

Battie pointed his gun at Jessie.

Fox raised his hand, a command to Battie not to pull the trigger. 'Go on.'

'He's telling the truth,' Jessie said. 'Joe Christie's house was broken into after he went missing three years ago. But the logbook wasn't there. And it was never found, because no one thought to ask his wife back then. She told us where it was hidden.'

'And no one knew this until you found it out?'

'That's the local bobbies for you.'

'And where's Christie's logbook now?' Fox asked her.

Jessie lowered her head and closed her eyes.

'I'm waiting,' Fox said.

'Heh. Over here,' Gilchrist said, and pointed his fingers at his eyes.

Fox jerked an angry look at him.

Battie shifted his aim.

Gilchrist struggled to ignore the gun pointing at him. He had nothing left with which to defend himself. Well, not quite nothing. His brain wasn't allowing him to think far enough ahead to work out the consequences of what he was about to say. But in a week or so, with big Jock Shepherd dead and a new man in charge, maybe it would mean nothing at all. And there was always the possibility – a ridiculously slim one, he knew – that Fox might just let him and Jessie go, once he'd been told the truth.

'We handed it over to Jock Shepherd,' he said.

Fox shook his head as if with irritation. 'Why?'

'For information.'

'Like an exchange?'

'Yes.'

'Information on what?'

'He told us about this place, Wren's Garage.'

If Gilchrist had stirred a hornet's nest with a red-hot poker he would have received less of a response. Fox removed a phone from his pocket and strode to the back wall of the garage, fingers tapping the screen. Wheelan and the other guy, the skinny one who'd carried Jessie to the garage, ripped a tarpaulin off a short stack of shelves and started pulling sealed packets off them, and placing them on a wooden pallet that Gilchrist hadn't seen until that moment.

Meanwhile, Battie raised his gun and stepped towards Jessie.

'Jessie's got a copy of the logbook,' Gilchrist shouted at him, and jumped to his feet, the movement so sudden that his world tilted for an awkward moment. Then it righted itself as Battie's arm swung his way until he was looking into the black mouth of the suppressor.

'We need them,' Fox snapped. 'Both of them.'

Battie lowered his gun and unscrewed the suppressor – if only cats were as well trained. He flipped his jacket wide, slid the suppressor into one leather holster, his pistol into another. Then he pointed two fingers at Gilchrist in imitation of a gun, and mouthed – *Later*.

Fox barked into his mobile, 'They're onto us. Get out. It's a set-up,' and hung up. He then nodded to Battie who stepped behind Jessie, and said, 'Up.'

Confused, Jessie tried to struggle to her feet. But urgency had taken hold of the gang, and Battie grabbed her arms, jerked them behind her back and, with the expertise of a police training officer, cuffed her – where had the plasticuffs come from? Then he shoved her towards the side of the garage, and turned his attention to Gilchrist.

'Up,' he said.

But Gilchrist was already pushing to his feet, holding his hands behind his back with an almost debilitating mixture of relief and despair – relief that they hadn't just shot the pair of them; and despair that they were being cuffed. The logical part of his brain had worked out that they were being taken away for disposal *off site*, to some place where the discovery of their bodies would not connect them in any way to Wren's Garage. Scotland's lochs and moors provided an unlimited number of places in which to dispose of a body or two, or worse, to spread body parts around.

The plasticuffs slipped onto his wrists with a tight tug that brought a grimace to his face, and a *Fuck you* from Battie. He glanced at Jessie, saw the trail of tears down her cheeks, and a dead look in her eyes that told him she knew everything was over.

They were both going to be killed. She would never see her son again.

And he would never see his children either.

No one would come along and save them.

They were on their own. And this was the end.

Which was when the garage door rattled.

CHAPTER 45

The wooden door rattled again, as if someone was trying to break in.

But if Gilchrist expected the gang to panic, he was sorely disappointed.

Mobile back by his ear, Fox spat, 'Stupid bastard. He'll wake the whole fucking town up.' Not that anyone was sleeping, Gilchrist knew. Then Fox turned his back to the door and carried on with his phone call.

Wheelan and the skinny guy continued stacking the pallet, wrapped bundles rising four feet high – which had to be the biggest stash of heroin to hit the British Isles, and put it somewhere in the eight-figure range. Battie strode to the door with grim determination, as if intent on telling the *stupid bastard* which leg he was going to shoot him in if he didn't keep the fucking noise down. But when he unlocked the garage door and pushed it open, he was confronted with the tail-end of a white van, exhaust fuming in the cold air, and the driver's door slamming shut.

Undeterred, Battie opened the other garage door wide, then stood to the side, in line with the driver's wing mirror, and guided the van back. Gilchrist didn't think the garage was long enough to hide the van completely. Not that it mattered, he supposed, as long as it was parked deep enough inside to load the pallet out of view of nosy neighbours.

The van eased back, edged into the garage and drew to a halt, brake lights casting a hellish glow over the scene, engine thrumming loud in the closed confines, exhaust pumping out grey fumes.

'Tell him to turn the fucking engine off,' Fox snapped at Battie.

But in the rumbling din Battie hadn't heard, or couldn't be bothered, and reached for the handles on the back of the van. Wheelan had only just lugged the last of the packages onto the pile, when Battie twisted the handle and pulled the van doors open.

Gilchrist would write in his statement later that it all happened with practised speed, and more terrifyingly, with an eerie, almost clinical silence in its unfolding.

Battie was dead before his body hit the garage floor, falling stiff-legged and straight-backed, as if his nerves had frozen from the single shot to his forehead. Fox was next, a burst of suppressed automatic gunfire – three rounds, Gilchrist would later recall – that turned the middle of his chest into a bloodied bullseye and blasted him full-force into the corner wall.

Battie's body hit the floor with a heavy thump as Wheelan squealed something for the last time, his face exploding from a single shot. The skinny guy managed to raise his hands shoulder-high in surrender before another short burst – two rounds as Cooper would later confirm – took the side of his head off.

Two men in black jeans, jacket and balaclavas – guns dangling from shoulder straps – leaped from the back of the van, and went about their business as if Jessie and Gilchrist were nothing more than invisible shadows. One of them remotely controlled a two-pronged forklift mechanism that extended from the van's interior and lowered to the garage floor. The other rolled out a length of plastic sheeting, and ripped off a perforated section. Then he picked up Battie's body as if he weighed nothing more than a bale of straw, and threw him onto the plastic. The ends of the sheeting were then folded in and over to form a nicely wrapped package. A strip of duct tape torn off a roll secured it.

He then ripped off another length of sheeting, and strode towards Fox's body.

A signal to the driver had the van easing back again, brake lights flickering, exhaust smoking as the driver slipped the clutch. The forklift scraped the floor, then juddered up an inch or so as one of the hitmen guided it into position. The van jerked to a halt, the brake lights vanished. The forklift raised the pallet, wobbling unsteadily from the off-balanced loading. A packet slid off, and split open, spreading a spray of white powder over the floor. Without a word, the hitman picked it up and tossed it into the van.

Fox's body was rolled onto the plastic sheeting as the driver entered the garage, all in black like the other two. He headed straight for Wheelan and carried him like a crumpled sack of meat over to another sheet of plastic that had been readied for him. Next came the skinny guy, picked up as if he weighed nothing, brains and blood dripping like wax as the sheeting was placed under him.

The back of the van settled down on its tyres from the weight of the drugs. The forklift was switched off and the remote control thrown into the back. One of the hitmen jumped in and anchored the stack to the floor with canvas straps that slid through metal rings fixed to the van's floor and walls. From the speed with which he accomplished this, Gilchrist could tell that he'd done it many times before. A quick jerk with one of the clamps, then another, and the stack was secured.

Just then, the two others threw the roll of sheeting that contained Battie's body into the van alongside the stack. Fox's body followed, dumped without ceremony on top of Battie's. Next came the other two, stacked like carpet rolls either side of the drugs.

With four bodies safely on board, the van doors were closed and the driver and one of the hitmen walked from the garage and jumped into the front of the van. Which left one behind, the largest of the group, who pushed his gun to one side as he fished inside his jacket. Then he walked up to Gilchrist and placed a padded envelope on the desk next to the computer.

'Jock sends his regards,' he said, then strode from the garage.

Instead of jumping into the cabin with the others, he slapped the side of the van. The engine revved, and the van eased onto the garage forecourt. As soon as it cleared the garage, he clicked the light switch, stepped outside, pushed the doors shut, one after the other, and snapped the padlock.

In the thick darkness, Jessie was the first to speak.

'Jesus fuck,' she said. 'What the hell just happened?'

Gilchrist was already shuffling his way across the floor, trying to visualise the layout in his mind's eye so as not to stand on any blood or brains or God knows what else was lying around. He kicked his shin against a shelf, but bit his tongue as he scuffed along in the pitch black until he reached the corner of the garage where the light switch should be.

With both hands cuffed behind his back, and in the inky black-ness, it took him some time to locate it, and several seconds more before he managed to flick it on with his forehead.

Light exploded over the scene.

Jessie was on the floor, lying on her side, arms behind her back, knees drawn up in the foetal position. Her face was tight and chalk-white from shock. In contrast, a dark smear of blood trailed from her nose to her chin and down her neck to disappear beneath her jacket. A bruise was doing what it could to colour her left cheek where Wheelan had punched her.

'Are you OK?' he asked.

She took a moment to unfold herself, and sit on her butt. 'Do I look it?'

'You look better than I feel,' he said, and hoped his smile would buck her up.

She hung her head, and said, 'Fuck sake, Andy. I really thought I was going to die. I mean, I thought I'd never . . .' She squeezed her lips, tried to hold herself together, but failed to stop her eyes from welling.

Gilchrist kneeled in front of her. With his hands cuffed behind his back, all he could do was press his head to the side of Jessie's, and let her fall into him. 'It's OK,' he said, as she let herself go, sobs wracking her body. 'It's OK, Jessie. We survived. Somehow. I don't know how. But we did.'

She nodded, took a deep breath, then another. Her sobbing subsided, then she sniffed, and said, 'Christ sake, my nose is running.'

'It could be worse,' he said. 'It could be your mascara.'

She chuckled at that, then pulled herself back from him. 'Sorry, Andy. I've messed up your jacket with blood and . . . and . . .'

'Snot?'

'Sorry.'

'It could be worse,' he said. 'It could be—'

'Don't go there,' she said, and chuckled and cried in equal measure.

'Come on,' he said. 'Let's see if we can get out of here.' He pushed himself to his feet, a bit awkward with cuffed hands, then walked to the desk on which the computer sat, an old desktop PC that had seen better days. Dust and greasy fingerprints marred the screen, and a glance along the electrical lead confirmed it had been snecked off and was plugless.

A brass handle on the desk drawer caught his attention, and he turned his back to it, gripped it with his fingers and managed to pull it out. It fell to the floor with a clatter of wood and metal, spilling its contents around his feet. At first glance, he saw nothing of use, but he scuffed the debris with his foot and uncovered a rusted blade for a Stanley knife.

'Can you pick that up?' he said.

'You never make it easy.' She shuffled on her backside, fingers scrabbling through the debris on the concrete floor.

'A bit to your left,' he said. 'Nearly there. That's it.' Then he squatted on the floor, with his back to her.

It took some time for Jessie to saw through Gilchrist's plasti-cuffs, managing to cut her fingers and Gilchrist's wrists from her groping efforts. Then it was Gilchrist's turn. With both hands free, it took less than five seconds to cut Jessie loose and pull her to her feet. They both looked at each other, as if surprised to find themselves still alive, relatively unharmed.

'Come on,' he said. 'We've got work to do.'

Jessie slipped her hand inside her jacket. 'They never took our mobiles.'

'They never needed to.'

While Jessie called the Office for help, Gilchrist picked up the padded envelope by the computer. It felt light. *Jock sends his regards*. Well, he was sure it wasn't a get-well card he had written. He tore it open and almost let out a shout of relief when his fingers wrapped around a small memory stick.

He slid the envelope inside his jacket and walked to the other side of the garage, to the corner where Fox had been killed. Blood and pieces of flesh and clothing splattered the back wall where Fox's body had crashed against it. A mess of crushed cardboard boxes, twisted lever-arch files, scattered letters, discarded business mail – one sporting the address: Mrs J. Duncan, Wren's Garage – covered the floor like the detritus from an overturned bin. Gilchrist leaned down and fingered his way through it, careful not to touch any gore.

It took him two minutes of picking and teasing his way through the mess before he found it in a discarded pile of computer leads and ethernet connectors, as if placed there for camouflage, intact and, incredibly, still working – Fox's mobile phone.

CHAPTER 46

Three days later, Thursday, 11.45 a.m.
North Street Office, St Andrews

Gilchrist could do nothing to prevent a yawn from stretching his mouth.

His body ached, his head swam, and tiredness swept through him in numbing waves.

After being freed from Wren's Garage, he and Jessie had refused to leave the scene for medical evaluation. Jessie claimed she'd had worse slaps from her mother, while Gilchrist downplayed his head wound. In the end, he'd worked through the night, and had less than ten hours sleep since. Other than a couple of Starbucks muffins and a pepperoni pizza delivered to the Office, he'd had next to nothing to eat, also. Even so, hunger eluded him. A piping-hot shower followed by a good night's sleep in a bed warmed by his electric blanket seemed ten times more attractive than food.

But that would have to wait until later that night.

By the end of Monday evening, Wren's Garage had been turned into a major crime scene. Teams of SOCOs had worked through the night and taken two full days to bag and log every item in the garage. Mid Shore for fifty yards either side of the pend had been closed to traffic, and had since become the local seaside attraction. Those residents closest to Wren's Garage had been interrogated by teams of police and given statements. Even now, door-to-doors were still being carried out around town. All leave in the Anstruther and St Andrews Offices had been cancelled, and reinforcements from other Fife Divisions, as well as from Tayside, Lothian and Borders, and Strathclyde Police, had been seconded to the investigation.

It seemed to Gilchrist that wars had been fought with smaller armies.

A white van matching the description and registration number plate given by Gilchrist and Jessie had been found in the early hours of Tuesday morning, abandoned in a ditch at the side of a dirt track off the A916 north of Bonnybank. SOCOs from Tayside had been pulled in to examine the van and surrounding area, but had found nothing substantive. Cabin, seats, dashboard, handles, switches and steering wheel had all been wiped clean, and the back of the van hosed down. Although traces of heroin were found on the walls of the van, evidence of any bodies having been wrapped in plastic sheeting was not found; nor was the original driver – presumed killed, identity as yet unknown. Gilchrist had hoped that the plastic sheets might have leaked blood or body fluids, but it seemed as if they'd been sealed good and proper.

Tyre tracks in the grass verges gave credence to the theory that a vehicle swap had been made at night in the dark of the countryside, and that three vehicles – best guess – had been involved. But the make and models had yet to be identified. One smart young constable questioned where you would find a water supply in the countryside, which had the CCTV teams in Glenrothes checking footage of garage forecourts, looking for a van being hosed down. But again, they came up with nothing.

A gang of ghosts could have left a clearer trail.

But what set this gangland assassination to the forefront of other investigations was the fact that Strathclyde Police and Lothian and Borders Drug Squads had spent the previous four months in a series of joint undercover operations planned to culminate in a major drug-bust that night in a barn on the outskirts of Blackburn, twenty miles west of Edinburgh, and just about far enough from Glasgow to make it look as if it was beyond big Jock Shepherd's reach. Known only to the necessary few, Operation Clean Out – aptly named in anticipation of doing just that to Scotland's drug barons – had moved relentlessly onwards. But as the deadline approached, four of Shepherd's men – Mann, Boyd, McBirn and Stooky Dee – had been murdered, which in an indirect way defined the beginning of the end of the drug bust.

Operation Clean Out was why Chief Constable McVicar had been instructed to assign Stooky Dee's murder investigation to Strathclyde Police. With only days to go, the integrity of the operation could not be jeopardised by the involvement of other constabularies. With months of undercover work about to culminate in a massive sting operation, there was too much at stake to let a murder investigation of a mere mutilated body on a beached boat interfere in any way.

But despite that, Operation Clean Out backfired in spectacular fashion.

It had been set to kick off at 7 p.m., the same time as the murderous attack in Wren's Garage. With everything in place,

Strathclyde's BAD Squad – under the command of Chief Superintendent Victor Maxwell – stormed the barn, an outbuilding in a farm close to the town of Blackburn. Bodies thick with Kevlar vests, armed with semi-automatic machine guns and X26 Tasers, and backed by police marksmen with night-vision goggles and infra-red sights, Clean Out kicked off with a precision that could have been the envy of any Army commander.

The barn where the drug cache was allegedly stored had been lit up like a banshee's party from helicopter searchlights. The door was battered down and teams of armed police, led by the BAD Squad, stormed inside, only to discover it was nothing more than a metal-framed structure for garaging farm vehicles – McCormick MC 115 Tractor with front loader; Bobcat 607 Backhoe; three flatback trailers – all later confirmed to be insured, licensed and roadworthy. Significantly, just enough traces of heroin were found in a corner of the barn to suggest that Operation Clean Out had been initiated a day too late.

In the face of an investigation into how such a carefully planned police operation had turned into a humiliating fiasco for several police forces, CS Victor Maxwell had tendered his resignation with immediate effect. Those who witnessed the moment reported that Maxwell had held his head high and his shoulders back as he left the scene.

But it had all been a ploy.

Maxwell had set up Operation Clean Out to fail, knowing that the drugs cache was not in Blackburn, but in Wren's Garage. He had controlled the whole faked operation, keeping details close to his chest so that he would be the one person to take the blame, the full blame and nothing but the blame for its failure. Having done so, he would then resign, and in that way initiate what he had believed to be his fool-proof early exit from the police force.

But the memory stick delivered to Gilchrist by one of the hitmen – courtesy of Jock Shepherd – provided recordings of phone conversations between Maxwell and others in his team, as well as video recordings of clandestine meetings in pubs and open spaces, in which laundered drug money funding overseas property purchases was openly discussed. But Gilchrist hit the motherlode with seven videoclips showing Maxwell and key members of his BAD Squad discussing the imminent gangland-style executions of Cutter Boyd and Bruiser Mann. Separate phone recordings backed these up, with two more confirming the successful hit on Hatchet McBirn.

But one other video nailed it for Gilchrist: the deeply disturbing and horrific murder of Stooky Dee. Although CS Maxwell never appeared in the frame, his voice could be heard over Dee's hysterical screams for mercy. Forensic analysis of that video would later confirm that it was Maxwell who had stuffed a folded five-pound note into Dee's throat, and Maxwell who gave the instruction for *Golden Plover* to be set loose on the North Sea – *to give the boys in blue something else to focus their resources on* – a diversionary tactic to stretch police resources to the limit as the deadline for Operation Clean Out approached. With such clear and incriminating evidence it seemed a certainty that every member of Maxwell's BAD Squad would end up in prison.

The powers that be did not hang around.

By two o'clock in the early hours of Tuesday morning, a warrant had been issued for CS Maxwell's arrest. Strathclyde Police, with the assistance of Lothian and Borders, quickly mobilised to make the arrest at Maxwell's home. Warrants were also issued for four other key members of his BAD Squad, and at 3 a.m. – only eight hours after the disastrous drug bust – five teams set off on concurrent missions to arrest and bring them all in.

The team assigned to Maxwell arrived at his home at 3.23 a.m. to find his wife, Alice, up and about, fully dressed, suitcases packed and in the hall, taxi parked outside ready to take them to Glasgow Airport for the early KLM flight to Amsterdam and onward connection to Thailand. When questioned, Alice explained that they were going on holiday. But when e-tickets were found to be for one way only, she broke down and confirmed they were leaving the British shores for good. It seemed that Maxwell and his wife had planned to retire to the Far East, and live out the rest of their lives in sun- and alcohol-soaked luxury.

Only problem was, Victor Maxwell was not at home.

According to Alice, Victor had returned from work at around 8.30 that night – CCTV footage would confirm his arrival at 8.42 p.m. – and had gone upstairs to shower and change. After that, they'd had a light meal, and just before midnight, Victor told her he was going to walk to the ATM machine outside the local Co-op and withdraw some more cash.

And that was the last she saw of him – so she said.

Gilchrist was having none of it. Dainty's words *as slippery as an eel in a barrel of oil* reverberated through his mind. It was another ploy. He was sure of that. Why would someone as sly and untrustworthy as Maxwell take his wife of almost thirty years to Thailand, when he could fly there himself and live the life of a bachelor with an endless supply of beautiful Thai women to take care of his every need? So Gilchrist ordered uniformed units to look out for Maxwell, travelling under a fake ID, at Edinburgh and Glasgow airports. But by 10 a.m. on Tuesday, Maxwell had still not been sighted or picked up.

It seemed he'd managed to slip under the net again.

By midday Tuesday, a nationwide search for Maxwell was well underway, but had to be redirected at 3.50 that afternoon when a sharp-eyed detective in Strathclyde's CCTV Unit, assigned to review early morning airport footage, noticed an incident in Glasgow Airport's long-term car park. A morning mist hindered visibility at that time – 7.33 – but she was able to watch the driver of a white car – a Ford Fusion – being confronted by two men as he was removing a leather holdall from the boot. The man then seemed to walk willingly to a waiting Range Rover – *sans* holdall – and climb into the back seat, while the boot was closed and his Ford abandoned where it had been parked.

The Range Rover then exited the car park.

Two hours later, an investigation into the abandoned Ford Fusion confirmed it had been rented from Avis by a Mr Leslie Duncan, too coincidental a name to be anything other than a pseudonym for Victor Maxwell. They had found their man. The Ford Fusion was forensically examined, but all surfaces had been wiped clean, with no fingerprints found in the cabin, on the handles or on the boot. The abandoned holdall – address label *L. Duncan* with nothing else – at least provided clothes from which DNA samples could be taken.

Despite having the Range Rover's registration number, no record of it could be found on either the DVLA database, the PNC or the ANPR system. A team was assigned to try to locate it on other CCTV cameras around the airport, but had no luck, the general consensus being that the plate was false and had since been changed. Without a definitive number plate to pin it down, the CCTV team soon found themselves tracking seven similar-looking Range Rovers through Glasgow's rush-hour traffic.

Gilchrist suggested they focus on any Range Rovers heading to the south of Glasgow, specifically to the Pollokshields area, where Shepherd lived. But even that turned up nothing. It seemed that the Range Rover had simply vanished, with Maxwell in it.

With the finger of mounting suspicion pointing at Shepherd for being responsible for Maxwell's disappearance, Strathclyde Police obtained warrants to search his homes – his main residence in Pollokshields and a luxury eight-bedroom villa in Murcia, Spain. Despite his poor health, Shepherd had been hauled into Govan Police Office again for questioning under caution, but been released. Gilchrist could not shift the image of Shepherd showing him photographs of four mutilated bodies, men on his payroll, and the memory of the anger that lifted off the man like heat from rock. Shepherd's team of lawyers might have bought him enough time to enjoy what was left of his life in his own home, but Gilchrist was convinced it was only a matter of time before he was found to be behind the murderous raid on Wren's Garage, and Maxwell's disappearance. Even though Shepherd had weeks, maybe only days to live, he was hell-bent on taking revenge on the man responsible for killing his men – Victor Maxwell. Of course, the boost to Shepherd's enterprises from the millions of pounds in drug money grabbed from Wren's Garage could be seen as the icing on top of the cake celebrating Maxwell's demise.

But one person who never featured in any of these videos or phone recordings was DS Fox. Without his mobile phone being recovered from Wren's Garage, he might never have existed. Forensic teams confirmed that Maxwell's phone – which he'd had to keep powered up during Operation Clean Out – had taken a call from Fox at 6.58 p.m. Fox's voice message had been subsequently deleted, but Jessie and Gilchrist were able to confirm Fox's panicked call from Wren's Garage, just before the arrival of the van at 7 p.m.

Four other members of Maxwell's BAD Squad – identified from the memory stick files – had been arrested and charged. Another seven were being questioned under caution. CI Jeffrey Randall, who had once interrogated Gilchrist over his alleged removal of critical evidence from an ongoing investigation, now headed up Complaints and Discipline, and with Maxwell's proven link to Wren's Garage, Gilchrist had pressed for an answer to how Lesley Jennifer Wren Duncan fitted into the equation. But Randall couldn't help. No one in the BAD Squad could provide any answers. Even Jackie – best researcher in the world – struggled to find anything conclusive on Duncan's name.

But by Wednesday evening, she'd provided Gilchrist with a number of possibilities.

Maxwell's wife had lost a child at birth, a girl they'd named Jennifer. Maxwell's grandfather, Duncan Maxwell, had a sister called Lesley. Not enough for definite proof, but sufficient to convince Gilchrist that the name had been devised by the man to create a false identity, a non-existent person who could fill the role of company secretary for Maxwell's benefit. After all, the fictional Lesley J. W. Duncan had access to a number of bank accounts through which millions of pounds passed annually. *Slippery as an eel in a barrel of oil* might not be considered close enough. By comparing the bank accounts noted in Christie's logbook with those noted in Tommy Janes's notebook, Gilchrist was able to confirm that transposing the first two numbers with the third and fourth number of each account had been the simplest of cryptographic keys. The FIU obtained warrants to freeze every one of these bank accounts, and had already set in motion legal action to secure all funds on the basis that they had been obtained through the illegal sale of drugs.

Now, another wave of tiredness swept over Gilchrist, and a glance at his wristwatch had him toying with either nipping out to the Central for an overdue pint and a rare spot of lunch, or calling Dainty for an update. Just then, his phone rang.

Without introduction, Smiler said, 'My office, DCI Gilchrist,' and hung up.

CHAPTER 47

Standing outside Smiler's office, Gilchrist thought he caught the low-pitched whisper of male voices from within. He gave the door a light rap with his knuckles, and cracked it open.

'Come in, DCI Gilchrist.'

As he entered he had the oddest sense of silence settling, as if he'd interrupted some secret convention. Chief Superintendent Smiley stood facing him from behind her desk. Her uniform looked as if it had been laundered that morning. The tall figure of Chief Constable Archie McVicar stood to her left, aristocratic and imposing as always. To Smiler's right, two men in dark-blue business suits, white shirts, red ties – model's dummies sprang to mind – followed Gilchrist's progress into the room like cheetahs calculating if they were close enough to make a sprint for the kill.

McVicar was first to greet him, his grip dry and firm. 'Good to see you again, Andy.'

'Sir.' He nodded to Smiler. 'Ma'am.'

She gave a tight smile in response, one he couldn't tell which way it fell – good or bad? He would just have to wait and see. Then she held out her hand as an introduction to the men to her right, and said, 'Mr White is with the Home Office, and would like to ask you a few questions. I've already advised him that we will of course provide all the help we can.'

Well, it seemed he wasn't being given any say in the matter. 'Of course,' he agreed.

One of the men stepped forward for a brisk handshake, and it took Gilchrist a few seconds to realise that he was not about to be introduced to the other man.

'Tell me how it happened,' White said to him.

'How what happened?'

'How four men were killed in Wren's Garage, and you and DS Janes were not.'

Maybe it was the English public school accent that made the question sound more accusatory than intended. But a glance at Smiler warned Gilchrist that it wasn't. No support from McVicar either, who stared at him with a look as direct as an eagle's. It didn't help, of course, that he'd failed to mention his first meeting with Shepherd, or Jessie having visited Shepherd's home and handing over a copy of Christie's logbook. Which was the problem with rubbing shoulders with the criminal element. Sooner or later you were going to be associated with them.

'They must have known we were with the Constabulary,' he said.

'How?'

'I couldn't say.'

'Were you in uniform?'

'No.'

'Plain clothes?'

'What else.'

'Display your warrant cards?'

'No.'

White smiled at that, a baring of uneven teeth that looked at odds with the sartorial perfection. 'So they couldn't have known you were with Fife Constabulary.' A statement, not a question.

'I don't think it mattered,' Gilchrist said.

White frowned. 'I don't understand.'

'Understand what?' he asked, which earned him a harrumph from McVicar.

But White was not up for playing games. 'Explain,' he said.

'We were tied up with our hands behind our backs.' Well, not strictly correct to begin with. But they had been in the end. 'Clearly no threat to anyone. So, why shoot us?'

'Why not?'

'You'd have to ask them.'

'I'm asking you.'

'I've given you my answer.'

'Them,' you said. 'Did you see them?'

'I did.'

'But you're unable to offer anything that might help us identify them.'

Again, not a question. Gilchrist glanced at Smiler, then McVicar, but he was on his own. Back to White. 'Have you read my report?'

'I have.'

'Did you understand it?'

McVicar harrumphed again, but White seemed untroubled. 'I did,' he said.

'So you'll have read that they wore balaclavas.'

'How did you know to go to Wren's Garage?'

Something close to anger flashed through Gilchrist at the change in tack. He was being toyed with, White's cat to his mouse, flipped from one paw to the other and back again. He felt as if he still needed to keep his distance from Shepherd, and said, 'We received a tip-off. It's in my report. I suggest you read it again.'

A pause, then, 'We're intrigued by your friendship with Mr Shepherd.'

Not what he wanted to hear, which told him they already knew about his contact with Shepherd. But he said, 'We're not friends.'

'More along the lines of, you scratch my back, I'll scratch yours. That sort of thing?'

Gilchrist thought silence as good a response as any.

'You met him in Dundee last week.'

Gilchrist struggled to keep his surprise hidden, but wasn't sure he pulled it off. Only Jessie and Mhairi had known he was meeting Shepherd. So for White to know, it must have come from Shepherd's side. Time to change tack, so he said, 'It's odd, don't you think?'

'What is?'

'The Home Office showing interest in Jock Shepherd.'

'We have our reasons.'

'Which I presume you're not going to share with me.' He glanced at McVicar, then Smiler. 'Or with us.'

For the first time, the other man spoke. 'When did you first meet Detective Sergeant Fox?' He stepped forward to stand next to White, but didn't offer his hand. 'Nathanial Fox,' he added, as if to make sure there could be no misunderstanding.

Gilchrist returned his gaze for several seconds, and came to understand that jumping from one line of questioning to the next was not a ploy to confuse him, but an attempt to keep the purpose of their meeting hidden. 'You're not with the Home Office,' he said. 'Are you?'

'DCI Gilchrist,' Smiler interrupted. 'We have agreed to cooperate with the—'

'It would help if I knew who I was cooperating with—'

'I would remind you DCI Gilchrist that—'

'If I may?' The second man had his hand inside his suit pocket, and retrieved a slim leather wallet, which he unfolded and held out for Gilchrist to read – *Bartholomew Winter* in an extravagant font, on a cream-coloured business card. Nothing else, just a name. 'Mr White is with the Home Office,' Winter said. 'I work with Joint Intelligence.' He flipped his wallet shut. 'Was your meeting in the West Port Bar the first time you'd come across DS Fox?'

The question was intended to shock Gilchrist into thinking he was being watched, that he was under suspicion for some criminal act, that they knew everything about him and what he'd been up to the last week or so. After all, this was the British government he was now dealing with. But Winter's question had the opposite effect, causing the sequence of events to slowly unfold for Gilchrist.

Fox had been a rogue cop, a maverick of sorts, whose investigative cases extended into that murky area between the law and criminality. And with government offices tracking Fox's every move since arriving in Fife, Gilchrist had by default incurred a tail of his own. Which explained how they knew of his meeting with Shepherd, and also their suspicions of how he came to find out about Wren's Garage. It might even explain how Shepherd had known they'd found Christie's logbook.

But it didn't explain the massacre.

Or did it?

He fixed Winter with a firm stare, and said, 'You know it was the first time.'

'No, I don't. Which is why I asked the question.'

'You think I was in cahoots with Fox? Is that what you're implying?'

'I'm implying nothing, Mr Gilchrist. Only asking a simple question. Was that the first time you met DS Fox?'

Gilchrist let his gaze shift to White, then back to Winter. 'You're with MI5,' he said. 'Both of you.'

Winter gave a wry smile. 'That's quite the quantum leap, Mr Gilchrist.'

'Detective Chief Inspector Gilchrist.'

Winter's smile held for a moment, then he nodded, the subtlest hint of apology.

Gilchrist had a sense of the mood changing, the air tightening, as if he'd landed some lucky punch and his opponent was about to let him have it back in spades. 'Your recklessness could have had you killed,' Winter said. 'Both of you. You and DS Janes.'

Gilchrist sensed a toughening in Winter's stance.

'We had Wren's Garage under observation,' Winter said. 'We knew Operation Clean Out was going to fail. We knew the consignment was to be moved that night. But we did not know to where, or to whom. We had a surveillance network that stretched from Edinburgh to Dundee, more than one hundred highly trained professionals on duty that night, watching and waiting. Then along you came with your associate, DS Janes, and your schoolboy antics, and blew millions of pounds worth of covert expertise to kingdom come in a few minutes.'

If Gilchrist wanted to know what that *something big* had been, well, there he had it.

But he wasn't through. Not by a long shot.

'Is that what you government people call a murder investigation? Schoolboy antics?'

Winter drew level with Gilchrist. 'Our inability to follow that consignment to its final destination due to your unwarranted interference could ultimately cost the lives of millions of innocent people over the years, *Mr* Gilchrist. Perhaps a great many more. So, yes, schoolboy antics would be an appropriate term.'

'And would cold-blooded murder be an appropriate term, too?' He thought it odd that neither Smiler nor McVicar stepped in to interrupt him, as if they were enjoying the show, eager to see how it played out. But not so odd, if you thought about it, for neither Winter nor White to answer. An image of the massacre in Wren's Garage flashed into his mind with such clarity that he wondered why it hadn't struck him until that moment, the deadly precision with which the hitmen dispatched their victims – single shot to the head; a burst of three rounds to the chest; all with pinpoint accuracy, without a single bullet wasted. Not Jock Shepherd's men, as he'd allowed himself to believe, but highly specialised military personnel. Battie might not have been the only person that night with SAS training.

'You didn't have to kill DS Fox,' he said.

Winter recovered his voice. 'You may recall that your own life was in danger, as was that of DS Janes. Would you rather such decisive action had not been taken?' A smirk tickled the corners of Winter's mouth. 'No,' he said. 'I thought not. You may also be interested to know that your meeting with DS Fox, and your conversations with Mr Shepherd . . . how do I say it . . .? *piqued* our interest in you. So when you turned up at Wren's Garage we obviously suspected the worst, that Fox had bought you off.' He glanced at McVicar, and said, 'But we were soon assured otherwise.'

Winter's flickered smile at McVicar told Gilchrist that the Chief Constable had stood up for him and Jessie, assured Messrs White and Winter of their professional integrity. Of course, if McVicar had taken Gilchrist into his confidence right from the get-go, none of this need have happened.

Winter turned to McVicar and Smiler, as if to announce the end of their meeting, when Gilchrist said, 'So you knew.'

White frowned, and faced him. 'Excuse me?'

'You knew DS Fox was a rogue policeman, and that he was in Maxwell's pocket, yet you allowed him into our Constabulary, gave him access to confidential files and records, and in doing so could have jeopardised the admissibility of critical evidence.'

Winter's eyes deadened. 'Our intention had been to track the drugs consignment to the buyer, not to have to abort months of work to step in and save your lives. I thought I'd explained that. Be as it may, we did. And for that, both you and DS Janes should be eternally grateful.'

Not once had Winter's voice changed tone, every word spoken with precise elocution, clipped and calm at the same time. If Winter had been a murderer, he could convince you he was doing you a favour by shooting you in the head. Gilchrist had the oddest feeling that he was expected to drop to his knees and give thanks to the government for blasting four people to death.

Winter pressed on. 'The government will of course deny any and all association with Wren's Garage. Much more convenient to point the finger of blame at Glasgow's drug lord, Mr Shepherd, who does not have long for this world and who will take all his deadly secrets with him to the grave, including all that happened in Pittenweem.'

Well, there it was. Winter was washing his governmental hands clean of any killings. No doubt, an official statement to the press would be made on the timely passing of big Jock, for which the government, and pen-pushing creeps like Winter and White, would come out squeaky clean.

Gilchrist managed to keep his temper under control, and he faced Winter and gave him a dead-eyed smile. 'Did DS Fox have family?' he asked him.

Winter blinked. White looked to his feet.

Gilchrist turned to Smiler. 'Will that be all, ma'am?'

A glance at White and Winter, who both stepped back, as if glad to be out of it. 'Yes, Andy,' she said. 'That'll be all. Thank you.'

Gilchrist nodded to her, and said, 'Ma'am,' and to McVicar, 'Sir.'

Then he turned and strode from the room.

CHAPTER 48

When Gilchrist returned to his office, he felt drained.

Winter seemed to have been always one step ahead of him, maybe more. Until that meeting, Smiler and McVicar *et al* had been praising Gilchrist for bringing Maxwell's BAD Squad to heel, a rogue band of killers, drug lords and money launderers that would disgrace the police force, and which would undermine public confidence and trust. The damage would take years to set right – if it ever could.

And now, here he was, Detective Chief Inspector Andrew James Gilchrist, the man who caused the collapse of a multi-million-pound surveillance operation that could have led the powers that be to uncover the drug empire of some global mastermind, and keep billions of pounds worth of drugs off the streets and save countless lives of innocent men, women and children. Christ, it really didn't bear thinking about.

From hero to zero in a matter of minutes.

He slumped into his chair and stared at his computer.

His reflection gazed back at him from a blank screen, a grey face with heavy eyes and a downward twist to the mouth that

spoke of unhappy times. Where had the years gone? His irrepressible zest for life, too. Now he felt tired of it all, tired of the
job, tired of being at the professional mercy of a hierarchy that
seemed more focused on fiscal management than on bringing
criminals to justice. Or maybe the lethargy that enveloped him
like a deadweight was nothing more than lack of sleep, or maybe
he was low on energy from having too little to eat in the past
three days.

He let his hand hover over the mouse, undecided whether to
open his emails and get on with the job, or just give it up and go
home. He closed his eyes for a long moment, let his body relax
and the need to sleep slide over him. Give it up and go home
sounded good—

His phone rang.

He jerked awake and stared at it for a moment, an old-fashioned handset that sat on the corner of his desk. He watched it as
it rang out, and felt a wave of relief sweep over him when the
caller finally gave out. He felt a wry smile tug his lips.

Was this how it ended? Was this what happened when you
reached the end of your career, the realisation that you're no use
to anyone any more, that the job is all too much for you, the
hours, the reports, the meetings, the endless fight for . . . for
what . . .? For justice? Or had you just been looking for a result,
any result, guilty or not, it didn't matter, so long as you could
close the books on one case and move on to the next? Or maybe
you just reached a certain time in your career and lost interest and
couldn't give a toss any more—

His mobile rang.

Out of habit, he reached for it – ID Dainty – then slipped it
back into his pocket, unanswered. Well, he supposed that told

him everything. At long last, he was through with it once and for all. He slid his chair back from his desk, pushed to his feet and walked from his office. In the doorway he paused to give his room one final, farewell look, a visual inventory of sorts for his memory.

Then he gripped the handle, and pulled the door shut with a satisfying click.

Outside, the wind had stilled. The air hung damp and cold. The sky spread grey and dull in all directions, a blanket of clouds as smooth as a bedspread. He turned into College Street as his mobile rang again. He slipped it out – ID Dainty – and surprised himself by taking the call.

'Fuck sake, Andy, I've been trying to reach you.'

'Was tied up for a while, getting my arse grilled.'

'You, too?' Dainty laughed, a throaty growl that could have come from a large man. 'I tell you, Andy, this fucking lot down here need to take a shite in the Clyde. And as for that wanker, Randall? Complaints and Discipline? Some fucker needs to complain and discipline that bastard's arse. Hang on a second.' The line scraped and rattled, as if Dainty had dropped his phone into a bucket.

Gilchrist walked on, mobile to his ear. He was tempted just to hang up, call Dainty back when he'd had a bite to eat and a couple of beers, but once again he was surprised by his need to know, his desire to ask one more question. He'd turned the corner at Market Street by the time Dainty came back.

'Sorry, Andy, it's fucking loony tunes down here.'

'Now you've called,' Gilchrist said, 'can I ask how well you knew Fox?'

A pause, then, 'Is that why you were getting your arse grilled?'

356

Gilchrist frowned. Not the answer he'd expected. 'I'm listening,' he said.

'Never met him before.'

'I thought he was one of yours.'

'No, Andy, sorry. With Clean Out about to break, we were on a need-to-know basis. Thought I was going to be read the Official fucking Secrets Act. Piss takers, the lot of them. No, Fox was sent up from London, some secret branch of some special department that had links to some other special fucking unit in Europe and Christ knows where else.'

'He was a plant?' Gilchrist said.

'That's one way of putting it.'

'And another way?'

'Sacrificial lamb.'

Gilchrist stopped mid-step, mobile hard to his ear. He turned his back to the bar and faced the cobbled street. 'Fox was dispensable? Is that what you're saying?'

'You didn't hear this from me, but Fox was more than dispensable. He was on their list of suspects right from the fucking off. If they hadn't shot the bastard when they did, they would've hung him out to dry for the rest of his natural. Fox was on the take, and in so deep he didn't know how to get out. He was toast, one fucking way or the other.'

An image of Fox's body being blasted into the garage wall, his chest exploding with blood, seared into his mind. Was that how the government of White and Winter terminated employment these days? Assassinate you, rather than go through Human Resources? He felt a surge of anger flash through him, and gritted his teeth with frustration.

But it was no use. 'Ah, for fuck sake,' he said.

'Andy?'

'I don't know, Dainty. I've just about had it up to here.' He took a deep breath, let it out. 'What's the point of it all?' he said. 'I used to think we were nothing more than numbers on some bean-counter's spreadsheet. But now I realise we're just a herd of simple scapegoats, being led to the slaughter house to be disposed of as others see fit, and to take the blame for someone else's cock up.'

'Fucking hell, Andy. You need to cut the psycho-babble. It'll do your nut in.'

Gilchrist let a chuckle slip from his lips. 'Yeah, I guess. But you were trying to reach me. So what's new?'

'You're going to love this,' Dainty said. 'Maxwell turned up an hour ago.'

'You found him?'

'Well, mostly.'

Gilchrist closed his eyes. This was what he wouldn't miss when he retired, news of blood and slaughter and all things gruesome. 'I'm listening.'

'I thought I'd seen it all,' Dainty said. 'But I tell you, Andy. There's some crazy fuckheads out there.'

Gilchrist tilted his head back, stared at the sky. Shepherd had got his revenge, he was sure of that. A shudder shivered through him at the memory of big Jock's hateful words – *when I take that cunt out by Christ he's gonnie suffer like this* – the way his finger stabbed the photographs of his men who'd been killed by Maxwell and his team. God only knew what Maxwell must have suffered. But his brain was barely capable of interpreting Dainty's words, a flow of verbiage so brutal and sickening that his mind couldn't take it all in . . .

'. . . found in a barrel . . . dumped in waste ground . . . wood-chipper used . . . nothing left, the lot . . . I've seen thicker soup . . . don't know what the world's coming to . . .'

Even then, his subconscious caught something out of place. 'An hour ago, you said.'

'That's right.'

'So no time to run DNA tests on . . . on . . .'

'That's right.'

'So how do you know it's Maxwell?'

'They left photos – before, after and *during* the mincing process.'

'Jesus . . .'

'It's him, all right. Poor fucker. Oh, and one other thing,' Dainty said. 'They also left a one-way ticket to the Philippines. Looks like you were right, Andy. He really was leaving the missus to rot.' Dainty coughed, a hard clearing of his throat. 'We're trying to keep the details away from the media, for obvious reasons.'

'Has anyone picked up Shepherd yet?'

'This is where it goes fucking haywire. It's hard to believe, but Shepherd's lawyers pre-empted his arrest by filing a claim against the force for harassment. I think they're just trying to keep him out of jail until the bastard dies.' Another cough. 'And once he does, fuck knows who's going to take over.'

Gilchrist had heard enough. He thanked Dainty – although whatever the hell there was to be thankful about, he couldn't work out – then he hung up. He slipped his mobile into his jacket and pushed through the doors to the Central Bar.

The ambience hit him like a kick to the chest – the background din of the lunchtime crowd; the rambling chatter of people talking, laughing, placing orders; the scraping sound of stools shifting; the sharp clatter of cutlery and plates chinking – everybody going about their business oblivious to the human slaughter taking place in the criminal underworld.

He found a stool at the end of the bar, and had to turn his face away from the heady smell of cooked food being served at the table behind him. He ordered a Fosters, lighter than a real ale, just looking for something cold and refreshing. But when he placed the pint to his lips, he caught sight of a couple at the other end of the bar spooning soup, and it was all he could do to make it to the gents in time before he bent over the sink and threw up. With not much in his stomach, he spat out bubbles of bile as he splashed water over his face.

Outside in College Street, he stuffed his hands into his jacket pockets and headed back to the Office car park. He would maybe call Smiler from home, tell her he wouldn't be in for the rest of the day, make an excuse that he was coming down with something, the flu, a cold, it didn't matter. And maybe he'd follow up with her tomorrow as well, tell her he was going to take Friday off, too, be back in the Office next Monday. And during that time off, when he'd had an opportunity to reflect on his life, past, present and future, he'd sit down and draft his letter of resignation.

As he turned into North Street, he smiled. He should have listened to Jack. He'd told him often enough that he was spending too much time at the Office, that there was more to life than just work and more work. Jack would be pleased to hear that he was chucking it. In fact, he should be the first person to find out about it.

He retrieved his mobile, and dialled Jack's number.

'Hey, what's new?'

Despite Jack's cheery opening, Gilchrist sensed an underlying sadness, as if Jack was trying to put a face on bad news. 'Fancy a pint?' he said, then remembered Jack was on the wagon. Well, except when it was his birthday.

'Can't. We're just about to leave.'

'Heading out for the day?'

The line fell silent for several seconds, then Jack came back with, 'No, Andy. We're moving. To Edinburgh. Me and Kristen. She's got a flat there.'

'That sounds like lock, stock and barrel.' He forced a chuckle down the line, but even to his own ears it sounded false. 'Where are you at the moment?'

'Mo's.'

'Is she back home?'

'Yeah.'

'Well, stay put. I'll be there in a couple of minutes.'

He hung up before Jack could object.

CHAPTER 49

Gilchrist would have been quicker walking to Maureen's.

By the time he found a parking space and skipped up the steps to her flat in South Street, fifteen minutes had passed since his phone call to Jack. Maureen surprised him by meeting him at the door, and giving him a heartfelt hug.

He buried his lips in her hair, and whispered, 'How are you keeping, princess?'

'I'm fine, Dad.' She stepped back from him, tucked a loose strand of hair behind her ear. 'Jack couldn't stay. He said a friend was giving them a lift to the station.'

'Leuchars?'

'I think so.'

He paused for a moment, then said, 'I thought Kris had a car.'

Maureen offered a grim smile, then said, 'I'm sorry, Dad. Jack said he'd call you when he and Kris had settled in.'

Well, there he had it. Jack had now resorted to excuses. He followed her inside, and found himself searching for evidence of male presence – Derek for one. 'Jack said Kristen has a flat in

Edinburgh. Does she own or rent?' Not that it mattered. He was just trying to find something to say to cover his disappointment.

'She owns it, I think. All hers. Used to be her parents'.'

'She inherit it?'

'I think so.'

'Only child?'

'She's never mentioned any siblings. So, maybe.' She walked into the kitchen, and said, 'Would you like a tea?'

'Sure.' He nodded as he let his gaze drift around her kitchen, as if searching for words to say. It surprised him how much it stung, Jack's departure without even a goodbye wish or a handshake. He never thought he would think it, but it would be lovely to give Jack a high-five and receive one of his shoulder bumps. An image of Jack leaving the Central Bar hand in hand with Kris came into his mind. Had he said something wrong? But whatever it was, he couldn't remember. He would need to ask Jack the next time they met.

Or maybe it would be best just to say nothing.

He placed his hands on the kitchen sink, gripped the stainless steel edges, and looked out of the window. From there, he couldn't see the sea over the rooftops, but the horizon had a hint of blue, as if the clouds were thinning and the sun would make an appearance before the end of the day.

'Are you all right, Dad?'

He turned to find Maureen eyeing him with concern. 'I'm fine, sure.'

'You look tired.'

'You got me there,' he said. 'I'm knackered. This case has done me in.'

'It's been everywhere on the news for days. Is it over now?'

He didn't want to say anything about Maxwell's wood-chippered remains being found in a barrel. Or that the case was far from over. You didn't kill police officers and expect them to drop it in a hurry. And the media would eventually learn the details of Maxwell's demise. So, no, the case wasn't over now. But it was for Gilchrist.

He smiled at her. 'I'm thinking of retiring.'

She set the teapot down. 'Thinking of, and actually doing, are two different things.'

'I'm going to hand in my letter of resignation in a day or so.'

She smirked at him. 'You written it yet?'

'Not quite.'

'See?' She handed him his mug. 'Here's your tea. Want a biscuit?'

'Any Kit-Kats?'

'Have a break . . .?'

'Have a Kit-Kat.' He chuckled at their old one-two act, from a TV ad years ago. Did they still run that ad? He couldn't say. He watched Maureen reach up to open a cupboard, her sweater sliding up to reveal a waist that was still whippet-thin. Ever since a life-threatening event a few years ago, she had become upsettingly thin. Not quite anorexic thin, but not far from it.

'Here you are,' she said. 'A couple left. Have them both. I never eat them.'

'You just buy them for your favourite dad?'

'Of course.'

She picked up her mug and walked through to the front room, and he realised he was supposed to follow. She sat in an armchair, leaving him with the sofa. He flopped into it, and waited while she tucked her legs up, made herself comfortable.

'So what's brought this on?' she said. 'Thoughts of retirement.'

'Getting old.'

'You don't look it.'

'But I feel it.'

'Jack'll be pleased.'

'Surprised, more like. Did you know he was leaving for Edinburgh?'

She shook her head. 'First I heard of it was about an hour ago.' She took another sip of tea while he nibbled a leg of his Kit-Kat. Then she said, 'I've taken your advice, and made an appointment with the doctor for next Tuesday.'

He sensed she was trying to direct the conversation away from Jack, but he decided just to go with the flow. He could phone Jack any time. 'Well,' he said, 'as I'll be retired by then, I can take you there.'

She chuckled at that, and changed tack again. 'Would you like something to eat? A sandwich? Tuna and tomato with some jalapeño peppers? Your favourite.'

'Why not?' he said. 'You talked me into it.'

Her hand brushed his as she slid from the armchair, and he watched her as she walked through to the kitchen. She was still too thin, way too thin. He needed to talk to her about putting on some weight, maybe even take out a subscription for the gym, work with a trainer and bulk up somehow. If he was retired, he could even go along with her. He picked up one of her magazines, browsed the pages, his eyes scanning the articles, his brain taking nothing in. The flat felt warm, and he plumped up a cushion as he rested his head against the back of the sofa, for just a moment . . .

A phone rang.

He came to with a start, surprised to see Maureen seated next to him, watching the TV with the sound muted. The curtains were drawn, and the room glowed with a mystical yellow from lighted candles and a lamp set in the corner. The spicy fragrance of potpourri swamped the air.

Maureen reached for the phone, lifted the handset. 'Hello?' Her whole being seemed to still for a moment, then she pushed to her feet and walked to her bedroom.

Gilchrist made his way into the kitchen, neck stiff, muscles hurting. He filled a glass from the tap, and took a long drink. The clock on the microwave displayed 7.34, which had to be the evening, surely. Had he been asleep for the best part of six hours? Force of habit had him fumbling for his mobile, which he found in his jacket hanging over the back of a chair.

He couldn't remember powering it down, but he switched it on to find he'd missed six calls, four of which were from Jessie. He was about to return her calls when Maureen came out of her bedroom, the tightness in her lips warning him that all was not well. He thought it best to say nothing, but she returned his gaze with welling eyes, and he found himself saying, 'Problems?'

She shook her head. 'That was Derek,' she said. 'We're finished.'

He didn't want to offer a joke about not knowing they'd even started. Instead, he walked towards her with outstretched arms, and she fell into him as the tears flowed. He said nothing, just held her, let her sobbing diminish her anger and her pain.

When he felt her recover, he stood back. 'Are you all right?'

She sniffed, nodded, dabbed a hand at her eyes. 'What is it about men?' she said.

'You're asking the wrong person.'

'I think I'm asking the right person.' She held his gaze, and in her eyes he thought he saw a flicker of understanding pass behind them. 'You're different, Dad. You know how to talk to women. It's as if you know what they're thinking.'

He kept his surprise hidden as best he could, and said, 'Now that, dear lady, is where you're wrong. No man knows what any woman is thinking. Least of all me.'

She laughed at that, a sweet ringing sound that he hadn't heard from her in years. Her eyes sparkled, and she kissed him then, a quick peck on the cheek. 'Love you, Dad.'

He had to say that he was somewhat confused. Where was her pain of only moments earlier? How could she go from tearful hurt to carefree happiness in ten seconds? Before he could work it out, he was saved by his mobile ringing – ID Jessie – and took the call.

'Where have you been?' Jessie said.

'Writing my letter of resignation.'

She laughed at that. 'Aye, sure, that'll be right. Write mine when you're at it.'

'No, Jessie, I'm serious.'

'So am I,' she said. 'Listen, you're needed here. Someone tossed a brick through the Office window a couple of hours ago—'

'I can give you the number of a glazier I know.'

'Very funny,' she said. 'The brick was wrapped in a pair of these wee skimpy thongs you wouldn't see me dead in. Victoria's Secret. Red.' A pause then, 'And covered in blood.'

Gilchrist found himself staring out the kitchen window, into the dark of night. 'That doesn't mean anything.'

'We got a phone call from the university early afternoon reporting one of their students missing. She never came home from a party last night.'

Gilchrist turned from the window and walked into the lounge. He didn't need to hear this. He was going home to write his letter of resignation. He was through with the job. Why hadn't Jessie listened? He glanced at Maureen who was watching him, concern etched across her face—

'She's only nineteen,' Jessie said.

Something tugged at Gilchrist's heart.

'Her parents are besides themselves with worry.'

Maureen smiled at him then, as if she could read his mind, understand his dilemma. Something in the way she looked at him – her thin build, as slim as a teenager, her wide eyes still reddened from tears of moments earlier – struck him. Where was he when she had been nineteen? How would he have felt if his teenage daughter had gone missing, with signs that something terrible might have happened to her?

'Jessie, listen.' He tried to hide from Maureen's gaze. 'I . . . I . . .'

'You should go,' Maureen interrupted.

'But . . .'

She pressed a finger to his lips to silence him. 'I love you, Dad. You know I do. But your job comes first. It always has.'

He shook his head. 'But I need—'

'At least for the time being.' She smiled at his confusion. 'You can write that letter of resignation later. Go,' she said, leading him towards the door. 'You've got another case to solve. I'll still be here when you come back. I'll even help you draft it.'

He leaned forward and pecked her cheek, then walked from her flat. 'Does she have a boyfriend?' he asked Jessie.

'A wanker of the first order. He's got form. And he lives in Inverness.'

Gilchrist skipped down the steps, pushed through the street door into the cold night. 'He could get the train from Inverness to Leuchars,' he said. 'In and out of St Andrews in a matter of hours. Has anyone spoken with him yet?'

'That's the problem,' Jessie said. 'He's missing, too.'

'Tell me everything you know,' he said, his mind firing alive as he breathed in the damp night. He pulled his jacket collar tight to his neck and walked towards his car. Mo was right, he thought. Retirement could wait for a little bit longer. Then he would draft his letter of resignation next week.

Or maybe the week after that.

Maybe . . .

He strode into the cold night air, Jessie's voice chirping in his ear.

ACKNOWLEDGEMENTS

Writing is often a lonely affair, but this book could not have been published without help from the following: Jon Miller, formerly of Tayside Police; Kenny Cameron (retired), Police Scotland; Gayle Cameron, formerly of Police Scotland; and Alan Gall, retired Chief Superintendent, Strathclyde Police, for police procedure; Peggy Boulos Smith and Al Zuckerman of Writers House for advice and encouragement when it was needed most; Howard Watson, for professional copyediting of the highest standard and for accepting my commas or lack thereof in dialogue throughout; Rebecca Sheppard, Desk Editor; Sean Garrehy, Cover Designer; Amy Donegan, Marketing Assistant; and John Fairweather, Production Controller – for beavering away behind the scenes in Little, Brown to give this novel the best possible start; and in particular Krystyna Green, Publishing Director, for once again placing her trust in me. And finally Anna, for putting up with me, believing in me, and loving me all the way.